THE LONG DARK ROAD

THE LONG DARK ROAD

P.R. Black

This edition first published in the United Kingdom in 2020 by Aries,
an imprint of Head of Zeus Ltd

A CIP catalogue record for this book is available from the
British Library.

ISBN 9781800249417

Typeset by Siliconchips Services Ltd UK

Printed and bound by CPI Group (UK) Ltd, Croydon, CR0 4YY

Cover design © Lisa Brewster

Aries
c/o Head of Zeus
First Floor East
5–8 Hardwick Street
London EC1R 4RG

www.headofzeus.com

For Rory

Prologue

It was only when the rain came down hard that Stephanie began to worry.

The pavement had come to an end at about the same time as the streetlights, and dusk had given way to darkness and gloom, with neither a star nor a single slice of moonlight to be seen. She had the whole length of the long dark road still to walk, with no houses on either side – just farmland, dry stone walls, and looming, rustling trees, rendered as swift-moving shadows in the night.

Stephanie put up her hood, thrust her hands in her pockets, lowered her chin to her chest, and crossed over to the right-hand side of the road. This was so she could better see any traffic coming towards her – but then the long dark road began to turn and twist in on itself, becoming serpentine, and a blind corner in one direction was as bad as one in the other direction.

Several cars passed her in the night, and the occupants all remembered seeing her. Stephanie thought, correctly, that a hunched, hooded figure bent into the driving rain might seem quite alarming given the conditions. Most of the time she was able to dodge over to the other side of the road, the sweep of headlights giving her ample time to make a move towards safety. There was hardly any verge to speak of, on the rare occasion when two cars passed each other in the treacherously narrow route; once, Stephanie hugged the lichen-infused dry stone walls, grimacing at the sensation of moss underneath her fingernails, hoping that the driver on her side of the road wasn't given to cutting a corner.

Once, someone beeped at her. She had a shutter-click impression of a jeering face, and then something was thrown from an opened window – an empty beer can, rebounding off the slate and rolling forlornly after her down a slight decline. Stephanie didn't even have to dodge it, but the encounter jolted her. *I have to get off this road*, she thought, and quickened her pace.

Soon she came to the bridge – the trek had seemed longer than when she had previously taken this route, in bright sunshine – and was reassured by its solid archway, as well as the white-letters-on-green-background that read:

FERNGATE – 2 miles

Two miles was nothing, of course. Back in the training days, two miles was the distance she would clock up on a rest day – a trot to ease her muscles on a treadmill, maybe, after some weights. As the rain grew more violent, trickling down the back of her neck and plastering her fringe to her forehead, it occurred to her to run.

Just cut your losses; tonight's not the night for it. Make an excuse later. You've got plenty of time to think one up.

Over the bridge, she glanced at the eerie phosphorescence of the rain-swollen river, a muted white explosion as the flow of the water met the boulders at the riverbank. *I wonder if there's a troll under here*, she thought, then quickly thought of something else.

Once she was past the bridge, the road grew straight and flat, bordered only by bushes separating farmland on either side. The rain eased off into a steady drizzle, and Stephanie felt comforted in the simplicity of the route ahead.

A big, heavy vehicle approached behind her. Even before its headlights picked her out in the road ahead, Stephanie could imagine the water it displaced, as if a tank was fording a river. Looking over her shoulder, all she could see were twin beams, painfully bright in the gloom. The vehicle slowed, and pulled up beside her, the rain cast in molten sparks through its headlights. Rain slicked the passenger-side window as it slowly lowered. A cheery, broad face appeared. 'You all right there, love?'

'I'm fine,' she managed, making eye contact with him. Then she spoiled this assertiveness by adding: 'I do wish I was a duck, all the same.'

The driver grinned. 'That's the truth. Don't suppose I can offer you a lift? It's a devil of a night to be out here on your own.'

'I'm fine, thanks. I'm just going along the road, here.'

'You sure?'

'Absolutely sure. Final answer.'

'Well… I had to ask. Take care. I hope your god goes with you.' The window buzzed closed again, and the Land Rover moved off, its tail-lights receding in the horizon, and then lost in a sudden bend.

His name was Jed Mulrine, and the police were very interested in him for a long time afterwards. They took great care to trace his movements, as well as examining his

Land Rover in quite literally forensic detail. These inquiries established firmly that Jed Mulrine had made no physical contact with Stephanie, that he was telling the truth, and that he was most likely the last person to see her walking on that road.

This final part of their conclusions was not correct.

After another half a mile of progress, a set of lights approached her from the opposite side of the road.

Stephanie had a long time to consider the vehicle. It had full beam on – understandably, given the conditions and the fact that she was out here in the sticks, utterly alone – and as the laser-bright beams flashed past her, she anticipated that the driver would douse them, upon seeing her. But the driver didn't, and Stephanie flinched. The light was unbearable, even with her eyes closed, searing through her eyelids. She had to hold up a hand to block off the unruly brightness.

The car slowed down as it passed. Then the brakes squeaked; she heard the backwash as it came to a complete stop.

Stephanie looked back to see the twin red eyes of the brake lights. Then the reversing lights blinked on, and the car backed up.

Something in this jolted her, and she quickened her step. But the car was quicker, of course, and soon it had stopped just a few feet before her.

The full beam was still on, and she could not make out any details, other than dark paint. The driver's side door opened, and a long, black silhouette appeared, the image as blurred and inconsistent as a lick of flame in negative.

Even before the figure lunged at her, Stephanie knew

what was about to happen. It was the same feeling as when she swam in the sea, and realised she was out of her depth. A yawning sensation, a realisation that what was beneath her might drop down for all eternity. That something that lurked down there might grab her.

She turned; there was a break in the treeline to her left, leading onto the farmland, and she sprinted flat out for it.

Footsteps pounded the road behind her.

No one reported any screams; no one drove past; and that was as far as Stephanie travelled along that long dark road.

So that's the mundanity of the move, and the mediocrity of my mother and father's farewells, over and done. I intend my time in Ferngate to be an adventure. Looking at the autumn-ready trees and the eager faces of the freshers reminds me of the stories I delighted in as a girl – school stories, friends, enemies, irritants, the masters you hated, the fairy godmothers who helped you. Anything's got to be better than Mum and Dad shrieking at each other.

From the diary of Stephanie Healey

Georgia watched the headlights slash her driveway in the early morning gloom. The tone of light was different, and the bulbs were spaced further apart than the car he used to drive. So, she was not altogether surprised when a brand-new, pistol-bright silver 4x4 tank crunched up the driveway. It barely made a sound; hybrid vehicle, into the bargain. Probably he thought this was subtle.

Rod looked grave as he got out of the car. With the connection that they might always have, he glanced up towards the window and their gazes locked. He did not look away, continuing to stare as he clicked the key fob. An empty holdall dangled from his hand, a deflated-looking thing that seemed to be as fresh out of the packet as the car.

Big, tall, dull, balding Rod. Ridiculous in his cycling gear, dull and abstemious in his habits, and back again for one last insult.

Georgia hadn't changed the locks, at the insistence of her solicitor, but he'd had the decency to knock. She didn't give herself time to rehearse an opening line, but swept the door open.

'Ah,' he said, 'you're dressed, great. I just wanted to pop over and collect one or two things.'

Georgia nodded to the silver-grey beast over his shoulder. 'Sure you'll get everything in that? It's big enough.'

He shrugged. 'Maybe. Maybe not. I just came for the CDs, in fact.'

'The CDs.' She sniggered. 'That's such a bloke thing to do.'

'I won't be long.' He moved forward, and Georgia stepped aside, cursing herself for her weakness, not wanting to get involved in a fight. Not today, not this early.

Stopping to take his boots off in the foyer, in the place where he used to hang his coat, he noticed the bags at the bottom of the stairs. 'Off somewhere?'

'Maybe. Maybe not.'

'Not heading to Ferngate, are you?'

'Stop interrogating me, Rod. Get your Hootie & The Blowfish best of, and bugger off.'

'I'm only asking.' He headed into the nook room, which was dominated by his CD towers. He snatched handfuls of CDs and shoved them into his holdall, seemingly indiscriminately, although she remembered that he had a strange knack of knowing just where his albums were on the shelves, in spite of there being no discernible order to how they were stored. 'Papers been in touch with you?'

'Of course. You know… you shouldn't really be here, Rod. I thought the lawyers were quite clear.'

'There's never been any need for lawyers,' he said, stiffly. 'Terrible idea to get them involved. Money down the drain. No reason we can't be sensible.'

'If you say so, Rod. Hang on – Carole King, that's one of mine.'

He paused, frowning. 'You sure?'

'Absolutely sure.' She held out her hand; he handed over *Tapestry*, warily.

'You know, Georgia… I also came here to talk to you about the next couple of weeks. I just want to… You know. Get a plan together.'

'For what?' She laid down the CD on top of one of the CD towers.

'Just, to present a united front. We have to do that, for the cameras.'

'The papers know what's happening with us. They printed a bloody story on it. What story do you want to get straight?'

'Just, you know… We need to show unity. People might lose sympathy if we don't. That's all.'

'I see. You heading to Ferngate?'

'I'm away on business, but one of the papers has been in touch.'

'They called you up, did they?'

'Yeah.'

'And they didn't call me. That's a strange one. How much did they offer you, Rod?'

'If that's your attitude, I don't want to talk to you.'

Georgia laughed. 'They did! One of them bought you up. I can't bloody believe it. And you wouldn't have told me. What, did you promise them an exclusive?'

'Please leave me alone now, Georgia. This is difficult for us both. I only want to get some of what's mine.'

'Don't let me stop you. I've been desperate to see the back of that stoner rock bullshit for years. If I never have to hear Neil Young's voice again, that's worth paying any price.'

Rod hesitated. 'Even the house?'

'Just get what you need and get out.'

She left him to it. He was quick, to give him his due; soon the holdall was full, zipped up, and perched on his shoulder.

'If you go to Ferngate, give me a call, right?'

'I'm not going to Ferngate. It's none of your business what I do, or where I go. And you'll need permission to get into the house. We agreed on that. I do have cameras set up – you appear at the door, I'll know, and I'll contact your solicitor about how you broke the terms of our agreement.'

Soon he was back outside, on the driveway. 'You let me know if you're going to Ferngate. Anything could help. Anything could give us a lead.'

Georgia sighed. 'I'll think about it, Rod.'

'Just call me. I mean it. Stephanie's bigger than us.'

'Is she bigger than you and whoever you're shacked up with, Rod?' It had come out on reflex, a snake rearing out of the bushes.

'Bye, Georgia. Take it easy.'

'Because, you know, she could come and sit in with us. Couldn't she? Maybe people will sympathise with her. Someone might take pity. Someone might call in with what we need.'

'Take a chill pill.'

'Bastard,' she hissed, but he was already in the 4x4. The engine turned over with that unsettling, sibilant sound, made a smart turn, and then drove away.

Georgia returned to the house, listening to the breeze whistle through the foyer. She stared at her bags for a moment, then searched for her car keys.

2

He's got the most beautiful hair for a boy. I am driven almost insane by its shampoo-advert perfection, and the way his freckles match its colour almost perfectly. I so badly wanted to run my hands through it, to feel it flow through my fingers like fine sand. So, I did.

From the diary of Stephanie Healey

Georgia Healey spotted the boy who'd first reported her daughter missing straight away, but she did it right – taking her time, getting very close, and remaining hidden until the last possible moment. For reasons she wouldn't have felt comfortable explaining, she didn't want him to see her just yet.

Yes, it was certainly him; the hair was a little longer than she remembered, a tawny red that would have been gorgeous on a little boy, but looked merely odd on top of his head at the age of – what was he? Twenty-one? Twenty-two?

He'd put on weight, too, a good stone and a half. The chin wasn't so square any more, and the dimples that Georgia remembered forming at the corners of his mouth when he smirked were now swamped in the flesh. Although Georgia didn't like beards, she wondered if one would have suited him – they were still the fashion, going by the other students who left the lecture theatre at the same time, although only just.

When the big moment arrived, Martin didn't know what to say. His expression said enough – said plenty, in fact. He paused, blinking rapidly when the flashbulbs went off.

'I suppose…' he faltered, licked his lips. Georgia laid a hand across his, and he clutched at it – a little too hard. Georgia always remembered how sweaty those hands had been, and also how small – an artist's hands.

'I suppose I just want to say – Stephanie, if you're out there, please get in touch. We're worried sick, your mum needs you home, and I need you back here, too. You promised you'd help me sort out my essay on George Orwell, remember? The Road To Wigan Pier?'

And then that smile, that awful grin, as if he'd snagged one side of his mouth on a fishing hook; the part-time grimace that would appear on all the websites. No matter that he'd broken down moments later. No matter that he had practically collapsed in that chair, right there, on the last syllable, his spine buckled along with his voice.

They took shot after shot, whirring, robotic long-lens digital cameras with humans optional in many cases, and they focused right in on him, more than they had with Georgia or the chief inspector. He knew, they knew, and everyone watching online or on TV or picking it up on Twitter or even cracking open a paper knew why this was. And so did Georgia.

*But she still clutched his hand, and held him fast as
the storm broke.*

He had tidied up the rest of his appearance since she'd
last seen him – battered old Doc Martens replaced by
smarter shoes, and new, at that, going by the glossy sheen.
Students' footwear did not remain unscuffed for long,
in Georgia's experience, even somewhere like Ferngate.
Tattered old jeans, embarrassingly frayed in places that
you tried not to look at, had been swapped for smarter
trousers that actually matched his long, brown corduroy
jacket. He looked like what Georgia supposed he was – an
arts student with too much money.

What was more surprising than his subtle metamorphosis
from scrubby late teenager to confident, if puffy young man,
was a new accessory; the girl who was holding his hand.

She was short, and if you were unkind, which Georgia
tried hard not to be, she was a little thick around the hips.
But there was no doubting her beauty; she had shoulder-
length hair that you might term lustrous, or describe as
a mane, or even, God help us, flowing locks – jet black,
probably dyed, and taking an awful lot of work in the
mornings in order to appear so thick, and yet be so easily
flicked. This was something the girl did quite often,
mussing her hair back over her head every few moments.
And quite right too. I'd do the same if I had that hair,
Georgia thought.

The face underneath was pale, but complemented the
jet-black hair perfectly. She had pale eyes and a long, thin,
but strangely elegant nose. They didn't speak a word to
each other as they came down the steps, although they

acknowledged one or two people as the class split off into groups.

Georgia waited until they were further along before she put away the phone she'd been pretending to study, took off her dark glasses, and crossed the street to approach them.

Digby Street was a long, ancient thoroughfare girt with cobblestones, the curse of many a cyclist and countless high heels wearers through the years. The young man and his girlfriend had emerged from the Crandbury Building, a red-brick addition to the university estate, which still cued a chorus of tuts and a brass section of sucked teeth whenever it was mentioned, more than fifty years after it was constructed.

In the background rose the spires of St Julian's and St Enoch's, gaunt, grey-stoned battlements that clasped the campus to the west and east. The young man and his girl were probably headed for the refectory at the bottom of the road, rather than the great fat loaf of the library building, acting as a bulwark at the very top of the pedestrianised road.

Georgia stepped in front of them; he noticed her immediately, and stopped.

'Martin,' she said, holding up a hand.

'Hey,' he said. 'Georgia. Jesus. Hello, how's it going?' She noted his reaction – understandable surprise, though falling far short of shock. He stepped forward, letting go of his girlfriend's hand. He did not move to shake hands, but rather his hand touched her forearm.

'I'm not bad, Martin. Sorry to just appear in front of you like this. Are you busy at the moment?'

'I'm… well.' Martin shifted his balance and glanced at his girlfriend. 'We were just going to grab a coffee, in fact.'

'Finished for the morning?'

'Yep.' He grinned. 'Been hard at it – an hour of Wordsworth, perfectly delivered by Mr Bellman. What a way to spend a morning!'

'Worse ways to spend it, that's for sure.' Georgia smiled, warmly, at the girl with black hair as she peered at the newcomer from behind her fringe.

'Oh – this is Colette, by the way. Colette, this is Georgia. She's a friend.'

'Hello there,' said Colette. North-eastern accent; Durham, perhaps. She took the time to shake hands. Though her hands were small and stubby – which reminded Georgia of moles, and cosiness and warmth – her skin was cold to the touch.

'What brings you to Ferngate?' Martin asked, cautiously.

'Just back in town for a visit, really. Tying up one or two loose ends.'

'Ah.' He hesitated, then said: 'Has there been any more news?'

'Not much – unless you've heard anything?'

Martin grimaced, then said: 'Nothing. Not a thing. There are posters up, of course, and I held a meeting the other day with the union president, a refresher, you could say…'

'I saw that,' Georgia said. 'That was kind of you. Clever, too, mingling it with a drinks promotion night.'

He tapped his temple. 'Yeah – best way to get the punters in, I find.'

'You're something to do with Stephanie Gould,' Colette said, her eyes growing wider. 'You're not her mum, are you?'

'That's right.'

'I hope everything's OK. So far as it can be,' she added, quickly.

'Everything's... well. You know. It's going, I suppose.'

'I feel so... God. I'm so sorry.' She sounded it, too.

'Well, it's one of those things that happens. You read about it, you see it on the telly, you hear a story at the top of the news on the radio – and then, one day, it happens to you. Or someone you know.' The wave threatened to wash her overboard, then. Georgia thought of it as a bow wave, a storm surge, something entirely unexpected that could put her in bed for the rest of the day. *Do not cry.*

Fortunately, after two years, she had learned to keep her feet. She held her head up straight, coughed once, allowed her eyes to mist over, and then smiled. 'One day you're news. Then one day... you're not news any more. And it's another story in the papers, another news bulletin... Someone else's daughter.'

Martin laid a hand on her arm again. 'Georgia... please, if there's anything I can do... Would you like to come for a cup of tea with us?'

'A cup of tea would be great, Martin – but not right now. I've got some business to take care of.'

'Oh – don't let us hold you back, then.' He took Colette's hand again, and she smiled at Georgia, for the first time. Her tiny little mouth had a cute way of cinching together, at the tips – as if her real smile was detained, and threatening to escape across her face.

'But later on, I'd like to speak to you, Martin. Just you, if that's all right.'

'Of course, any time.'

'Would you mind giving me your number? I didn't have any contact details for you, you see. Couldn't see you on social media anywhere.'

'Well… yeah, I'm not too fond of it, in fact.'

'That's very rare, these days.' Georgia pulled out her phone; on cue, he recited his phone number. 'That's great. I was thinking The Griffony – I take it it's still open?'

'Sure.' He grinned. 'Where good drinkers go to die.' The crassness of the expression struck home, then, but Georgia spared his blushes.

'That's brilliant. I'll see you at eight o'clock, if you've nothing pressing?'

'Not tonight.'

'Great. And it was lovely to meet you too, was it… Colette?'

'And you.' The girl smiled.

'Speak to you soon. Enjoy your coffee.'

3

It strikes me that – and you might want to sit down for this – I have Friends. That is a cap F.

From the diary of Stephanie Healey

The Griffony hadn't changed much in the thirty years and more since Georgia had first set foot in it. Its oak panelling bore the scars of decades of graffiti, scratched into the surfaces with penknives, or maybe just pens. The framed photographs that adorned many parts of the walls were strictly unmolested, too – records stretching back to the 1950s, with haircuts running from the Elvis/Teddy boy era to the long hair and loon pants of the flower power era, and then – with a sudden flashbulb shock – colour came into the frame, although Georgia associated the shades and tones on show as matter that she often saw in a clinical capacity – things that had to be washed off or wiped away. Ochre, beige, avocado, clotted browns and burnt purples.

Brass plates, brass taps, brass railings gleamed in the early evening light of the squared bar space that dominated the centre of the pub. Even if the pub wasn't quite ready to host major surgical procedures, The Griffony ran a tight ship as far as its brasses went – a neat trick, Georgia supposed. As before, a galaxy of single malts lit up the central plinth, back-lit in mellow gold. The bottles looked barely touched; then, as now, students had ignored these drinks, but Georgia had to admit she was tempted.

In the centre of it all, of course, was Reg the barman. He had seemed unchanged at first, but the closer Georgia got, the more wizened he seemed; the white hair had probably been there when he was in his forties, but the thin, heavily lined features were new. She had always remembered the landlord as a brawny character. Someone who really suited a big heavy Scandinavian jumper, with a savage beard perhaps grown to mask a double chin. The spare flesh and the whiskers were gone, now; Georgia wondered if he had been ill.

Georgia was slim, a little taller than average with a blonde bob, a reckless flight of fancy by a trusted hairdresser, which had angered her at first, until the compliments started coming in. She wore a Breton shirt that had perhaps seen too many washes, but she liked it and wanted to feel comfortable – ditto the skinny-leg jeans, a little too pale now, but snug. She had considered wearing some heavy boots, before she'd realised what she was doing.

Lots of people told her she didn't look as if she was the wrong side of fifty, and she always demurred, but she had supposed it was true – until she came to The Griffony and saw some real young people, their unfathomable hairstyles, the band T-shirts and slogans that might as well have been in Sanskrit. *I'm a fish out of water, no doubt about it*, she thought – and felt even more so when she ordered a soda water and lime, right after a tall boy surely only just turned eighteen, if he was that, ordered what looked like a prehistoric tar pit in a Perspex pitcher called a Jägerbucket.

She chose a tight alcove that had only one way in or out. The bench was bolted on to the wall just above a locked-up cabinet filled with ancient medical textbooks. In the corner, just over Georgia's shoulder, was a lacquered carving of a griffin. It was difficult to gauge whether it had been carved with a sense of irony or not; she could see someone creating it in deadly earnest, which somehow made it funnier. Its chest was puffed out, beak set in a grim line, the shoulders of its forelegs thrown back somewhat imperiously. It had a comically peeved expression on its face – perhaps in response to the tattered striping of sticky tape on one shoulder that someone had been too lazy to peel off after the Christmas decorations came down.

Martin Duke had gotten changed for her – another jacket that he'd be embarrassed about in a few short years, plum coloured with pale blue silk visible at the cuffs. It wasn't too warm for this jacket, but he was sweating as he sat down.

'Martin,' she said. They air-kissed, the warm skin of his cheek making a feather-light connection with hers.

After they'd gone through the pas-de-deux of who should pay for what drink, he said: 'You're looking well. Still doing the running?'

'Just for fun,' she said. 'I'm not so fast these days – I feel guilty doing it for charity when I've trailed in behind a man in a Loch Ness Monster suit. That actually happened, you know,' she said, catching his grin.

'Well, at least you're still doing it.' He slapped his paunch. 'Unlike me. You on your holidays?'

'You could call it that.'

'So – any developments?'

Georgia shook her head. 'I'm afraid not.'

'I saw you on the telly.' He sipped at a pint of flat, warm beer. 'The T-shirt campaign. It was a good idea – I still see a few of those on the campus.'

'It was just something to try. Maybe a bit silly. She'd hate that, you know – the idea that people had her face printed on a T-shirt.'

'Did you get many tips on the phone line?'

'Mainly abuse.' She smiled, thinly. 'Every single call was checked, though. Some of the abusers had a visit from the police.'

'Serves 'em right.'

'I take it you guys came down here a lot?'

'Everyone did. You matriculate, you come down here. It's a rite of passage.'

'I came down here, too.'

He raised an eyebrow. 'I didn't know you studied here.'

'Oh yeah. Medical school. Loved it here, I'll be honest. Every Thursday, we'd all go to The Bus Stop. Snogging, snakebite, the occasional fight.'

'The Bus Stop?'

'You know it as Benjy's now.'

'Ah – I should have got it from the description.'

Georgia tapped the edge of the bookcase with her fingernail. 'But this was the starting point – ground zero. We used to come in here to get started. If I'm telling the truth, I preferred the pub to the club. You could talk to people. They weren't out of their minds and turned into werewolves, you know that way? Reg was the barman back then, too.'

'No way! He's even older than I thought!'

'He was a young guy back then. That's how long ago it was. Well… youngish.'

'Reg has been embalmed, they say – reanimated many times. Served pints for the Romans.'

'Still miserable with it. *Sodes Tempus*, gentlemen.' They chuckled at that, and Martin at least looked as if he understood. Then Georgia said: 'I recommended this place, you know. Truth be told, I pushed Steph to come here. I felt safe here, and I thought she'd be safe. Can you believe that?'

'It's the classic, isn't it?' He gestured towards the oak panelling grid above his head. 'Classic university town, classic university spire, classic university quadrangle, classic university pub. She told me her grades, you know. One of the first chats we had. She could have studied anything. She wanted to do English Lit. Writer. All those A's…'

'Oh, don't I know it,' Georgia said, a touch sharply. 'I told her – "brains coming out of your ears, and you want to be a poet!"'

'She was a great poet, mind,' he said.

Georgia didn't like the tense Martin was using. She said: 'It's a piece of writing I'm here for, in fact.'

'Yeah?'

'Yeah. I'll tell you a thing about Steph… She always, always wrote. She had no problem putting letters together even before she started school. We used to call her the Little Prodigy – though never out in public.'

'She had the talent, that's for sure.'

'Yeah – but she had the skill, too. And all through her school days, she wrote – stories, little comic books. She drew the illustrations herself in felt tip and crayon. I remember them to this day. The adventures of Stephanie Selkie. She had a Scottish granny who told her about selkies, and the name stuck.'

'Selkies? Are they like mermaids, then?'

'Kind of. Though they could turn on you. Stephanie Selkie was a mermaid to start with, a princess who lived under the sea. She had brothers and sisters. I admit this bothered me a lot at the time, as Stephanie didn't have brothers and sisters. She was the one who looked after them all. She had a magic necklace that I think fired lasers. She could wrestle sharks and killer whales. But as she grew up, Stephanie Selkie turned into a normal girl who could go on land. She had adventures with Lana Lake – her real-life little friend was Lana Price.'

'That's sort of common, I think. When I was a kid, I used to put myself in these little comic books. Socking baddies on the jaw and all that.'

'Later, she got into writing her own adventures down, in real life.'

'You mean like a diary?'

'Yeah. A secret diary, which she kept hidden. Really, really well.'

Martin coughed a little on his pint. 'But not well enough, right?'

Georgia grinned. 'Hey, don't knock the mummy radar. We might be nosy buggers, but it's usually for the right reason.'

'I remember my mum finding a packet of condoms once, and I just had to applaud her. She should be on the team to find Shergar and Lord Lucan.' He put his head in his hands. 'I don't know where to start with my apology for that statement. So many crass things. I'm sorry, Georgia.'

'Don't worry. Happens more than you'd think.' Georgia stared at her own drink; soon it would be time for another. Did she dare get a pint for herself? 'Anyway. It turns out, Stephanie wrote a diary.'

'Is that right?'

'Yeah. Embarrassingly enough, the police never found it when they searched her old room. She had hidden it behind a loose board in a wardrobe. They took their time, completely renovated it, pulled the place apart. No one wanted to move into that room, as it was. Because of what happened to Steph. They went in with the sledgehammers. That's when they found the diary. The person who got her room in the halls the next year. There was just enough room to hide a sheaf of notepaper in there. It ran all the way back to school days. The girl who found it passed it on to the cops right away. It's only just been sent to me. Truth be told, when she was writing it, as a kid... I knew about it. It was mostly school stuff – boys she liked, girls she didn't like, speculation that her headmistress was a vampire's familiar.'

'And you read it from cover to cover.'

'Guilty as charged.'

'You're dry there – can I get you another drink?'

Georgia paused. 'No, I'm fine. Anyway, the diary continued through primary school and then into her teenage years at high school, but she got smarter about hiding it. I missed it in a way, you know? A bit like a TV show you've really gotten into.'

'Heh – I bet that was frustrating.' He drained his glass

and set it down on the table. 'There's a point coming soon, I suspect.'

'Yeah. The later entries is where it gets interesting. She wrote part of it at our house – Easter holidays, right before she vanished. I remember her being shut in her room for hours on end, with the radio on. I thought she was studying, but loads of it must have been taken up with writing her diary.'

Now a look came into his eye – not quite discomfort or alarm, but a renewed interest. 'Was there anything new?'

'Bits and pieces. It covered the people she'd met so far in her first year, her opinions of them. It's funny – there was something in the tone that reminded me of the baby diaries. "That Jessica Jerome… what a show-off. I can't abide that!"'

'Jessica Jerome was a show-off!' he spluttered. 'She dropped out, in fact. Last heard of spending her time at stage doors, hoping she'll be spotted.'

Georgia made eye contact, and held it. 'Some of it was quite frank. I shouldn't be shocked, really. It was the eighties when I was a student, so, you know… it wasn't the Victorian era. We had AIDS to worry about, but we tended not to. Sorry, I don't want to make you feel uncomfortable.'

'You don't make me feel uncomfortable.'

Except she did. His stance had shifted; the left hand had come away from the back of the chair, where he'd left it dangling, and linked with his right on the table.

'She mentions someone called Neb. Do you know who Neb is?'

He shook his head. 'Can't think who that would be… There's Katie Neville, a classmate of ours. That's about as close a match as I can come up with. Off the top of my head.'

'No, Neb's definitely male.'

'Any other details?'

'Yeah – Neb is you, in fact.'

'Neb? She never called me that.'

'It was a pet name. The person called "Neb" is definitely you. She mentions the red hair – I remember the words she used: "like a really interesting crayon, the one you would eat first out of the pack". She mentions the freckles that you're embarrassed about, but she finds quite cute… mentions your jawline, how square it was. The dimples. You're a classmate, you're friends from almost the first day, you spend time together. She mentions that your favourite writer is George Orwell. You want to write a great social document for the twenty-first century… Don't look so embarrassed! It's all good stuff. But you're Neb. There's no doubt.'

'What on earth is "Neb" short for? I don't know what it means…'

'I think she means "neb" as in nose. Northern English or Scots, I think. Not too popular a phrase down here. We're back to Stephanie's Scottish granny again, with that one.'

'I didn't realise I had a big nose,' he said, a little tartly. He restrained himself from touching it.

'You don't have a big nose. It's used in terms of being nosy. As in, "Keep your neb out of my business."'

'Nosy?'

'Yeah. I think she meant that you were a little too keen on her. She felt a little bit uncomfortable about it.'

'…Too keen on her? Excuse me?'

'Yes. That's why I wanted to talk to you, specifically. It pointed out a few things. Such as, that even though you said you were her boyfriend, and you described yourself as such in direct quotes with the police... that wasn't really your relationship. Was it?'

'Hey... we were lovers, if that's what you're asking. We spent all our spare time together. That's boyfriend and girlfriend, isn't it?'

'Not according to Stephanie, no. I mean, she goes into details... Lots and lots of details. She mentions that you kissed her one night in the Acropolis, a club out of town that you all went to. She mentions that she didn't really want to do it, but felt as if she had to. She felt sorry for you; she thought it was a mistake. A fumble. She mentions that you slept in the same bed, but never actually had sex. You were too drunk. Not that you couldn't perform or anything – you literally couldn't get your clothes off. But she says that after that, you were always hanging around. And this is what puzzles me, because she says that nothing happened after that. That you were a fixture, you came around for coffee, but you weren't really... Well, you weren't lovers, were you?'

'Listen – what she writes in her diary is up to her, but we were together when she went missing. That's it – that's the truth.'

'It doesn't sound like it, Martin. I don't want you to be upset, I just want you to explain some things to me. She says she wants rid of you – that she hopes that after your first-year exams are over, you'll find someone else to hang around waiting for after lectures. She says you used to do this a lot – popping up outside classes that she'd taken, but you hadn't. I remember the exact phrase, now, she was good at that stuff. "Waiting for her inside phone boxes no one even pisses in any more", waiting for her to pass by. She said you surprised her once or twice. She found it creepy. She says – pointedly – that she's quite repulsed by you. That you're the last person she wants to sleep with. And she said… what was the wording, again? She says she can see herself ending up inside a fridge on a landfill site if she lets you into her life.'

Martin Duke's bottom lip trembled. He bit it, took a breath, then said: 'Bullshit.'

'Bullshit? So, Stephanie was making it all up, then? It sounds to me – and I don't know the truth, here, I'm just going by what she wrote – that you weren't remotely boyfriend and girlfriend. She is exasperated when you show up one afternoon and she's sleeping with another boy. Did you know about this other boy?'

Martin's jaw dropped. 'Other boy? When was this?'

'February morning – sunny, but very cold, she said. She said she had to wear her hiking socks and three layers of clothing because the boiler packed in. But she had someone else with her. You were at the security door to the block of flats. She said she'd already tried to get rid of you for the day by text message. But you were persistent, she said.'

'Listen… This was a while ago.' He licked his lips. 'Stephanie and I didn't sleep together until April, after the Easter holidays. After that, she rarely stayed in her own flat. If you must know.'

'I must know,' Georgia said.

'We were together, when she disappeared. I don't know about other boys, or whatever else she was doing. That's down to her. I can't answer questions about that, or how she felt. We had a relationship – it might not have happened right away, but we were together. Boyfriend and girlfriend. That's the truth.'

'So, you didn't actually become lovers, in the sense that most people would understand it, until right before she disappeared?'

'If you mean had sex, and you aren't counting a "fumble", as you termed it, then yes. That's true.'

'Thing is, this isn't quite what you told the press and the police. You said something like, "When we first laid eyes on each other, it was like an electric shock… We couldn't stay away from each other, or keep our hands off each other." That's what you said.'

'That's how it felt to me. And I'll tell you this, if we're being frank… You reckon Stephanie said that she wasn't that into it? Not how I remember it, Georgia.'

'"We had made plans together… We were looking to a time past when we were at university." You said that as well, or words to that effect, didn't you?'

'I know the report you're talking about. I was encouraged to say that by a reporter. He put a lot of words in my mouth.' Martin shrugged. 'I didn't think too much of it at the time. We were trying to find Stephanie. That was the priority. That was the only thing I could think about. The idea was to jog people's memories, to find out if anyone had seen anything or knew anything. It might have helped put a human face on me, after everyone accused me of killing her. But it wasn't to provide a step-by-step record of every single encounter we had. If that's what interests you.'

Georgia's pulse was racing. She wanted to reach out

and grab that head, to clutch at the loose flesh around his cheeks, to hurt him. *What's in there?* she wanted to ask. *What do you know about my daughter?*

But instead, she said: 'I don't know the full facts. But if I was building some kind of argument, then I'd say to you: "I think you're a fantasist. I think you were chasing my daughter, but you didn't succeed."'

Martin smiled, surprising her. 'I'm well-schooled in this, you know. You should have heard some of the stuff the police put to me. You'd think they wanted me to make a confession. They built up all these scenarios. They said I was jealous, in fact. A jealous boyfriend. So I did away with her, out of jealousy. That was it. No, wait – I was a creep, a weirdo. A psycho who reads too much Edgar Allan Poe. Obsessed with death, because I read Keats and Shelley and Byron. Or, what was the other one? Oh yeah, you've just told me – I was a fantasist; they said that, too. That I claimed we weren't together when we were. One or two other theories came out, too. They claimed I was secretly gay, because Stephanie had short hair, therefore I liked boys, really. Then they claimed I was secretly into her pal – what was her name, Adrienne? – and I was using Stephanie to get at her. So of course, I killed Stephanie, because she got awkward about it. They mentioned other boys, but I didn't know anything about them. If you've learned anything new, you should take it to the police. You have taken it to the police, haven't you? These ideas of yours?'

Georgia said nothing for a moment. Then: 'There's an inconsistency, Martin. You said similar things to me, when we spoke. You'd think you had been together for years. But you were only together for a matter of days, really, when you think about it. A blink of an eye. That's going by what you've just told me.'

Now he looked angry again. He drummed his fingers on the table, then said: 'I don't know anything about what happened to Stephanie. No – look at me. Look at me, please.' His small eyes flared as wide as he could make them, as he recited: '*I – do – not – know – what – happened – to – Stephanie.* It haunts me. I considered transferring, taking a year out – but didn't. I was persuaded to stay. The university were kind. Especially when it was proven that I had nothing to do with it. You believe that, don't you?'

'The police were very thorough.'

'No, say it, Georgia. I want you to say it. "The police proved that you had absolutely nothing to do with what happened." Say those words.'

'I can't say it, because I don't know it for a fact, Martin. If you don't know what happened to Stephanie... someone does. Even if no one actually abducted her, and the suicide theory checks out...'

'It wasn't a theory, Georgia. I'm sorry, I'm going to have to...' He looked around, as if for support.

'... Even if the suicide theory checks out, then someone knows what the circumstances were.'

'It's not a theory. I'm sorry, but we're done here, Georgia. Please don't hang around outside lecture theatres waiting for me again.'

That stopped her. 'I was just trying to catch up with you.'

'You sure? You know, Georgia, if I was building a theory about *you*, I'd say that you were a bit obsessive. Hanging around lecture theatres, arranging to meet me for drinks... It's a bit strange, isn't it? Paints an ugly picture.'

Georgia ran her hands through her hair. Her voice broke, as she said: 'I want to know, Martin. I want to know the details. Even if I've heard them before, I want to go over them again and again. I want to see the inconsistencies. It doesn't add up, Martin.'

'It does. Stephanie killed herself.'

'Then where's her body?' This came out shrill; Reg and one or two others looked in their direction. 'Where's her body, Martin?'

'You know where it went. I'm sorry, I... Look, a lawyer told me a while ago, when I sued the papers, that I shouldn't speak to anyone about Stephanie. I'm breaking that, here. I'm so sorry.' He signalled towards the front door.

It was Colette. She frowned at the pair of them, then grew concerned as she noticed the tears kindling at the corners of Georgia's eyes.

Colette laid a hand on Martin's shoulder. 'Everything all right?'

'Fine,' Martin said brightly. 'We've been having a catch-up. It got a bit emotional.'

'My God... can we get you something, Georgia?'

'She's fine,' Martin said, getting up. 'I think she was just going.'

4

'And this is…'

Before I could say her name, or even say 'This is my mother,' Adrienne launched herself at Georgia.

'Mummy!' she cried. 'Look at you!'

The girl kissed my mother hard on the cheek, and hugged her uncomfortably across the throat. 'You could be sisters! Look at you, you're a fox! You're coming out, aren't you? Stephanie, please instruct your mummy to come out with us. You'll knock them all dead! We'll have a trail of stuttering boys to follow in your wake, then we shall dine on your scraps!'

'I guess… I'm going out,' Georgia said.

Adrienne squealed and hugged her harder.

Over her shoulder, I shared a look with my mother.

From the diary of Stephanie Healey

Georgia locked herself in the car and sat in a car park behind a KFC drive-through, and cried and cried. These were best places to do it, she had found – alienating, dispiriting, grey blocks and white lines cramming in people stuffing their faces, oblivious to what was going on around them. She had suffered an anxiety attack so acute just two months after Stephanie had gone missing that she had thought she might actually die – despite all her training, all her experience in trying to help people manage the crushing weight of life and expectation, the deep breaths and the safe spaces and the mindfulness, she had sunk on one knee in a clothes shop when she had read a sign that said: 'New season stock in NOW!' and she had looked at the row of models in the picture – some blonde and cherry-cheeked, some edgy-looking and scowling, all different shapes and colours except for the geometric perfection of their teeth, and something in this new season and new line taking place without it being possible to imagine Stephanie wearing these clothes, having these friends or indeed attempting these smiles had strangled her.

So it was now after a quick drink with Martin. She had thought about eating, but this afternoon's encounter had stripped her of any desire to do so. This car park was just out of town, and incongruent with the ancient structures stretching up into the sky over the wall in the background. Unlike the new buildings on the campus, no one had objected to the out-of-town shopping complex, the beige brick blocks with their well-known arches and primary colours and logos. Georgia cried and cried, until she felt better, then cried a little more. She gripped the steering wheel of her car, but did not batter the horn, as she felt she must. Across the car park, in the space opposite, a woman was feeding fries to a three-year-old still strapped into a back seat. She did not glance once in Georgia's direction.

She waited until the windows had steamed up, before blowing her nose, using a wipe to clear the tide-mark horror beneath her eyes, waited until her eyes were marginally less bloodshot, then she took the car back into the centre.

The new buildings in the centre had messed with her sense of geography; the Bryant Tower was a strawberries and cream coloured fibreglass building that she was sure would be a residential property. It turned out it was the new arts block, and at the top of this, in what appeared to be an actual penthouse, was where the student newspaper was produced.

Georgia had only hazy memories of the student newspaper back then – a scandal sheet of sorts, which scored one notable coup where it turned out a physics professor had been selling his services as an escort through the small ads in the town's proper newspaper. She had only seen the outside of the *Ferngate Ferret*'s offices in the old union building – a reptile tank of a room, the glass reinforced with mesh like an off-licence in the centre of Dodge, its windows blotted out with Bauhaus, Slayer and Morrissey posters. When she passed through the intimidatingly clean and spacious reception and got to the top, she was surprised to find a working space that resembled an Apple store rather than a newspaper office. It was clean, for a start; there were also a load of computers, which had been in-built into the desks – Macs for design, Windows machines for word processing, with few signs of debasement or debauchery.

Four or five people were in there, curiously spread out, and everyone seemed to be actually working, heads bent to the task. A television set high on wall showed Sky News; in the opposite corner was a gigantic poster of a shirtless Justin Bieber. Whether this latter had been installed with any sense of irony, it was difficult to say, though it had been defaced a hundred times as seemed appropriate. This was the music desk, surely. The one everyone wanted to work on.

Georgia spotted Adrienne right away. She had changed little since Georgia had seen her last – still well dressed, the only change being that she was wearing clothes for work, not the editorship of the *Ferngate Ferret*.

The girl had a face like a heart that had been scrawled in haste – pale and pretty, with good high cheekbones and something of a sullen mouth. Her hair was cut a little shorter, but the colouring was the same – reddish shot through with blonde. It was the first thing you noticed upon entering any room she inhabited, a colour that demanded a double-take, then a closer look. She had the same sapphire necklace Georgia could remember, a chill pulse that caught the light about her throat – an heirloom from a grandparent. Georgia remembered it had been one of the first things they had spoken about. Adrienne had invited her to handle it – a sturdy thing, set in tarnished metal. 'I don't think it's worth very much,' she had said, thereby guaranteeing that it was worth a lot.

Adrienne Connulty was the type of person who greeted people she knew much as a bowling ball might greet a set of skittles, but she was more reserved this time upon seeing Georgia. 'And there she is! Hey!' She hugged Georgia close, patting her on the shoulder. 'How you been?'

'Bearing up. Sorry to spring this on you at short notice.'

'No problem at all. Let's head into my office.'

'You've got an office? My God, they treat you well in here.'

'Perks of the job, Georgia, perks of the job.' She turned to a young man with a flap of hair on top of a tight-cropped back and sides, one of three other people who were in the office, all spread out across the desks. 'Josh – you mentioned you were making tea?'

'Yeah, well, about two o'clock…'

'Tea for us both, soon as you like. Milk and no sugar for Georgia, is that right?'

'It's no problem if you're busy,' Georgia averred, catching a sullen look from the young man. 'I won't take up too much time.'

Adrienne's office was as advertised, a glass booth set into a far wall with a decent view out the window over the slated rooftops of the campus. Georgia didn't like the feeling of exposure. She wondered if it would get too hot on an especially sunny day.

Georgia took a seat facing Adrienne over two mugs of tea. Adrienne faced her, hands folded on the desktop, absurdly formal-looking. Georgia had a feeling she had been invited in to the headmistress's office.

'I love what you've done with your eyes,' Adrienne said. 'You've gone for a natural look. What is it you're using?'

Georgia thought of the ochre stains on some wipes in her purse. 'Just a little bit of concealer. Blurs the lines. Best you can hope for at this age, I'm afraid.'

The younger woman reached over and took her hand. 'Knock it off – you're gorgeous,' she said. She held on for an absurdly long time, then said: 'To bring you up to date,' Adrienne said, 'we've got a new event for the campaign. I've set it in stone – it comes out every year for the anniversary, until we get a result. "Bring Steph back home". I hope you don't mind the contraction?'

'Contraction? Sorry?'

'Steph. I truncated the name. Diminutive. Makes it more informal. Like someone you would know. Even if you don't.'

'Oh, I see – no, that's fine, I'm all for that. I know most of her friends called her "Steph".'

'We're having a get-together in the centre of town. Nothing major, just a desk set up, with some flyers posted over town, with all the usual social media suspects. The union sprung a few quid for us, and the local council's helping, too.'

'That's superb – thank you so much. Every little helps.'

'And get this: the Megiddos are coming to do a little set. Just the two of them, an acoustic number. That guarantees some national press coverage, too. Keeps it fresh.'

'They sound like a band… Should I know them?'

Adrienne's mouth twitched. 'They're going to be huge. It's all happened for them really quickly, but they're on a steep trajectory. They had an album just outside the top ten, but they're going places. Played at Glastonbury.'

'I'm so sorry – this is the thing about getting old. The last *X Factor* winner I can remember was Leona Lewis. I still think U2 are a kind of newish band.'

'Didn't one of them die recently?'

'What? U2? I hope not.'

'Anyway. Yeah, the Megs. Local boys done good. You know that Riley was a classmate of ours?'

'Riley Brightman, you mean? Yes, I know about that lad. I think he even sent us a letter. Beautiful handwriting, I recall. And GPs appreciate good handwriting.'

Adrienne was perhaps too young to appreciate jokes about doctors' illegible script, but she smiled anyway. 'So, what brings you here today? I'm assuming you're not just here for a couple of drinks and a dance… but I can do that too, if you like?'

'I wanted to talk a little bit about a couple of loose ends, really. I won't take too long.'

'OK.' Not one change in her demeanour.

'I spoke with Martin Duke earlier on today.'

'The Duke of Dull! Poor lad. How is he?'

'Thriving, it seems. He'll be in his last year – same as you?'

'That's right. After that summer, it was strange… He came back fat. A strange one, given all he'd been through.'

'Depression can do all sorts of things to people. You'd be surprised.'

'Would I now?' She said this a little too quickly. This was the Adrienne that Georgia remembered – *spiky enough, love.* 'It's a shame. People know about him as The Boyfriend. People will talk. And they do talk. I'm sure you had your doubts about him after what happened to… well, when Steph disappeared – everyone did.'

Georgia said nothing.

'But the police completely cleared him. He was at a do with the writing society that night. The Hephaestians. Witnesses, social media, the lot. You still get people who think he might just have been able to sneak away. There's a five-minute window where people think he could have gotten into a car, you know… I doubt that, myself.'

'I doubt Martin Duke had much to do with Stephanie. Full stop.'

'What do you mean, full stop?'

'I have my doubts that Martin and my daughter were even a couple.'

'They spent a lot of time together,' Adrienne said, and sniffed.

'I think you know as well as I do that a lot of what he said was a sham.'

'I do believe they had their moments. I was there for a few of them.'

'I am led to believe they had a bit of a drunken fumble one night. Then after that, he attached himself to her like a puppy. What I need to know from you is whether or not they were actually lovers, or whether he was just some sad case who trailed around after my daughter.'

Adrienne laughed. 'Well... you're not talking about a lot of time here, really... Rome wasn't built in a day, you know.'

'Did they sleep together, Adrienne? That's what I'm asking you.'

'A drunken fumble, like you said. It caused a big scandal at the time. Kids. You know.'

'A fumble. Yeah, that ties in with what I heard. So it's true, then – they weren't really an item?'

'What's an item?' Adrienne cocked an eyebrow. 'I remember them being cuddled up together in the park, one day. Seemed cosy enough, to me. If they weren't together, they could have fooled everyone else. Everyone said how good they looked. As a pair.'

'They weren't together. I'm pretty sure of it.'

'So why are you asking me, then?'

Georgia cleared her throat. 'It's an inconsistency in what I was told. It's something that doesn't add up. That means it's worth investigating. I want everything checked. To look at what he said at the press conference… to read what he said in the papers – and I've read it all – you'd think they were inseparable lovers. I don't think that's the truth, and I find that interesting. Anything that doesn't add up in this case is interesting. You know what that's like, don't you, Adrienne?'

'What… being interesting?'

'No. Being in love. The real stuff, I mean. Have you had a proper boyfriend by now?'

'That's a bit frank of you, Georgia. But I'll answer you. Yes. One or two.'

'Then you'll know the difference between a lover and someone you had a drunken fumble with. And you'll know the value of investigating things that don't add up, don't you? Especially in your line of work. You're going places, aren't you? Be blind not to see it. I can see you turning up on the telly, you know. Ah, don't look so modest,' Georgia added, more kindly. 'I've seen that article in the *Telegraph*. That's a feather in your cap, for a student.'

Adrienne actually blushed. 'It was something worthwhile. Something I like to do.'

'A bold idea. People trafficking? Here? Who knew there was such a sleazy underbelly in a town like this? I guess it goes on everywhere. You just have to know where to look.'

'I was worried about those girls. You know how it is.' She shrugged.

'They must really like your work, to give a gig like that to a student. A two-page spread!'

'I'm going to join their traineeship after I finish.'

'It's a great paper. Or it used to be, last time I read papers. Isn't everything online, now?'

'They still do all right,' Adrienne said, a trifle sharply. 'So. Apart from Steph and the Duke of Dull's little dalliance, was there anything else you wanted checking?'

'Yeah. Who's Cornfed?'

'Who?'

'Corn... fed. Written like one word. Cornfed. It's a pet name I've discovered.'

'As part of your inquiries?'

The term was clotted with sarcasm, and there was no mistaking the coldness between them, now. Adrienne was sat perfectly still, perfectly composed, but there was something in this comportment that repelled any sense of warmth. *She doesn't like this*, Georgia thought. *She's not exactly defensive, but this is not a comfortable experience.* 'Yes. I've looked into one or two things. Cornfed was a lad who Stephanie was involved with. Someone she was very keen on indeed.'

'Really?' Adrienne sat forward. 'I have to say that name means nothing to me. And I didn't know she was seeing someone else. Was this when she was with Martin?'

'As I say, I don't think she was with Martin. Not the same way she was with Cornfed.'

'This is news. I'm intrigued. Any details?'

'Just that he was a brilliant singer.'

'Oh.' Adrienne swallowed. 'That could cover a lot of bases.'

'That he's a music star in the making. A lyricist first. I imagine someone blond and handsome – solid. Someone you could see mucking out on a farm, instead of hitting the library. That's what Cornfed suggests to me. Does that ring any bells?'

Adrienne focused on the far corner. 'Search me. Only contender is Riley Brightman, of course. You know – the Megiddos. The letter writer. You'll meet him at the fundraiser. He's in town the next few nights, in fact.'

'The... what were they called again?'

'The Megiddos. There's two of them, but Riley's the singer.'

'Riley Brightman...' Georgia made her spell it, taking notes in a journal she'd bought at the stationer's on Hopkirk Road.

'But – I strongly doubt it's Riley Brightman.'

Georgia's pen stopped on the page. 'Whyever not?'

'Because Steph and Riley weren't... well, they weren't on the same page.'

'In what way?'

'Well, you know... They say opposites attract, but this kind of thing isn't true in real life. Riley was a big character, even before the record deal. He was a star, everyone could see it; people notice him. And Steph was...' She scrambled to save the situation. 'What I mean to say was – look, Steph was hardly one of life's extroverts. You must know what I'm getting at. She was... is, a lovely girl, once you got to know her. But she wasn't the type to live her life at the end of a loudspeaker, you know? God knows, you had to light a fire under her to get her to speak at tutorials. Not that she was timid; she was just *quiet*.'

'That's a fair comment. It seems to me like you're saying that this Riley lad was too good for her.'

'Not at all,' Adrienne said, genuinely appalled. 'She was too good for *him*. I don't think Riley was the kind of lad she would have enjoyed being with. I just can't see them together. And I would have known, if they were.'

'Clever like that, are you?'

'We were besties. Besties don't have secrets.'

'Oh, but they do.' Georgia leaned forward in her seat. 'She does say that you were good friends, that's true. But things got a bit awkward when she got together with Cornfed.'

'Sorry, go back a bit, Georgia… when you say, "she does say", what do you mean? In a letter, an email… phone messages? What?'

'Some correspondence that I found recently. She says that you were really into Cornfed in a major way. She felt guilty when she got together with Cornfed. But she said she couldn't help it. She said that for all his bluster, he's charming. That wasn't quite the word… beguiling, that was the term. A very beguiling person. And he certainly showed interest in her, however it appeared to you. She was flattered, and she was very keen on him in return. But she was keen to keep what happened between them away from you. This wasn't just for the sake of concealment – she was worried about how you would take it. Now, you say it isn't this Riley person, the lad in the band. Have you any idea who else it could be?'

Adrienne's mouth twitched. Her eyes locked with Georgia's for so long, and so intensely, that Georgia began to fear an explosion was coming. But at length she said: 'Honestly, I've no idea.'

'OK.' Georgia tapped the notepad. 'There's one or two other things Steph mentioned… about you.'

'This is intriguing. Just to be clear, though, Georgia – you've been to the police with all this?'

'Oh yeah. Don't worry, I'm no Nancy Drew. Well… maybe I am. I'm just curious. I want to figure one or two things out for myself; I won't do the police's job for them. But I want to look at something Steph mentioned, about this project she'd set up for herself.' Georgia gestured expansively. 'It was nothing to do with her course – more to do with a personal project she had. Something she just wanted to write about. Information she wanted to pass on. She's such a great writer, you know. About everything and nothing – plays, little stories, outlines for novels. I think that was her calling. Later on, though, she got really into non-fiction. A lot of it was just observational stuff. Then she started writing about some of the girls who work in The Strand. That's the red light district, isn't it? She wanted to write about some of the women who worked there. She spoke to a girl from Kosovo who was on the street there. Does that ring any bells, Adrienne?'

'Of course it does. You read the *Telegraph* report.'

'I did. Fascinating stuff. Only, it looked very close to an idea for a feature Steph wanted to write. Very close to the one I read in the *Telegraph*, in fact. She'd already done quite a bit of work on it.'

Adrienne folded her arms. Some colour had flooded her cheekbones. 'What are you implying?'

'I'm implying nothing, Adrienne. Just stating facts. This working girl she knew… it seems she had a nickname, too. Curly Sue. Do you know who Curly Sue is?'

'No idea.'

'Shame. If it jogs your memory, or you find anything in your contacts book – do let me know, won't you?'

'I'll get right onto it.' Adrienne drummed her fingers. Her cheeks were still red. 'I really hate to be a nuisance, but we put this month's paper to bed in a couple of days. That's why it seems almost busy in here. We can catch up later, maybe? I do hate to chase you out.'

'Don't worry. I totally understand. Thanks for your time.'

As Georgia got up to leave, Adrienne bit her lip, then said: 'About this Cornfed... I might have an idea who it is.'

'Go on.'

'Did she definitely say it was a student?'

'Definitely someone attached to her classes. Someone very clever and knowledgeable.'

'Not a lecturer, by any chance?'

'Could be, now you mention it. Though the fact that she didn't outright mention it made me discount it. But you could be right. It was someone who spoke in tutorials very well.'

'The man you might want to speak to is Tony Sillars. He was plain Mr Sillars back then, but since then he's become Dr Sillars. He was one of the lecturers. Specialising in contemporary novels. He's corn-fed, all right. That's a good description. Wish I'd thought of it.'

'A lecturer? With Steph?' Now it was Georgia's turn to sound incredulous. 'Isn't that illegal?'

'Frowned upon, but not illegal... He's only about three years older, or something, before you freak out.'

'Even so... It's unlikely. I don't get the impression Cornfed was on the teaching staff. Were they...?'

'Lovers? Like proper lovers, not quick-fumble lovers? I don't know. It wasn't for lack of trying on Steph's part. That's my honest opinion.'

Georgia wanted to argue with this, but she reined in her response. 'Thank you. I'll check that out.'

'Sorry, that's the only tip I've got. Her and Riley... believe me, it's just out of the question.'

'I'll take your word for it.' Georgia got to her feet. 'Thanks, Adrienne.' Their handshake was formal, and there were no hugs. 'I'll look forward to the benefit show, it sounds amazing. Do you have a contact number for the Megiddos?'

'Sure. But you can meet the Megiddos tomorrow – they're up at the union, giving us an interview. You can come along and say hello.'

Georgia took one last note. As she put her journal back into her handbag, Adrienne asked: 'Did Steph have a pet name for me? Just out of interest.'

'She did.' Georgia zipped the bag closed. 'Magpie. I'll be seeing you, Adrienne.'

5

URGENT APPEAL OVER MISSING STUDENT

By Amanda Rees, PA news agency

Police have appealed for witnesses after an 18-year-old student went missing on a remote stretch of road during stormy weather.

Stephanie Healey vanished last Friday night after apparently going out alone for a walk along a rural route just outside Ferngate.

She was last seen making her way along the A928 road, close to Ferngate Bridge.

The road has no footway for long sections and police are said to be combing the area for any sign of the teenager. Police divers are also assisting the search in the River Dalton.

A first-year student of communication and media studies at Ferngate University, Stephanie's disappearance during bad weather is said to have been out of character.

The 19-year-old, who is originally from Manchester, is described as 5ft11in, with short-cropped dark hair, dark eyes and a fair complexion.

At the time of her disappearance, Stephanie is thought to have been wearing a light green military-style jacket, blue jeans and sturdy hiking boots.

Senior investigating officer Detective Inspector Neal Hurlford, of Ferngate police, said: 'While Stephanie's disappearance is out of character, we would like to stress that we are keeping an open mind as to her whereabouts.

'At the moment there is nothing to suggest foul play, although the investigation is fast-moving and liable to change at any moment.

'Currently, we are focusing our efforts on the River Dalton and the countryside surrounding the A928 where Stephanie was last seen.

'Weather conditions at the time were wet and windy, and anyone driving along the A928 is almost certain to have seen Stephanie if they passed her.'

Anyone with any information regarding Stephanie's disappearance is urged to contact Ferngate Police, or the Crimestoppers charity.

Lectures. I've gone to every single one. Swotty, Neb called me. Something sour in him. Maybe he can see it; maybe he knows. I don't really care. Yes, lectures. I've been to them all. I pay particular attention to one lecturer. And I don't hear a word. That's the thing about a Kingfisher. Hard to look away. Beautiful, even with a wide-eyed little fish in its gob.

From the diary of Stephanie Healey

After Georgia had another coffee, she put on fresh make-up, anchored her sunglasses on the bridge of her nose, and stalked the lecturer.

His office, where he held tutorials and occasional meetings of the New Barbarians poetry society, was in a very handsome part of town. It was away from the squat, functional arts block and in a leafy sandstone area. In the early spring sunshine, with that vibrant virginal green tending towards yellow, it looked wonderful.

Despite the warmer weather, Tony Sillars was still wearing a long astrakhan coat that suited being a little shabby, its hemline flailing at his shins like a needy child. He had what Georgia would have recognised as a record bag slung across his shoulder, a brown leather holdall with an incongruously fearsome buckle gleaming in the middle.

He was handsome, which Georgia had been prepared for, but also laughably young, for which she was not. He had a long Roman nose, which suited the hollows of his face underneath high cheekbones, and a strong jawline that was chiselled rather than craggy. Curly black hair he must have worked hard to control each morning shone in the sunlight, straggling this way and that, a glorious mess. Thin-framed round glasses softened an otherwise heroic countenance. She couldn't help but think: Clark Kent.

He nodded and smiled at just about everyone he passed – men as well as women, Georgia thought, to be scrupulously fair.

She grew tense as he came into the café, and although he had a good look round the seats to see if there was anyone he knew, he did not recognise Georgia. *And why would he?* she thought.

After a long conversation with a plump, beaming barista, he took a large Americano to a seat in the opposite corner and pulled out clumps of printed paper from his bag. Essays, she supposed. He read with his nose very close to the text, darting forward now and again with an unholstered red pen to make notes.

Georgia had thought through several approach scenarios, each one equally lame. She laid her takeaway cup on the table in front of him and went with the simplest option: 'Dr Sillars?'

His reactions were the opposite of what most people would have displayed. At first there was warmth, and an easy smile. And then surprise – and not pleasant surprise, either. *He recognises me.*

'Dr Healey?'

'That's right. I see you're busy – I can come back another time?'

He laid the pen down and straightened in his seat. 'What is it you want?'

'Just a few moments of your time.'

'I'm extremely busy.'

'As I say – I just want a few minutes to talk.'

'I'm not supposed to speak to you.'

Georgia smiled. 'Who told you that? A lawyer?'

'That's correct.'

'Well, this isn't sworn testimony or anything. I just want to update you on one or two things.'

Sillars looked around; took in the other faces in the café, ones he knew and ones he didn't. They were all turned towards Georgia and the lecturer.

He smiled at last. 'Of course you can sit down. If you

want to come back to the office, we can have a chat there. I was taking a few minutes to get some marking done.'

'What's the theme?'

'Consumerism in Martin Amis' *Money*.'

'I think I've read that one. Is that one of the funny ones?'

'Very much so.'

'Does the 1980s still count as contemporary literature, though? I'm, eh, asking for a friend.'

Sillars huffed like a child asked to explain the plot of his favourite movie. He holstered the pen in his inside pocket, closed over the stapled printouts, and fed the papers back inside the bag. 'Let's take a walk, shall we?'

He was certainly the more awkward of the two as they made their way from the coffee shop to his office building. Georgia felt the late afternoon sun on her face and felt a treacherous burst of peace and contentment. The walk up the boulevard, the world beginning rise, stretch and yawn after the winter, the blue in the sky, all served to cast a spell over her, if only for a moment.

'I need to invest in a coat for the spring,' Sillars said, squinting into the sun as it drained through the leaves above. 'Gorgeous, all the same, isn't it?'

'Going to be hot, so they say. For the next couple of weeks.'

You would have sworn his office was a residential flat with a communal entrance; he unlocked a sober police-box-blue door, and sorted through some mail in his cubby hole. 'Late entries,' he said, almost apologetically, brandishing plastic wallets filled with more printouts. 'This is where I have to make a decision; do I go in tough, or take pity?'

'Take pity, of course,' Georgia said. 'Always.'

He smiled at this. 'I'll sleep on it.'

She followed him up the spiral staircase. Each door had a brass nameplate, with sometimes florid titles. Behind the door of Dr Rubens, Department of Philosophy, Georgia was delighted to hear raised voices, laughter and derision.

Sillars' office was at the very top, beneath a skylight. He unlocked the door and took her into a cave crammed with books.

'You know, this place… this would have been an Aladdin's cave to Stephanie.'

'It was. She really caught light in here.'

'Loved books. From the very first. I mean I always read, always enjoyed reading, always encouraged it, but she's something else. Story time was treasured when she was a little girl. And it wasn't long before she was making up her own.'

'Let me take your coat.' Sillars took his own off his shoulders with a comical flourish, like he was a courtier, or perhaps a matador, and hung it on a hook beside a standing shelf crammed to the front and back with books. Georgia ignored his outstretched hand and hung her coat on a spare peg.

Despite the riot of spines and titles all around him, his desk was tidy. He bade her sit in front of him and offered her tea, which she refused.

He took a relaxed pose, and asked: 'What can I do for you, Dr Healey?'

'First of all, I wanted to thank you for all your efforts in trying to find Stephanie.'

'It was the least I could do, honestly.'

'You and the Hephaestians were wonderful in setting up the search teams. I remember that. I remember your face in among them.'

'As I say… it shocked us all. But I was glad to help. Still am glad to help. I believe she may still be out there.' He stared right into her eyes. 'I believe it.'

His sudden sincerity shocked her. She swallowed and said: 'I feel the same way. It feels the same way some people must feel about an afterlife, or a god. I have to believe it. It's kept me going.'

He looked for a moment as if he might reach out across the desk and touch her. Then he said: 'I want to help in any way I can. I was warned by a solicitor not to speak to anyone. She meant "don't speak to the press", specifically, but she did warn me to be careful when speaking to anyone.'

'I understand perfectly.'

'Great.'

'I don't understand why there's any need to be guarded. Just tell the truth and you'll be fine.'

A nerve jumped on the side of his neck. 'The reason I'm guarded is because, for a long time, I was suspected of having something to do with your daughter's disappearance. As I'm sure you're aware. People think she was murdered. People think I had something to do with it.'

'That's one scenario. It's possible I am talking to my daughter's killer, right now.'

Somewhere in the room, a clock ticked.

'It's not the truth, though,' he said, in a calmer tone. 'I had nothing to do with what happened to your daughter. I want her found. Wherever she is, whatever the truth might be.'

'That's why I'm here. I think there's a detail or two that was left out. I want to go over things, carefully. There's something that might have been missed. There's a chain of events out there that don't make sense. That goes from the Friday afternoon she went home from the pub, early, without drinking anything. Then – when the thunderstorm began – she puts on her heavy walking boots, she leaves her phone behind, and goes out for a walk along that damned road. Somewhere along the way, she vanishes. There are lots of elements there that don't make sense.'

Sillars released a long, low sigh. 'I cannot imagine how frustrating and awful it is. Sure, if I can help, I'll help.'

'I want to know about the Hephaestians.'

'It's my dedicated writing group. We meet twice a semester. Everyone's welcome – undergrads, postgrads, staff... We had a physics professor in here. She's on the telly now, in fact. BBC4 every other night it seems, explaining how the universe works.'

'Dorothy Pettifer. Yes, I know.'

'Anyway... that's the size of it. I lectured the first years on the modern American short story, and that's where I met Stephanie for the first time. She was assigned to my tutorial group. She was quiet at first, but you could tell she had a passion for it. You don't often get that, especially in freshers. I get loads of time-wasters... songwriters, people who come to university without any idea of where they're going. People who think being a poet will make you a lot of money; people who want to write thrillers you can buy at an airport.'

'Nothing wrong with any of these things,' Georgia said, mildly.

'The point is – Stephanie had a passion for writing. I guess you know that, from what you've told me.'

'Oh yes. Everything had a story attached. When she was a little girl, there was playtime with her toys. It always fascinated me that she worked out every little relationship between them – who liked who, who didn't like this person or other... Who was in love. Who was jealous. I was never sure where all that came from. She might have seen it on the soaps or in the movies, except we didn't let her watch a lot of television, so it didn't come from there.'

'Maybe just from life,' he said. 'Children sometimes see more than we do. And take in a hell of a lot more than we realise.'

'She was fascinated by stories. It was almost as if there were no minor characters in anything. My husband's a hoarder – he kept a lot of his childhood toys, soldiers, action figures and the like. We dug them out of the loft one day and let Stephanie have a look. You'd be lucky if she'd started school by this point. She got into the idea of fighting and setting up the soldiers, she played along with that. All the guns, the noises they made. But once the battle was over, she went back to check on every single soldier who got killed. She made them "better". She brought over her little Sylvanian Families – they were the nurses. All the soldiers were asked about their mummies and daddies, brothers and sisters, their friends... Some were told they could go home. Some had to stay in hospital forever.'

'Nobody died?' He smiled as he said this. 'That's a sunny nature. I remember that. Do you know, she wrote a poem about all the dandelions who lose their seeds in the wind? The tragedy of being plucked. The delight in seeing the seeds sail off into the wind. It was beautiful because it was like something a child would write. Enchanting, that was the word I wrote in the margins. We published it in our Christmas Review.'

'I saw it. She was so proud. So was I.'

'It was the first thing she submitted to the group. She had the touch. Quiet, maybe a bit too much so, to start with… That's how I found her, anyway. But once she starting talking about her subject, she really came alive. Everyone could see it. There was talent there, lots of it. She'd hardly be the first writer to have a quiet nature. On the outside.'

'I'm intrigued by the writing. This is mostly what I'm here to talk about.'

'Well… I look at a lot of writing.' Sillars gestured towards his record bag, dangling from one of the hooks on the wall. 'The dandelion poem sticks out, of course. I remember some bits, but not in terrific detail. I'll help where I can.'

'I'd like to take a look at some of the writing, if you don't mind.'

'I'm afraid I can't let you take away essays or manuscripts. They're university property, really. It would be improper. The police might even have them.'

'The Hephaestians isn't an official club affiliated with the university. So you wouldn't be breaking any rules, there. I've checked.'

'Of course you have,' he said, a little sharply. 'Look… if

you'd given me some advance notice, I could see if I could dig something out from the files.'

'You've got a filing cabinet there, I see.'

'That's right, but... I don't really have the time to pick my way through it.'

'I can wait... When is your next lecture?'

'Four o'clock.'

'So, you can go through a filing cabinet, can't you? How long does it take? Unless your filing cabinet is actually a secret passage into Narnia or something.'

'Mrs Healey, the answer is no. To all of your questions.'

'Dr Healey,' she corrected him. 'It's all right – the things I'm most interested in won't be here. They aren't part of the Hephaestians, either.'

'No?'

'No. The things I'm most into are the pieces of writing she submitted to you, off the record.'

'I'm not sure what you mean.'

'Her big project. The writing project she was putting together. She worked on it all the way through her first year. I know about it... but I don't know what it is. She refers to it a lot. In her diary.'

'Her diary?'

'That's right. Her private and personal diary. She wrote one during the Easter holidays, right before she vanished.'

'I don't know anything about that.'

'Well, no, you wouldn't. It's a diary.' She laughed, but he didn't join in. 'She talks about the Project – and she gave it a capital P – but she didn't actually refer to it too much. I know it was non-fiction – something to do with the New Journalism. The kind of thing Tom Wolfe or Ken

Kesey might have written. It had a subject – the underbelly of Ferngate. The freaks, the outcasts. Sex workers. And I can't find any sign of it around our house, and the police don't know anything either. It's something she says quite a lot. "I was working on the Project today. Got another two hundred words into the Project..." but she doesn't talk about what she wrote on the day, and bar one or two little details, I don't know a great deal about it. It's very frustrating. I'd like to find out what that is. Do you know what the Project is?'

'I don't know, Dr Healey.'

'Thing is... she mentions having shown it to you, in some form. Are you saying this isn't the case?'

'I don't... I recall plenty of writing from your daughter. There was a short story about a girl who communicates telepathically with a dog. There's one about a dominatrix who wants to travel back in time to shit on Hitler...'

'Oh – that's a cracker. I really liked that one. She somehow managed to be quite tender about it. That's a difficult sell for a love scene involving Hitler... and shit. And then there's the story about the tinker who sells bottled dreams to people at a country market. I've read all these. I've read the notes she made on the stories. They were all carefully based on real people, did you know that?'

'I don't think it's uncommon for people in fiction to have real-life antecedents.'

'She wrote detailed true-life character studies on these people. She said she wanted to fuse fiction and non-fiction... It didn't strike her that this was something new. It was like she'd invented pointillism, or expressionism, or the wheel. But she was always careful to keep a note of character, in real people. Did you know, for example, that the bottled dream-seller is based on you?'

'No, I didn't.'

'The dream-seller turns out to be selling shoddy dreams, you might recall. Good for a little while, but the effect quickly fades. After a while people figure him out, and he gets left behind in favour of someone with better products. Someone younger. Someone better at bottling dreams. She called you Kingfisher. In her diaries. And in her notes for the story.'

'Dr Healey, I have a lot of paperwork to catch up on.'

'I know. I won't take up too much more of your time. What I want to know is, how long did it take for you to start sleeping with her?'

'I'd like you to leave.'

'It's good you haven't denied it. That tells me you might be open to an actual conversation about things, instead of playing footsie.'

'I can't say any more about your daughter. I'm sorry.'

'I mean she was what… eighteen? When you first got together.'

'I did nothing wrong.'

'Oh, but you did. It's right there in the code of conduct. You were given a disciplinary, weren't you?'

'I did nothing wrong, and there was no finding of impropriety.'

Georgia's shoulders slumped. Here it was again; the moment her façade crumbled. It had happened too many times, the past few days, and she didn't want it to happen now. Her eyes misted over, but this made Sillars more anxious. He got to his feet.

'Please...' he said.

'Look. I don't care what happened between you. You were what, twenty-four at the time? Not a huge age difference. I met my husband when I was nineteen, and he was twenty-seven. A junior doctor and a student. So, I'm not judging you on that. I know people who slept with their teachers, for God's sake. I'm not saying it's right. I know it happens. And I don't think you had anything to do with what happened to Stephanie.'

'I was at the Hephaestians' cheese and wine night, that night. There are dozens of witnesses. I could not have had anything to do with it.'

'I know all that. But there's something wrong. She mentions that she had made the Kingfisher jealous. She was with someone she called Cornfed, and that annoyed you. Do you know who the Cornfed might be?'

'Riley Brightman certainly looks Cornfed.'

'He was part of the Hephaestians, wasn't he?'

'As I'm sure you know, yes. My most famous pupil. Even ahead of the physicist.'

'It's odd that Stephanie didn't go to the Hephaestians' cheese and wine night, don't you think? It was her favourite element of academic life. She loved it. Loved the social reach it gave her. So why wasn't she there?'

Sillars paused. 'Something happened after the last meeting of the club. The cheese and wine was going to be something of a damp squib as a result. But there was a bit of a row, as it happened, between two of the boys.'

'What kind of row?'

'I've told all this to the police.'

'What was it that *happened*?' Georgia's voice broke on

this last word. 'I'll beg you if I have to. I don't care that you slept together. I really don't. She was an adult – just. It's up to her to make mistakes, to have these experiences. I don't grudge her them. In a way I'm proud she came out of her shell enough to appreciate herself and to get on with life. I always wanted that for her. She was shy, introverted. Deep as the ocean, but not everybody sees that in a beautiful girl. I think you saw that. She said you told her that. She said you loved her work, even if you didn't say that you loved *her*. She hurt you, though, I suppose. I'm sorry she hurt you. Just like she hurt Martin Duke. He was in the Hephaestians, too, wasn't he? Was there something…?'

'At the pub trip after our last session, Riley Brightman beat Martin Duke up.' Sillars was tense, his fingers splayed out on the desktop. 'I think it was meant to be a fight, a confrontation Martin had engineered, but it was ugly… Martin started it, but Riley finished it. Though it's fair to say his bandmate was involved and helping out. That troglodyte who plays guitar along with him. It was all a bit of a mess.'

'You saw this?'

'I did. I tried to break it up.'

'Was he hurt badly?' She thought she remembered Martin Duke with a thick lip at the press conference. This had seemed suspicious, to everyone.

'Not really. I'd say Riley Brightman looked worse for it. He had a bloody nose. But Martin Duke ended up on the floor, I'll say that. There was only one winner there, if you're wanting a boxing score.'

'Do I need to ask what the cause was?'

'You tell me. You're the one with the secret diary.'

'Was it Stephanie?'

'So far as I understand.'

'Please be specific. I need you to be on the level. You've got no idea what this is like.' Georgia gestured out of the window, where a phalanx of trees was discomfited by the wind. 'I can't have sunny days. I can't have weekends off. I can't take pleasure in the seasons. Or a cup of tea. Or just drawing breath. There's something fundamental missing. It's like someone took my lungs, or my heart, but I kept going. An evil force keeps me alive. And it's torture. Torture.' She was weeping now. This caused him horror, and he shrank away from it.

'I'm sorry,' Sillars said. 'Truly I am. I am sorry.'

'I think she had an appointment to meet someone. I think that someone might have caused her harm. I want to believe she's alive, but I'm a doctor and I'm trained in realities and I know the realities in this case.'

'Dr Healey, there is a theory that Stephanie caused herself harm. There's a poem she wrote. You'll know it. It's called "Where The Dark Waters Flow".'

'*Where the dark waters flow... under the long dark road...* yes. I know that one. I could recite it for you. If you can bear it. I understand the connotation. But that's the part that I think is least likely to have happened.'

He shook his head. 'That's not the official line from the police.'

'You think she'd have honestly done that without leaving a note? Without telling anyone else? Without writing anything to her *mother*? You think that was in her personality, because she was a *bit quiet*? You think I wouldn't have *noticed*?' Georgia was sobbing, now. She fought the clasp on her handbag, then struggled to pull out a clean tissue from the pack.

Sillars clenched his jaw. Then he said: 'I can't say anything else. That's it. We're done. Finished.'

'If you find the Project, let me know. If you have a copy, let me know. There could be a clue. Even if you only read it – anything. Any detail you can spare. Please. From the bottom of my heart, I'm begging you. Tell me.'

His head was in his hands, briefly. She thought he had broken down, too. But when he looked up again, he was angry, seething. 'I already told you. I don't have anything to say. Now take your coat and get out. If you don't, I'll call security and have you removed. Then I'll be going straight to the police.'

6

One day a horseman came by while Princess Melinda was gathering wild flowers. He brought his steed to a halt and tried to get her attention with a loud, braying, 'Hello there!' But Princess Melinda simply continued to gather the wild flowers.

From 'The Stubborn Princess', by Stephanie Healey,
aged eight (on my next birthday)

A quick dash through the meadows with Cornfed. There's a purity, here, something you'd struggle to explain to anyone but your fellow lovers. It sharpens everything.

From the diary of Stephanie Healey

Georgia was falling, or spinning. Lights followed her around and then spurned her, the diamond spark of a distant star that was getting further away by the second.

When she settled, she realised she wasn't in space, or falling, or spinning, but held fast in the ground. Perhaps a mine shaft, or a grave. Somewhere dark, rank and crawling in any case. There was just enough light to see the pinpricks of moisture on black soil. It was hard to say whether any creatures moved in there, or whether the ground simply sweated. She couldn't say where the light came from – a thin effulgence perhaps from a phone.

Georgia felt around and to the side, and finally up above. She was in a crawlspace, a natural tunnel gouged out of the earth, perhaps by a giant earthworm. The edges of stones nicked her fingertips, but by and large the tunnel was smooth. There was a little give in the earth above her head; this frightened her more than anything, the notion that she might be buried down there.

She edged her way forward, where the light grew a little brighter. The soil trickled down as she edged forward on her sodden knees and elbows, tickling her nose and dusting her hair. All the while she was aware of her slow, deep breathing.

Georgia reached what she was sure was a dead end; then she saw that the wall of the tunnel curved to her right. It was surely too narrow to go down, but she knew she had no choice. The lights to the right were a little brighter, a flickering pale blue. A phone, surely. A way of calling for help.

She noticed that the space above her head had increased – nowhere near enough for her to stand up, but certainly an improvement. Georgia kept going, until the space suddenly broadened out. Then she saw the source of the light; not a mobile phone or a laptop computer, but an old analogue TV, tuned to static. It made the gritted surface of the tunnel wall dance, and seem to writhe.

In this stroboscopic glare, Georgia could see a head

sticking out of the earth. Black-haired, with fine cheekbones, eyes closed.

Stephanie.

Georgia doubled her speed, elbows braking painfully off raised stones. 'Steph!' she yelled. Her voice sounded muffled, as if a blanket covered her face. 'Oh Steph, I'm here!'

Stephanie's eyes opened. Black and liquid in the weird light. She smiled. She was buried up to her neck in the rank earth. Two hands appeared, clods of soil clinging to the fingertips like tiny bin bags slung over the dustmen's shoulders, black grime seaming the fingers and knuckles. Stephanie smiled.

Georgia gripped the hands. They were cold and slick, as if she'd gripped the belly of a fish. Stephanie grinned, but the eyes were blank. Georgia had seen those blank eyes before, the frank glare of an elderly woman who had passed in the night, a cancer patient whose body had finally quit like a flickering old bulb, and once, a little boy whose asthma had finally choked the life out of him after he was put to bed—

'Steph, let's go. We have to go back out.'

Georgia couldn't be sure if her grip became tighter on Stephanie, or vice versa.

Stephanie shook her head, slowly, not blinking. Her mouth brimmed with dark liquid, as if she'd taken a brew made with the earth that swallowed her, and finally spilled over in inky rills.

Stephanie began to draw Georgia down.

She would not let go. 'No! You're coming with me!'

Georgia pulled, as hard as she could, teeth gritted. Something tore, and split; Stephanie's wrist bones escaped her pallid flesh. Then the smile grew wider as the skin split along her cheeks and the hinge of her jaw. Her teeth emerged, gums grey rather than pink, then the flesh pulled away from her skull. The skin was retracting into the earth, though the bones remained. Still Georgia clung on, watching the hair yanked off her daughter's skull, the skin undulating backwards into the final darkness.

'All you have to do is let go,' Georgia heard herself say. 'Let go – or go with her.'

That was the end of it. That's when she woke up.

Later, Georgia took tea at a vegan restaurant, which she vaguely remembered having been a video shop back in the day. It was simply furnished, clean and wholesome enough, and the hummus, spicy tomatoes, home-made bread and oil-drizzled rocket salad was filling enough, but as usual she only managed about a quarter of it before giving up. She paid up, apologised to the waitress, then took herself on a short walk across the square to the police station.

It was quite a new building, but she was familiar with this one, having been driven in and out of it a few times in a near-stupor when Stephanie had first gone missing. The queueing system at the main reception was maddeningly laid-back, a fact pointed out more than once by an agitated-looking man in badly soiled sweatpants who Georgia took great care not to make eye contact with.

Finally, she was called through to the security door and then taken to a side office down a long dark corridor. It was an interview room, she realised with an odd thrill.

She was left waiting long enough to have stretched and yawned, before Detective Inspector Neal Hurlford appeared.

He was much as he'd appeared the last time she'd seen him – only a little above average height, but bald, bullet-headed and very thick-set. She wouldn't like to guess at his collar size, with a powerful neck and shoulders betokening someone who certainly made an effort at the gym, whenever he decided to go. In build he was a doorman, one who you would obey should he raise his voice, and possibly even before that; but the eyes and the set of the cheeks were kind, even cute, and even allowing for the circumstances in which they had met, she remembered someone who had been prone to wide-eyed surprise and quick mirth.

He nodded at her and grinned. 'Mrs Healey – it's been a while.' His handshake was warm. He sat across from her and sat back in the chair, scratching the back of his head and stifling a yawn. 'Excuse me! Long day, here. How have you been keeping?'

'Well... all right, is the expression, I suppose.'

He drew a long breath. 'All right is as good as I could have hoped.'

'I know you're busy. I just wondered if you'd been able to have a look at my thoughts on the paperwork that was turned up.'

'The diary you mean?'

She nodded. 'It's not much, but...'

'It's a lot. I'll level with you, I was excited when I found out about it.' He opened up the buff folder and pulled out some printed sheets. 'It's a lead, no matter how small. Something new. Something we can work with.'

Georgia felt a blossoming of that treacherous creature whose name she dared not vocalise; a strange levity in her breast that she had learned not to trust. Still, there it was: hope. 'Have you found much else? Can you say?'

'We certainly had some new conversations with people.' Hurlford's eyes met hers. 'It did help clear up one or two loose ends we'd struggled with.'

'I understand. You can't say much.'

'We have some procedures, I'm sure you understand. What I can say is it helped give a clearer picture on one or two incidents that had been bothering us.'

'But no new leads.'

'Not quite, no. But it was useful,' he said hastily. 'This "Cornfed" character... it gave us an insight into one or two things. We had to conduct some new interviews. It didn't exactly tell us new information, but it did make the picture that bit sharper.'

'I'll bet you can't divulge the details, et cetera et cetera.'

He smiled, shyly. 'There's no fooling you, missus, is there?'

She met his smile and raised one of her own, but she said: 'You could have told me that over the phone.'

'True. But what I'm interested in, is what you got out of the diary.'

'Come again?'

'You have some ideas of your own, I bet.' Hurlford pulled his chair closer, bending his head conspiratorially towards her. 'Share them. Don't keep them to yourself. I'll listen to any theories, anything that gives me a more complete picture.'

'All right then. Cornfed, I think was the musician who was in her class. The one who's going to Glastonbury next year. The one who was in the top twenty the other week, and got interviewed by Steve Wright. I'm sure you know who I mean?'

Hurlford made no indication of agreement or disagreement. 'Go on.'

'I think my daughter was involved with Riley Brightman – obsessed with him, for sure. She talks about him all the time. Now, admittedly, a lot of it is in abstract terms, so I can't be sure. But I think she was carrying on with this Brightman boy, at the same time she was supposedly going out with Martin Duke. That's point one. Point two is that I don't think my daughter was as closely involved with Martin as he made out. To look at him, to hear what he said, you'd think they were a close item. I don't think they were. If anything happened between them, it was a drunken fling that he took far too seriously.'

He took no notes; but he paid close attention to Georgia. 'What else?'

'I think she may also have been having a fling with Tony Sillars – the lecturer, contemporary literature.'

Hurlford took a little longer before replying: 'I see.'

'None of this is news to you, I suppose.'

'We've looked into a lot of aspects of the case. We've had hundreds of officers, over thousands of hours, looking into every aspect of it.'

Georgia smiled. 'You're really good at this, you know. I can see why they wanted you to front the investigation. Have you thought of entering politics?'

He did not appear to take this as a slight, and certainly Georgia hadn't intended it as such. 'Nah, I think that level of villainy is beyond even me, Mrs Healey.'

'Is sleeping with students a crime? Abusing his position of power?'

'It's not illegal for consenting adults to develop relationships, regardless of how it happens. It is, however, unprofessional, and lecturers are required to notify their governing body if they have a relationship with a student. To avoid an obvious conflict of interest. To make sure they are blocked from marking the work of a person they are romantically involved with. If they break those rules, then they could face losing their job. So there are no laws, exactly, but there are rules, and they have to adhere to them.'

He's rehearsed that line, Georgia thought. 'And I take it he did notify authorities about my daughter?'

'I'm not at liberty to disclose that. I can say that Dr Sillars still has tenure at the university, and the full support of his colleagues.'

'So – he did report it. Or, he reported something.'

'Dr Sillars is married, did you know that?'

She hadn't noticed a ring. Certainly, there were no pictures on his desk. 'Really?'

'Yes – to a former student.'

'I have heard that he's somewhat fluid when it comes to relationships.'

'As I said, Mrs Healey, Dr Sillars is held in very high regard among his employers and his students. I understand that he has an agent. He's been in talks to appear on a television documentary.'

He hadn't mentioned that, either. 'Well. So long as you're aware of what he's like.'

'It can be very hard to prove relationships happen between lecturers and students.'

'He must be a suspect, though.'

Hurlford sat up, and grew very serious. 'Dr Sillars' movements have been accounted for on the night Stephanie disappeared.'

'But not all night. He was at a party, wasn't he? A cheese and wine event. I know that. But there's every chance he could have got away, got into a car. He could have driven down there. By car it's not far at all. He could have done this.'

Hurlford sighed. 'Dr Sillars' movements have been accounted for, and we are not treating him as a suspect in the case.'

'How about Cornfed – Riley Brightman? And Martin Duke?'

'We are aware of Stephanie's social background – we've gone into it in some detail. We've interviewed just about everyone she was involved with at the university. We have made no arrests at present.'

'Then you think she was abducted?'

Hurlford pinched the bridge of his nose – the first outward sign of any agitation. 'We are keeping an open mind about what happened to your daughter.'

'I know that. You say that. I've been told that so many times. We have to keep an open mind, because we don't know. But you must have an idea, or a suspicion.'

'Gut instinct, you mean?'

'Yes, if you like.'

'I'm not qualified to make a judgement on that. But you are.'

'Excuse me?'

'I go by facts. I back everything up with proof. It's not

an exact science, I leave that to forensics. But I have to make the events fit together. It all has to make sense – it's a matter of times, dates, locations, corroboration. Physical evidence, of course, if I can have it. Your gut instincts can deceive you – that's my experience. I've looked right into the eyes of killers, and you wouldn't believe how trustworthy they can seem. How they can act innocent. Even if they've got one or two tells, they'd swear blind that they didn't do it. But I would listen to other people's gut reactions. They can give me a steer. They can open a door to something I hadn't considered. Especially when it comes from the mother of a missing girl. So, go on. Tell me what you think happened.'

'Well... the strong theory is that she killed herself.' Georgia swallowed. That faint tremor began again, seizing both her hands. Her voice shook a little, as she continued. 'Several people have said she seemed ill, withdrawn. She went to her GP and complained of depression, just after Christmas. I didn't know this at the time. She was given a course of citalopram, which she collected from the pharmacy but didn't take, going by the medication that was found in her room at the halls. She had been out of sorts. Something had happened between Martin Duke and her that might be related to a fight he had with Riley Brightman. Something that really upset her. She also had her end-of-term exams coming up, and she hadn't been studying as hard as she might. It seemed her essay marks were mediocre and she had only just started cracking the books at Easter time. That's not the girl I knew. And yes, she had seemed withdrawn in the Easter holidays. She stayed in her room, slept a lot. She was writing a diary. So yes, all these factors do fit in...'

she took a deep breath '…with the theory that she went up that road, on that awful night, with the intention of heading into the moors and taking her own life. And her body is still out there, somewhere.'

Hurlford reached across the table and offered his hand. She took it, nodding once, choking back tears.

'Then there's the other theory. That at some point, on that road, in the six- or seven-mile stretch in between Ferngate Bridge and Raeside filling station, she came across someone who caused her harm. Maybe it's one of those awful random events, a random bloke, someone who had a moment of madness, a guy with a time bomb in his head, something out of a horror film… Or worse, someone who's done it before, someone who took a chance, and she was just very, very unlucky. Or maybe it was a hit and run. Somebody panicked, lifted the body off the road. But that's the second scenario. I'm realistic enough. I don't think she did a Reggie Perrin. She was a wilful, imaginative girl, but not that wilful. She'd have come back to me eventually. And she didn't run off with a handsome stranger. She didn't ride off into the sunset on a weird quest. She isn't on a kibbutz somewhere, or paddling a log canoe up the Amazon. I imagine all these things, of course. I imagine all the good outcomes, the ways it could have worked. The ways she could come back to me. But suicide and abduction are the two realistic theories. Does that make sense to you?'

He had let go of her hand by now. At length, he nodded. 'Those are two common theories. But I'm always open-minded. Not exactly positive – I am not going to give anyone false hope without good cause – but I have to be open to every possibility until the facts change. And the facts are that your daughter vanished on that night. We have no new leads. It's a terrible mystery. I am still working on it. I am still talking to people. I am trying to pick up new things. This...' he held up the buff envelope, which held a scanned version of the diary '...did fill in a few gaps. But it didn't give any definite clues. Not yet.'

Georgia nodded. 'You knew all this, in other words. Everything in the diary. It all came out in the wash, at the time.'

Hurlford didn't reply directly, but he said: 'We spoke to everyone she encountered... everyone who was in the pub with her on the nights leading up to the disappearance... We retraced her every move, we saw her on CCTV from multiple directions, we traced every single bit of data we could on her. And we spoke to literally everyone. Her friends... their friends... the men she knew... Everyone, Georgia. We haven't made any arrests, and we don't intend to yet. We'll keep looking. That's what I can tell you. That's a guarantee. We'll keep looking. We'll keep talking to people. We'll keep going to the public.'

'People don't just...' *Vanish*, she was going to say. But she knew that was false. Of course people vanished. She'd read the Wikipedia pages. She'd seen the smiling faces of those who'd disappeared, the passport photos, the school portraits, the graduation gown mantelpiece images. Analogue smiles, blood reds faded to ochre. And she'd seen the faces of those who'd lost them. The mothers and fathers, gaunt, drawn, haunted. Like her.

'Don't give up on us. We are working on it.'

'You're not magicians, I know.'

'Are you here for the appeal? I think the Megiddos are

playing. Very big deal – they're an up and coming band. Riley Brightman's done well for himself.'

'I haven't met him. But I think I'm going to.'

'He's a nice lad.'

'Stephanie thought a lot of him.'

'Cornfed… yeah. It could be him. But it's vague. We can't be one hundred per cent. She was very keen on Cornfed, that's for sure.'

'Cornfed could be the one. The person who took her.'

'The men you mentioned – including Riley Brightman – have alibis for that night.'

'Alibis can collapse. Loyalties can change. So can the big picture.'

Hurlford took a sip of water, never taking his eyes off Georgia. He placed the cup down on the table, then said: 'I would caution against approaching Riley Brightman.'

'I can hardly avoid him at a concert, can I?'

'I just don't think it's a good idea for you to approach people. Every angle in this case has been explored. Ones you've thought of, ones you haven't.'

'And ones you won't tell me about.'

'For very good reason. Now, it's not a big warning, or an edict, or anything like that. I just think it's not healthy for you. How long have you been in town?'

'Since last night.'

'And when are you going back?'

'In a couple of days, maybe. I've got things I want to work out. In my head.'

'In what way?'

'Places I want to go. Steps I want to retrace. Places I want to pay a visit. Memories I want to kindle of the times we spent here. Moving her in. Taking her to lunch. Coming over to check on her. Things parents do.'

'I understand.'

'Do you?' She said this a trifle sharply. 'You know as well as I do, Stephanie's probably dead. She's in the ground, somewhere. Or in a freezer in someone's garage. Or worse still. I won't see her alive again, I know that. But until I have her body back, there's a tiny doubt. A little flaw in the logic. I know this because I dream about her. Sometimes it's… not so good.' She shuddered, at the thought of her dream earlier. 'Other times, it's lovely. She's alive. She tells me she's fine. We have a little chat, and I give her a hug. "Don't leave it so long," I tell her. Usually this is about the time an alarm goes off in my head, and I wake up. Once or twice, I even screamed.'

'I'm sorry, Georgia.'

'Because you can't really know. There's a doubt. And your brain will seize on anything. If you're lost in the woods, and you see a plume of smoke, then you'll go towards it. You don't know who lives in that house. It could be a wicked stepmother. But you'll go. You'll take any hope that's going. Once or twice, in the past two years – I don't mind admitting this – I've had a little bit too much to drink. And I had this fantasy of ways that she could be still alive. Each one sillier than the last. It's the old kibbutzes and canoes idea. Maybe she was pregnant, and decided to raise the child off-grid, an earth mother. Maybe she became a self-sufficiency buff. All sorts of fantasies. Because you can't know for sure; even though, of course I do know. That's my gut instinct, as a scientist, as a doctor, as a person who deals in the harshest realities. And it's also my gut instinct as a mother. But I still hope. Though it's wrong and it's stupid of me. I hope. I can't exactly grieve. And I can't exactly be optimistic. I'm stuck. I'm in limbo. That's why I've come here.'

'Leave it to us. Trust in the professionals. This is pretty much what I told your husband. I'm sure you know.'

'What? When was this?'

'Well… six or seven months ago. Start of the last academic term, this would be. He told me you knew?'

'What did he say? Did he find out anything?'

'Um… no, he didn't…' Hurlford blinked, then reached for the water. Discomfited, for the first time. He hadn't looked nearly so uncomfortable when modelling death scenarios. Interesting that he did not know this. 'Rod didn't provide any new information. Just checking in, really. Much as you are now.'

'I did not know that.'

Hurlford sat back and folded his arms. 'I'm going to give you… an opinion.'

'Go on.'

'You've lost a lot of weight since I last saw you.'

'I try my best. Not easy once you get to fifty.'

'It wasn't a compliment, Mrs Healey. It looks like the kind of weight loss that you get through stress, anxiety… and depression. I've seen it in mothers, fathers and partners before. You say you can't grieve, but you look like a person in grief, to me.'

'I'm a general practitioner with more than twenty-five years' experience. I know these signs better than you.'

'Then I would hope that you'll recognise them in yourself, and take any help that's offered. If you've split from Rod… divorce in itself can be hell. I remember my parents splitting up well enough. My advice... I mean, my opinion... that's all it is... is that you should go to the concert, leave nice and early, get out of Ferngate, and have a holiday. Somewhere you can be distracted – somewhere very loud, or somewhere very peaceful. Because I can see the change in you. I can see what Stephanie's disappearance is doing to you. Above all, I want you to stay away from that road.'

'I didn't mention the road.'

'You mentioned retracing steps, and those are the obvious ones. It's not a good road. It's the kind of place you'll find flowers tied to trees every few miles. I attended a lot of RTAs on that road, when I was in uniform. That's before we think about what happened to Stephanie. So will you promise me that? Stay away from the road. And stay off the moors, too. Particularly the ghyll. Will you promise me that? Don't go near the ghyll. It's not safe.'

Now she was angry. 'I'll go where I please. Unless you're giving me orders, now?'

'Of course not. Georgia...' He was exasperated. He raised his hands, as she got to her feet.

'Don't worry. I'm not planning on staying here long. And I think I'll see myself out.'

7

There's a place of adventure – somewhere in my head, quite separate to whatever physical spot I happen to find myself in, and I can't help but feel drawn to it. I need to reconcile this need for romance in my head with a physical reality. I feel this is the essence of Cornfed's appeal. I was such a quiet, withdrawn girl. All the excitement took place in my head. Now I find myself living these quests and romances, and it is delightful to me. If there's a source of all adventure then I have to make my way towards it. But I'm rambling here.

From the diary of Stephanie Healey

Georgia took a room in a small apartment block, an unlet student property that did well on the online pop-up room services. It was at the top of the building and seemed all quiet, despite the presence of young people below. A bed, en-suite bathroom and a TV stand were just about all it permitted, but Georgia was glad of the close confines. A bigger room would have given her imagination space to play, and that was something she didn't need in the dark, with the heavy curtains blotting out everything but the dull glow of her fitness tracker. She imagined she was at sea, tightly packed but secure in a cabin, nothing outside but cool waves.

The next morning, she put on her walking trousers, a good base layer and a training top, cinched the laces of her new boots, and set off on the road her daughter was last seen.

It was a bright morning, and she congratulated herself on having the foresight to pack sunblock. Its coconut smell was treacherous, a reminder of foreign holidays from long ago. She fit a baseball cap over the top of her tied-back hair, and made her way through the town centre. The market was set up over by Slumbers' Yard, with its intriguing mix of fresh fruit and veg, seafood and bongs. From here there was a lane that ran alongside the river. Here, surely, was the place Stephanie would have entered the water. Even now, in dry conditions, it ran fast here; there had been up to nine inches of rain on those two days, a freak hangover from an Atlantic storm that had battered Britain. The river would have been close to bursting its banks, and treacherous. There had been a suggestion that Ferngate Bridge might have been washed away. But the only thing that had been taken away had been her daughter.

The weather factor about that night irritated her. It complicated things. It meant that there could have been a more mundane explanation. Treacherous conditions, very easy to slip, lots of ways she could have entered the water along the river. There had been extensive searches, but...

Georgia passed some dog walkers and runners on the path alongside the river. One of these was a rather alarming young man with eyes screwed tight shut who was reciting things to himself, point by point, counting on his fingers. Finals coming up, Georgia supposed. She remembered this well enough.

Stephanie hadn't been that way inclined. She did have an intense, swotty phase around about the time she'd started secondary school, and she'd been top of the class for a while. The onset of the teenage years had changed that. Not that Stephanie had tried to fit in with the wrong people, but more that she learned not to stick out too much. That to compete and to try to reach the top was to draw unwanted attention. Tall poppies tended to suffer the same fate, even though the school Georgia had sent her daughter to was far less razor-edged than the one she'd attended. Much better to miss out the homework occasionally; to forsake the studying for a night out with Mel or Izzie, the two girls who'd stuck around for the early years. But not the latter ones.

Though both girls had come to see her after the disappearance and their tears had been real enough when they saw Georgia, they had lost touch in the senior years, the make-up years, the boyfriend years. Stephanie had not followed them. She'd gone strange; gone into herself. Tall, with good legs and sharp features – *a model*, Georgia had said to her, more than once; *you could be a model* – Stephanie had never made the most of it. There had been one comically nervous lad who came around for studying and tea one night, only once, but never again, and never anyone else. Stephanie had taken more to writing, scribbling in her diaries, branching out into short stories and plays, none of which she'd ever attempted to have published.

To Georgia's dismay, her daughter had pursued this into

higher education, putting her disappointing exam results to some use, if not good use. Oxbridge was out of the question – something Georgia had never known she wanted for her girl, until it became something denied – but she had followed in her mother's footsteps and ended up at Ferngate. At the time, of course, this had seemed cute.

Journeys and quests; adventures, castles and magic. These had been some of Stephanie's fleeting obsessions as a youngster. She hadn't joined the hillwalking society, but she had instead taken journeys on her own. This was something that had been pieced together later, by the police, but it hadn't surprised Georgia. There was a walking route through the town, and Stephanie had gone on it, enjoying the exercise and her own company, as usual.

Weirdo was the nasty verbal spit Georgia often resorted to. It was always there, a spear ready to throw whenever things grew tense. To Georgia's shame, she'd even said it to her daughter during some of the worst teenage rows. *If you won't study properly, then you could at least go out more and get a social life, like a normal girl your age!*

Then Rod's voice, meant to be soothing, but always slightly arch: *'Let her develop at her own pace, Georgia. She's her own person. She'll find her own path. She's not going to go into medicine. Forget it. That's not what she wants. It never was. Never will be.'*

'Then she could do something useful, for God's sake! A writer... how do you become a writer? Who studies to be a bloody writer? Poetry? Tone poems? What in God's name is a tone poem?'

'Well, someone's got to do it,' Rod said. *'Writers are out there, and people read. So why not Stephanie?'* And maybe

he'd have sighed. This would have become a condescension too far. And that would have triggered another row.

The path grew more crooked, with the metal barriers at the edge of the riverbank seeming to become warped, as if remoulded at an idle moment by a giant with twitchy hands. This emptied out onto the road itself, with a narrow pathway also marked for cyclists on one side of the road. Taking this path, Georgia trooped past a mix of big houses and bungalows on the opposite side, with smart driveways and immense gates. Some of the houses were hidden behind trees and bushes, the odd window appearing through the gaps like a nosy neighbour. Millionaire's row, Georgia supposed.

Every single door knocked. Every single person interviewed. Every single movement traced, checked to the minute, noted, accounted for, logged. They knew what they were doing. What had Hurlford said? *Hundreds of officers, thousands of hours*. The answer was not to be found in these homes, these people. Knocking these doors was a waste of time.

But Georgia knew, if no answers came, that one day she'd be knocking those doors, all right. She'd want to speak to everyone. She might take years to do it, but she'd do it. She'd look into every face, every pair of eyes. She'd watch and listen very carefully.

But Stephanie had not stopped at these houses. Like a wraith she had drifted past them in the pouring rain. One or two people at their kitchen windows or upstairs in their rooms had seen her shade passing by, walking into the storm. The weather had made her passage memorable for them. *Who'd be out here, on a night like this?*

Here and now, Georgia was beeped by a leering teenager as the footway disappeared – a nasty shock, a brief encounter with the kind of unpleasantness that Stephanie might have run into. She had to cross the road several times to avoid blind corners. Her shoulders were tense, alert, as she anticipated traffic, straining to hear the sound of an engine. Sometimes the road kinked and warped, so that Georgia felt herself stranded in a knot of road, quite unable to do anything should she be rushed on either side by traffic.

As she'd been told by DI Hurlford, there were a number of places where the trees were garlanded with dead flowers and limp streamers. At one of these spots a wind chime played its melancholy fanfare. Perhaps it had been there when Stephanie had walked this same path, spinning and swaying in the maelstrom. This road wasn't busy, even at this time of day – a bypass had been completed about ten years ago, diverting much of the traffic. It would have been a draw for every lunkheaded teenager in their daddy's Beamer for miles around. The ancient tributes were testament to that – the places where the cars had left the road. Georgia had prescribed antibiotics for one boy back home who had lost his lower left leg in one such accident. She knew that the two teenage girls who were in the back of the car at the time had not even had that wretched luck. Stone dead; blunt-force trauma. The boy had seemed utterly indifferent, even contemptuous of Georgia as she examined the wound, and the nurse had said the same, later, after she changed his dressings.

Stephanie had never driven, or shown even the remotest interest in owning a car. Georgia had paid for a few lessons as soon as her daughter was old enough, but the girl had begun to feign illnesses when the sessions came up, and soon enough she understood the signs. Pony riding and trekking had been more her thing, but again, the girl had retreated from that as soon as the teenage years had kicked in. She went into herself – a phrase Georgia had remembered from her Scottish granny. Private worlds had taken precedence over the real one. She was a wanderer at heart, a gypsy spirit, someone who liked hills, mountains, lakes, freedom, and not too many people. She was—

A bum, Georgia had told her, after she came back home from a camping trip, as she dumped a load of stinking gear in the washing basket then left it to fester. *A stinking bum. My beautiful daughter, a bum.*

She bit down on the memory. When she was alone – which was more and more often these days, now she was out of the blast zone of shock and trauma in the immediate wake of the disappearance – these sour recollections could flood in. A sharp word or a raised hand when Stephanie was a child; the exasperation of an exhausted parent when she wouldn't behave in public; a catty remark, or even the full-blown rows. One exchange particularly haunted Georgia, a physical altercation when she'd grabbed her daughter by the scruff of the neck. Those dark eyes had widened in shock, the mouth dropping open. *You are failing*, she'd roared at her. *Why did I have to have a failure as a daughter?*

Whatever, she thought. *Whatever happened, she's my daughter and I love her. Wherever she is, whatever circumstances put her there, alive or dead, I will have her back.*

The bridge came sooner than expected. It rose on the horizon, the slow undulating back of a whale, pretty in the fresh afternoon light. It was something you would use in the background if you were the type of person to take selfies, which Georgia was not – a Checkpoint Charlie for people trying to get to Ferngate by this route, rather than the motorway slip road on the far side of town. Unless you took the turn-off about two hundred yards past the alarmingly narrow throughway on the bridge, that was you until a roundabout seven or eight miles further on. Unless you parked in an overgrown lay-by forsaken even by the truckers.

Georgia took a deep breath and cleared her mind, listening to the patter of the river underneath as she crossed the bridge.

There was a theory Stephanie had entered the water here, whether by accident or design. Again, with the amount of rain that had doused the whole region over twenty-four hours, the waters would have been swollen and greedy, and there was a chance that her body had been carried downstream for some considerable distance before it was strained through Paveley Weir.

Georgia accepted that the theory was sound. There was a chance that Stephanie's body was under the water somewhere over the course of miles, snagged on a tree root perhaps, buried under mud maybe, but there. Somewhere. Still tossed this way and that by the flow of the water. Suspended animation.

Short of dredging the whole river by herself, there was no way to be one hundred per cent sure. *Maybe it'll come to that*, she thought. *Maybe there will come a point where I'm wading through it, inch by inch, hoping to find something that isn't there. Groping around in the riverbed. Hands full of stones and silt and things that wriggle.* Similar to the knocking of every door. She'd present a flyer, maybe, a picture of a girl three years out of date, five years out of date, ten, fifteen, twenty years out of date. *Please*, she'd say. *Please help.* These derangements were not impossible, even likely.

Reaching the crossroads after the bridge, Georgia checked her OS map before taking a left, up and over a set of steps in a limestone wall. The land rose surprisingly sharply here; there was farmland all around, and Ferngate itself was flat as a Monopoly board, but the land inclined sharply heading east towards the crumbling coast. After bypassing some sheep and their nervous newborns, the trees closed in. She followed an old train track, long ripped up by Dr Beeching, that led through a defile in the earth. Rock began to appear here, mainly slate and limestone, poking through new ferns and bracken. It was a fine dry day, but the rock was slick to the touch.

Georgia was following a hunch, but a good one. If Stephanie had been following one of her old quests, then she would surely have passed through the cut in the earth. Even on a horrible night, or perhaps even because of it, this is where she might have gone. If she'd taken a notion. And 'taken a notion' was as good an explanation as any for why her daughter had walked up that lonely road, with no text messages or social media trail to follow, no other indication why she had gone where she'd gone.

The other reason Georgia had come here was because, even if Stephanie had a destination in mind along that road past the bridge, then if she'd been abducted, this was a place where she might have been taken. Where would you go to hide a body? The notion still triggered a primeval reaction in her, deeper than instinct, a stiffening of the muscles at the shoulders, a mild sense of nausea. You'd dump it around here. Even with the sniffer dogs, the scores of volunteers, the foliage and the ground literally scoured, this seemed like a good place for wickedness to be concealed.

The path was reasonably well kept, but stony. Georgia's calves gave her more trouble than she might have supposed, and the new boots began to pinch in the traditionally awkward spots. After half a mile, she reached the first point on the map that had fascinated her – the cave.

Cave was a misnomer; it was more of a gap in between two immense boulders, overgrown with moss and lichen, with a lip of rain-worn stone protruding overhead. It provided cover for anything the size of a man on down, and indeed there were signs that a fire had been lit outside it recently. Names and obscenities had been carved there, blurred over time into a Sanskrit highway across the rock. Georgia paused and crouched low, after making sure she was quite alone. You would sit comfortably inside, though the overhanging rock would be something on your mind. It would be wet to shelter in here, although the ground in there was soaked up by a natural carpet of pine needles, but you could do it – you'd perhaps need to do it, with the rain coming down in the dark.

Perhaps it was here that something had happened; something unspeakable. Though the police were sure no one had passed along this way.

Georgia moved on. The next step along the journey would be her last along this route – the ghyll.

She heard it before she saw it – roaring water carried

through, some run-off for the source of the river. The ghyll was a waterfall contained within a rocky gap in the earth – a peephole at the top of a hill that gave a view into what was either a vision of hell, or a natural wonder, depending on your viewpoint. Signs had been erected there, warning passers-by of the danger. Georgia had read there was some opposition to these signs among ramblers and local people, some disdain over the incursion of the modern world even as it served to warn people of the danger of death.

People had died in the ghyll. It was a popular spot with cavers; once you squeezed yourself through the aperture at the top of the hill, a flat slab of rock pitted with holes formed over the last ice age, there was a very tricky climb down to a cavern, and a downward-sloping tunnel into fast-flowing water that eventually emptied out into the river below. Two cavers had been killed in a collapse in there, in 1985. They had been trying to squeeze through the narrowing, water-logged passageway down, down and down into some unspeakable darkness, when some rock had fixed them fast under the water.

Georgia was not claustrophobic – not so you would notice, anyway. She was not arachnophobic either, but she was certain what her reaction would be if a bird-eating spider was to land on her face. So, too, for this gap she stared into now, at the head of the ghyll.

'That is one great big pile of nope,' Georgia said, aloud.

She heard the water through the black hole; caught a faint impression of silvery light as the water bounced off the hollow rock. Georgia could not imagine being in that gap even if she had wanted to go down it. The idea of being trapped down there, with no space to move, no way of getting in or out, was almost too nasty to properly consider.

There were other statistics, apart from the luckless cavers from 1985, pointillistic black and white newsprint photographs she'd seen only the past few weeks, when she'd looked into the background of the ghyll. There were the suicides.

Once you had squeezed through a narrow passageway with a bit of a kink in it, you were through a drop of perhaps twenty yards down to a hard, jagged stone floor. That's where many people were found.

It was a theory that this is where Stephanie had been heading, on the night she vanished. It was the second most popular theory surrounding her disappearance, according to every single message board, website, Facebook group and forum Georgia had haunted. There was the idea that her daughter, in the depths of a despair few could imagine, had come to this place in the dark in the middle of a storm, had lowered herself into the gap – perhaps helped by the sudden flow of water – and had fallen around seventy feet. From there, the turbid waters had carried her spindly body through the channel where the cavers had dived, stuffing her in like a child cramming a toy into a dollhouse too small for it, and then dumped her into the river, there to continue her journey to her unknown destination.

Like all of the most popular theories, Georgia had to admit it was plausible.

No body had been found there; and the police had looked. Specialists had been called in, cavers who had gone through the now-widened passageway where that luckless pair had died in 1985 – and that was after robots had been sent down, insectoid sentinels with camera lenses for eyes, and they had established there was no Stephanie there, and no traces of her there either, neither primary nor secondary – no tell-tale fibre threads snarled up on the rocks, no footprints on the softer earth above. If there had been any sign, it had long been washed away by the remorseless torrent.

Georgia moved closer, pleased at the solidity under her feet on the thick, flat rock. Some daring souls had tattooed their names into the stone, here, close to the gap. It was bigger than Georgia had supposed, looking at it online. Even a bigger man could easily go down that gap, she thought. Swallowed up in the earth. She looked forward into darkness, chilled by the echoes of running water, the connotations of depth, of a sudden end to a fall.

She edged forward, and then she read the warning sign planted in the ground once more, and then realised that someone could shove her into that gap without much trouble.

Just as she hesitated and turned her head to check that no one was preparing to do this, someone did, and she plunged down the hole, screaming.

8

The hound of hell's call carried all across the moors, and Princess Stephanie was afraid. But she knew that she had a chance with the Sword of Destiny in her possession.

From 'Princess Stephanie's Journey', by Stephanie
Healey, aged nine

Someone asked me if I was into hiking. It felt cruel to laugh, so I did.

From the diary of Stephanie Healey

It was a joke, a pratfall. Except she was about to die.

Georgia was wedged into the hole in the earth, in the place where the suicides jumped; where Stephanie might have fallen.

Her legs were dangling free in space, her thick-soled boots a sudden and terrible drag against crude gravity. The lip of the cut in the earth that reached into the ghyll was at her waist, her backpack wedged tight against her.

Then the ground seemed to swallow her, and it was at her chest. Her fingers grasped at the rock, hard, and slowed her progress. She arched her back, wedging herself into the hole. The backpack was quite full at the base, but if it should slip by as little as two or three inches, then Georgia would lose her leverage. And then, only her fingertips and whatever strength she could retain in her shoulder joints would be all that stopped her from disappearing.

Her chin hurt; she supposed she had bashed it against the rock. She caught her breath, threw back her head, and cried out: 'Help!'

Only birdsong answered her, and the rustle of the trees.

Someone shoved me, she thought. *Someone hit me on the back of the knees and I slipped forward. Someone ran up behind me, quiet as you like.*

'Help!' she shrieked again. 'Someone help me!'

And an answer came. One quick, terse bark from a dog.

'I'm at the ghyll! I'm falling! Help me!'

Even as she said it, her fingers lost their grip, and she slipped an alarming distance. As she regained a hold on an aeons-old rill in the slab of rock, she knew that the backpack was a hair's breadth away from dislodging. She scrambled with her feet and knees to find some purchase on the rock, and from there to boost herself back to safety, but the gap fattened in front of her; she could only find the merest touch on the ends of her boots, but it simply wasn't enough to take her weight.

Turn. I'll have to turn around; there's rock at my back. But doing so would remove the wedging effect of her backpack.

I might have no choice.

'Help!' she screamed again. And again, a dog barked.

Closer this time. 'Somebody help me! I'm stuck in the ghyll! Help me!'

With a great spasm around about her midriff, she tried to edge upwards – and this was what finally dislodged the backpack.

'Oh no,' she gasped, as a terrible strain gripped both her shoulders and her wrists. 'Oh no, please, please.'

The dog barked again, closer this time, but Georgia couldn't cry out. She tried to turn around to her right, to find the stone that touched her backside, and to somehow brace her feet against that. But in the turning, her hand slipped.

She screamed as she fell. The dank walls around her stole the sound, bouncing it off the face of the stones.

She did not fall far, but wedged again in another gap, the side of the wall scraping her ear painfully and taking some skin off her hand. She was caught again, in a secondary gap. Again, the backpack had stopped her from tumbling into the gap.

And below that, the seventy-foot drop. To the place where they found the bodies in 1985.

'Someone help me! I'm stuck! Help!'

There was some purchase in the unseen gap ahead of her, but her boots slithered off it – and this drove Georgia deeper. There was little to hold on to, and no way to brace herself. The black rock rose up five or six feet above her head. Daylight presented a mocking face in the cut above her; birds even flew overhead, an added mockery.

'Help! I need help! Oh God!' She slipped again. One hand found a cut in the rock, something to hold on to. The backpack was no longer tight against the rock. Her feet were swinging free.

This is it. This is how I go.

She held on, muscles straining, but there was no way she could last even two minutes, let along as long as it might take for someone to reach her.

Something blocked out the light above.

It was a dog's head. An Alsatian – with comically cocked ears. It barked once, loudly, the roar of a dragon bouncing off the wet stone.

'Is someone up there? Help me!'

'Hey there,' someone said. 'What's going on? Is there someone down there?'

'Yes! For God's sake, get help. I can't hold on!'

Another head took the place of the Alsatian's; that of a man, though she could not make out the features. 'Wait a minute,' he said. 'Oh Jesus. Hang on, if you can – just hang on.'

'I can't! I'm going to fall!' Panic turned her voice into someone else's, the oscillating shriek of a banshee, or a lost soul.

Georgia felt her fingers slip; the rock scraped painfully up her back, breaking skin. She was slipping. She was going. The rock touched her throat, almost delicately. Then her chin, rougher still. Something strained and snapped somewhere in her bicep, though she felt no pain.

Then the edge of a rope hit her on the top of her head.

'Grab on!' shouted the man above.

She needed no further invitation. She had no other choice. Georgia gripped the thick, knotted hemp with one hand; finding the tension to its satisfaction, her other hand joined it. She scrambled up with a nimbleness she would never have credited herself with even five minutes beforehand. She rose fast, out of the lip, over the edge, and then she was gasping, scrambling and sobbing, on her knees, then on her feet, her entire body quaking.

The man at the edge of the ghyll had tied a rope around the base of a thick tree, about five yards away, and then hauled her up once she'd taken a grip. His dog was big enough to put its paws on Georgia's shoulders – and it did, licking her on the face. She did not mind; she even braced herself against its weight, until the man stepped forward into the light and drew it away.

'Bad girl!' he said, seizing the dog by its collar, dragging it down. 'Not you, I mean,' he said, patting Georgia on the shoulder. 'Are you all right? Did you get hurt?'

Georgia shook her head. She felt the side of her face and her ear; her fingers came away spotted with blood, but not much of it. 'I think I'm OK... maybe tore a muscle in my arm. I guess I'll know soon.' She laughed, an odd sound, a hysterical sound. 'Thank you. Thank you so much.'

'Not the first time I've had to do that,' the man said. In the light, his features took shape – he was tall, broad without being particularly athletic, with a weathered face and high cheekbones. His ears stuck out, and there was something in the curve of the nose, the narrow chin and the thick brows and the delicate blue eyes that made her think he had some Irish blood in him. It was a friendly face, the face of a farmer – although his green wellies, dark green jacket and working trousers were a large component of this assessment. 'What were you doing at the lip? Didn't you read the signs?'

Georgia didn't answer him. She glanced around, at the gently swaying trees, and the gaps in between. 'Someone pushed me,' she said. 'I'm fairly sure of it.'

The man who'd rescued her looked around. 'Shoved you? There's no one here, love.'

Then the dog strained at the leash, and barked.

'Who's there?' the man said.

No one answered. The dog barked, cocking its ears, in the direction of the thicker forest, leaping up once. Then it abruptly turned and began to jump up at Georgia again.

'No one there,' the man said. 'Saoirse here's just a bit agitated. Come on, I've got a car just up the road. Come with me and I'll get you a cuppa tea at my hut. Let's get you warmed up. That's what I call a cliffhanger, love, and no mistake.'

'Someone's just tried to kill me!'

'If they did, they're long gone. Come on, let's get out of here.'

Georgia was too tired, too sick, too frightened to disagree. After he unlooped his rope around the tree and fed it back into his own bergen, he led her up the hill and out of the treeline, into bright sunshine.

9

HUNDREDS ATTEND CANDLELIT VIGIL FOR MISSING STUDENT

By Peggy Hoffman, BBC News

Students, staff and local residents have turned out at a candlelit vigil for missing teenager Stephanie Healey.

The 19-year-old vanished after going for a walk during a storm just outside Ferngate on Friday 20th March. Stephanie is a first-year English student at the university there.

The chancellor of Ferngate University, Sir Oliver Chessington, led the proceedings outside Ferngate town hall, which was lit up by hundreds of candles as an estimated 200 people took part in a minute's silence.

'I would appeal for everyone in Ferngate to think back to that night.

'There was a storm – in a lot of ways that'll help jog people's memories. It was a wild night, very difficult conditions to be out in. No one knows where Stephanie went, but we do know she travelled up the A928, on foot, alone.

'If anyone remembers passing Stephanie on that road,

please get in touch with the police.'

English language and literature student Stephanie's face is visible the length and breadth of the town, in a number of missing posters arranged by volunteers, led by Stephanie's boyfriend and classmate, 20-year-old Martin Duke.

'We haven't given up hope,' Mr Duke said. 'It's possible she has decided to take off on her own somewhere. If you're out there, Stephanie, please get in touch – with the police, with your family, with anyone. We just want to know you're safe.'

Stephanie's mother, 50-year-old Georgia Healey, said: 'I know my daughter. She isn't the type to take off somewhere on her own. She wouldn't do something silly, either. I would appeal for anyone who knows anything, or even thinks they might have seen something, to get in touch.

'It doesn't matter how insignificant they think it might be – a door unlocked, or a strange car they didn't recognise parked up in their street… anything. We're desperate for information. We need to know where Stephanie went.'

The Rev Stacey McAllister of St Eunan's Church, who helped co-ordinate the vigil, said: 'Stephanie Healey's family are desperate to find out what happened to her – you can see and hear what this means to them. It's heart-breaking.

'We have no idea what happened to her – there could be a perfectly reasonable, innocent explanation. But if someone does know what happened, I would ask them to examine their conscience and help ease the suffering of Stephanie's family and friends.'

Rod Healey, Stephanie's father, said after the vigil: 'This is a sad situation and we have to get to the bottom of it.'

When asked what message he had for his daughter if she was watching, he said: 'Get back home. Your mother's worried to death.'

(Online report, dated 31st March)

I went into the church one morning, on my own. I made sure I went early to watch the old ladies lighting candles. There was a man there, middle-aged, Catholic, something out of HE Bates. I took a shine to him. He was very pious; the pews groaned under him. It was around about this time I noticed the girl, staring at me.

From the diary of Stephanie Healey

The Land Rover appeared through a clearing, off the road, parked at an angle on a slightly sloped dirt track through the trees. It could have packed two versions of Georgia's first car inside, at a push.

Saoirse the dog had taken to Georgia. Not quite wanting to throw herself into her rescuer's arms, she had thrown herself into the dog's, delighted by the contact.

Her rescuer had been wryly amused by this scene. 'She's supposed to be a killer, you know,' he said. 'Big softie when you get down to it. She knows when someone's in trouble. By the way, I'm Jed, Jed Mulrine. I'm the gamekeeper.'

She knew the name, of course. She swallowed, then said: 'Gamekeeper? This is private land?'

'Yep – this is Sir Oliver's estate. There's a public path through it, of course – you're not trespassing or anything.'

'I didn't think I was.'

'You sure you don't need a doctor? You must have taken a bit of a beating down the ghyll.'

'I'm fine – and I guess that's official. I am a doctor.'

'Ha!' Jed's laughter was a little like the dog's bark, she thought. Half-surprise, half-enthusiasm. 'Then – heal thyself!'

Georgia let Saoirse lick her once more, before they reached the Land Rover. The dog snapped to attention after Jed had clicked the key fob, and the doors snicked open. There was a caged section at the back of the vehicle, and the dog leapt into its allotted space after its owner released the back door. It sat, contentedly, and chewed on a length of thick hemp rope identical to the one he had used to pull Georgia out of the ghyll.

'In you get,' Jed said. 'I've got some of the perfect medicine inside.'

In the expanses of the passenger seat, all her cuts, bruises and abrasions raised their hands and made themselves known. Her bicep throbbed, but Georgia was now sure she had simply strained it, without tearing the muscle tissue. Her hands still shook as she took off the backpack and laid it in the well at her feet. Threads had been picked away on the waterproof material, unpicked by the rock much as a cat might have worried an old sofa.

So close, she thought. *If I hadn't been wearing the backpack, I'd be down there now. Or God knows where.*

Maybe I'd have ended up in Stephanie's arms.

Jed got into the driver's seat, then pulled his bergen off his back. Reaching inside, he brought out a silver flask. 'Now, don't worry – there's no alcohol in this. But I do have to warn you that there's some of the strongest tea in existence. It might draw the teeth out of you – I let it stew in the pot.'

'It sounds perfect to me.' And it was. He unscrewed the cap and poured her a measure, still steaming hot. Strong, invigorating, its warmth reaching her very fingertips.

'I've got some antiseptic wipes, if you want to take care of those cuts,' he said, indicating her scratched hands.

'That'd be great.' She accepted these, thoroughly cleansing the wounds, wincing a little at one section where the skin had been pared back at the edge of her thumb.

'Now I'm going to ask you the sixty-four-thousand-dollar question... What brought you to the ghyll?'

'I'm having a look at the area. I'm on a project.'

'Project, yeah?' A certain sourness had crept into his voice. 'What kind of project, if you don't mind my asking?'

'I don't mind you asking. My daughter went missing in Ferngate, two years ago. Her name was Stephanie Healey. You must have heard of her?'

Jed's face fell. 'Stephanie Healey. The girl who vanished on the A-road. Of course I remember her. I'm the guy who spoke to her before... I spoke to her on the road. I saw her. I offered her a lift, in the rain.' He suddenly looked stricken. 'I helped out in the search. We scoured the woods, the ghyll, everything.' He suddenly clutched her hands; the gesture was meant to be a comfort, but it was too abrupt, and Georgia's heart leapt as he lunged forward. 'I thought your face was familiar. I remember you, at the time. I was at the vigil.'

'I don't remember a gamekeeper... I do remember Sir Oliver, though. He was very kind.'

'Spent a fair bit of time on the ground, himself. With the search and that.'

'I'm hoping to be able to speak to him. But he's busy around about this time, it seems.'

'Aye – he's got a lot on. Not just with the university. Busy man. I have a job of getting hold of him myself.'

'The hall is miles away from here... I had no idea that the grounds stretched so far out.'

'Oh, the family's owned the land around here for generations. Name's in the Domesday Book, or so they tell me. Old, old money.' He started the car, and reversed the Land Rover back up the way it had come, before it reached a passing place buttressed by limestone walls. Georgia was alarmed at how quickly he turned the Land Rover in such a tight space, instinctively recoiling as the jagged tessellations of the walls surged towards her in the mirror. But Jed Mulrine must have done this hundreds, if not thousands of times; without the vehicle lurching or coming to a sudden halt, he spun the wheel confidently and soon had the Land Rover heading back up the uneven road. 'Be a bit bumpy here – though you'll be used to that, given what happened this morning!'

Georgia nodded, taking in the rest of the capful of tea so as not to spill it. She screwed the top back on the flask. 'Where are we going?'

'I've got a shepherd's hut just up the road a-ways – you can get your breath there, then I'll drive you back.'

'I don't need to stop, really. It's fine if you take me back.'

'It's totally up to you – I can't get onto the A-road back the way we came; we'll have to head back up this way. My shed's on the way. If you like, I might even be able to call in at the hall, see if Sir Oliver can see you.'

Georgia failed to keep a plaintive note entirely out of her

voice. 'Really? That would be good, if you could manage that.'

'Then we'll call the police. About the person shoving you in.'

'No...' Georgia hesitated. Would Hurlford even waste time sending someone up here? Would it point to some instability on her part, chasing phantoms that weren't there? She was sure of it, though. She was sure she had been pushed. 'Maybe I was wrong. It seems strange that someone could do that... The fall, the shock...'

'I understand. Still. I'll also have to make note of what happened in the ledger. Health and safety – sorry, them's the rules. I am responsible for the land.' The jocular note was gone from Jed's voice, all of a sudden. It brooked no argument, and Georgia did not offer one.

'I understand. If you could call through to the hall – I wanted to speak to Sir Oliver only briefly.'

'There's a do on up there, soon,' Jed said. 'He is around, but you'll be lucky. He takes a hands-on approach to most things. Some of the time I'm having to check something out in the woods, and he's in there before me with the dogs. Sometimes I wonder why he bothers paying me...' He grinned. 'I shouldn't have said that out loud, should I?'

'I wouldn't mention that at your next appraisal,' Georgia said, smiling. 'I don't even know if I said thank you, back there. I guess you saved my life. That's no exaggeration.'

Jed raised a hand. 'You'd be surprised the number of times I've done it. Some of the time, they even do it deliberately. I've found bodies, there. I guess you don't need to hear that.' He flushed suddenly. 'Anyway, you're lucky. I was only there because I was told a deer had gotten itself stuck there, would you believe. No sign of any deer. Then Saoirse must have heard you calling – she set straight off. I didn't hear a thing. If you need to thank anyone, thank the dog.'

'I already have. She's obedient, isn't she? A monster, but obedient.'

'Yep – she was part of a litter that was meant for the cops. I kept her for myself, though – bit naughty of me, but she was clearly the best of the bunch. Got to have a dog, in this job. Three years old, would you believe?'

'Still more growing to go? Christ, on her hind legs she's nearly as tall as you are.'

'Yep! I could put a saddle on her, I reckon. Save me the petrol in this wagon.'

The hilly road levelled off, and the ground flattened again, revealing sparse farmland with flocks of sheep within. There was no sign of another human being out there. Even the trees seemed less civilised in their form, out here in the open – stunted against the wind, misshapen somehow. It was a warm, bright day, but a sharp wind rocked the Land Rover.

'Must be about two years now since that girl of yours went missing,' Jed said, almost too quietly to be heard over the engine. 'To ask a silly question… you bearing up?'

'Kind of. In a manner of speaking.'

'Can't be easy. I can't imagine what it's like… I don't want to imagine what it's like. I've got a boy myself. Probably round about the same age. The idea of him going missing… You got other kids?'

Georgia swallowed. 'No. She's my only daughter.'

'Shocking. I can't say…'

'Say what?'

'Well, there's something about it doesn't fit right with me. I've heard the stories – and stop me if this upsets you – I've heard the stories about, you know, her maybe having taken her own life.' He swallowed, and narrowed his eyes into the road ahead.

'Of course,' was all she said in reply.

'They searched the ghyll. I was there, advising the cops. Hurlford – that's the detective's name, isn't it?'

'One of several. They had hundreds of officers working on that case. So he told me, anyway.'

'I could believe it. Hurlford, that was the lad, though – he coordinated the search. We didn't find anyone in the ghyll. Had you fallen, you'd have most likely ended up in the cavern below.'

'But the two potholers, who died – they were caught in the tunnel leading to the beck, weren't they?'

'They were – but that was by design. I haven't been down there, but I saw the footage they broadcast – it's a narrow path, but some people like to go into those caverns, those tight spaces. It's a hell of a space to end up in by accident. You know this, I'm sure.'

Georgia paused. 'Go on,' she said, finally.

'It's possible, I conceded that. Totally possible that your girl, somehow, chose to walk up that hill, in the dark, in the middle of a storm. And maybe she went into the ghyll, and maybe she ended up being washed into the river, with the rain and all. It is possible. But it's not bloody likely.'

'What are you saying?'

'Not saying anything. I have no idea what happened.'

'So, why say it's unlikely she ended up in the ghyll, then?'

'Because it's something that bothers me… and you're not from here, are you?'

'No. We live in Manchester.'

'So, I'm guessing you've come here for a look around. To find out a few things.' Mulrine took a deep breath. 'Look, this is my way of saying – I don't think your daughter ended up in the ghyll. I don't think she went into the woods. I think something else happened to her – on that road, back there.' He jerked a thumb behind him. 'I think she might have met with some harm.'

'What do you mean by harm? What do you think happened? Don't hold back – tell me. I'll listen to anything, any idea anyone has. It's not like I haven't gone through every scenario.'

'What I'm saying is I think someone took her. From the road. Probably in a car. Whatever happened to her, it happened far away from here.'

Georgia said nothing. In the back, the dog snorted in its sleep.

'We're here,' he said. 'Just up ahead.'

10

Turns out, she knew Cornfed, too. From the party. I was thrilled at the discovery. We clung to each other like sisters. Or what I imagine sisters are like. Then she told me there was a job going.

From the diary of Stephanie Healey

It wasn't what Georgia had expected – a new, freestanding structure, actually still on wheels, sat in a clearing in front of one of the limestone walls. It was dark green, with a corrugated effect, although it had clearly cost a fortune. Inside it was a large room with a couch on it, a low-hanging light, some tight-packed bookshelves, a kettle and a mug tree. The shepherd's hut was plumbed, going by the sink in one corner, and connected to the grid. It was cosy; Georgia particularly liked the old-style mahogany-effect radio set into one corner on the table, next to the window; only the pale blue stand-by light gave away that it was actually a digital set, fashioned to look like an ancient wartime wireless, complete with dials.

'Another tea?' Jed said, hanging up his jacket on a peg.

'I will, thanks. Just milk. Is there a bathroom through here?'

'Yep – dead ahead.'

Saoirse sat in a basket near the door, and seemed to grin at Georgia as she limped into the door and locked it behind her.

There was even a shower cabinet in the tight white space. Perhaps he lives here, Georgia thought. She could see the attraction, especially in the summer – a cosy space, but with the promise of travel and adventure. Perhaps it was like Enid Blyton; perhaps he used the Land Rover to transfer the shepherd's hut here and there on the estate.

She peeled off her jacket and her training top, surveying the injuries. Some scraping along her back, angry red scratches and raised skin that would form a nasty bruise; a nick taken out of her ear, still bleeding. She pressed some tissue paper to the wound, and winced. In the mirror she spotted a rough patch on her chin, but it felt worse than it looked. 'Used to do that to myself with a pumice stone, voluntarily,' she said to herself.

After she'd bathed her wounds again and tried to look like someone who hadn't just been eaten alive by the earth, she came back in to find two steaming mugs of tea on top of the table, and a chair pulled out for her.

Jed filled in a logbook as she sat down. He looked rangier with his jacket and wellies off – though not quite diminished. He was lean as a gunslinger in a red plaid shirt, angular and clearly physically fit, despite the bony bonhomie of his face. He looked kind, though. There was something in him, bizarrely, that made Georgia think of a younger, slimmer version of the late Sir Terry Wogan, though Jed had to be well into his fifties.

'Sorry,' he said, pushing the logbook towards her. 'Details.'

'What do you mean?'

'This is an accident book,' he said, colouring slightly. 'You'll have to put down what happened to you, and sign it... Also, you need to check to see if what I say seems correct, from your perspective.'

'Oh, I see.' Georgia scribbled down a rough version of events, signed it, and after a pause, added her name and address.

'I have to take note of everything that happens – it gets reported. Particularly to do with the ghyll.'

'It's a dodgy place, that's for sure.'

He tapped the sheet with a finger like the head of a shovel. 'I know you said you weren't quite sure, just then, but... I still have to contact the police.'

Georgia paused. 'I guess you do.'

Jed nodded. 'If anyone's out there trying to shove people into the ghyll, I want to know about it. I'll take a look anyway, with Saoirse. If anyone's around, I'll see signs of them. But there was no one around, apart from you. That was my feeling.'

Georgia sipped at her tea. 'Next you'll say, "I know these woods like the back of my hand".'

Jed chuckled. 'Yeah, something like that. Been working for Sir Oliver for nigh-on thirty years. I was a tree surgeon at first, if you can believe that – out of the forces after five years, then answered a job application. My folks are from Ferngate originally, but they got divorced. I hadn't been back since I was twelve, maybe.'

'You must have started round about when I was getting close to my final year here.'

'You went to Ferngate? The university?'

'Yep. Medical school. Best days of my life, believe it or not.'

'I can't imagine the brains it takes to do that – amazes me how someone can be so well read and well qualified, to do something so skilful. I admire that, that's the honest truth.'

'It's all to do with graft, really – it gets pretty hands-on. You have to put in the hours. It's like everything else – do the reading, find the answers, practise all the time, then apply everything you know in the field.'

'That said… I would question how smart someone was, going right up to the ghyll, and ignoring all those signs. The ones saying Danger of Death, and such like.' He took a long draught of his tea. Nothing had changed in his tone of voice, but there was something in his eyes that made Georgia feel as if the temperature had dropped a little. Just for a second, the shepherd's hut felt a little less homely.

'I came here to find out more. You were right first time,' Georgia said. 'I'm retracing Stephanie's steps. Or, the steps she was supposed to have taken, according to the theories.'

'And what do you reckon to those theories, now you've done that?'

'I'm in agreement with you. I think on that night in particular, in the middle of a storm, it's unlikely she would have come anywhere near the ghyll. The only reason she would have done that is if she had a pressing need to be there – meaning, she meant to kill herself. And as you say, there's little evidence that she did that, and there was no sign of a body. There is that slight chance she got washed out into the river, but even at that, it would be unusual for a body to completely vanish from the waterway. Not out of the question – that's the bit that tortures me. But unlikely. There's a chance that's all I'll ever know. That's all I might have: that it's possible she jumped down the ghyll during a storm. That's what the police think, you know.'

He placed his mug on the table, then leaned forward. He moved his hand, and might have touched Georgia's arm, but he stopped himself, then said: 'For what it's worth... well, I already told you. I don't think she came onto the land, here.'

'Do you remember that night?'

'Of course.' He scratched his chin. 'I guess this is where I provide you with my alibi?'

'If that's the way you want to put it, I won't stop you.'

He chuckled. 'You know something? I admire your honesty. For that reason, I'll tell you – I was working on the flood channels up at Chessington Hall. It's flat, up there, even though they're at a higher elevation – had problems with drainage in the past. Too many trees chopped down, you ask me, but Sir Oliver had this idea of a showground. Somewhere people could hold weddings, or even a festival. He's a canny man – but losing the trees around about the hall leaves it prone to flooding. That's just my opinion. He told me what I could do with it. So anyway, that night, the Friday, me and some of the farm workers helped dig a trench. At one point, we wondered if it was ever going to stop raining. Sir Oliver even wanted to come out and help, the mad bugger, but we talked him out of it. Me and the rest of the boys who work with the sheep were all there, digging the ditch, well into the morning. Lots of witnesses.'

'That's a little bit defensive, Jed. Just a little bit.'

He shrugged, amiably. 'If I was you, I'd be a little bit

suspicious. The cops certainly were. I'm the only person around here, after all.'

'But they cleared you.'

''Course. I don't know what happened to your daughter. Anyway, the day after, I helped coordinate the search. It was my job to take a look at the grounds, scour as much of it as possible, talk it over with the cops and walkers' groups and God knows who else to think about where she could have gone. Or where she might have been taken. Sir Oliver and the previous groundsmen were called out, too. No sign of her. And I might add, they turned my place over, too.'

'You actually live here?'

'In the warmer months, yeah. See that sofa over there? It opens out into a comfy bed.' He coloured again. Strange, Georgia thought, that he should have such a shy reaction, and yet talk over Stephanie's possible murder with barely a stutter.

'You're not married, then?'

'Nah. Kicked that habit a while back. Missus packed up and left. Haven't seen her in, God, fifteen years now. I don't blame her, in a way. It's not an ideal life, this, for some. But it suits me.'

'I can see the appeal, sometimes. You live rent free?'

'Yep. I love these hills and these woods. Best place in the world, far as I'm concerned.'

'I used to think that, too. I used to have a dream of coming back here, and opening a practice.'

He nodded. 'They all say that. Great place to study – or, it would be, if I was the studying type. My boy is. You'll probably see him out and about. Some head of hair on him – he got my hair, but he's been dying it all colours. Jesus.

Anyway, beautiful town. All this countryside nearby... breath of fresh air.'

'Bit lonely, though. Compared to the big places. It was for Stephanie, anyway. Horrible how it's turned out, really. That I used to think this place was a dream. Now it's the opposite.'

Her voice hadn't cracked this time, but Jed saw something in her that prompted him to pat her arm. She didn't stop him; didn't mind. After a pause, he said: 'I'll make a quick phone call. See if Sir Oliver's around. He's not a bad guy, so far as they go. Bit abrupt, but I always kind of liked that about him. He didn't skirt the issue. He was gutted, you know. What happened to your lass. Devastated. He puts everything into this town. It's his birthright; the university and the town and the Chessingtons are hand-in-hand, over history. He took it personally, you know. Close to depressed as I've ever seen him.'

'I spoke to him at the time. But I don't remember much about it. A handshake. A promise to do all he could. Everything is a bit blurred, really, from that time. I wouldn't mind a longer conversation with him.'

'You could've gotten in touch through the university. Or Twitter; I think the estate has an account, now they're looking at holding weddings and parties in the hall.'

'It's all short notice, this,' Georgia said.

'Trying to catch him out?' Jed caught her look, then said: 'Ah, I'm just joking! I'll make a call. Hang on now.'

He went outside to do it, leaving the door ajar. She couldn't make out much of the conversation.

Saoirse watched her with one wary eye, chin resting on her front paws, as still as stone.

Jed gave her the thumbs-up when he came back inside. 'You're on – this afternoon, in fact. Finish up your tea and I'll drive you over. He's got a spare hour.'

11

There's a world out here you couldn't dream of. But you'd smack your lips over it, just the same. Cornfed's the key to it all, really. I shouldn't be so surprised. One door leads to another, each one narrower than the last. But we all want to go through them. Come on. Don't lie.

From the diary of Stephanie Healey

It was a grand building, several miles away from Jed's rolling shed. The house was open to the elements with the nearest trees perhaps one hundred yards away on three sides; it had two storeys but was broad, Victorian in scope, with grandiloquent Greek pillars up a short flight of steps. The stonework was a mellow colour in the bright sunshine, and had surely been cleaned not too long ago. A long gravel driveway enhanced the building's sense of grandeur and broad scope. An ornate fountain provided an obstacle in the middle of the driveway, depicting what seemed to be a mermaid and a porpoise at play, amid jagged waves, the patina on the face of the carving rendering it all in aquamarine. The effect was so extraordinary that Georgia only realised as they turned around it that the water in it had been stilled. To the right of the house, a candy-striped marquee loomed, larger than the house itself, and behind that thick, forbidding forest, as far as the eye could see.

The grounds were busy, with white vans parked to the side of the house, and people making their way into and out of the tent. Others worked on the periphery, tending to the lawns that fringed the driveway, although to Georgia's eyes these looked immaculate as they were.

'I had no idea this was here,' Georgia said. 'I had a vague idea of the chancellor and I think he'd appeared on the local TV now and again. But I didn't know this house was here. It's incredible.'

'Private estate,' Jed said. 'The Chessingtons had plenty of money swirling around – no need to open it up to the public, like so many of the stately homes. They liked to keep themselves to themselves. Sir Oliver's a bit of an oddity in that regard. He doesn't need the income, but he wants people to come and see the place. He's even thinking about donating it to the National Trust in his will, though his kids weren't amused by that, I can tell you.'

'It looks like the best hotel you ever fantasised about staying in.'

'That's one thing Sir Oliver didn't want,' Jed said, sternly. 'He doesn't want the house proper turned into a hotel. He's open to the idea of hosting weddings and conferences, but he wants the place to keep its... what's the word? Mystique? Allure?'

'I get what you're saying.'

Jed pulled up at the front steps. A woman in her early twenties whose wide-lapelled trouser suit made her look as if she'd dressed up from her mother's wardrobe came down the steps to intercept the Land Rover. She had glasses and wild curly hair, clipped down and tamed, but only just. She already had her hand held out, ready to shake, by the time Georgia had gotten out of the car and before Jed had even opened his mouth.

'You'll be Mrs Healey?' She smiled, her red lips struggling to contain her teeth. 'I'm Susan, Sir Oliver's personal assistant.'

Georgia shook hands. 'Thanks for letting me come over – I appreciate Sir Oliver's a very busy man.'

'Not at all, we're delighted to see you. Follow me, please.'

'This is goodbye, then,' Jed said. He shook Georgia's hand more heartily. 'You take care now, lass, you hear? However it all works out, be well.'

She was absurdly touched. Now that her nerves had settled since the incident at the ghyll, she felt on the verge of tears again. 'Thank you. You probably saved my life.'

'Ah not at all. You'd have found a way to get out. You've got the good stuff. I can tell.' Then he was gone with a last wave. In the back of the car, Saoirse barked joyfully as her master returned.

Heading up the stairs and into the doorway behind Susan, Georgia spied a long, rich red welcoming mat, with marble underneath, and a white spiral staircase at the far wall. Everything gleamed. Georgia looked down at her Frankensteinian boots and shivered.

'Um... should I take these off?'

'No, you'll be fine,' Susan said. Then she paused, and stared. 'Um, actually... If you wouldn't mind?'

'I'd be the same,' Georgia said, unlacing the boots. It was a relief to dump them in the doorway and stretch her toes.

She half expected white-gloved servants to fly out from the doorways to right and left, bearing silver dust pans, brushes and moues of disgust as they picked up her shoes between pinched fingers. No one appeared.

'Sir Oliver's on a break at the moment – he's helping prepare the grounds. There's a lot going on, as you can see.'

'A wedding, I think Jed said?'

'Private function, yes.' Susan indicated a creamy leather sofa in an alcove. 'If you'd like to wait there for a minute or two, Sir Oliver will be along to see you.'

'Thanks.' Georgia took a seat beneath a granite statue of a figure from Greek antiquity, short sword poised, preparing to take a swipe at a terrible monster with a tessellated hide that reminded her of the Crystal Palace dinosaurs. Looking at the face, she snorted in astonishment; he had the exact likeness of a young Clint Eastwood, down to a cheroot perched on one side of the mouth.

'Do you like it?' A voice boomed across the space – incongruously northern. 'That there's Hercules fighting the dragon. I had it made when I was going through a Sergio Leone phase. Some days I think it's awful. Some days I think it's the best thing I've ever done with this place. It usually depends on whether or not I'm drinking.'

Sir Oliver Chessington was not quite the man Georgia remembered – he had been in a sober suit, with his silver hair neatly parted, short but wearing well for his age, every inch and every ounce the country squire he was.

That had been two years ago, in the days and weeks following Stephanie's disappearance. The man who came down the spiral staircase now might have been a completely different man, in utterly different circumstances. He was short, possibly even shorter than Georgia, with a jumble sale off-grey polo shirt over the top of boot-cut blue jeans frayed at the hems, which did nothing, nothing at all for him. The toe-tips of his black socks peeked out from beneath these unruly hemlines like a diffident mammal in two minds about leaving its burrow. The once well-groomed white hair was in all directions now, and the all-salt-no-pepper stubble completed the picture of a tradesman approaching retirement who still enjoyed his work.

'I heard *The Good, The Bad And The Ugly* soundtrack, when I noticed the cheroot,' Georgia said, rising to meet him.

'I'll have it piped in at the front door for visitors.' He stuck his tongue out, and grinned as they shook hands. 'How lovely to see you, Mrs Healey. You're looking very well.'

'And you – thanks for agreeing to see me. I know you've got loads on.'

He brushed this aside. 'Ah not at all. You're always welcome here, always. How is your husband? Rod, wasn't it?'

'He's fine – away on business at the moment.'

'Keeping busy, keeping busy. A man after my own heart. Now – you're a milk, no sugar type person with the tea, would I be right?' He clapped his hands and pointed his index fingers at her.

'Ah, no tea for me, thanks. Jed made me a couple of cups in his shed. That's plenty for me just now.'

'You had Jed's tea?' Sir Oliver grimaced. 'Good Lord, that'd take the enamel off your teeth. I was going to get him to brew a vat of it for me – it'd clean those front steps a treat. Probably make copper pennies all shiny again. Well, I'll get you something else, then?'

'Just a glass of water.'

'Still? Sparkling? Or soda water, with a little something extra in it?'

She smiled. 'Just still is good for me, thanks, and out of the tap.'

'Your wish, my command. Follow me, we'll go to the cocktail room. The cocktail room's cool.'

12

Some idiot – it might have been Neb – made that stupid comment about how, if Cinderella's shoes fit perfectly for the ball, then why did she leave one behind? It's cretinous when memes become common currency. Bad enough seeing them online. This actually seemed to stump him. Probably he just wanted to start a conversation with the group. He struggles a bit without these starters for ten. So, he got quite upset when I laughed. I told him straight out – nothing happened in that story that Cinderella didn't want to happen.

From the diary of Stephanie Healey

'I should thank you, really,' Sir Oliver said. 'It gets me out of the game for a little bit, probably just as well. I have this recurring fantasy I'm a working man, which I can't seem to shake. The site foreman will be delighted to see the back of me.'

They were sat in an almost comically ornate bar-room, filled with more classical sculptures in recessed alcoves. Marble was all around them – black, white, or a threaded composite of both colours. It was ostentatiously expensive, but Georgia wasn't sure she liked it. She didn't want to say it was vulgar, but it had the feel of a nightclub she would have felt uncomfortable in.

'You've got a lot of work going on outside. I think Susan said something about a wedding?'

'Oh – private party. Just a gathering we have every year, round about this time. I've expanded it a bit this year, though. To give you a bit of a scoop – I'm using it as a testing ground for holding weddings and other events here. We've had a few people married on the grounds – I was one of them, a good forty years ago now – but I'm having the place opened out a bit. We shouldn't really keep the place to ourselves, is the way I look at it. Funny, if you'd asked me the same question when I was twenty-five, I'd have told you to get on your bike. I've mellowed, as I've got older.'

Georgia had difficulty in finding the time to break into Sir Oliver's flow of speech. He was quite mesmerising with it, although she imagined that he'd become tedious after a few drinks. 'It's quite a place. I was saying that I'd never realised it was up here.'

'Oh, I know – that's what I mean. My old man, he turned away BBC crews and all sorts. I think there was talk of one of those TV adaptations being filmed here at one point – *Brideshead*, or something Jane Austen-y. Charles Dickens, you know the drill. I wish he'd said yes! They used a house just like this one for one of the Batman movies. You know, the house he hangs out in when he's not in the Batcave. Anyway, before I say too much…' He cocked his head at her and raised an eyebrow.

Georgia wondered if she'd missed something; if she should have paid closer attention. 'I'm sorry?'

'Uh… what can I do for you?'

'Well, I just wanted to pass on my thanks. I understand there was another awareness campaign raised in the past six months. It appeared in all the national papers, advertising too – which wouldn't have been cheap. Whenever I tried to find out who had funded that, I was told not to worry about it. So it doesn't take too much deduction to work out who was behind all that. Given that I don't know too many people with Bruce Wayne levels of wealth.'

Here Sir Oliver grew sober, even serious. 'Ah no, don't mention that. It was the least I could do. And I'll do it again, next year. And the year after that. Until we get an answer for you.'

'You're very kind. These things can make a difference.'

'I hope so. You know, when I heard the news that Stephanie had gone missing… I don't want to say anything that upsets you, or make any claim to being close to what you're going through… but I took it personally. You know that way? It happened on the university my family built up. The one I'm in charge of. On my patch. That sort of thing doesn't happen on my patch, you understand? I can't have it.'

'What sort of thing?'

'A disappearance. A mystery. Now I'm not saying there was foul play; there's no evidence of that. I hope I'm not speaking out of turn, but there is a chance someone abducted her, and that idea…' His voice seemed to boil, as he struggled to sum up his outrage. 'Well. I just can't have that, as I say. Students are students, young people are young people. People get beaten up, and there have been one or two murders. But this is something else. This is in the realms of the sinister. It's a feeling I have. But I'll say this – we'll find out what happened to Stephanie. This is my guarantee.'

'You're a good man,' Georgia said simply. There it was, that choking feeling again. She swallowed it.

'Take it easy, lass,' he said. 'I can't imagine the strain… I can't imagine the sense of shock and loss. I've got kids of my own, and it's still beyond what you've experienced. But you need some down time occasionally. How's work going?'

'Ah, it's fine, all good. Very busy.'

He nodded. 'You're down on holiday, I take it?'

'Just a few days.'

'You know, it hadn't escaped me that the anniversary is coming up. There's a concert being held tomorrow night, did you know that?'

'I did – the Megiddos are playing. I must confess I'd never heard their records, but they seem to be a big thing these days.'

Sir Oliver snorted into his tea. 'Yeah – believe it or not, I hadn't heard of them either, until I had the CD in my hand. But I am old hat beyond old hat. There's things out there now, the internet, streaming, whatever… I've no idea what's going on. You don't hear the charts any more. You get locked out of it. It's technological as well as cultural, I find. At first you don't understand the appeal of certain things, then you're totally shut out of it. That's the thing about getting old, isn't it? The years roll by and you stay stuck. My wife's barely gotten over Elvis dying.'

'To be fair, it was a blow for everyone.'

He giggled again, and gestured around the room. 'It's a shame this isn't a proper pub, you know? I was thinking about putting in a fire, making this room a bit cosier... A cocktail lounge is all very well, but it's not homely, you know? Cool, warm, polar opposites. I'd love to get a proper pub going in here. Maybe once we expand it, that's just what I'll do.'

'It's stylish, all the same. I could see it as a nightclub.'

'Yeah – it's the kind of place I could see myself getting thrown out of, as a twenty-one-year-old. Or not being allowed in, in the first place. Probably be the first landlord to get barred from his own boozer, if I opened it out. So...' He made that gesture again, quizzical, ironic, and Georgia bit down on her rising irritation.

'So...?'

'That was all you came here for? Just to say thank you?'

'Well. That, and to ask if there had been any updates whatsoever.'

'I'm sure you'd have heard before I did. Nothing I can report, alas.'

'I had a chat with Jed, earlier on. He spoke about the night Stephanie went missing.'

'Remember it well. A Friday in March. They say that about March, don't they? Arrives like a lion, leaves like a lamb? Well it was a bloody tyrannosaurus that night, never mind a lion. Uprooted a line of trees on the west side – took down some guttering. You see that creek running along the side of the house, about two hundred yards away? Well it was more of a tributary at the time, and it was close to bursting its banks. Part of the fencing had already been washed out. Jed helped co-ordinate a dig. Him and some of the lads working on the farm dredged it out. Had a digger on site, and Jed dredged the banks. Dangerous – I didn't want him to take the responsibility. I could see the whole lot ending up being swept away, digger, Jed, the lot, like a kid's toy. He wouldn't let me take the controls. Wisely, because I had no idea how to use them.'

'He cleared the site?'

'Jed, and some of the guys I had working on the house that day.'

'Do you know much about them?'

'Who – the boys on the house? Not a lot, just hired hands. One or two boys from Australia, as I recall. You know who does know a lot about them, though? The police. They questioned all of us, they checked the security footage, you name it. And they searched through every single nook, cranny, drawer, attic, crawlspace, basement, barn, shed, trapdoor and even secret Scooby Doo passages that exist in this house, just after Stephanie disappeared.' He smiled again, not unkindly. 'I'm gathering that's why you're here, really? To ask a few questions?'

Georgia decided to let her mask slip, and gave a tired smile. 'I'm not exactly Columbo, am I?'

He laughed, delighted. 'Georgia, I'm only surprised that it's taken you so long to come up here. I'd want to know everything about this case, if it was me. I wouldn't blame you for that, at all. Feel free – ask me anything. I'll put your mind at rest, if I can.'

'OK. This dredging work… is it possible that it might have caused something further downstream? Like a landslide?'

'No – it was close to flooding up here, but the land does slope down and it emptied out into the river eventually. There was a bit of localised flooding, but nothing spectacular. The ghyll was full that night, and treacherous – but for my money, too treacherous. If Stephanie had decided to go up there, for whatever reason, then it would have been too dodgy underfoot to go on. Even if she was really determined, I don't think Stephanie would have gotten there, coming up the hill from the A-road. Different if she had been coming from the top of the hill, up here, and making her way down the path. But we know that this definitely didn't happen. Just a theory of mine – a way of saying that she didn't end up in the ghyll, like the police reckon.'

Georgia almost gave a start. She said: 'You've been making your own inquiries.'

'Of course. After the police had been through everything – and they did go through everything, sniffer dogs, you name it – I went through everything, too. Inside and out. Front and back, and both sides. It's a big old remote estate, that's for sure. There are plenty of hiding places. But I can tell you, and the police can tell you, that whatever happened to Stephanie, it didn't happen to her on this estate, or my house. And the staff were all here, when she disappeared. I know exactly who was here that night, and what they were doing. Jed and those boys were out all night, and the serving staff helped out at home. I know, because I was there with them.'

'This is something I'm told all the time, everyone I speak to. Whenever I think there's a place to look, or a piece of information someone missed… a door closes. I'm on the wrong track. I've had to get used to the idea that I might never know. You read about these people in the papers, or you see them on TV. The people who never find out what happened to their loved ones. And I've got to accept that this could be me, now.'

'And your husband,' Sir Oliver said gently.

'Yes, of course,' she snapped.

He sat back a moment, and took a swig from his mug of coffee. 'You know, you can take a look around, if you like.'

'God... I don't have that much time off!'

'I'm serious.' His tone was hard to read, though. Georgia remembered this was his house. She remembered that he appeared every year on lists she went out of her way not to read in the *Sunday Times*. Georgia remembered her manners.

'It won't be necessary. I... I'll tell you the truth. I'm desperate.' Her face crumpled. She let it happen. It was rare for her not to fight it.

'Oh, lass.' He was out of his seat, and around the black and silver-threaded marble table. He took her by the shoulder, and she leaned into his chest, her face in her hands. 'Oh, lass. This world. What has this world done to you? This world,' he repeated.

After a few moments she fished in her bag for a tissue. The white and grey faces of the gods and heroes seemed insolent, rather than indifferent. She suddenly didn't want to be here, in this gigantic doll's house, with this well-meaning jack-in-the-box. 'I'm sorry. Coming back here was a bigger struggle than I'd expected. I have my own memories of Ferngate, and I thought they'd be foremost in my mind. But in every corner, I see somewhere Stephanie might have been. A place she might have had fun, or been happy. Or even somewhere she wasn't happy. A room she might have studied in. Somewhere she might have worried about her exams. She never sat her end-of-term exams, you know.'

'I know, lass.' Finally, he let her go, and moved back to

his seat. She didn't feel condescended to. She wondered where he had gotten the accent from. There was talk of him having worked on building projects since he left university, sometimes working on the site in actual construction instead of in the planning – an engineering graduate, something of an oddity in the Chessington family, who had a long male lineage of art students, failed poets, and finally 'patrons of the arts'.

'Look, I'm going to tell you something,' Sir Oliver said. 'I trust the police. I know DI Hurlford – he's in charge of the investigation, and he's thorough as you like. I knew his dad – good man, local boy. He's left no stone unturned. And yet...' He gestured with empty hands. 'No results. There's one stone that hasn't been left unturned. So, I've decided to put a private detective on the case.'

Georgia said nothing. Sir Oliver hesitated; he'd expected her to say, or do something else.

'Well, it's just an idea. Someone on a full-time payroll, exploring one or two theories. Maybe asking a few questions. Doing what you're doing here, in fact.'

Georgia drank the last of her water, then said: 'I've already hired a private detective, Sir Oliver. It cleared out a fair chunk of my savings. He was very expensive. He was also very thorough. You know what he concluded?'

He shook his head.

'That Stephanie most likely killed herself by jumping in St Anthony's Ghyll. That the water was so strong that it propelled her right through the system, all the way into the river, and possibly even out to sea.'

'Well.' He seemed stumped. 'That's the common theory.'

'And I suspect that like me, you don't quite believe it.'

'No. And not just me. Jed – he knows the ghyll like no one else. He could write a book about the land over there. What he says in these woods, goes, and I take Jed's word over everyone's. He doesn't believe she ended up in the ghyll, either. If she did, it wasn't by her own design. They say she walked through the woods a fair bit, took hiking trips on her own… but at that time, in the dark, with that storm? I'm not buying it.'

'No,' Georgia admitted. 'Me neither.'

'Think about it,' he said, finishing his coffee. 'What I said, about the private detective. A different one could turn up a different conclusion. And it'd be all on me. It's my mystery, too. This was one of my own, on my patch. I'm not having it.'

She nodded. She was touched.

'Listen – you can stay for lunch, if you like. It's going to be the old ancestral classic, made by my own fair hands. Know what it is?'

She shook her head.

'*Le fromage et jambon* toastie. With the special ingredient, Henderson's Relish. What do you say?'

She laughed. She was tempted. Her mouth had watered – and there were few foods that held much attraction for Georgia. 'I'm afraid I can't, Sir Oliver. I'd best be heading back into town. I need to get ready for the show – and I'm already running behind schedule, today.'

'How about a little bit of pickled onion in there? Not everyone's favourite filling, I'll give you that, but it adds that touch of zing.'

'No, that's very kind. Another day I'd like to.'

'Well, I'm taken up with this bloody party over the next

couple of days. I can't make it to the concert tonight, but the hoi polloi are going, such as they are in Ferngate. If you're still in town next week, I could fit you in then? Proper lunch, my treat. Champagne. And a taxi ride home. Speaking of which – I'll get someone to drop you off in town. Think Jed's off doing what... well, whatever Jed does. Man of mystery.'

Georgia cut him off, before he could find another tangent. 'You've been very kind in giving me your time, so far. I should be back home by the weekend, but if I'm in town I'll give you a call. You have a number...?'

'Ah – Susan does the phone stuff. And lots of other things to do with websites and Twitter and God knows what. She'll sort you out – call her, I'll consider my diary, and then she will tell me precisely what to do, and when to do it. Every household needs a Susan.'

'And thank you for your other kind offer. If you do decide to hire a private investigator, I'd be grateful if you could share any new information you find.'

'Yep – you and the police. That's for sure.' His eyes grew flinty all of a sudden. The laugh lines around his eyes suddenly dilated, along with his pupils. 'I'll sort this out for you, I promise.'

He got off his seat to greet her as she rose – then grimaced.

'Everything all right?

'Truth be told, it's my back. Buggered it a few weeks back.'

'Let me have a look.'

'Bit frank, Mrs Healey, isn't it?'

'It's Dr Healey. You forget – I'm a GP. What happened – did you feel it go?'

'Kind of... But the pain didn't really come in till later.'
Sir Oliver turned, and she put her hands on the small of
his back.

'How about here?'

'Ouch! Yep. I was on a ladder, you know, checking out
the scaffolding on the tent outside. It was out of nothing –
I twisted to look at something and there was that sort of
grating feeling. Didn't realise I'd popped anything that
badly until I got out of bed the next morning.'

'I'm going to say something to you that you won't
like – you've got to rest it for a few days, and take some
Ibuprofen. You can expect it to be painful for a couple of
weeks.'

'Ah, that's not quite what I want to hear. Got lots to do,
you know.'

Georgia nodded towards Susan, who had somehow
appeared at the doorway to the cocktail lounge, entirely
unbidden but absolutely on time, so far as Georgia could
see. She frowned at the sight of Georgia's hands on the
small of her boss's back.

'I'm sure Susan could climb a ladder or two for you, Sir
Oliver.'

13

How to look good on a night out, in the era of Cornfed:
1.

(rest of the page is blank)

From the diary of Stephanie Healey

*A*n *age-old problem*, Georgia thought, staring into the mirror back at her apartment. It was a long time since she'd worried about dressing for any occasion. In the end she decided to go with comfortable over presentable. Boots – knee-high, not the beetle-crushers she'd taken out onto the wilderness. Oil-effect jeans, which were getting a little long in the tooth, and which Georgia knew would be like parting with a beloved pet once they gave up the ghost. A maroon bodysuit that she had sometimes worn to work on the odd occasion, and which had drawn comments from Dr Owens, easily the biggest sleaze she had ever worked with. Over the top she wore a short-sleeved blazer, which would have done quite nicely at work or if she'd decided to go to the pub quiz at The Drake with Rod.

This triggered a memory of the time Stephanie had gone with them, one Tuesday during the Easter holidays. She'd still been at school and still under-age, but they'd gotten her a wine or two, and their team, The Wise Old Owls, had finished a creditable third. There had been lots of other mothers, fathers and children – people they knew, familiar faces. Georgia knew many of them through her practice, of course, both inside and out, but she'd known a strange pleasure in seeing Stephanie speaking to a schoolmate, a tall rugby-playing lad with fair hair and long eyelashes. She had been confident and pretty with a slight flush at her cheek. Credit Pinot Grigio for the blush... or maybe not. Georgia had been delighted with her daughter that night, even surprised at how much she'd known for her age. They'd gone home in the taxi, all quite merry, all quite happy. Was it the last time? Hadn't there been a Christmas or two in between?

Georgia sat down, and her head spun. After a time, she clicked on the kettle and tore open a sachet of instant coffee... and then another, doubling down. It wasn't her coffee maker back home, but frankly nothing was. She was tired. Sitting down on the bed was dangerous; lying back on it would be fatal. *I almost died today*, she thought. *I can have a night off.*

But not tonight. Not with these people.

She looked up the Megiddos online, of course. Though she hadn't had the time, nor particularly the inclination, to get used to their music, she'd watched the top videos on YouTube. They'd been at Glastonbury just that summer. The top video, for a song entitled 'Tears Never Dry', saw the band performing at just the right time, as the sun sank in front of an absurd sea of heads, with a sky from a Turner painting above turning everything a crepuscular crimson, purple and gold. There was a backing band on bass, drums and keys, but the two main men were front and centre, and the only two permanent members: Riley Brightman, and Scott Trickett.

Brightman, Georgia knew of. He'd even made his way into the newspaper gossip columns and magazines she occasionally flicked through during a tea break at the surgery. Beautiful, rather than handsome, taken to shading his eyelashes in black, but with a firm jawline and short, pure black hair with the sheen of a house-cat's coat. He was just pretty enough for girls to fall in love with, just alternative-looking to get away with the boys' vote, too, with irresistible blue eyes. On stage he wore what appeared to be a Byronic, loose chemise, which someone had attacked with scissors. Onstage banter between Brightman and Trickett had revolved around how Brightman kept getting the material caught in his guitar strings. Later on, they'd brought on someone from Coldplay or Mumford & Sons for a duet, but Georgia hadn't kept watching for that. Brightman was an engaging stage presence, polite – and a fine counterpoint for Trickett.

Scott Trickett was only twenty-two, the same age as Riley Brightman, but looked a good deal older. Or perhaps he hadn't weathered as well; he was stout, and wearing black T-shirts most of the time, with a reddish hairline. Georgia couldn't be sure if he was receding, or if his jowls and chin had grown too large for his forehead. She could spot a drinker; he was probably a precocious one. If this was how he looked age twenty-two, then God knows how forty-two would look, or fifty-two. He had small eyes, too, and the temptation was to feel sorry for the bigger, but shorter man, playing guitar and singing back-up to a star.

Their stage banter belied this. 'How's it going so far?' Brightman had inquired, at the end of 'Tears Never Dry'. While the audience had responded with typical enrapturement, Trickett stepped up to his mic and asked: 'And how much of a nonce does Riley look tonight?'

Brightman seemed the fall guy for the jokes, and he took it in good part along with the audience. But while he sang, Brightman was clearly the star, the one the camera focused on. His voice was good, Georgia had to admit, throaty and deep, belying his age, and capable of some gymnastics that made her think of Jeff Buckley, maybe the last male singer-songwriter she had secretly adored. Screams regularly greeted his every utterance, in between songs, but he was perhaps too well aware of how good he looked, in typical rock god pose, his guitar neglected for the moment, both hands clutched to the mic stand, neck corded, legs splayed.

Georgia smiled at this. It was something you didn't dare vocalise, along with finding policemen awfully young these days. She'd seen it come and go, these rock stars, these fads. Most of them had one album and two or three singles, a little bit of time in the sun, and as often as not they were gone. For a brief period, their number-one singles were attached to car adverts, and their agent might set up jocose appearances on panel shows. But before they knew it, they were dumped by record labels. It didn't seem to be so different in the digital era. They were just as disposable, although not as liable to clog up your shelves or, ultimately, your loft.

When had she last gone to a concert? She'd accompanied

a widowed aunt to a Michael Ball show a while back, but she'd done that under duress (though he had been tremendous, to be fair). How about bands? She'd done a festival in Hyde Park headlined by Lionel Richie, so it could have been that, but that had felt sanitised, as if she'd actually seen it on television and misremembered having been there in person. A real concert, a real gig – with drinks before it, and excited chatter in the queue, then a club night afterwards. When had it been? What decade?

It was a mild night, and the streets seemed unusually busy. The venue was The Orchard, a cavernous space that had one been a warehouse, converted by some canny operators into a concert venue and exhibition hall five or six years ago. It was the sort of place that might host youth theatre during the day, with mother and baby events in the café, and welcome bands in at night. A decent-sized venue, about two thousand capacity. Walking up to the venue, with its spotlit billboard, black letters on a white background, Georgia realised that the crowds and the young girls in particular were there for her daughter.

CONCERT FOR STEPHANIE, read the billboard. Beneath that, simply: THE MEGIDDOS, plus SPECIAL GUESTS.

The queue was already around the front of the building when Georgia took her place. The audience was mainly young and female, and she tried to swallow that increasingly familiar feeling of looking her age. Three girls just ahead of her did offer her a swig of a pre-mixed gin and tonic from a can, which she politely declined.

One of them, a tall girl with a graceful equine neck and

wonderful smoky eyeshadow, asked her: 'You seen the Megiddos before?'

'First time. I'm looking forward to it though.'

'I've seen them six times,' she said. 'I entered the ballot for Glastonbury – I think they'll headline this year. You must have seen that, last year. They were the best band of the day.'

'I did see that – 'Tears Never Dry' was amazing.'

'It always is. God knows how it didn't make number one. I think this is an acoustic show tonight – just Riley and Trickett. I reckon it'll suit a lot of their stuff. Riley writes songs on an acoustic. It's better for working out the harmonies, he says.'

Georgia had run out of things to say about the amazing Megiddos and their cosmological career path, and she certainly didn't want to get into a discussion with a superfan who knew everything about them, including their favourite toothpaste. 'Who's the support band, do you know?'

'Some local chancers,' the tall girl said, taking a swig. 'Who cares?'

One of her friends, a short girl in a shorter dress who shivered in spite of the mild conditions, said: 'You into Riley, then?'

'He's a great singer. He could be a star.'

'Could be?' the second girl spluttered. 'I think he's there already, love. I reckon you could be his mother. You're not his mother, are you?'

'No. Not his mother.' Georgia felt herself shrivel. There was something feral about the shorter one. This, and the sweet smell of the drinks they were necking, made her feel insecure. *She's basically a child. Get a grip of yourself. And tell her to fuck off, if necessary.* 'Are you his girlfriend?'

She did laugh at that, all credit to her. 'Hey, terrible about that lass, wasn't it?' she said. 'The one they're having the concert for, I mean.'

'They never did find out what happened to her,' said the girl with the long neck.

'Must be awful for her family,' the shorter girl said. 'Looks like she killed herself. But imagine not knowing.' Then, bless her, she offered Georgia a drink from what purported to be a bottle of pink gin and tonic.

'No thanks, I'm driving,' Georgia lied.

'I reckon someone's done away with her,' the tall girl said.

'Yep. Long gone.' The shorter girl grinned, finished the last of her bottle, and screwed the top back on. 'She'll be in someone's freezer, by now. In different drawers.'

Georgia took out her phone, and pretended to be busy with a text message.

When they reached the front of the queue, the three girls were vigorously searched, with the doormen having watched them finish their drinks and then stuff the bottles into a bin before rearranging their clothes. Georgia grinned as the tall girl unbuttoned her top a little. She knew what was coming.

'Are there any spaces on the guest list?' she asked one of the doormen.

The bouncer was, to his credit, utterly impassive. 'I'm afraid the guest list is full tonight.'

Georgia had a flashback to when she had gone to see Suede, when they were popular the first time around. She'd seen people behave the same way. Things didn't change quite so much.

When she stepped up, she made sure she said, loud enough for the three girls to hear as they continued into the venue: 'I'm on the guest list tonight.'

The doorman consulted his phone. 'Name?'

'Georgia Healey.'

The doorman looked up, blinked, then smiled for the first time. 'Please step through the barrier to my left, Mrs Healey. You all right?'

'I'm fine, thank you.'

Every head turned to follow her progress. The three girls, who were in the process of being frisked by a female steward, looked at her as if she had sprouted a second head. Georgia wished she'd kept her voice down, as she took a trip up the stairs.

The VIP area was floodlit in purple, with a soft-lit bar that wasn't particularly busy. It was a broad space on a balcony overlooking the entire area – the kind of place Georgia would have preferred to watch any show, these days. A band was already playing down below, a droning outfit with a floppy-haired singer on a Rickenbacker guitar that seemed broader than he was. He was almost offensively blond, a shade of hair difficult to look at under the rudimentary light show, like staring into the sun. When he dragged his hand through his floppy fringe, which was often, he had a big forehead, Georgia noticed. No one seemed particularly interested, and neither was Georgia, especially after the big screen dominating the space at the back of the stage suddenly lit up, in sharp white and black.

'Find Stephanie Healey – missing, 22 March 2017. Call now if you have any information.'

Then a number.

And then, in the white space below, a montage of images Georgia knew very well. A clear-faced student union card ID, the hair clipped back, the chin thrust forward, a strangely confident aspect for such a quiet, diffident girl. Then a cropped image of her cuddled up to a friend whose hair was visible – she was certain this was Adrienne Connulty, with bright red lipstick on that didn't suit her and a silly grin that she wore even worse. Then her wearing a football strip, part of a team she had decided to try out for. So far as Georgia knew, she hadn't played a single game, but in a strange way the football kit had suited her angular features. She had her arms folded, in classic team photo pose. Had she just enjoyed the aspect of dressing up? She'd barely even kicked a ball as a child, huffed her way through every PE lesson, made every excuse not to take part in high school. Had she done it for a dare? Was there someone involved that she fancied?

And then a picture of Stephanie and Georgia, heads leaned into each other, from three Christmases ago. The last Christmas? They had all gone to midnight mass, the biggest laugh being that only Rod was a Catholic, but he'd long gotten out of the habit. It had been a gorgeous moment, on a frigid evening with the night skies having put on their Sunday best with an extraordinary scattering of stars above. Epic, sweet sadness, even while Stephanie was there, in between her and Rod, and the three of them going home in time for a brandy and a Baileys and the fire on, joking that Santa had already been, gazing at the piles of presents and tinselly wrapping, and Georgia had to look away at that point and check her phone.

Someone touched her elbow, and she jumped.

Adrienne Connulty held up a hand. 'Sorry, Georgia, didn't mean to startle you.'

They both had to shout, as the support act began their latest drone. 'Quite all right.'

'Hey,' Adrienne said, 'I thought they called this type of thing a warm-up act? If it gets any cooler out there, I'll ask them to stick the heating on.'

'You know, someone once told me that the big aim of a support band is not to be better than the headliners.'

'Mission accomplished. Get you a drink?'

'No thanks.'

Adrienne drank from a bottle of beer. She wore a denim jacket and had changed her hair, quite radically, since they'd spoken the day before. She looked like an eighties teen magazine cover star, fresh-faced, blonde and slightly frizzy. Georgia had to admit this suited her. She particularly liked the pin badges on her lapels – 'The Megiddos', and also 'Prat Spaniel'.

'Prat Spaniel? Who are they?' Georgia asked, pointing to the badge.

'You're watching them now,' Adrienne replied, indicating the stage. 'Or trying to. Local outfit. Riley's done them a favour, I think.'

The band finished at that moment to lukewarm applause. The band linked arms and bowed as if they'd finished a residency at the Royal Albert Hall, before the blond singer palmed sweat off his broad forehead and said: 'Remember why we're here, folks. We'll be collecting for the Find Stephanie fund, while the main men are on stage later. We even take contactless. Uh, score one for the digital age. Anyway, enjoy the Megiddos, we're Prat Spaniel, come and say hello if you see us!'

Before he left the stage, he raised an expensive-looking camera, and shot the crowd. Even from that distance, Georgia could make out the grin underneath the camera. But neither it, nor the camera's flash, could quite outshine the stark blond hair.

'Click,' he said, into the microphone, after taking some shots of the crowd. Then they were gone.

'They were OK, I guess,' Georgia said, applauding gamely. 'Probably sound better on record.'

'Not sure I'd take the gamble. Anyway... Georgia. I want to say sorry about earlier on. We got off on the wrong foot... I'm not sure what happened. You're upset, I'm upset... Look, we just want to find out what happened to Stephanie, all right?'

'Of course. Goes without saying.' Georgia sighed. 'Look, forget about it. I'm on the lookout for answers. We both know there probably aren't any answers. I'll go on like this for as long as I live. I know that. Sometimes it gets to me. I try to hold back, but I can't. Sometimes things boil over.'

'I get you – I totally get you,' Adrienne said, leaning an elbow on the balcony and moving closer. 'I'm a results-based person. You are too – you've got to be in your game. Same with me. I want answers; you want a diagnosis. Am I right about that?'

'Sure.'

'And we both want the same thing – am I right about that?'

'This isn't part of the show, Adrienne,' Georgia said, scanning the faces that were turned towards them. 'Don't bother with a call and response.'

'If you just turn that way, we'll help you out a little.' Then Adrienne leaned close, her cheek brushing Georgia's, and an arm snaked around her shoulders. Blades of hair jabbed into her nose. She turned to look at what Adrienne was grinning at; a flashbulb erupted in her face.

By the time a second muzzle flash had spiked her eyes, Georgia had a grip of herself, smiling, chin upthrust.

'For God's sake,' she muttered. 'If you'd just asked for a photograph, I'd have posed for one. You didn't need to try and trick me.'

'No one's tricking you,' Adrienne said, with the fixed grin of a fairground carousel horse. 'Connor here jumped in without asking.'

The photographer was one of Adrienne's officemates at the student paper offices. He had unusually light, carefully groomed hair, close to a pudding-bowl style from the early 1980s. The fringe must have been difficult to see through. He gave them a thumbs-up, then turned away to survey the results on his phone.

'Are you sure I can't get you something?' Adrienne asked, softly.

'Maybe a white wine spritzer.'

'A what?'

'A white wine spritzer.'

'Yeah.' Adrienne giggled. 'I heard you – I just don't know what the hell it is.'

'You know what, maybe just a white wine. A small one.'

To Georgia's surprise, Adrienne merely raised a hand, gaining the attention of a woman dressed all in black at the side of the bar with her hands folded. She came over and took an order, then disappeared to the bar. Georgia saw that it was filling up – not much space at the bar, at any rate, although the seats lining the edges were sparsely populated.

'It looks like we'll have a massive boost from tonight – enough to do some more advertising,' Adrienne said. 'You sticking around for the after-show? They're having it up here.'

'I suppose I will. Are Riley and Scott coming?'

'I bloody hope so. I told the paper that they would be – I'm in trouble if I don't get some words.'

'I'd like to speak to them.'

'Oh – they'll want to speak to you. I guarantee that. Riley said he couldn't wait to say hello. He texted me.'

'Did he now?'

A tall man in a cloth cap and a long grey jacket that was surely too warm for this time of year approached. A digital recorder was already in his hands as she said: 'Hi – I hope you don't mind me interrupting. I'm Ben Lotherton from the *Daily Mail*.'

Adrienne stepped aside, but only slightly; Georgia noticed that she had a digital recorder in her hand, too.

Georgia smiled. There was a group of them, before long. Then some more photos. She posed, smiled – not too broadly – and had the presence of mind to make sure the glass of wine was put down well out of shot, and didn't take a sip of it while she spoke to the journalists. She remembered the media training provided by the police officers; she even remembered some of the lines she'd used. 'Anything can help us at all,' she said. 'It's been a devastating time for the whole family and personally very hard for me, of course it has. But I want to thank Stephanie's friends for rallying round, and in particular Riley Brightman and the Megiddos for setting up this concert. I want people to keep searching. We'll find the answer, one day. We'll find out what happened to Stephanie.'

Soon they drifted away to the far corner of the bar. A couple of hundred words was all they needed, the police officer had said. You didn't have to give your life story. All they wanted was something to hang quotation marks onto, to justify the hassle and expense of covering the story, of spending the time at a press conference, or indeed at a tribute concert.

Charity concert, Georgia corrected herself. *It's not a tribute. Not yet.*

She allowed herself a sip of white wine.

'Bet you've been looking forward to that,' Adrienne said, as she clinked her bottle with Georgia's glass.

'Just a sip or two. To tell you a secret, I never drink.'

'Oh… given up?'

'No! Nothing evangelical. I never drank so much when I was younger, and pretty much nothing at all the past few years. I wasn't even too bothered about it socially, after a while. I'll take a glass at Christmas. It's not that I don't like it – I just don't like the lack of control.'

'I must admit, I like a beer now and again.'

'Well, you're a student, love.'

'People don't like getting out of their heads so much,' Adrienne said. 'Most boys I know would rather be in the gym. People want to look good, not get wasted. Myself, I blame the selfie generation.' Adrienne fidgeted with her hair as she said this, oblivious.

'Not drinking so much – I get you,' Georgia said. Spying the three girls from the queue making their way to the front of the crowd below, she added: 'You could have fooled me.'

'What does this mean to you, Georgia?' Adrienne asked. 'Sum it up, if you can.'

'You're still rolling the tape, aren't you?' Georgia's shoulders relaxed. 'It's all right. I don't mind giving you some quotes. This means the world to me. I hope it'll help jog people's memories, though – this isn't about me. This is about finding my daughter. I notice you took a lot of pictures of me. I don't mind that. But make sure Stephanie is front and centre. You're selling your story to the *Telegraph*, or wherever it was that head-hunted you – is that right?'

'Well, not exactly,' Adrienne said, drawing back a little. 'Not that it matters, I suppose.'

Georgia raised her hand. 'It's fine, Adrienne. At the end of the day you're helping me. So I'll help you help me.'

'I'm happy to help.' Adrienne grinned. 'Your husband said the same thing.'

'What? You spoke to Rod?'

'Yes.' Adrienne's eyes narrowed. 'Isn't he here with you?'

'No, he's not – not so far as I know.' Georgia hoped Adrienne couldn't see her blushing. 'When was this?'

'I called him earlier on today. He's been in touch throughout the campaign. Been really helpful. He gave us a cracking interview. Said how hard you'd been working, how much you'd been throwing yourself into your practice. Coping mechanism, he called it.'

'I see. That's interesting. Hopefully he didn't talk about me too much, and focused on Stephanie.'

'I'm just surprised he isn't here with you.'

Georgia smiled. Clearly it didn't fool anyone, but she said: 'Oh, he's busy, himself. He's got his business to look after. Too busy to come over tonight. Anyway... I brought something that I thought you might use. I meant to hand it over when we last spoke. But, you know...'

Adrienne's eyes lit up as Georgia dug into her jacket and produced a photo. It was a printout of the original, a reasonable copy. It showed Stephanie while she'd been studying for her A levels. She'd taken time out from – supposedly – making notes on *Romeo and Juliet* to have a cup of coffee out in the garden, her elbows on the rickety fence post, looking at the farmer's fields across the road. The light had been gorgeous, and Stephanie had been distracted and distant, but this lack of expression had heightened her beauty – an alien beauty, taking more after Rod's side than Georgia's. Not knowing herself observed, she had a more natural look than her silly faces or the mock-ironic pout she had affected at the time for social media. There was the long jawline, the big cheekbones, the clear brow and the pale, pale skin, and the Elf Warrior ears, as her school friends had christened them – this latter feature being the only justification for the pixie haircut that Georgia loathed.

How much more beautiful she'd be with longer hair, Georgia had thought. Still did think, in fact. *If only she'd grow it out.*

'You can have this. I found it recently, on an old phone. I forgot I'd changed phones not long before Stephanie disappeared. This is one of the best photos of her. I caught her unawares.'

Adrienne took the photo. She bit her lip. Tears brimmed. 'Gorgeous girl. Big skinny malinky Stephanie. God, Georgia. Thank you for this. Thank you.'

'I'll get a digital copy to you. I just had this one printed out recently... I really like it. You can see why.'

'No, we can scan this, don't worry yourself.' The photo disappeared inside Adrienne's bag. 'Anyway... Looks like it's showtime here.'

14

The thing about Cornfed is that the more appointments you make, the more you miss of everything else. And you don't mind one little bit. In the mornings is best, in the afternoons is OK too, and in the evenings it's a necessity. I want to trace my fingers down Cornfed's face, and leave a slight impression, as you would on fine sand. I want to know Cornfed in every dimension.

From the diary of Stephanie Healey

'Thanks so much for that, thank you.' Riley Brightman had on a tight-fitting black T-shirt and grey jeans – different to his usual fey, sometimes androgynous style. He had even done without the eyeshadow for a change. Everything was centred on his T-shirt, and the message stencilled in stark white capitals across his chest. 'FIND STEPHANIE', it read, followed by the helpline number. A fine effort, Georgia thought, even though his black rhinestone-studded guitar strap obscured it most of the time.

The cheers went on and on, after the opening number, a raucous affair stripped back to just two acoustic guitars and the performers' harmonies. Georgia didn't know the song, but was impressed by how well their voices worked, away from the *sturm und drang* of bass and drums and distorted strings; there was something of the Everly Brothers to them, although the two front men seemed as chalk and cheese as ever. If anything, having Scott Trickett wearing the same outfit as Riley Brightman accentuated their differences – Scott was ill at ease in a T-shirt, the curving script stencilled on the front highlighting a monumental egg of a belly that might have gotten him a seat on a packed bus had he been a woman. Trickett was sweating heavily under the lights even before the first number began, and he gulped down a bottle of beer set up on a table beside the mic stands as it finished.

'I'm going to bang on about this,' Brightman said, palming away his own entirely imaginary sweat, 'but we're here for a reason, and it's up on screen behind me. This is Stephanie, my beautiful friend. She went missing just over two years ago, in this town, right here in Ferngate. Someone out there must know a little something about her – anyone, anywhere, if you even think you know about what might have happened to Stephanie, please give this number a call, or send a text, or drop an email. Any information you could have could help us find her. Please…' His voice hitched; the crowd roared all the same. Brightman ran a hand through his hair, then clutched the mic stand. 'OK. This one is called "Sunrise With Dawn".'

'Bit rude, this one,' Adrienne whispered in Georgia's ear. 'Not too appropriate, I guess.'

'Wait till you hear about this guy I used to listen to called Prince,' Georgia muttered. She took a sip of the wine, and leaned on the balcony rail, watching the show.

Brightman was the star, of course – she knew that already. But then something strange happened, amid the thrashing of the acoustic guitars, augmented by the beautifully constructed chorus lines and middle eights; Georgia forgot about things. She was genuinely enjoying the show, the good-looking boy working his way through his poses, one minute the rock god, the next an awkward foal, all stringy muscles, fringe and shyness. He knew just when to sink back, and when to spring forward. It was as much physical theatre, even restricted to the acoustic guitars and a few lighting effects – but they were good songwriters, and they could play.

Georgia had gone through a phase in her freshman year of wanting to form a band, and had tried to learn how to play with a battered acoustic and a songbook-for-dunces out of the library. She had no aptitude for music, but she did have one for stubborn slogging and dogged study and practice, and from that phase she knew enough to recognise that what they were doing wasn't easy, with Scott Trickett taking on most of the heavy lifting. The stout man wasn't quite a guitar hero or hair metal fret wanker, but his skill was clear. What was especially odd was that he said very little, staring into space, or merely applauding away from the mic whenever Brightman spoke.

They played for about forty minutes – just about all of their songs. A new tune Brightman said was called 'She Said', or 'She Says', Georgia couldn't be sure which – met with a rapturous response. 'This is the first time anyone's ever heard it…' Brightman looked to the big man to his left, and when no response was forthcoming, he said: 'Outside of our own festering minds, anyway.'

They ended with 'Tears Never Dry', pausing during the second chorus to hear the audience singing every word. A sea of camera phone lights dappled the crowd below. 'My God,' Georgia muttered, 'is everyone recording this gig, or watching it?'

Adrienne, who was still stationed by her side, said something like: 'Cheer up, Grandma.'

The applause was thunderous. After a short encore, which took in a two-guitar rendition of 'She Moves Through The Fair', Brightman raised a hand and looked right into the gallery. Georgia straightened up.

'This is for Stephanie, OK?' he said. Then he sang Robbie Williams' 'She's The One', solo.

Georgia did not know what to do, or what to say. She felt frozen to the spot, mortified for a spell, then a little bit angry.

Then Adrienne's hands were over her shoulder, and then something broke in her. More than one person came over to hug her; one might have been the journalist with the cloth cap. She wanted to flee, but held her ground, and joined the applause, tears streaming down her face.

'All right?' Adrienne asked.

'Coping,' was all Georgia said. Instinctively she reached for the glass of wine – it had barely been touched the whole night – but something in the dry bite and the sourness afterwards suddenly disgusted her, and she laid it down on an empty table.

Brightman and Trickett took their bows before the crowd, with the stout guitar player hurling picks from his stand out into the audience, before they both disappeared backstage.

Various pictures of Stephanie's face scrolled past on

the video screen at the back of the stage, with the contact details beneath.

'How long will it take them to come upstairs?' Georgia asked Adrienne, as the audience filed out of the hall below.

'Hard to say... Don't think it'll be too long. Don't reckon Riley would keep you waiting, anyway. Oh! Hey!'

Adrienne flailed somewhere over Georgia's shoulder. This alarmed her, as if a bird had fluttered at her ears, and she cringed a little.

She cringed a bit more when she saw who Adrienne was signalling.

Martin Duke and his girlfriend, Colette, were stood at a pillar nearby, each sipping a beer. They both looked surprised, then a little hesitant. Colette whispered something in Martin's ear, and they came over. Colette was wearing long black culottes that didn't suit her at all, and her lipstick was certainly eye-catching – thick and burgundy. She'd painted her nails black, and her hands were laden with silver jewellery, Celtic symbols, it seemed. Martin Duke was looking better than Georgia had seen him before, but looked a bit of a sight, truth be told. He wore a tatty off-white band T-shirt – Aerosmith, it looked like, most likely worn ironically – underneath a brown corded jacket that looked like it had been stolen off a lecturer's peg, having hung there for maybe fifteen years. His trousers also appeared to be flared, with sequins and roses stitched into the sides of the thighs. Had he been as slim as he was a couple of years ago, he'd have gotten away with this look, but if anything, it underlined that he had lost his looks a little, his definition softened.

Adrienne practically smothered both of them – it

bordered on assault. No fresh air kisses for her; both were smooched on the cheeks, more than once. 'You guys! It's lovely to see you! Sit down, have a drink.'

'We're fine,' Martin said, cutting her off with a hand and addressing Georgia. 'We just wanted to come along and show our support.'

'It's appreciated, Martin. Did you enjoy the show?'

Colette answered for him. 'They're all right, I guess. Not really my cup of tea. Did you see Prat Spaniel, the guys who were on before it? They're more my type of thing.'

'Interesting sound,' Georgia said. *Yeah. While you're at it, tell them you thought they had a good beat, Grandma.*

'You know what?' Martin said, leaning closer, a mischievous set to his lips as he spoke. 'I reckon they've got a hell of a good beat.'

Georgia mock-applauded. 'I asked for that! Yeah, to be fair, I was just being polite. It sounded like my dishwasher on a long cycle.'

'Oh – you can tell the singer that, if you like,' Colette said. 'He's right beside you.'

The blond singer who'd been struggling with the Rickenbacker on stage was staring right at Georgia, maybe five yards away. Georgia had no idea he'd been there. She drew in a deep breath as he raised a bottle of beer at her in salute.

'Hey, hi,' Georgia said. 'Very interesting sound your band has.'

'Thanks. I thought we had a great beat, too,' he said, and laughed uproariously with everyone else.

'I think I'll go home, and hide under the covers,' Georgia said. 'It's not been my night.'

'Ah, don't be silly,' the blond boy said, not unkindly. He stuck out a hand, and Georgia shook it. 'I'm Howie Abbot, by the way. Pleased to meet you, though these are terrible circumstances.'

'Don't mention it.' Close-up, he had the look of a bit of a jackanapes – tall and wiry, with fine blond hair seeming stolen from a two-year-old. On stage he had come across as a bit of a bumbler, a little preppy, out of place on stage with drums and flashing lights behind him. He seemed more confident in person.

Georgia was aware of a change in the atmosphere over her shoulder – like a sudden change in air pressure. People on the periphery of her vision sighed and shifted.

Riley Brightman came forward. He'd changed out of the white-on-black T-shirt; now it was black-on-white.

'Well now,' he said rubbing his hands together, after a firm clap. 'It looks like the band's all back together.'

'Good show,' Martin Duke said. 'You pulled it off.'

In the unearthly atmosphere the pair's proximity generated, it was impossible to know if there was any irony intended in the remark, even down to the level of double entendre. Unconsciously, Georgia had taken up a more defensive stance.

'Well, you'd know all about that,' Riley replied, finally. 'Want a drink? Someone get this guy a drink. Best poet in the university, this time last year.'

'I'm fine, thanks. Got a beer, here.'

'Have another, then.' Riley stepped forward and slapped him on the shoulder. 'You deserve it. Been a hell of a year. And one for you as well, princess – Colette, wasn't it?'

He turned on the most dazzling smile. She couldn't help but respond with one of her own. 'That's right.'

'You fancy another beer, Colette? I remember you loved to chug 'em down. Back in the Hephaestian days. Beer monster, weren't you?'

'No thanks, Riley.'

'What a pair of stick-in-the-muds! Changed days. Well, Colette, we'll need to catch up some time. See if we can't get the beer monster out of you, eh?'

Unfortunately, Martin Duke was still young, and took the bait all too easily. That's when Georgia knew the situation was lost. 'She said she doesn't want a beer, Riley.'

'Bit controlling of you, Martin, if you don't mind my saying so.'

'I do mind you saying so.'

Georgia stepped forward. 'Look, everybody...'

'Nah it's OK,' Riley said, warding her off. 'Martin's a little bit hot under the collar. I shouldn't try to get his goat. It's easy to get his goat, mind you. Not to mention everything else.'

'Only goat you're getting is the one you're sacrificing to your daddy, cheese dick,' Martin said, almost pleasantly. Then he smiled.

One or two people laughed within earshot at this, and it might have been the catalyst for what happened next. Riley Brightman's eyes locked on Martin Duke's. Then, without warning or preamble, he attacked.

15

I sometimes feel I've enraged them without trying; yet when it boils over, no attempt at pacification seems good enough. I think I'll leave them to it, next time.

From the diary of Stephanie Healey

Riley launched himself at Martin as one dog would at another. He had no set goal for his attack, no end product, motivated only by a desire to annihilate.

People were already shouting and screaming by the time he took a grip of Duke's off-white second-hand ironic band T-shirt. The collar sheared off the material quickly and cleanly in Brightman's fist; with the material bunched up between his fingers, he then darted his hand into Duke's face.

There couldn't have been much contact. Martin seemed to grimace, rather than flinch, at the blow. Then he tugged himself free of Riley's grip and swung an arm, hard. The connection was clear, and brutal, and then Riley Brightman was down on one knee, blinking. It had happened in less than three or four seconds. Georgia darted forward instinctively. 'That's enough!'

Colette then got involved, as Martin Duke stood his ground, his T-shirt collar askew and loose round his neck like a Jacobean ruff. The girl's culottes flailed as if in a high wind, and she pummelled Riley Brightman's back as he tried to get to his feet.

'*Bastard*, you fucking *bastard*,' she screeched.

Bouncers in hi-vis flooded the scene like laser beams; Colette was borne away with her legs pinwheeling, a child lifted out of harm's way. Martin was huckled out roughly by two absolute brutes who wouldn't have looked out of place in an American wrestling ring.

Arriving just a bit too late to get his hands scabby, Scott Trickett bowled forward, jabbing a fist at Martin Duke's retreating back, bellowing, until a female steward laid a hand on his shoulder and gently, but decisively, pushed him back to where Georgia stood.

Riley Brightman was back on his feet, and utterly in control, despite a comically fat lip. He was fully aware of the camera phones that pointed in his direction, and the fact that journalists were in the room. He seemed to focus on Adrienne Connulty's mobile searchlight before the others, as he raised his arms in a placatory fashion, saying: 'It's all right folks, show's over. Bit of a scuffle. Party's not a party without one. Everyone have a drink, eh? It's on me.'

He came forward and seized Georgia by the hand. His own was small and delicate, the touch soft. It was like handling a wren; Georgia didn't want to squeeze too hard. 'Sorry you had to see that, Mrs Healey. Unsightly stuff. I've no idea how that clodding idiot managed to get on the guest list.'

'Are you all right? I think you've got a cut lip.'

'Must have done that to myself, when I fell.' He touched his lip and stared at the blood a moment, fascinated. 'Headlines, in the next five minutes: "Brightman punches self in face".'

'Hold on a second.' Georgia dug into her pocket for some tissues, dabbing at them. 'I think you'll live.'

'Let's have more drinks!' Riley bellowed, to no one in particular. Georgia was discomfited to see that the girl in black who had brought Adrienne a drink earlier snapped to it on the double. Then Riley turned back to Georgia. 'Let's you and me have a sit-down and a talk.'

He steered her towards the back bench, waving away any other attention that came his way. Including from Adrienne Connulty, who said, much too brightly: 'Hi, Riley!'

He was over-familiar, but not creepily so. Tactile; a hand on the arm or the shoulder, head bent close enough to kiss at times.

Georgia felt disorientated for a moment or two. *Do I want to kiss him?* she thought. It wasn't every day that you sat next to a living poster on someone's wall. It wasn't like seeing famous people in concert – there was still that barrier between crowd and performer, in those circumstances. She remembered being in a Japanese restaurant for her birthday one weekday off with Rod, and she'd turned around to see a Premier League footballer and his reality TV star wife there. There was something surreal about it, a moving image you were used to seeing on the television, or in pixels on news sites, or static in whatever papers you could be bothered reading. It was like they were ethereal beings, creatures who lived in picture books or within the gilded frames of high art, suddenly become flesh.

Riley betrayed no clear signs of anxiety or stress, despite having been in a physical altercation moments before. His preamble seemed decent and sincere, although he locked eyes and hands with her to do it.

'I know this might have been uncomfortable for you, and I'm sincerely sorry about that. I thought it was the best thing to do in the circumstances. It was the least I could do. Me and Stephanie... we were close. It was a brother and sister relationship, that's for sure. I just couldn't believe it when I heard.'

Georgia pulled back with her hand – just a little. Enough for him to get the message and release her. 'You certainly seemed close enough. She spoke about you now and then.'

'It was a great year. Good group. Lots of friends, lots of socialising. You were a student here, Mrs Healey, is that right?'

'That's right. Too many years ago now.'

'Not at all. But you remember what it was like. It's a good town, a party town, but a quiet town, too. Somewhere you'd settle down.'

'Yes. A funny old town.' She smiled. She did remember. It was something she had blotted out of her mind. That she had loved the place. That she had subscribed to all the alumni publications, even made a donation or two to the medical school. Enjoyed reading about it, following the papers it published in journals. The last Home Secretary had been a Ferngate graduate, and although the man hadn't been fit to line a cat litter tray in Georgia's estimation, she'd known the reflected glory of someone from her alma mater doing well.

And then I sent my only child here. And that happens.

'But it didn't look like you were very close to Martin Duke. What happened there?'

He laughed, slapping his thighs with both hands. 'That dick? Excuse my French. But that guy… You know, I'll say this frankly, and I don't want it to upset you. I know the police cleared him. They checked where he'd gone, they cleared him, but that guy… I had my suspicions about him. They weren't as close as he made out. In the press conference, in the papers. I thought he had something to do with it, somewhere.'

'The police are quite clear about it, Riley.'

'All the same, he's a weirdo.' Was that an Elvis sneer? Georgia thought it was. 'He sniffed after her. I think she gave in and let him trail along behind her because she felt sorry for him.'

'That's not the first fight you've had with Martin, is it?'

'Fight? That wasn't a fight.'

'I mean the last time you had a punch-up. The night Stephanie vanished.'

'Well. That wasn't a fight either. It was an ass-kicking. And I wasn't on the receiving end of it.'

'Really? He looked as if he can handle himself, just then.'

'He got lucky.' Georgia had struck a nerve with that, though. 'He was all over the place, that night. At the Hephaestians' do. Let me tell you.'

'Maybe he was drunk,' Georgia mused. 'Reminds me a bit of old Thommo. Rugby player I knew. Scrum half – one of those guys about five feet six if that, but broad as they come, and muscular, with it. The type of guy who can drink about six pints before the night's even got going, and not look as if it's done any damage. I remember him getting a beating, one night. He was too drunk to do anything about it, basically. Got kicked up and down the car park by someone not much heavier than you. We didn't speak about it much, once he'd healed up.'

But Riley Brightman had already drifted away somewhere else. He nodded towards a phalanx of well-dressed young women who were stood near a table. Their way was barred by two bouncers, perhaps the same two who had given Martin Duke and Colette their cards. They filed forward, and Riley posed for a series of selfies. Photographers from the media took shots of this, too. Riley made great play of his fat lip, posing with his finger pointing towards the slight swelling – even making a boxing pose with one of the women who wanted selfies.

'Sorry about that,' he said, sliding back into his seat. 'Anyway – I hope this helps the fund in some small way. It's the very least I could do, Georgia.'

She had the horrendous feeling that he was preparing to jettison her.

'I loved that song you wrote for her. "She Said", or "She Says" – was that it?'

'Yes.' He nodded solemnly. '"She Said". It's about Stephanie.'

'I'd like to see the lyrics, if that's OK.'

'I'll get those to you – my PR is hanging around in the background somewhere. She'll get your email address. I promise.'

'Stephanie was a poet, too, you know.'

Riley had been poised in the very act of getting off his seat – but here, he stopped, and sat back down. 'That's right. She was. A great poet, too. We used to write together. We were talking about her doing some lyrics for me. I was just starting out.'

'Just starting out – and here you are, already. Glastonbury, the top ten...'

'Number one in the streaming charts, as we speak,' he said, a little too quickly.

'Absolutely. I just wanted to know, though – did she ever talk about big projects?'

'How do you mean?'

'Like writing projects, plays or novels.'

'Oh, all the time. She was a creative whirlwind. She would have... Sorry. Sorry. She will have a career in the creative industries. Someone will pick her up, I know it. There was just... something about her. You know that way?'

'Of course. She radiated something, but I didn't know what it was. The word I want to use is "enigma". She's an enigma to me. Not something you'd say about your own daughter, but she was.'

'That's as good a word as any. Listen, I have to...' He clapped a hand to her shoulder.

She took his hand between hers, and held it, tight. He frowned at this. 'I want to know about the Hephaestians, Riley. Specifically, about Tony Sillars.'

'Sillier Soddus! Yes, he's an enigma too, I guess. Not what you think he is, I can say that. But a great man, in his way. He looks like one of those wise seraphs, you know? Beyond the ken of mere mortals. Says all the right things – feminism, equality, calling out prejudice, your racists, your homophobes. He was Mr Woke. And you suspected he was nailing all the students, but...'

The blond boy put down a pint of lager on the table before Riley. He all but wrinkled his nose at the drink as it slopped partly across the surface, but he said: 'A gentleman and a scholar. You'll always remember meeting this guy, Mrs Healey. This is... Howie...' Riley's face scrunched up in mock concentration.

'...Abbot,' the boy said.

'Howie Abbot – that's right. Remember the name. This guy's the future, Mrs Healey. Take a look at this face, here.'

The blond singer seemed absurdly drunk. 'I will climb the stony path to the summit of Mount Pop!' he declared, his arm still around Riley's shoulders.

'You will, you will.'

'With you, as my wise Sherpa!' The blond singer sat down, untidily.

Georgia tugged Riley's sleeve. 'Sorry – before we lose the thread, here. You were saying about Tony Sillars?'

'Oh – just that he's a top man. Encouraged me with my poetry. Encourages everyone. You don't get many teachers like that in life. I thanked him, in the sleeve notes of our album. He got in touch, wrote a letter – like, on paper. All formal, like. You know what the bugger did? He asked us for backstage passes!'

Riley laughed aloud. Then he was gone. Georgia noticed Adrienne collaring him before he made his way through a thickening crowd of onlookers. The bouncers, possibly seeing what had happened earlier as a failure and a cause for a reprimand the next day, looked very nervous as he hugged, shook hands, posed for photos, and signed ticket stubs.

The blond boy sighed and sat back. He sketched something on the sheet of paper with the thick marker pen. Georgia saw the words 'FORMAL LETTER', in capitals, in the centre of what seemed to be a crude impression of a gilded frame. He turned to look at Georgia, and smiled. 'Hey there.'

'Hey there yourself. How's your night?'

'It's going swell. Absolutely no one has come to take my number, or pose for photographs. Don't suppose you want to pose for photos?'

'You seem friendly with Riley.'

'Oh yeah. Go back a-ways.' He leaned closer. He smelled of booze – and not just beer; that awful, almost folk-memory taint of vodka was on his breath, uncut. 'I think Riley sees me as a little brother, you know. He's helping me out. I get it. I get it. It's a big gig, this… although it's for a cause.' He looked ashamed of himself. 'Sorry.'

'It's all right. You've dedicated your time and your effort to it. Don't feel bad. It's good you're getting this exposure. I'm glad.'

'Thing is, you've got to stick in,' the boy said. 'You've got to stick in with Riley. His dad's the thing, you know. It's how things are done. It's how you get a deal. Dirty world, but it's the same everywhere. It's a snake that eats itself.' He made a grand gesture, one hand clenched in the other. It was the gesture of a children's TV presenter, something he had probably practised. Had he done it on that stage, earlier on? Georgia couldn't remember.

'Riley's dad? Who's his dad?'

'You don't know?' His features softened, and he giggled. 'It must be the worst-kept secret in the music business. It's up there with Linda McCartney and the Eastmans.'

'That was hardly a secret. Who's Riley's dad?'

A great, booming voice caused both their heads to snap up. 'Right then you, Nancy boy, budge up there, let me sit next to the lady.' Scott Trickett appeared, three pints of landfill lager clutched between his hands, slopping out onto the floor.

The blond boy budged up as he was told. Georgia suspected Trickett wouldn't have broken his stride in any case, and would have flopped down on his lap, had he not gotten out of the way. The big man slumped like a walrus beaching itself, slammed the pints down, and offered the one with least spilt out of it to Georgia, eyebrows raised.

'No thanks, Scott, I'm driving.'

'Ah, that's no excuse. You could walk home... Oh, sorry.' Before Georgia realised what he meant, he wiped his hands on his white campaign T-shirt, and offered a hand. Whereas Riley's hands were those of an artist, Trickett's were those of a bricklayer. She felt something sharp jabbing the pads of her hands, and recoiled.

Trickett held up his hand. His nails were long, and wicked sharp on the right hand. 'I'm so sorry, again. I'm an idiot. I forget about these.'

'For guitar picking?'

'Banjo, actually. But you're on the right track.' Trickett had his back turned to the blond boy, who, whether or not he was drunk, took his cue, and also his pint, retreating in the direction of the crowd. 'Hey – you hear any more about how the inquiry's going?'

'No news, I'm afraid. Just got to hope this jogs people's memories.'

He shook his head, gulping half his drink down, and suppressing a belch. 'Terrible times, something like that can happen, I tell you. It's an awful road you're going down. Oh... sorry again.'

'Quite all right,' Georgia said. 'You don't have to keep apologising.'

'I've got this thing, where I say inappropriate things. What do you call it again? Being a dickhead.' He grinned. White foam clung to his beard. Although he surely hadn't long put on the white campaign T-shirt, he smelled as if he had been wearing it for a few days. Georgia, who was well practised in not showing discomfort whenever less-than-well-groomed patients took their clothes off in front of her, did not retreat.

'Not at all. Hey – I was thinking Riley's dad might be here tonight. Is he here?'

'What – Sir Oliver? Nah, he's busy tonight. Rotarians, Masons, Satanists, something like that. Some kind of party going on up at the hall. I had a suspicion it was for Riley. Not long had a birthday. And he was just not telling me. Or daddy wasn't inviting me. That'd be right.'

'He can't go without you, surely. There's no him without you.'

'Beautifully put! Yep, we're brothers. Wouldn't want to be separated, though I'm sure he wants to kill me most nights. It's like family. Wouldn't be right without me. It can be a wrench, can't it, when you're parted from the person you're closest to? Like an umbilical cord being cut... Ah, Christ.' He drew a hand down his face. 'Can we start again?'

'If you like.' The bottle of water Georgia had ordered had appeared by her side, unnoticed, and she swigged from it. 'Maybe it's for the best if you start again.'

'I am truly, truly sorry. You sure you won't have this pint?'

'Nope. You go ahead.'

He did, too, gulping at the second drink at the table. 'I get a real thirst on, you know. Like the thirst for knowledge, and the truth.'

'How did you meet up with Riley? He never told me.'

'Ah, I was an engineering student at Ferngate. Was going to work in construction. Until I met Riley and the Hephaestians, and he set me right. I always played guitar. You wouldn't think it with these hands, would you?'

'You were at the Hephaestians?'

'Excellent cheese and wine nights, that's for sure. Truth be told, I didn't go much. Not one hundred per cent my scene. They were all so *into it*, you know? Tight-knit bunch. There's always going to be trouble stemming from that, I guess. Boy-girl trouble.'

'Like with Riley and Martin, just then?'

'Martin Duke isn't trouble. He's a ponce. Look at the state of his T-shirt. What was he trying to achieve with that?'

'Seems there's a grudge there.'

'Yeah. Your daughter had a lot to do with it.'

'She was a big fan of Riley's – is that it?'

'Well…' The big man scratched his chin, sipped a beer, and thought carefully. 'They were good friends, you know? Both into the poetry.'

'You must have been into the poetry, to join the Hephaestians?'

'Me? I'm a pragmatist. As I said, I like booze. Cheese goes down well, too. But mainly, I was looking for a lyricist. Or, to learn how to write lyrics. It was an open society, you know. Most of the time there was just a hard core. People like me popped in and out, dropped off their work, had it marked. But mainly it was Riley, Martin Duke, Sir Percival de Insincere…'

Georgia smiled. 'The lecturer? Tony Sillars?'

'Yeah, him. Team leader. Dude actually looked like a novelist's photo, you know? The glasses and that. Hand on his chin. Sir Creepy de Hands. Goes by many names. Then there was Martin Duke, of course. Plus the chick he goes out with, now. Scary goth girl. Never took to her, really. Too quiet, you know? You never know what's going in those heads of theirs, the quiet ones.'

'Stephanie was quiet.'

Trickett shook his head. 'Not when she got going. Not in my book. Not when she got into her stride. You should have seen her performing her stuff. That's what it was, a performance. She cared about it. She wasn't there for a laugh. It was spooky in a way – not spooky-creepy, just… She was more intense than quiet, you know? They were all crazy about her. I suppose I was, too, in a way. I thought she'd be an actress, I really did. There was some talk of her trying out at the drama society; she was thinking about it. She had an amazing look. Thought she'd bob up in theatre.' He appeared to deflate. 'I am truly sorry. "Bob up"… what's wrong with me?'

Georgia hurried him on. 'There was a fight at the Hephaestians, you said. The night Stephanie vanished.'

'Yeah. Well-known story. Stephanie didn't show up,

and that took everyone by surprise. It was the last meeting before exam season. No answer on her phone. So then, out of nowhere, Martin "The Dick" Duke starts going on about how upset she'd been the other day, how he'd had to comfort her. Riley asks what he's trying to imply. It all goes off from there. Tables flying, the lot.'

'What was the gist of it?'

'That Riley had been sleeping with her. Riley says, "So what? You're not her boyfriend." They square up. Tony Sillars tries to appeal for calm. So do I, for that matter. Martin Duke says, "Don't act the innocent with us. You're the biggest tart going." Sillars raises his hands and walks away. Then the two main contenders get stuck in. Biff, kapow, thwack. I didn't think Riley had it in him, you know? Artist's hands. Little dainty things.'

'He beat Martin up?'

'Yeah. In a manner of speaking.' Trickett chuckled. 'You know how you get someone giving it, "hold me back, hold me back", when stuff kicks off? When he doesn't really want to fight? The pair of them were at it for a bit. Then Riley really lost it. I don't think he laid a hand on him, but he upended a table and bashed him a couple of times with a chair. Could have really messed Martin Duke up. Lucky he didn't get him on the head.'

'And what then?'

'Then, it's fair to say that particular meeting of the Hephaestians dissolved. I think Colette tended to Martin's wounds. Me and Riley went on the sauce. Creative fires were set, though. We wrote our first big single that very evening. "Classical Studies Society Barn Dance". Shortened the title to "Classical Studies". Wise decision.'

'So, you write the music, Riley writes the words?'

'It's a bit of both. Riley's a great songwriter. He's more into the melodies. I sometimes come up with the key, the chord progressions. And the solos. Though truth be told, I don't like the spotlight.'

'You didn't seem keen tonight.'

'It's not the occasion for showing off.' He looked thoughtful. Then he cocked his head closer. 'You in town for a while, yeah?'

'We'll see. I've got a few days off. I might stick around.'

'Good. You could do some digging. For Stephanie. I mean...' He slapped his forehead.

Georgia swallowed back a pulse of anger. 'I'm beginning to wonder if you have an actual condition.'

When Trickett drew his hands down his forehead, she could see he was laughing. She didn't like this at all, or the size of his pupils. 'Now you know why I don't sing lead!'

'What did you write at the Hephaestians?'

'Ach, doggerel. Comic poetry. I wrote these paragraphs of monotone stuff, made out it was verse. Sillars was kind about it. I used to joke that I was actually Hephaestus. Cos I can actually build stuff. When the apocalypse comes, they'll all come to me for help, and shelter. They'd not survive, otherwise. They'd get picked off, one by one. Oh. Sorry.'

'I said before – you don't have to apologise. So, you must have known Stephanie's work?'

'Not loads. Just the poetry. I remember the performances rather than the actual words. She was a bit of an enigma to me, I guess. I knew her, just to see her. Nodding acquaintance. She didn't take to me, I have to admit. For obvious reasons.'

'Like what?'

'Well... look at me.'

'Don't be silly.'

'Like I say... great writer.'

'Did she ever mention any projects she was working on?'

'Well, I don't know for sure. She said she was spending a lot of time on Bewley Street.'

'Bewley Street?' Georgia struggled to recall what the place was. Somewhere in her consciousness, an alarm pinged.

'Yeah. She mentioned spending time among the girls, there. Doing what, Christ only knows.'

'No one else mentioned this. The girls on Bewley Street... Is that the place down by the old corn exchange?'

'Yep, that'd be the place.' He drained his drink, and grinned. 'Don't quote me on it, though.'

'It's the red light zone? Jesus. What was she doing there?'

'Some project. I don't know what, exactly. Guess the cops would know.'

Her heart was racing. Here was something new; the thing she'd been looking for. The flaw in the picture. 'You're sure? How did you find out about this?'

'Someone told me. I can't remember who. I'm not the guy to ask. I'll be honest, I didn't know her that well. Not as well as Riley knew her. Or Martin Duke. Or the lecturer. Or that other guy, what was his name now?' He placed a finger to his lips.

It was only then that Georgia knew for sure she was being mocked. She took a deep breath and sipped at her drink, trying to stop her hands from shaking. 'What other guy was that?'

'It's just a figure of speech, Columbo.'

'Signifying what, exactly?'

'I'm sure you're bright enough to figure it out. Some guy, any guy, lots of guys...'

Before she could stop herself, she took a bite. 'Lots of guys – but not you. Correct?'

He smiled. 'You know... I wonder, how do you keep functioning? I have to know.'

'Excuse me?'

'Knowing that she's almost certainly out the game. How do you keep going? Do you fool yourself? Do you cling on to hope? Or do you think of the practicalities?'

'Practicalities? I think you should leave, son, before I lose my temper.'

'I mean – the meat and bones of it. The harsh reality. You've got to be thinking – is she underwater? Is she in the ground? Is she in separate pieces, somewhere? Is she an ornament? Did she fulfil her destiny and become a chili con carne? Was she a good meal for someone? Or for the pigs?'

Georgia had never, strictly speaking, punched anyone in her life. She made a fist of it now; a poorly constructed one, thrown overhand, downwards, into that bloated, mossy face. He didn't even try to dodge it; merely said, 'Ow!'

'You evil, miserable fat bastard. How dare you!? How dare you say that to me?!' The plastic water bottle rebounded off his chest, and rolled to the floor, spilling out the mouthful or two she had left. Only after seeing this did she realise that she in fact had thrown it, in reflex.

'Help! Police!' The big man was giggling, his breasts wobbling beneath the tight white T-shirt. The bouncers hesitated, seeing Georgia, knowing who she was.

They parted to let Riley through. He sat in the seat

vacated by the blond boy from Prat Spaniel. 'Hey, rock stars. What's going on? You're spooking the horses, brothers and sisters.'

'That big girl, she hit me!' Trickett spoke in a Shirley Temple falsetto, affecting a shaking hand as he pointed at Georgia.

'Your friend's sick,' she hissed at Riley, 'and I'll be telling the police about him. I think it's time I was going.'

Now, Trickett affected solemnity. 'I was just saying, we have to be honest about things, Stephanie's probably...'

Riley punched him – a much better blow than the one she'd thrown; probably the cleanest of the night. It thwacked him plumb in the left cheek, a meaty contact that turned the big man's head and drew gasps from onlookers.

'Mind your manners,' Riley said.

The punch could have dislodged some teeth, or detached a retina, had it been an inch or two higher or lower. But still the big man laughed. 'I'm being beaten up here! Call a constable.'

'Apologise,' Riley said.

'Ha ha. What? Fuck off. Bitch is crazy, man.'

'I said, apologise,' Riley said, taking Trickett's shaggy head in his hands and leaning close.

Trickett stole a kiss – uncomfortably tender. 'Sorry, Daddy.'

'Not to me, schmuck.' Riley's eyes were hard, and he kept the head in his hands. He turned it, a puppeteer, and the big man looked into her eyes.

'I'm truly sorry,' he said. 'I'm an idiot. Please forgive me.'

'I'll say this for your bandmate,' Georgia said, her voice

quaking, 'he's a delicate guitar player, for such a clodding tit.'

'Ha! Very true.' Riley let go of Trickett, and then budged up beside him. Trickett grinned and hugged his bandmate. It was as if nothing had happened. Then he got up, gathered his drink, waved heartily at Georgia, and left.

'Aw, he's a big cuddly bear,' Riley said. 'He does, unfortunately, have a sense of humour. His default mode is inappropriate. I would have tried to stop him. I didn't want him to sit next to you.'

'Does he get punched a lot?'

'Yeah. Between you and me – I believe he likes it.'

'I'm not sure I like him, at all.'

'He's harmless.' Riley shrugged. 'You coming to the party?'

'What party?'

'My place. I live in Ferngate, you know. I'm a local boy.'

'Oh I know,' Georgia said. 'I know that, for a fact.'

Then she giggled – a high, out-of-control sound. Riley smiled and nodded. That was the first, and perhaps only indication that something was wrong.

16

Stephanie Selkie dived deep, deep. Her eyes were used to the dark, and she could see the creatures that lived there from a long way away. Some had flashing lights like a Christmas tree. Some slithered in the slime at the very bottom, where no light ever came. Some were huge but gentle, and they sang their sad songs to each other out in the deepest of deeps. And some had teeth, and bit you just for the joy of biting you.

From 'The Chronicles of Stephanie Selkie,
Princess of the Sea'

The big lump followed me home the other day. The Trickster. His modus operandi *was frighteningly similar to Neb's – so much so I wonder if he'd been following us both, and taking notes. I saw him waiting for me outside the phone box, which got converted into a mini library, which was then of course converted into a latrine. It suited him. I dodged him quite easily. Every time I think of that dense expression on top of his dense facial foliage, I still laugh. I had half a mind to walk past him once or twice, to mess with his mind, but I'd already wasted enough time.*

From the diary of Stephanie Healey

'I'm sorry,' Georgia kept saying, every time Scott Trickett's face swung into view. She fussed over him, asked for some ice, tried to create a cold compress for his face. It was difficult to tell if there was any swelling thanks to his general condition and the mossy beard.

'Could you get me a bandage?' he asked, his head cocked for his audience. 'Could you do me up like Mister Bump?'

And she did – rummaging in kitchen drawers, picking her way through old bills and plastic bags.

Adrienne Connulty caught her by the wrist. 'God's sake, Georgia. What's going on, here?'

'Nothing,' she'd said. 'I'm perfectly high. I mean fine.' And she giggled. 'What's your story, Adrienne? What's going on, exactly?'

'Just take it easy. Do you fancy a cup of tea?'

'Yeah, why not? Cornfed tea – how about a nice cup of that?'

Adrienne frowned, but only a little. 'Hang on, I'll put the kettle on.'

They were in what Riley had called his flat – in fact, it was a huge, detached house, somewhere out of town. It was a new design, clearly not more than a year old, spotlessly kept. The kitchen was whitewashed, open plan, with gigantic windows looking out into an indeterminately large garden space, swallowed up by the night. The fittings on the kitchen were clean, to the point of clinical, and there were dozens of seats lined up around the worktops and plinths, without any clear sign of a proper kitchen table. Wood seemed alien to those surroundings, utterly incongruous, and most of it had been stripped out bar the sideboards.

The space was dominated by an atrium and a raised area, which it took Georgia far too long to realise was a stage. Two stools were set up, and two guitars as red and shiny as freshly peeled conkers stood on stands.

The stage had an audience. Males were strictly in a minority, here. In fact, the only men were members of the support band, Prat Spaniel. Howie the singer was already sitting with one of the many young women who were sat around waiting for the secondary show to start. 'Select invitation,' was all Scott Trickett had said on the matter, to Adrienne.

They were all so horribly young. Some surely not old enough to drink, and yet they'd been at the concert. When she'd been driven along to Riley Brightman's house, not long after midnight, she'd gone past the three girls who'd been stood in front of her in the queue. They were still stood at the door of The Orchard, quite alone, waiting for Riley or Scott to appear. They'd already left by another exit. The three girls peered into the car, straining to make out who was sat there.

Now they were in Riley's kitchen, and although Georgia realised that she wasn't quite right, she couldn't quite figure out why. She took on a Mother Hen persona, a warped version of what her husband had called her GP stage act. She fussed over some of the girls, who all reacted to her with some alarm. Almost without exception, they were sober, very well dressed, with perfect hair and make-up. 'Are you Riley's mother?' one of them asked, with incredulity. A girl who Georgia could have believed was 13 years old – a daffy, naïve question.

'Not Riley's mother,' she had sneered. No one had cottoned on whose mother she was, of course. No one twigged. They weren't there for her, and they weren't there for Stephanie. Some of them screamed when Riley and Scott reappeared. Most of them had their phones poised, ready to film.

Riley had gotten changed into a blood-red shirt, just messy enough to look fashionable, in some kind of gypsy style, Georgia supposed. He had reapplied his eyeliner, and his pale, thin chest poked through a gap in his shirt. Scott Trickett still wore the white campaign T-shirt, stained in patches with what Georgia hoped was beer. But there was something wrong with the garment. Something was written on it, in black marker.

The "FIND" in "FIND STEPHANIE" had been crudely crossed out. "STEPHANIE" had been amended to read "STEPHANIE'S DEAD".

As the two men appeared on stage to rapturous applause and even screaming, Riley Brightman had spotted this for the first time.

All those mobile phones, held up to record.

He crossed over to a kitchen drawer and brought out a pair of scissors, as shiny bright and barely used as everything else in the cavernous space. Then he appeared to grip Scott Trickett by the chest, who grimaced through his beard. Pulling out the material, Riley snipped off the offending word and stuffed it into his pocket. Trickett remained where he was, mock-crestfallen, examining the furry chest space exposed by the surgery.

'Welcome to our, uh, soiree. I want to start with a slower number for you,' Riley said, nodding towards Georgia. 'You might have heard it earlier when we played it at The Orchard. It's called "She Said", and it's about a friend of mine.'

But Georgia was not moved, impressed or even flattered by this new rendition, echoing out in that weird space, brightly lit by the spots up in the ceiling. She moved in among the spectators, engaging them in conversation. Some were polite, a few ignored her, and one girl with chestnut hair and blonde streaks seemed to shriek: 'I mean, I'm just sat here not bothering anyone, and you're here getting in my face and screaming at me!'

'No one's screamed at you,' Georgia said. 'Don't tell lies.'

Adrienne steered her away. 'I've got your tea here. Have a seat and listen to the show.'

'Did you know who Riley's father was? I didn't know. No one said.'

Adrienne's grin was fixed to her face. 'Darth Vader? That was a joke.'

'Funny how it isn't well known. You'd think it would be well known.'

'It's no big deal, Georgia.'

'We sure about that?'

'Maybe I should call you a cab?'

'No thanks. I'll stick around. What are you doing here, in fact?'

'I'm a fan. I'm also a journalist.'

'Riley giving you an exclusive?'

'I'll ignore that tone of yours, for now. I'm going to call you a cab.'

'And I said, don't bother.'

'Georgia love, you're out of your head. It's about time you went home to sleep it off.'

'How many meetings of the Hephaestians did you attend?'

'Most of them.' Adrienne applauded as the Megiddos finished another number.

'You weren't part of the hard core, then?'

'Hard core? In the poetry society?' Adrienne burst out laughing and sipped at a beer. 'No, I suppose I wasn't. I showed up now and again. Sent in one or two lines, but poetry's not particularly my thing.'

'Good cheese and wine though, eh? That's what I heard.'

'Yeah, to be fair. Those were always good nights. You got a lot of folk attending. Like Scott Trickett.'

'So you weren't so much into poetry, but you got into the poetry society? Funny, that.'

'What's funny about it? I like socialising. Most young people do. Even people your age, I guess. It's not a crime, is it?'

'Just seems a bit off. If it was something like skiing, and I wasn't into skiing, then I'm not sure I'd join the skiing society.'

'I work hard, Georgia. I didn't come to university to have a laugh and act the fool. I don't have time for poetry. It was a useful society for me, though. I discovered I liked to write about real things, real people, in a way most people can understand.'

'So, poetry's not your thing? You don't get it?'

'Oh, I get it all right. It's just not my thing.'

'To be fair, that was an interesting piece you wrote about

drugs on the streets of Ferngate. A good exposé of, what was it – people trafficking?'

'Sure.'

'Based around Bewley Street, I'm guessing.'

'Yeah, something like that. It's in places you'd never expect, in this town. Or any other. But Bewley Street was an obvious place to start. I'll call you that cab now. They'll be here in about ten minutes. I know the manager.' She pulled out her phone and started dialling.

'Was this an idea that you and Stephanie had?'

'I'm sorry?'

'Bewley Street. People trafficking. The working girls there.'

'I don't know what you're talking about.'

'Someone told me that Stephanie's big project was something to do with Bewley Street.'

'I don't know a thing about what Steph was doing on any project.'

'It's interesting that you were such close friends, and you were examining the same kind of project.'

'It's interesting, but I don't know anything about it.'

Georgia considered her a moment. She was enjoying the other girl's discomfort. 'Stephanie had a diary, you know. She'd written in it since she was a girl. But the later entries weren't found until recently. Somehow the police missed it. Amazing that that could happen, but it did. She wrote quite a lot about you.'

Adrienne's jaw worked. 'That a fact? Nice things, I hope.'

'Some nice things, yes. She wrote about a project she was working on. Capital P, Project. Going by what she wrote, I think the girls on Bewley Street had something to do with it.'

'News to me, Georgia.'

'You know the codename she had for you? In her diary? Magpie. That was you. The Magpie.'

'Yeah. You told me that already. I'm truly sorry for you,' Adrienne said, sincerely. 'I hope you find what you're looking for. I've got a cab ordered for you on my app. It'll be here in about fifteen minutes, tops. I can't remember where you said you were staying.'

'I didn't.'

'Get some sleep. You look so, so tired.' She laid a hand on Georgia's arm.

'Yeah. And you,' she muttered, and got off her seat.

The room seemed to tilt. Georgia grabbed hold of a worktop. There were a few sniggers from the dozen or so spectators. Someone held her up.

'Time someone was leaving,' the snarky girl with blonde streaks said.

Georgia held up her hand. 'I'd just like to say… Thanks for having me over. And thanks so much for helping me look for Stephanie, my daughter.'

Silence from the stage. All eyes were on her, now. A dreadful quiet descended. 'I think that Cornfed and his friend have been… instrumental. That was a joke. Ha.'

Riley and Trickett's heads snapped up at this; they shared a look, then burst out laughing.

'Cornfed!' Trickett said. 'That's the very man! Hey, that explains a lot, Riley, I have to tell you.'

'You OK, Georgia?' Riley said. 'Maybe have a lie-down, yeah?'

'Absolutely fine, thank you.' But she did sit down. Georgia planted herself on the still-slick black and white tiling. All the shoes lined up at the far wall, worn by his adoring crowd, she supposed. She hadn't been able to afford shoes like that when she was a student here. Assuming they were students, of course.

'Georgia...' Riley carefully placed his guitar on the stand, then approached.

'No, absolutely fine.' She looked for something to hold on to, to get back to her feet. But suddenly, staying on her backside seemed like the best option. 'I think I have a cab on the way.'

Then a bloated, fuzzy face appeared on her lap. 'Are you my mummy?' Scott Trickett yelled. 'Will you be my mummy? Can I nuzzle you, Mummy?'

The shrieking laughter seemed to crystallise, coruscating from every surface, reverberating off the glass above and to either side. Outside a security light clicked on and off, flaring a long flat lawn in yellow-green.

Georgia shrugged him aside, found a chair leg, and got to one knee, then the other.

Riley tried to steer her towards the door, but she shook him off, and staggered out of the door. Adrienne Connulty, finally, took her by the arm. 'Your car's here,' she said.

'I'm absolutely fine. You don't have to worry about me.' But the dark out in the hallway disorientated her. She had come from a place of light into one of darkness.

'God almighty, Georgia, please look after yourself. Go home. I would go home, if I was you.'

'That's mighty suspicious of you.'

Adrienne gave a cry of disgust, as if she'd discovered

Georgia had soiled herself. Had she, in fact? She hadn't had much to drink... she hadn't had anything to drink.

'I think someone gave me a dodgy drink somewhere,' Georgia said. 'I don't feel drunk.'

'You're wasted, Georgia. You don't remember swigging the whisky? The cocktails and the wine?'

'What? I didn't do that!'

'Here we go.' A door opened, and another security light blinked on. A car was at the bottom of a long driveway, lights washing red gravel. 'Take care, Georgia. Call me if you want anything. But not anytime soon. Safe home.'

'Yeah. Safe and sound.' She didn't look back. The driver, a tall, thin, middle-aged man, intercepted her halfway down the driveway, alarmed.

'Sure you're going to be OK, miss?'

'Quite sure.'

'Fifty-quid charge if you're sick.'

'I won't be sick.' She slid into the back seat of the car, groping for the seatbelt, and she thought: *I might be sick, you know*. She took a deep breath, focused on the lights of the house until her head steadied, then said: 'I'm absolutely fine.'

'Glad to hear it. Where to.'

'Bewley Street.'

The face turned slowly, its look incredulous. 'Excuse me?'

'You heard what I said.'

'Whereabouts on Bewley Street?'

'I'll stop you when I know.'

17

Magpies are such a pretty bird up close; the black feathers have an iridescence to them, a hint of blue and green. It's wrong to call them black and white, but then – cliché klaxon alert – nothing is, boys and girls. It's unlucky to see one on its own, you know. My Magpie is never alone, of course. She's always paired up with someone, and if she isn't, she'll soon be paired up with someone else's someone. I wouldn't want her any other way. Some people were just born to be material. A gift, although, thank God, not in the way they imagine themselves.

Magpies also have one of the ugliest calls in the whole bird family. Second only to the vulture, I guess.

From the diary of Stephanie Healey

Grey light filtered through the curtains, and Georgia woke up with a gasp. She was fully clothed, on a bed, beneath a thin quilt without a cover. The room smelled of cigarette smoke; there was nothing in it bar a scarred bedside table and a lamp that hadn't been dusted in aeons. The carpet might have been purple, salmon or cerise at one point; it too was covered in cigarette burns.

Georgia threw off the quilt, and began to check her pockets; no sign of keys or phone, no sign of purse, no sign of shoes, no sign of—

Already in tears and panicking, she sat up, holding a shaking hand to her mouth. The mattress she was sleeping on was thin, like a camp bed, and the legs felt unsteady.

Underneath the bed was her shoes, one lying on its side, and her bag.

She tore it open. Everything was there: phone, purse, cards, even money. She hadn't spent anything last night.

And now to the question of where the hell she was. She snatched open taupe curtains the texture of an old dishtowel and looked out of the type of windows she didn't think existed any more – single-glazed but steel-reinforced – staring out onto a flat pebblestone roof space garlanded with birdshit.

In the background was the clock tower; still in Ferngate, thank God. But where?

Memories flooded in. As if in a mist, approaching women standing by a brick wall at the site of a long-demolished bakery. The women hostile at first. Then she had pleaded: 'Please, please, I'm looking for my daughter, you have to help.' And they had. Until a man had come along and told her to get lost. Georgia had been cheeky to him but his hand had been firm on her upper arm. And then...

A gentle knock at the door. Georgia sat up straight. She didn't feel hungover exactly, but a spasm of pain travelled along her temples. She pinched the bridge of her nose. She felt frozen, unable to speak.

Another rap at the door; then the handle turned.

'Hey... you awake?'

A black girl with close-cropped dark hair came in. She was smartly dressed in a grey trouser suit and white blouse, open at the collar. Georgia would have put her in her twenties, but only just. She held out a huge mug of tea and a packet of paracetamol in her hands.

'Reckon you could use these?'

Georgia's throat was dry. She nodded numbly, and accepted the cup as the girl bent down. She popped two pills, dry-swallowed them, and then held the tea, willing her hands to stop shaking. The varnish on her thumbnail was tarnished, she saw.

There was no way out but to be straight with the girl. 'I have no idea how I got here.'

'I'm not surprised.' The girl smiled. 'For double points, I'm going to guess you've got absolutely no idea where "here" is.'

'Correct.'

'I'll take it from the top. I'm Lil. You're at a hostel.'

'Homeless hostel.'

'If you like.'

'You're a resident here?'

'In a manner of speaking. I help run it. I was on last night.'

'Jesus. What am I doing here?'

'A good question. You're in the wrong end of town, that's for sure.'

'My name's Georgia Healey. I'm here because my daughter, Stephanie, she…'

'It's OK love – I know who you are and what your story is. You told me, lots of times.'

'Last night, I… It's complicated.' Georgia dared a drink

of the tea. It was scalding hot, but she needed to wet her mouth. 'I don't know what happened to me. Someone said I was drunk, but I don't remember…'

'You were on some kind of drugs, that's for sure. Maybe roofies. I can't be certain. I did wonder if you'd taken K. You got confused, kind of spacey. You wouldn't let me take you to casualty, though. Kept saying you were a doctor. I almost believed you.'

'I am a doctor. And I think someone spiked my drink. I'd only had a sip from a glass of wine, then a bottle of water… I was at the benefit concert last night.' How long had the bottle of water been sitting there beside her? It had been opened, beside the glass. Or perhaps the wine glass that she'd left behind for a moment. She had returned to it briefly. That was all she'd had to drink. But what had Adrienne said? About her necking Scotch? She couldn't remember that. But then most of her recollections had been foggy, like half-remembered dreams. It might have been a movie she'd watched half-asleep one night.

'How did I end up here?'

'One of the girls who was working out on Bewley Street contacted me. Said you were going to run into trouble. Some of the lads who look after them wasn't taking too kindly.'

'God, I could have been killed.'

'They were worried about you. More along the lines of what you might do to yourself, rather than what someone else would do to you. I came out to pick you up. You took a lot of persuading to get into my car and come back here.'

'Thank you. You say you work here? How much do I owe you?'

'It's not that kind of place.' Lil raised a hand. 'It's a

volunteer service. A lot of women from foreign parts end up in Ferngate. Lots of them don't have a place to stay, for one reason or another. Some can't speak English.'

'Trafficked?'

'Afraid so. The lucky ones end up at the Knees Up club, which is exactly what you might imagine it is. The unlucky ones end up here a few nights a week. The very unlucky ones end up on the streets, and on the gear. It happens here the same way it happens in London, Las Vegas, anywhere. Sometimes we help move them on. Sometimes we get to send them back home. Some of them have to go back out onto the streets.'

'Jesus.' Georgia looked around at the sparse room, once more. Just a bed, a table, a lamp, the curtains.

'They don't operate out of here, if that's what you're thinking,' Lil said, at length.

'I'm just glad someone was here to help me. You say it's community-run?' Georgia fished for money in her purse.

'Don't give it to me,' Lil said. 'Do it through the online portal. It isn't cash and carry. You want to freshen up?'

'No… I'll head back to my room.'

'You kept saying you didn't have a room. You said there was no one for us to call, either.'

'I don't know why I said that.'

'I do. You said you weren't going to sleep until you found your daughter. You kept saying it, right up until you passed out. I got your shoes off OK, but you tried to fight me when I went to get you undressed, so I thought it best to leave you as you were.'

'Sweet mother of God.'

'If I was you, I'd take a day off or two.' Lil's voice

grew kinder, less sardonic. 'You know, I remember that case. The missing girl. I saw the posters for the concert. I even remember your face. Don't you have a husband, or someone?'

'Yes... He's, kind of... out the scene.'

'I see. I'm sorry. It must have been tough for you.'

'It happens. It might have happened anyway. Probably.' She took a sip of the tea. It lit a cosy fire in her belly, and her shoulders relaxed. She began to sweat immediately, hands shaking.

'Well. I've got to get some sleep myself, Georgia. Long old shift. I think it's time for you to go.'

Lil led Georgia out through a musty-smelling hallway that hadn't been dusted in a long time. She was tall but not elegant, viewed from behind – something in the set of her back and shoulders made Georgia think of an athlete, but perhaps more suited to the javelin or discus rather than track events. A woman in a white towel with wet hair coiled about her shoulders nodded at Lil as they passed; Georgia stared straight ahead, not wanting to meet her gaze.

The stairway had a surreal slant to it as she made her way down the stairs, and it was here that her balance suddenly, shockingly shifted. Her nails scraped down a length of 1980s Artex with nicotine stains in between the swept arches before Lil caught her.

'Hold your horses, party girl. Everything all right?'

'I think so... my head's spinning, here. I'd love to know what they slipped me.'

'Who?'

'Doesn't matter. Some tits at a party.'

'No, it does matter.' Lil's hand on her back was a little

more than concerned. 'If someone really did spike your drink, you need to get in touch with the police.'

'I'd rather not. They already think I'm mad. And anyway, I can't be sure.' A cold sweat broke out across her body, and she stopped short.

'You're not going to be sick, are you? Because if you are, you know... get outside before you do it. This place isn't the Palais but if you blow chunks, this is the most awkward place. Crook of a staircase? I wouldn't want to get on hands and knees with the carpet cleaner in this space, love.'

'I'm fine, thank you. Just tell me where I am and how I can get some transport.'

'You head for the clock tower, you'll go past the train station. There's a taxi rank outside it.' Lil steered her towards a door with a man in high-vis standing outside it. He eyed Georgia carefully as they went outside. The morning had a little bite in it, and there was some mist in the air. The last traces of winter, she thought; she checked her phone. Before 7am.

'And... here's my card. You get in touch if you need anything. But I won't expect to see you back here.' Lil passed her the paperwork. *Lil Baikie*, it read. *Manager, Ellwood House.*

'Thank you,' Georgia said, putting it in her bag. 'I owe you a lot.'

'It's my job.' Lil shrugged, nodded at the doorman, then walked in the opposite direction.

Georgia's head spun again as she shuffled into the taxi and gave the directions. *If a spiral staircase is the worst place to be sick, then the back of a taxi is surely a close second*, she thought, willing the roundabouts to ease up.

'OK back there?' asked the driver, a concerned pair of eyes in the mirror.

'Just about.'

'Big night, eh?' She sensed rather than saw the grin.

'Plenty big enough.'

'Was it an eighties night, then?'

'What makes you say that?'

'Eh, the hair. Bonnie Tyler? No?'

Jesus. She felt her hair. It had in fact gone crazy. And she hadn't even checked. 'Yeah. It was a tribute night.'

'Hard life, eh?'

'Whatever. Turn around, bright eyes.'

He laughed in unaffected mirth, but Georgia's stomach was churning. Had she been drinking? It wasn't something she could remember, but there was a sweet and sour aftertaste at the back of her throat that could have been spirits. She didn't feel especially hung over, though. Had she drunk a shot or two? Perhaps, when it was passed to her. But Georgia was almost certain that she'd been slipped something. K was a possibility, although this was only something she'd read about like most other parents, rather than having experienced herself.

She paid up and hobbled into the lobby of the lodging house. The pretty girl with the eastern European accent at the front desk looked up in some alarm when she entered.

'I know, I need a shower, and I need a mechanic for my hair. I apologise. I haven't looked this much of a fright since I was last on the telly with the police.'

The girl got up; it took Georgia a while to take in what she was actually saying. 'No, there was a man here for you, asking for you.'

'What did he look like?'

'He was white, white-skinned. He had a hat on, like a beanie hat, like you'd wear when it was cold. I'm sorry, I don't remember too much more.'

'Young or old?'

'Forties, maybe fifties.'

'Was he tall? Wearing glasses?'

'No glasses. Quite tall.'

'He didn't leave a name, or anything?'

'No, he left before I could ask. Said he would be back later.'

'And this happened when?'

'This morning.'

She checked her watch. 'It's not even nine o'clock yet.'

The girl shook her head. 'I'm sorry. I don't know anything else.'

No glasses? It could have been anyone. It could have been someone from the party. Or... It could have been one of those jackals who featured in her murky memories from Bewley Street. She pictured them with yellow eyes, but few other details came to the fore. God, she'd been screaming and shouting. *I want to know about my daughter. Who knew about my daughter?*

In her room, Georgia flung off the rank clothes, then blasted with scalding water in the shower. Soon she was dressed in fresh pyjamas, her hair dried, saddled and shod. She looked at her phone, and realised it was dead – she had barely had time to check anything, after her original appraisal at the party. She plugged the phone into the wall, then rooted around inside a zip-up section, hidden at the back.

'Special reserve. Thank God nobody found you boys,' she said, addressing a blistered pack. Georgia hadn't had cause to open these for a while; she popped two of them into a glass of water and watched them fizz, before knocking the cup back.

Within a minute or two, any lingering hangover had gone, replaced by a certain controlled calm. That was better.

She lay back on the bed, luxuriating in the sense of numbness, welcoming the dark to come. These were something she'd had been prescribed by a colleague who should probably have known better. She hadn't resorted to these of late, but now was as good a time as any. *Take the edge off. Maybe take the rest of the day off. Back into it tomorrow.*

Then, seeing a couple of energy bars reappear on the phone, she switched it on.

And saw the messages. The new ones filled the screen, from many sources. The names involved made her heart kick: Rod, of course, with the majority. Then her friend and colleague since medical school, Barbara. Then one from Neal Hurlford's personal number.

Fear came in slow waves – it was something she was aware of without having direct experience of it, like the sound of an alarm breaking through the walls of a dream. She sat up; then she was on her feet. All the missed calls, too...

Then the door was battered.

'Who's there?' she could barely say it. She stuffed the blister pack back into her bag, her fingers taking on the consistency of plasticine, so slow were the movements.

'Georgia, open up and let me in.'

She did so – and there was Rod. Over his shoulder, the girl at reception's face swung into view, pinched tight in anxiety.

'I'm so sorry, he barged in – shall I call the police?'

'It won't be necessary, thank you. He's my husband.' She turned to Rod. 'And without glasses, as I live and breathe. You got contacts? New girlfriend, so soon?'

'Georgia…' he sighed. He looked like he wanted to put his hands on her, but restrained himself. 'They've found a body.'

18

I sank again the other day. I'd call it a fugue, but it's so much better than that, so much more resonant. Some days with Cornfed, that's all you want. That blissful fade-out. There is a price to pay after we're apart, though. A phone call or a text message can't cut it.

From the diary of Stephanie Healey

'What do you mean? Body? What body?'

Georgia felt herself sinking to the floor in stages, like bad animation. Rod caught her before she got there. 'A body,' he said. 'They found it yesterday. In farmland, not far away from here.'

She let him sit her on the bed; let him hold her hand. She guessed from looking at the indentations his fingers made in her skin that he was holding it tightly, but she couldn't feel it. 'It's her, isn't it?' she heard herself say. 'It's her. It must be her.'

'Is everything all right, Mrs Healey?' asked the receptionist. Her eyes might have been on stalks.

'I'm Mr Healey,' Rod snapped. 'And she's quite all right.'

'It's OK, honey. I'm fine.'

Rod stretched out one long leg and swung the door to, cutting off the girl from reception. 'They don't know if it's her,' he said gently. 'They're carrying out some tests, but nobody can be sure just yet. Hurlford said they were waiting until they got in touch with you before releasing any information at all. He said, off the record, that it's unlikely – but he wanted you to know they'd found something before a story appeared in the media and you put two and two together.'

'It's her,' Georgia said again. Was her heart beating faster? 'It must be.'

'He said not to leap to conclusions. He wouldn't be drawn on any details, but said the word "unlikely". I don't know why he's saying that. I don't know what state… We have to hold on to that for now.'

'I want it to be her. I want this to be over, now. I can't stand the not knowing. I'm turning my cards in, Rod. I've had enough.'

Rod took her by the shoulder – gently – and turned her to face him. He looked into her eyes, expressionless, for several seconds. 'Where are they?' he said.

'What?' She remembered to blink.

He got up and tore through her bag. He unzipped, pulled open compartments and emptied the bag out. 'The pills. The fucking pills! Where are they?'

Georgia got up; the room seemed to swell and tilt, but she kept her feet. 'You've no right. You never had the right. Get out of my bag, get out of this room, and get out of my life!'

'This is going to end up with you dead. Do you even read the news? A GP, addicted to painkillers. In the name of almighty God…'

She found her voice, and drenched him with it. 'How dare you judge me? You of all people!'

'What happened to you? The girl at reception said you were out. I saw you staggering out of a taxi this morning. Where were you?'

'Wouldn't you like to know?'

Rod hurled the bag with some force against the headboard. What he was looking for was still inside. Always the last place you look, she thought. 'Don't play games with me.'

'For your information, there was a benefit concert for Stephanie last night. At The Orchard. This band, the Megiddos…'

'Nice of you to tell me.' He folded his arms, and ground his teeth.

'This band, the Megiddos, they were Stephanie's classmates. It was a benefit gig for the fund to help find her. If you'd been in contact with me, or if you'd been keeping in touch with the case, then maybe you'd have known that already!'

'I've been busy,' he said.

'Oh yeah. With the new model. Taking your mind off things, is she?'

'Let's not do this here. I'm here for you.'

'How did you know where I was?'

'Hurlford told me. He contacted me, when he was trying to get in touch with you last night. He said you'd been in town. I came straight down to find you. He thought I might still know where you were.'

Georgia stared at her pyjamas, her bare feet. She knew her heart was beating, but it was like taking a patient's pulse, a distant percussion. 'I need you to get out of the building, Rod. I'll get dressed, then we'll contact Hurlford. He must know the score by now...' Clothes, Georgia was going to say. Perhaps they could tell by the clothes? But then of course, she might not have been wearing any. She heard Scott Trickett's Year Four bullying voice, a fly orbiting her ear: *Wonder if she's in a shallow grave? Or a deep one? In one piece? Or half a dozen?*

'I'm staying right here.'

'I'll call Hurlford.'

'You're wasting your time – he's been diverted to answerphone the whole morning. Last time I spoke to him, he said he would contact us.'

She stifled a yawn. Even here, at a time like this, this is what the pills could make you do. She regretted taking them, full stop. 'I'm not asking you again, Rod. I'll call the police and tell them you're intruding – which you are. I might even tell them you've been acting threateningly.'

'No one's been threatening you!' he scoffed.

'I might ask them to speak to the receptionist you just barged past and slammed the door on. The one who's probably been listening to raised voices. If she's a clever girl, she might even have called them already. I think I'd rather call the cops, than ignore the shouting and bawling and have something nasty happen.'

Rod pursed his lips, and nodded. 'Very calculating. That's the Georgia I remember, all right.' He applauded, sarcastically.

Looking at him now, she could pinpoint when it was that she first realised she'd fallen out of love with him. It must have dated from the time he'd started wearing the glasses, and got paranoid about his receding hairline and cropped it as close as it would go. He'd lost weight, having gone down the angular, bendy rabbit hole that was semi-serious cycling. She'd gone past his cycling troupe one day, four of them going two abreast on a windy back road Georgia took to get home from the surgery to avoid traffic. She thought she'd recognised Rod's bony arse pistoning above the flat blade of the saddle; when she saw the branded helmet and shades there was no doubt. She'd wanted to blast the horn at them, to scatter them like starlings.

Later on, the preamble to that night's argument had been, 'I know cyclists have every right to be on the road, but...'

He'd gotten paranoid about his weight round about the time Stephanie had gone to high school, and to be fair he stuck to exercise and dieting and removed a spare tyre he'd developed. The tragedy of it was, Georgia hadn't minded the spare timber on him; some nights, when they still cuddled up on a Friday night to watch the chat shows, eat crisps and slurp wine, she had even liked it. The more weight he lost, and the fitter he became, the more pleased he became with himself, the less Georgia had liked it.

Stephanie closely resembled him; there was no doubt they were father and daughter, although you would never have made the same call about Georgia and her own girl. Oddly, the angular features, the long nose and the pinched, but bright black eyes that looked so awkward on his face suited hers perfectly. The ideal ugly duckling, once she'd grown tall like he was, everything had fallen into place about her appearance. The long legs, the cheekbones, even the ears, which she'd been distraught about at age eleven or so, once the bitchy little friends had found an easy target. Even the teeth and the short hair and the long nose all made an appealing picture. Georgia hadn't wanted her to cut her hair short, had hated it, but was forced to admit the effect was even more striking. Boys had adored her, particularly in her senior years at school. If only she'd realised.

And now they had found her. Perhaps the features were no more. *'Is she a skeleton?'* Scott Trickett's voice, again. *'Did someone smash the skull up?'*

Georgia slapped herself, hard. It certainly got Rod's attention. 'My God. Take it easy, Georgia.'

'Take it easy yourself, you patronising twerp. I told you to get out. Final warning. I'll meet you in the foyer. Wait there. I'll be ten minutes.'

'Where are we going?'

'The police station, dummy.'

19

You should see my dad, running. He has the most comical run. He thinks he can do it with a bit of style, with proper structure, with his palms held flat I guess for the sake of streamlining, and his trousers flapping about his stork's legs. He runs like he is trying to avoid each individual drop of rain; he has no forward direction. He's a disaster in progress, a crane crashing through some scaffolding. He's a video game character with a bug, out of control, in need of a reboot. All that effort to catch a bus. I told him, once I'd caught up with him, with the tail-lights over the hill: Never, ever run for a bus.

From the diary of Stephanie Healey

Georgia must have started crying because she saw tears drop onto her jeans, making dark little patches. It was something to do with the smile on the face of the female police officer in plain clothes who came into the room; the smile angled downwards, following the cast of the eyes perfectly. Georgia had wanted to make a joke about Princess Diana's smile, but the police officer might have been too young to remember Princess Diana. There was a reason for that smile, its slightly smudged quality, a long way short of a grin, bereft of sincerity.

'It's her,' she heard herself say. 'Isn't it?'

The female police officer said nothing. She only leaned close, and took Georgia's hand. Georgia allowed herself to be led into the dance, her head on the girl's chest.

Rod said nothing. His hands were linked on the table, his shoulders relaxed, staring straight ahead.

Hurlford came in. He had a folder, much like he had in the office when she'd spoken to him recently. She wondered if it was a prop, something to divert the attention. He cleared his throat before he said: 'Thank you both for coming – I appreciate this is another difficult moment, on top of a lot of difficult moments. I'll get it out of the way – it isn't her.'

Georgia's emotions fluctuated, seeming to roll over the skin of her face, much as a cuttlefish might change colour when spooked. 'What? It's not her?'

Rod's hands unclenched. He took a slow, shuddering breath. Tears glinted behind his spectacles.

'I'm so sorry – we couldn't say for sure over the phone, before we knew for certain. It's the body of a young woman in her early twenties, but we are certain that it's not Stephanie.'

'It's not Stephanie?' She was incredulous. After all this. 'You brought us out here to tell us that? I was sure this was it... I was sure...' Still, she couldn't quite extricate herself from the policewoman's grasp. She wasn't sure she wanted to. *Just sleep. To sleep... You need to sleep...*

'I'm sorry – I have a policy that I don't just tell people over the phone, if at all possible. It's better if you're prepared.

I can't give people news of that nature while they're on speaker phone in the car, say, or in the middle of doing something dangerous or important. I had to bring you in.'

'I'll tell you why you had to bring us in.' Rod brushed a tear from his eye, before replacing them. 'You wanted to have a look at us, didn't you? Me in particular.'

DI Hurlford showed no discomfort at this. 'As I say, we have a clear procedure in place.'

'Was the girl murdered?' Rod asked. 'Or can't you say?'

'We won't be one hundred per cent certain until the toxicology report is in, but we would have to say that at the moment there don't appear to be any suspicious circumstances.'

Georgia said: 'She was found at farmland, you said – whereabouts? Anywhere near the Chessington estate?'

'No,' Hurlford said. This piqued his interest though. 'What made you say that?'

'I'm thinking, close to where my daughter disappeared.'

'No, it was the far side of Ferngate, to the south. The flatter part. Think cornfields, out that way.'

'She killed herself, then? That's what you mean when you say "no suspicious circumstances", isn't it?'

'I can't say any more. You're both educated, experienced, professional people, so I think you'll appreciate the need for operational secrecy and discretion.'

'Can you say if the girl had anything to do with Stephanie? Was she local?'

'I will say that she wasn't a classmate or a contemporary of Stephanie's. This case looks unrelated to the missing persons inquiry over your daughter, Mrs Healey. Though of course, we can't say for sure. Please... Stay for a few moments and get your bearings. Even a result like this in such a long-running and complex case can have a traumatic…'

Georgia fought clear of the trained officer and stood up. 'I think I've wasted enough time. Thank you, though. Oh, and one thing I should have made clear when we spoke before…' She pointed at Rod, who appeared to have shrunk in his seat with the tension and pressure released. 'Do not release any information about me to this man. Technically we are married – but not for long. He does not speak for me, and vice versa.'

'Mrs Healey, I'm truly sorry,' Hurlford said.

Rod intervened: 'Just before she goes – can you tell us if there's been any breakthrough thanks to the anniversary campaign?'

'One or two leads that we're following up. Again, I can't say any more than that.'

'Exciting leads?' Georgia asked. 'You can say that, can't you? Promising leads?'

'That's all I can tell you.'

'He's got nothing.' Georgia turned to her husband and gave a sad smile. 'That's polite-speak for "he's got nothing".'

Hurlford was unfazed. 'Mrs Healey, I would advise you to get some rest, and then follow the advice I gave you the other day: go home, and take a few days off if you can. I'm experienced in cases like this, and the stress involved can be too much for people to bear. Especially if they involve themselves in the inquiry. Sometimes you can make problems for yourself, and for other people.'

Georgia frowned. 'You been following me?'

'I have not. I'm simply saying…'

'Just find her,' Georgia said. 'You wanted a new lead – it's right in front of you. Look into that. Find "Cornfed". He's my top suspect.'

DI Hurlford opted for his right to silence. He merely folded his arms and met Georgia's gaze, unflustered. 'I'm working hard on this case, Mrs Healey.'

'Hang on a minute,' Rod said, getting up to follow her. 'Paperwork? What paperwork are you talking about? What do you mean by this "Cornfed"?'

'I think I'll refer you to a lawyer,' she told her husband. 'Probably you should follow DI Hurlford's advice, in your own right. Maybe get out of town. Before sundown, or whatever it is they say in westerns.' She didn't hang around for the comeback, or even for the reaction. The door to the interview room was appallingly heavy – or she had become appallingly fragile. She had to put her back and shoulders into opening it. *Soon, soon, you have to lie down and sleep soon. Can't go on. Like Dracula racing the sunrise.*

Heads snapped up as she passed. She kept her head high and dignified, all the way down the stairs, through the security door and then the revolving doors at reception and out into the open air, which is where Rod caught up with her.

He appeared flustered, but his voice was soothing as he caught up. 'I'm sorry, Georgia. This was a complete mess. And totally unnecessary. He wanted to see my reaction, I'm sure of it.'

'And why would that be? Still having trouble putting together your movements on the night she vanished? Hasn't your squaw given you an alibi, by now?'

'Actually, yes.'

She paused. 'I see. So, you were playing away that

night after all. Lied to me beautifully, didn't you? Had me convinced. Told me I was a nutter – that's the exact word you used. Nutter. And I believed you. It seems my life was actually in tatters before my only daughter vanished. That's refreshing. Lovely to see.'

'Georgia, please. Listen to me. I want you to come home with me. I think you need to get some rest, and try to put all of this out of your mind. Hurlford's right, it's got to be difficult to come to terms with, however you slice it. Seeing all those photos of Stephanie on that website nearly broke me. God knows how you feel about it, being here all this time.'

'You know, I've just put it together. You came here because he told you, didn't you? Hurlford? He got in touch with you first. It's true, isn't it?'

Rod said nothing.

'And that made it easier for you to find out where I am, and what I'm doing.'

'I was worried about you. It's the truth. You're still my wife. Our history together won't just evaporate. I wanted to come over here and see you were all right.'

'Looking at houses, Rod? Nice family home for that little blonde piece to move into? Happy families? She got kids of her own? What was her name, then? Was it Evelyn? I forget. Maybe that was another one.'

'Let me at least drive you back to the hotel you were staying at.'

Georgia was so tired, she was tempted. Just sink down into the seat… company car, she noticed, when she got in; a definite upgrade on what he was running before the split… let the pills wash over her, and finally, God willing, sleep.

'No. It's not far, I can walk.'

'Georgia, you should have let me know about this concert thing. It's not fair to lock me out. Whatever's happened between us, we have to stick together over Stephanie. I want to find her as much as you do. Surely we can stick together on this? Until we find out what happened? You should have got in touch.'

It was difficult to feel angry, as such, given the dose she'd taken, but she came close. She stopped in the street, outside the front door of a vintage specialist shop, next to some racks of fruit, veg and fresh flowers from the same family business she remembered from years ago. 'Why didn't you know about it? Someone as computer-savvy as you... don't you have alerts set up on your mobile phone? On search engines? Or when you're flirting with some trollop on social media?'

'That's unfair. I'm a busy man. I can't be expected to know everything...'

'You should be plugged into it! This should be as near as you can get to having something wired directly into your fucking *brain*.' She tapped a finger against her own forehead, savagely. He actually flinched. 'You should be in contact with every available agency, every available person. You should have every number *memorised*.'

He bit his lip. 'Some of us have to work, Georgia.'

'What's that supposed to mean?'

'As opposed to you. How long is it since you were in at the surgery? They've got a locum in to cover for you. I asked Barbara, and she said you'd been away on a course. Except I kept checking, and I was told you weren't back yet. I forget all the excuses, but here's a few. "She's doing work up at the hospital… She's on a break for a couple of days… I think she's on a training day". It didn't take a genius to spot you had been off on the sick.'

'That's none of your business. Absolutely none.'

'So, what is it then? Time off to recover? In a way I welcome it. It's the best thing for you. You should have taken time off when you had depression. After she was born. It lasted months, a year even. Obvious to everyone but you – a bloody GP!'

'I don't do time off for illness. I've got too many people to look after.'

'Yeah. Except your daughter.'

'What?'

He was getting ready for a burst of rage. Everything in his stance and his features foretold this. Rod was a tall, imposing man, even with a bit less meat on his shoulders than Georgia remembered. She was braced for it. 'I mean, you couldn't wait to pass her off into the hands of a childminder, could you? You simply couldn't be bothered.'

'How dare you?' She turned away, thought better of it, turned back, and got in his face. 'How dare you? The absolute nerve of you to say that. Away four days here, three days there… yeah, you signed some deals. You got lucky. They still pay management consultants. But you were never there in the first place. You basically expected me to give up a career and do the childcare like your absolute drudge of a mother, didn't you? Nursing a kid in one hand, doing the washing up with the other. Are you out of your mind? All those years of training, working as a locum all over the place, and finally, *finally*, I get a practice in a nice part of the city, and you expect me to give that up? To facilitate *you*, carrying on with your bloody dandy highwayman act in turbocharged fucking telesales!'

They had drawn a lot of attention from passers-by. The woman running the till at the fruit 'n' veg shop viewed them with detached interest at first, but now she seemed alarmed.

'You're dreaming,' he said. 'Who paid off the mortgage? Oh, that was me. Who got Stephanie into her school? Oh, that was me. I paid the price for all that. My bonuses, my share dividends. That was all my own work.'

'Yes, I earned money too. Hello? Doctor? GP? Yes? I have a good, responsible job. Which facilitated *you* in your wheeler-dealer fantasy lifestyle. Buying your fancy car, while you were in a dry patch. And your new suits. You got six of them once. Wonder how many trollops were in the back of that car? I bought into your dream lifestyle. I backed up your fantasy. So, factor that in.'

'It's not a fantasy, love. Check my bank statements, you want a dose of reality.'

'Oh, sod off. You know something? There's a part of me kind of wants the economy to tank again. If it takes out bores like you, it'll be worth it.'

'I see. Georgia's rage overrules the general good. How very narcissistic of you.'

'If there's any more room up there, cram your pop psychology books up your arse. And how nice of you to put things in terms of money? It's almost as if it's the only thing that matters to you.'

'Not the only thing. But it is a thing. You know what else mattered to me? Family. I might have been away three or four days a week, but at least I was there the other times.'

'And I wasn't?'

'Frankly, no, you weren't. Yeah, you've got a busy job. It's tough work being a GP. I know that. Underfunding and what have you. I get it. But part of me thinks it was an excuse.'

'Oh, you are off at the deep end now, old son.'

'Really? Who took Stephanie to swimming and horse riding? That was me. Who went to all the school plays and concerts? That was me. Who made sure the uniform was ready for school? Who made sure the uniforms still fit her, and bought more when she needed them? Who cuddled her in the night when she was scared? That was me. Who took her out shopping for clothes? That was me. Who made her a nice breakfast and made sure she had a cake and candles for her birthday? That was me. Who took her to her mother's own fucking GP practice when she was sick, where her mother passed her on to a colleague? Oh, that was me.'

'You're out of your mind. If you think for a minute that one or two little things here and there were any substitute for the work I did and the effort I put into that girl, you are in need of a fucking prescription, sunshine. I'll write you one, if you like.'

But Rod was winning; he usually did. And he enjoyed it, in his traditional way. 'We're straying off the point. I get that you're playing Nancy Drew out here. Trying to tie up loose ends. I get it. I've done it myself.'

'What? Bollocks.'

'I've been here. I've asked the same questions. I've gotten the same results: zero. So, what's this paperwork that was found, then?'

'Not really a concern of yours.'

'It will be a concern of mine, and my solicitor will agree.'

'Stephanie's diary. It was hidden in her old flat, and hidden well. The police only just found it. They passed it on to me.'

Now he looked as if he wanted to hit her, during a long pause. 'Well? You saving it for the next episode, or something? Never mind the suspense! Out with it! What did you find out? And when were you going to send it to me?'

'I've got a copy. I scanned it in, and backed it up. I'll send it to you.'

'Are there any leads? *What – did – you – find – out?*'

'Nothing we didn't really know. She knew a lot of boys, as well as Martin Duke. Look, it's complicated. I'll send it to you – Hurlford already has a copy. You can make up your own mind.' Georgia was on the back foot, now. She shouldn't have let that slip in the interview room. Damn it, she needed to sleep.

'Yeah. Send it to me today. Right after we're done here. Look, Georgia – I'm here to find her, the same as you. I want to know what happened. But believe me, there's no link you can uncover Hurlford and the rest of the team don't know about. There's dozens of officers, you know. Hundreds, maybe. Still asking questions, still knocking doors, still checking tips. At some point we're going to have to accept it. Stephanie was a depressive. She was on medication – you know that, surely.'

'She had a very brief course, when she was fifteen. That has no bearing...'

'She was severely depressed. It was undiagnosed. You said so yourself. A quiet nature masked a lot of turmoil. She was down, most of the time. As you were, after you had her. It runs in families. She took after you in that regard. You know what hurt the most, that time she turned into a bloody zombie? It reminded me of you. There is a good chance that she took her own life. The walk up that road... who in their right mind would walk up that road, on a night like that? It's like those poor people who park up their cars and walk along bridges. Except they don't appear at the other side. You know what I'm talking about. You've lost patients to depression; you've told me about it. One day they decide they've had enough. And they take the road out. You have to accept this is what happened.'

'I accept nothing.'

'Please, Georgia. I mean the best for you. I know it's hard to believe, but it might be time to shift how you see all this. You need to start accepting that Stephanie is most likely gone. And we might never find out how she did it, or where.'

'If she's gone, find me her grave. Stick some fucking flowers on it!' A dash of purple caught her eye; she lunged for a plastic bedding container of petunias from the rack outside the fruit 'n' veg shop, taking the flowers by the stalks as she might have gripped an opponent by the hair. She swung the entire load at him but, as on so many other occasions, he was fast when it came to a dodge. Clumps of soil erupted across the pavement.

'Hey!' The woman in the shop came out. She took Georgia by the arm – but not to remonstrate. 'Calm down, there, love. Take it easy. You can't be doing that. Now I don't know what's going on here, but I suggest the two of you step away for a bit and calm down. OK?'

'I'll pay for the flowers,' Georgia said. 'I'm sorry, this

has been... This has been a terrible few days.' Her face crumpled; then the woman at the till was holding her up.

'No,' Rod said, 'I insist.' He snapped a twenty-pound note out of his wallet and handed it to the woman at the till. 'Get a nice herbal remedy for my wife with the change, would you?'

Common sense, after a fashion, prevailed. She allowed him to take her in the car. She sank into the leather seats, again. The seatbelt was like a comforting arm around the shoulder. The air conditioning was just right. She almost dozed off.

Then Georgia realised that Rod had driven past the turn-off for the hotel.

Trees enclosed them, buds erupting in the sunshine.

'I know this road. Take me back.'

What she could see of his eyes were blank. He didn't even blink – just gazed into the unfurling grey carpet. 'This is the way, isn't it? This is the road she would have taken out of town.'

'Rod... I want to go back to my bed. I've had a long day...'

'This is where she would have gone. Right turn here, at the sign? Weird old sign, that. Something out of a horror film. Must have looked even worse in a storm. Wonder if it shook in the wind? Did it creak?'

'Rod. Stop this car, turn in the road, and take me back.'

'Won't seem so long by car, this,' he said. He was breathing hard, his temper seething through the cracks in his demeanour. 'Take you a few minutes from here to the petrol station. Different story if you're on foot. It's like if you're running. You run up a slight incline, you know all about it when you get to the top. If you're in a car, you barely even notice you're driving at an angle.'

'Rod. Please.'

'So, she walked all the way along here, and then we get to the bridge... You might feel some butterflies in your stomach, apologies. Am I breaking the speed limit?'

'Yes, you are. Slow down. Stop.'

'Over we go. Whahey! Nice little bridge that. They say it was at real risk of washing away, that night. It's very old, you know. Then we get to the path. There we go!'

Rod brought the car to a halt. The engine sounded like a giant snoring, his foot on the clutch and brake.

'There it is,' he said, 'right up there. You've walked up there, right? Walked up that path, haven't you?'

'Yes.'

'And you know it's difficult, a tough climb, but a very determined person could do it. Then there's that crack in the earth, and the water running through it. If the fall didn't kill her, then the water did. She's in the water somewhere, Georgia. This is the truth. Hardly anyone was out in that weather. One or two people who passed by, and were caught on camera. The farmhand up at Chessington Hall was traced and eliminated. Everyone in a vehicle who went past the garage or past one or two houses who have security cameras has been accounted for. She wasn't put into a car by anyone. And no one threw her over their shoulder, either. She could even be out at sea, Georgia. With the river in spate, it's not out the question. She'll turn up. But she's dead? You got it? Dead. Go home, and try to get on with your life. I'll help you in any way I can.'

'Was it you, Rod?'

'You what?' He bellowed these words, shrinking Georgia back in her seat.

'At the ghyll. Was it you who knocked me in?'

'What are you talking about? Seriously, are you out of your mind on diazepam or whatever it is you're on? Has it addled your brain? Knocked you over? No, I didn't get to Ferngate until last night. After Hurlford called me. Worried about your mental state. So I came over to get you out of this dump. Only to discover you were out enjoying yourself! Thinking of number one, as usual.'

Georgia raised her phone. 'I'm about to dial the office at Ferngate and tell them that you're keeping me prisoner in the car. Turn around, and take me back.'

'Oh, I aimed to. That was my intention.' He swung the car around in a sudden arc; there was a car coming in the opposite direction, which had to drop anchors. Rod ignored its blaring horn, as he took her back down the road. 'But my point, I hope, is made. There's nothing more to discover. Stephanie killed herself. You know that, don't you? Deep down?'

20

So easy to slip into roles. We all do it. Fluidity of character. One minute my head's bent close to a book; I'm defacing the margins with a pencil, pushing an imaginary pair of spectacles up my nose. The next I'm naked with lightning in my eyes. You get into it so easily. Like listening to your favourite song, you know every beat. Eyes to the left. And forward. And walk. You'd do it too, if you could. Don't lie to yourself. Maybe I should be an actress? That's what he told me, anyway. Flirt. And smile. And flash. And thunder.

From the diary of Stephanie Healey

Georgia slept most of the afternoon. She woke in stages, listening to her own breathing, becoming gradually aware of a misty light making its way through the curtains of her room. Into the evening of early spring; pleasant outside, not too cold in the room, a harbinger of better conditions to come.

Clarity of a kind had come back to Georgia, and with it, feelings of loss, shame and depression. Flashbulb images came back to her of her time lost in the hole of the previous night – the benefit concert, and its aftermath at the house of the pop star. All those fresh, scrubbed young faces, within touching distance of their idol. They looked like the kind of girls who had mothers and fathers waiting for them in big cars as they spilled out of nightclubs; who wanted for nothing, with dance lessons and pony trekking behind them, the kind of girl you instinctively feared for in the orbit of people like Riley Brightman and Scott Trickett. People like Stephanie, she realised. Were they home now? Were they waking up at the same time, feeling the same way Georgia did right now?

One of them spiked my drink. She knew it. Georgia hadn't been out of her head for a long time, but she knew her own mind and her own body. She'd been slipped something in one of her drinks. And she knew Trickett was the likeliest candidate.

She took a painkiller – this one regulation use, not military grade – and shook out a sachet of coffee into a bleached mug. Was Adrienne right? On top of the pill she'd been slipped, had she been drinking, too? There was a cloudy section where many things could have taken place. She remembered something; sharp bite of whisky, the sour taste of retching, dredged from teenage memory. But there was a reason she'd drank the whisky. To sharpen herself up, she realised. To give her a jolt. She'd been aware she was going down the plughole.

Most likely someone had slipped something into her water. What had it been spiked with? She had a suspicion it might have been ketamine. She'd had no direct experience of the drug but knew the signs. She had been zombified, and at one stage would probably have forgotten her name.

Bright flashes of light were somewhere in her memory. This had happened round about when things faded into a long dark tunnel, after she got to Bewley Street. Where she met a very different set of faces and demeanours among girls stood under streetlights, the polar opposites of the girls at Riley Brightman's house.

'Dear God,' she said aloud. 'They might have killed me.'

Her hands shook; she kept her wrists relaxed on her thighs and willed the tremors to stop, in tandem with a breathing exercise. *Calm it down*, she thought. *You're here for a reason. Focus. Get back on it.*

She wasn't sure what she'd been given. But she had a fair idea who had given it to her.

Her phone went; irritated, she snatched it up. Adrienne Connulty's caller ID flashed up.

'Yes?'

'Georgia? It's me, Adrienne. Listen, I just wanted to make sure everything's OK. You seemed pretty out of it at the party. I think a couple of drinks went to your head, maybe.'

'Yeah, you can say that again. I'm sorry if I was a little bit lairy.'

'No, you were fine... It was an emotional evening for you. For all of us. I just wanted to be sure you're OK. I couldn't get a response on your phone. I was worried for a little while.'

'It's nice of you to check. I've had a good sleep and I'm raring to go, really.' She checked her watch. 'Well. As raring as I can be at this time of night on a weekday.'

'You got time for a coffee?'

Georgia peered at the thin dusting of granules at the

bottom of her mug. 'Actually, a real coffee would be just the job.'

'I want to meet up… I feel there's a tension between us, Georgia.'

Georgia allowed a few blissful seconds of unease. 'Like that, you mean?'

'Yeah.' Adrienne laughed. 'Something on that level.'

'I'm just fooling. We can have a coffee. Maybe you can talk me through what happened at the after-party? I'm a big foggy on the details.'

'Sure, I can do that. There's another thing… Well. Something I found after you came round to our offices. It got me thinking. There was a fashion special we decided to do… a showcase of the art and design college, that sort of thing. Truth be told it was an excuse to get some girls in their undies, see if we could boost circulation. And it worked.'

'In this day and age, too. I thought that stuff went out with the nineties?'

'Young male audience, even in this day and age, you'd be surprised, Georgia. Or not.'

'So, what's the significance?'

'Stephanie was involved… you'll see. I'll get you at Turbo Joe's. It's open till ten o'clock on a week night. You know where that is?'

'No, but I'll find it.'

'Great. How soon can you be there?'

'Give me half an hour. I'll need to repair my face and hair.'

*

Turbo Joe's must have been a bookshop of some kind – the kind that kept itself in business by whatever it had upon request up in boxes on the top floor, rather than the paperbacks down below. She could vaguely remember a place she had been into once or twice to look at posters, but had been put off by an all-too-attentive man in half-moon spectacles.

Now it was a thriving coffee shop, with dark-stained corners and candlelight. It was busy – one young mother even had a baby out in a pushchair, no doubt hoping it would fall asleep, while she nursed a lemon-scented tea.

Although she wore a hat and a heavy coat that was surely too warm for the weather, Adrienne was looking perky for someone who must have been up late the night before. She remarked in kind to Georgia.

'I've had a bit of time to recover,' she said. 'I'm not quite sure what happened. I do remember a whisky or something. Someone offered it to me.'

'Yeah,' Adrienne said, 'you said, "this one's to clear my head."'

'That's about right. So... you mentioned something about photos?'

'Yeah. But before that, I... I heard something about a body being found. But,' she added, before Georgia could interject, 'I hear tell that it's a traveller or something. One of the seasonal workers on a farm. Nothing to do with Stephanie.'

'I heard that too. The police told me.'

'Ah that's a relief. It's only hit the news wires just now. Standard police release, really. Body found, twenty-two-year-old woman, not a UK national, no suspicious circumstances. "No suspicious circumstances", don't you think that's a horrible phrase?'

Georgia shrugged. 'The police have to follow procedures, I guess. It's one of those things they have to say. It can tell you a lot by saying very little. Sounds like a suicide. Or drugs. Sorry, am I keeping you back from something?'

Adrienne had clicked on her phone the moment Georgia started to speak. One side of her mouth curled upwards. 'I'm sorry. Got a few things on the go. Last night was a really good night.'

'Yeah. Good show.'

'I mean, in terms of content. I got an exclusive from Riley.'

'Oh, I see. Sold it, have you?'

'Oh yeah. Had something in place with the *Telegraph* already. But he didn't know that.'

'What was the exclusive – or can't you say?'

'Well there's exclusives and there's exclusives.' Adrienne sipped at her coffee. 'I had a long interview. Put it like that.'

Georgia could barely believe it. Here she was, smirking over the fact that she had probably copped off with the man who might have killed her daughter. 'Well. That's something to tell the grandchildren, I suppose.'

'We haven't planned that far ahead,' Adrienne simpered. 'But who knows?'

'It must be exciting. You guys an item?'

'He definitely wants to see me again. In fact, I'm going up to the house tonight. After I finish up here.'

Georgia took in the hat, the heavy coat. She was genuinely intrigued as to what a person like Adrienne would wear on a promise with a rock star. She wasn't quite crass enough to be wearing nothing underneath the coat, but you couldn't rule it out either. 'Well. Exciting times.'

'I know.' Adrienne tapped something into her phone, a near-stupefied expression on her face, and Georgia felt a spasm of anger more terrible and urgent than the one that had led her to attempt to crown her husband with some nice bedding plants just a few hours before.

'Adrienne,' she said, simply.

'Sorry. Here.' Without breaking concentration or even looking at Georgia, the younger woman fished in a deep pocket in her jacket, finally emerging with a USB pen drive. She handed it over.

'And can you explain what this is?'

'It's photos of Stephanie. From the shoot I was talking about. The fashion show, ahead of the summer season. We had a risqué section. Got into trouble for it. But it boosted the circulation. One of the girls went on to get a modelling contract out of it, in fact. Worked out quite well. I understand there was a photographer or two who were very impressed with Stephanie.'

Georgia weighed the pen drive up in her hand. 'Where did you find this?'

'It was in a cupboard with some old gear. I remembered it – when I took over as editor, I'd already checked out the pictures. They were in a box with an old machine or two we were going to recycle. Quite careless – you shouldn't be cavalier with old pen drives. You might see one or two naughty ones of me in there. You won't be posting them to the internet, will you?'

'I'll try to keep my hands at peace.'

'It's all I could do, really,' Adrienne said, fixing her hat.

'Another thing for you to remember her by. I think the pictures are all the photographer took, so you'll see lots of other girls there.'

'Is there an internet café round about here? I don't have a laptop with me. You get used to phones doing all that for you, these days.'

Adrienne pointed around the corner. 'They've got some here. Not many, you might have to wait. I think I only saw one guy sat there.'

'That'll do. Thank you for this. It's kind of you to think of me. Sure you don't want a copy?'

'Already done and backed up,' Adrienne said. 'Should have been archived on the system, really. Photographer was a bit naughty. They are good shots, mind you. Nothing too rude – excellent for his portfolio.'

'Thanks.' Georgia zipped the drive up inside her bag. 'When you say risqué… how risqué are we talking? Seaside postcard? Something that'd end up on the internet?'

Adrienne made her eyes as big as possible. 'Artistic. Most definitely. I'd say they were beautiful. You're not a prude… Well. I don't think you're a prude. But I think you should be proud of them. And I think you should be proud of your daughter. You know, she made the most of what she had, and…'

'Excuse me?'

'I mean, she had so much talent and my God, she took a great picture. Great lines, you know?' Adrienne nodded earnestly. 'I think it's a complete picture of Stephanie, a side to her you maybe didn't know. I think you'll love them. If you're broad-minded.'

'I used to think I was broad-minded, until the moment I

gave birth,' Georgia said. 'But I'll look at these. And thank you. So... when's the big date?'

'Not too far away. I'll get a taxi up to the house, I think.'

'Hopefully Scott Trickett won't be there to make things interesting for you.'

Adrienne screeched laughter – waking up the baby in the buggy. Its mother darted a look at her that might have transfixed a whale, but Adrienne was utterly oblivious. 'Oh my God, no, he's out of the picture. They are quite close, Riley and Scott, but not that close. At least I hope not. Nope, Scott's out and about tonight in town. I'm surprised you can't hear him from here.'

'Whereabouts is he?'

'He's having a soiree at Cronus. Be there most of the night. You know it?'

'Sounds like the kind of place you'd have a snakebite and black.'

'A what?'

'Never mind. I'll find it.'

'It's where they got signed.' A compact mirror appeared in Adrienne's hands – Georgia might have blinked and missed the movement. *Quick Draw McGraw*, she thought. 'Bit grungy but you'd enjoy your night. Well... Maybe you wouldn't, after last night. You get my meaning, I hope.'

'Cronus. Was that after the titan?'

'Not sure who he played for.' Adrienne bared her teeth. 'That was a joke, Georgia.'

'Of course.' Georgia raised a hand, acknowledging her own pomposity. 'Take care now, Adrienne. You'll be careful, won't you? Don't get into bad situations. Times have changed and there aren't many rock stars about now, but I'd be amazed if the behaviour was any different.'

'You sound like my mother,' Adrienne said, giggling.

'Well. Someone's mother.' Georgia sipped at her coffee. 'Last night... I hope you don't mind me being frank.'

'Oh, please be frank, Georgia. You don't have to be shy with me.'

'Last night, you got together? With Riley Brightman?'

Adrienne plunged right in. 'Right under the noses of his little harem. By the end of the night a few of them had to be thrown out. They'd lost their minds. One of them clawed her own *eyes*. Can you imagine? We had to get the minders in. It's mass hysteria, isn't it? It's like they think they know him. Or they have a chance.'

'They get themselves into some states,' Georgia said, thinking of the three girls ahead of her in the queue. 'So had it been building up over time? You always kept in touch, you said.'

'Kind of. If you must know, we'd been together before. Last year. Back before he was anyone.'

'Oh. You had history?'

'Yes. It's difficult to say... You know, Stephanie adored Riley, we all did, but nothing happened between them.'

I bet you did your very very best to make sure nothing did, Georgia thought. But she said: 'He's charming. Most people would be smitten with him.'

'If you must know... the night we got together was the night the Hephaestians had their final meeting. The night Stephanie disappeared.'

'Oh.'

'Yeah. If you were wondering about where Riley was that

night – same as the police – I can account for his movements. If that's what you're asking. And he can account for mine. Come to think of it, so can the people who lived next door to me. The walls... very thin.'

'I see. That's interesting. Thanks for telling me. I don't mean to pry. You know how it is.'

'I do.' Adrienne nodded solemnly. 'Just before I go, there's one or two things I want to ask you. Bearing in mind the conversation we had the other day.'

Georgia shook her head. 'About that... I'm sorry. This has been stressful. Just being here is an ordeal. I...'

'I told you not to worry about that. We all go off at the deep end, once in a while. That's kind of why I want to speak to you.' She scrolled through her phone again. 'Ah. Here it is.'

Adrienne showed her the handset. On it was a series of pictures. Bright morning sunshine. Familiar buildings. Racks of fruit and veg. And facing each other like two fighters on a video game, Rod and Georgia.

'What the hell is this?'

'These were taken this morning. You and your husband had quite a row. What was that all about?'

'Eh? Is this a joke?'

'No joke. It seemed you were having a real set-to about Stephanie. I think he was accusing you of... and if you'll forgive me, I don't have any notes, but it was something like: "You weren't there for Stephanie when she was growing up." Was that it?'

'You little bitch. How dare you... How did you get these?'

Adrienne snatched her phone back as Georgia reached out. 'No you don't, Georgia. You said some incredibly hurtful things to me the other day. As if I'd done something wrong. As if I'd been hiding something from you. So I'll ask you – were you a good mother to Stephanie? Were you there for her, or were you sort of absent, as your husband alleges?'

'I've a mind to speak to a lawyer. You've no right...'

'You were in a public place, and anyone has the right to photograph you in those circumstances.'

'It was a private conversation!'

'Hardly private. Anyway, I spoke to your husband later on. He dropped by at the offices in fact, to find out what's going on, on the ground. I was indisposed, but I got his number. Interesting chat we had. Anything to add to his claims? That you drove Stephanie away? That you were in fact quite cold with her, never quite bonded properly? He mentioned something about depression, but that's quite personal information, so I wouldn't dream of publishing it.' And here, Adrienne beamed.

'You print one word of this, I'll sue for defamation. That's a promise.'

'Newsflash, Georgia: in order for it to be defamation, it has to be untrue. Here's a funny thing: what Rod said to me struck a chord. That time you came over and had a night out with us, when you came to check up on Stephanie. I got that sense from you, too. There was a real distance between you and her. I'd never have said that to your face, until you had the nerve to come into my office, and say those appalling things to me. You all but insisted I had something to do with it. I had *nothing* to do with it. So, I'll do it now. I will say it to your face. It's best not to have regrets, isn't it? You know all about that now. You were cold, and Stephanie knew all about it. Said she was *dreading* you coming to visit. Dreading it.'

'Oh, you're a piece of work, Adrienne. My nose is never wrong, you know. And why have you given me these photos, incidentally? You going to sell them somewhere? What are you getting out of giving them to me? A dig of some kind, obviously. That's it, isn't it? There's some insult attached. Something that makes Stephanie look bad, and you look good. I'll bet everything I have on that.'

Adrienne chuckled. 'I wouldn't bet on anything, if I had your luck.'

'Get out of here, Adrienne. Or I will do something that I might regret. Possibly.'

'Not to worry, love. I was just going.' Adrienne got to her feet. A waft of perfume reached Georgia's nostrils as she did so – not at all unpleasant. Her attire was perfectly arranged, but she seemed to take an age to be sure she had all her belongings and her coat was properly fastened, with her hat positioned time and again. Once she had everyone's attention, she said, at the top of her voice: 'Have to go. It's not every day a girl gets to have a date with a rock star. Can't keep him waiting.'

21

Technology was meant to make things clearer. But the more pixels we can cram onto a screen, the less definition we have.

From the diary of Stephanie Healey

The computers looked old, in that the monitors were in three dimensions, with wheezing motherboards and fan units. Also, they were that weird grey/beige colour. They appeared to have been upgraded to latest spec, though, as she booted up the computer. It felt almost quaint to be given a password on a piece of paper by a barista. There was only one other customer at the tight-knit bank of monitors, a young Asian man who typed, seemingly without pause, his eyes fixed dead ahead. Finals time coming up, Georgia reminded herself.

She plugged in the pen drive and, after an automated scan certified there was no virus lurking within, Georgia opened the folders, marked 'TOKYO DRIFT'

Sub-folders appeared, all marked with names. 'KYM BURLEIGH', 'CONNOR URQUHART' and of course 'ADIE CONNULTY' appeared. 'I'll restrain myself from looking at your accidentally leaked candid shots,' Georgia muttered drily to herself, and here, at last, the student sat in front of her stopped typing and looked up.

Georgia clicked on the folder marked 'STEPH HEALEY'. Thumbnail images opened up, all black and white. Georgia clicked on the first. There was Stephanie, but not Stephanie. Her hair had been cut into a fringe that traced around her face, as if trimmed around the rim of a bowl. It had something of the Evil Teacher about it, and didn't suit the girl Georgia knew. But this didn't seem to be the girl Georgia knew, full stop. Stephanie was dressed in fishnet tights and absolutely nothing else; she was contorted into an S-shape, accentuating her legs and trim bottom, easily her best features. Her arms were crossed over her breasts, but Georgia gasped when she saw how thin Stephanie was – the terrible detail of her ribs, visible beneath her elbows. The small dark eyes were given more prominence by heavy use of black mascara, and she had been shot against a white background, making the light and shade all the more stark. Georgia did not recognise the set of the eyes. There was something not exactly feral, more malevolent; a challenge in the narrowed gaze, like Clint Eastwood flinging his poncho off his hip in the middle of town.

The other shots were in the same vein; in the next one someone had given Stephanie an extraordinary spiky haircut, fanned out on one side. She posed with one finger to her temple, and grinned. She was wearing only a pair of underpants and heels, with an ancient studded bikers' jacket unzipped to the navel. Again, the pigeon hollows of her breastbone caused Georgia to clutch her own chest. Again and again, Stephanie wearing very little. In one shot she was wearing PVC boots up to the tops of her thighs, and was even cracking a whip.

Only one shot could have been called explicit, but there was something arty in it – just Stephanie, nude, facing the camera. Her hair was wet and her skin was glistening, though this latter was clearly the effect of oil rather than water, as intended. Here the hollows, ridges and bones of Stephanie's undernourishment were apparent – the hip bones and pubic bone and the non-existent stomach, the almost mechanical bulge of the shoulder blades, were the most painful to see.

Georgia checked over her shoulder; no one was watching. There were at least thirty shots to go through, some separate angles in the same study. The last one, though, was most troubling. It was Stephanie, again wearing the fishnet tights along with a pair of patent leather pumps with an immense silver buckle on the instep. She was almost folded in half, forehead resting on her knees, arms, hands and fingers loose, trailing across the white-tiled floor.

Georgia chewed the inside of her mouth. Then she saved all the pictures to her email's online drive, zipped up the pen drive, then checked her watch.

'Little bitch,' she muttered. 'Shaming her. That's all this is about. Shaming *me*. Shaming her after she's...'

She dropped some coins into the tip jar on her way out, noting with satisfaction that the young mother had the baby asleep at last, and was getting her things together as carefully as she could.

'Hey,' she whispered to the barista. 'Do you know a place called Cronus?'

'Oh yeah,' the girl whispered back, 'there's usually a

band on in there. I heard the Megiddos might be playing this week – secret gig. They're still in town.'

'Really? That'd be awesome. I'd love to see them play. Can you tell me how to get there from here?'

22

*A whole afternoon then the night after it drifted away.
This might be what it's like to be famous. It's certainly
what it's like to be wasted. You're plugged into something
else. You start to believe that you're special; you're a star.
I think they call it self-actualisation. All the big stars
manage it – they become who they want. Maybe this
is the path. But it's nothing really, I know that. A slutty
assignment. But what a rush. There's a shabby glamour
to all this, like tinsel at a school dance. But when those
lights fade, ah, dear.*

*Cornfed, just lie with me. Just lie quiet, and let me
hold you, as long as I can.*

From the diary of Stephanie Healey

Georgia walked past the doorway several times. It was
in one of the older buildings in town, what looked like
a smart Georgian town. There were decent businesses either
side of it – a nauseatingly cute cake shop with strawberry
red and white tablecloths and doilies and a fine art centre, its
walls curiously naked in a way that denoted affluence. She
double-checked her phone; nope, it was there somewhere.

Then she saw the sign on top of an innocuous-looking doorway. Greek-style lettering, the upper and lower curves of the letters pointed like a short blade: *CRONUS*. The litter bin to the front, with polystyrene cases poking out, and the squat, brutish young man in the doorway should have been the giveaway.

The bouncer grinned as she approached. 'Got any ID? Over-twenty-ones only, I'm afraid.'

'Will my pension book do?'

'In you come. Mind if I give your bag a search? Regulations.'

Faint stirrings of panic; Georgia smiled broadly to keep them at bay. 'Sure.'

A cursory search, thank God; he was nowhere near the hidden compartment. 'If you've got any guns or drugs in there, can you let me know how you hid them on the way out?'

'I'll put something on TripAdvisor.'

Something of a flaw in either the planning or design, the doorway led to a rising staircase, rather than descending. The walls were poorly lit, and blood red in the places closest to the light fixtures. The carpeting was scuffed, worn and weathered like the faces of rough old men.

After a welcome from a surprised-looking female steward through another door, Georgia emerged into a long, blacked-out space that she recognised from her student days. A dank place where quieter-natured people would gather; blacked out at the windows, a long bar dominating one wall. A small stage dominated one side of the room, but it was empty for now. It was quiet – Georgia supposed it was a week night, at the beginning of exam time, with only sparse pockets of people here and there.

She couldn't quite make out every face, and she supposed it might be too much to ask the girl serving at the bar to turn the lights up for a minute or two. Instead, she asked: 'Hi there. I heard the Megiddos were in tonight, is that true?'

The girl pursed her lips, a patronising smile Georgia wanted to slap right off her. 'I think you'll find it's only one half, I'm afraid. And he won't be performing, he's made that clear.'

'Mind telling me where he is? I'm a massive fan.'

'Right. Well. He's over in the alcove. That's his spot.'

'Many thanks.'

That pursed smiled again. 'Not of the crazed variety, are you?'

'Excuse me?'

'A crazed fan. A stalker. *Yee! Yee!*' She mimed stabbing someone, in harmony with the serrated *Psycho* notes.

'Oh, much worse than that. I'm his mother.'

There being no further comeback after that, Georgia followed the barmaid's directions. A set of alcoves were set into the walls, reminding her of railway sidings. Benches were set up inside, furred over with some unspeakable carpet that surely constituted a health hazard. These were empty except for a couple conversing with bowed heads over the sound of the music, and one with about three people in it, one of whom was the man she was looking for.

Shouldering her bag, Georgia approached. As well as Scott Trickett, there was a man Georgia didn't recognise, a good-looking young man with long hair and gypsy eyes, who had a seamed, lived-in look to him that stopped him from being truly beautiful. Beside him was a young girl who looked as if her body had outgrown her features, dressed in black with a sleeveless top, cut low in the front, a short black shirt and thigh-high cowboy boots. For a disorienting second, Georgia was reminded of Stephanie; she flashed back to the photoshoot she'd just seen on the memory stick Adrienne Connulty had given to her. She blinked to clear the vision.

Sitting across from these two was the bovine, red-bearded bulk of Scott Trickett. Georgia heaved herself over alongside him, smiling at the surprise of the two newcomers sitting opposite.

'Hi,' she said. 'I'm carrying out a spot-check of ID. Don't suppose either of you have your NUS cards on you?'

The pair traded looks, part confusion, part irritation. 'We're not students, love,' the long-haired man said, in a Scottish accent like pebbles ratting down a drain.

Scott Trickett frowned hard at Georgia, then, once he recognised her, threw back his head. 'Aw, I don't believe it. This is my mummy! Everybody, say hello to Mummy!'

The young woman wearing black took him at face value, and proffered a hand. 'Oh, lovely to meet you. It's great you can get out to see Scott.'

Georgia shook her hand, and said, in all earnestness: 'I'm not really his mother.'

The girl looked confused, but her companion was baleful. 'Not sure what you are, exactly, if you're not his mother. A joker? You aren't a copper, I can tell you that right away. I can smell them. And you smell...' the young man inhaled, brutally, more of a snort than a sniff '... really flowery, in fact.'

'Folks, this is an old friend,' Scott Trickett said, amiably. 'Could you leave us for five minutes? Promise we won't be long.'

'Sure, mate. We'll be right back.' The man with the gypsy eyes winked at Georgia, then gestured for the woman in black to move. Still embarrassed by what had happened earlier, she tutted and then slid along the seat with some reluctance. They both headed for the bar.

Scott Trickett swirled half a pint and sipped at it. 'Surprised to see you around here. You should still be out of the game, by rights.'

Georgia made an effort to soften her features. 'I didn't feel too bad when I woke up. I hadn't really had too much to drink, you see.'

'Ah, right. It's strange – cos you looked completely out of your head.'

'It was some night. A very emotional one, too.'

'That's right. A long party. Would you believe, I haven't been to bed?'

'I would believe it.' She grinned.

'What brings a nice lady like you to a place like this?'

'Well, first of all, I heard you were in town, and I really wanted to say sorry.'

Trickett put down his pint glass and arched an eyebrow at her. 'What for?'

'Well… hitting you.'

'Don't apologise for that. I was a prick.' He shrugged. 'Fair play. *Everyone* hits me.'

'I didn't take your comments too well, and also, I didn't thank you properly. You and Riley throwing that party… It's a great, kind thing that you did. It means a lot to me.'

'Well, we just want her found,' Trickett said. His eyes lost focus for a moment; Georgia glanced over her shoulder, and realised he was staring at the girl who'd been sat across from him a moment before as she waited to get served at the bar. She rested one of her feet on part of a high stool, her thigh muscles flexing. 'Wherever she might be. X marks the spot, so they say.' He blinked, and returned to the present. 'Oh… sorry. My mouth has a way of tripping me up.'

'I remember that detail, yes. You don't have to apologise to me.'

'Some things should just stay buried, you know?'

'You're right about that.'

'In a manner of speaking. Uh… sorry?' He grinned weakly. It was difficult to know whether or not this entire Tommy Tourette routine was just that, an act, or if it was a natural condition. Georgia decided it didn't matter. She glued an easy smile to her face, and didn't make eye contact, for fear that she might claw his out for him.

'Can I get you something?' she asked.

'Uh, that's a hellova kind offer. Just whatever beer they've got. A bottle.'

Georgia brought him back a pint of lager. 'Oh – sorry. You said a bottle, didn't you? Damn it.'

'Don't worry, Mrs, ah…?'

'Healey.'

'Mrs Healey. I was going to call you Mrs Stephanie, there.'

'I'll answer to anything.'

'How about Milfy? Can I call you that?'

'Excuse me?'

'Never mind. Bad joke. I'm all about the bad jokes. I can't stop. I should be kept away from a microphone, I really should.' He accepted the pint and sipped from it, grinning with a fresh growth of foam across his lips.

'Your bandmate not out to play tonight?'

'Brightman? Nah he's got some local entanglements. There's a big party up at his dad's.'

'And he hasn't invited you? Curious.'

'I didn't say it was tonight.' Some irritation, here.

'What is it, a birthday or something?'

'Yes. That's what it is. A birthday. That's right.' Trickett sipped his beer, and glanced at the girl with the black boots. She was having a very animated conversation with her long-haired male companion. Neither of them looked particularly happy. 'Now, have a look at this situation, here. It's quite finely balanced.'

'What do you mean? The couple who were sat with you?'

'Yeah. It could go either way. Look. They're a couple. But it's dodgy.'

'They're arguing. I don't get what you mean, though. How is it dodgy?'

'I mean, whether or not she's going to be in my bed tonight.' He cocked his head. 'Hope that doesn't shock you.'

'Believe it or not, sex has been around a while.'

Trickett clinked his plastic pint glass with Georgia's bottled water. 'Touché! I like you. I mean – look, the guy's quite good-looking and all that. I can say that quite happily. The pair of us go to a blind casting audition or photoshoot, he'll be in the reckoning – I wouldn't even get a picture taken for the file, unless it's for the office Christmas party. But I've got something he doesn't. And his little gothy pants girlfriend wants it. And he's not happy.'

'You've been in this situation before?'

'One time I had a super-fan come over, a guy. Waited hours to see us. Brought his little girlfriend. Nice little piece.

Bit plain. Short hair, not my usual thing. But anyway, at the after-show party, I tongued her right in front of him. He stood there watching. Couldn't do a thing about it. See, what I've got is… a bit of magic and sparkle. Show business, baby. Accept no substitute.'

'That sounds like a quality evening. Maybe the girl thought she was going to meet Riley? Maybe that's why the girl with the boots came here, in fact. To see the main man. Not you.'

'Sure,' the big man said, with no hesitation or discomfort. 'I totally accept that. I take what Riley leaves. Shit, I was *banking* on it. And sometimes, I take what Riley doesn't leave. That's the way it goes. He's a good-looking boy – but he can't shag them all.'

'How about when he was a student?'

'Oh, he was a busy lad at university. I'm sure you know all about it.'

'I don't. I'd like to know more.'

'Maybe you should ask him, then.'

Over at the bar, the girl clattered out towards the main door. Her boyfriend sighed, shook his head, drained a drink, and followed her. He waved towards Scott Trickett, who responded with a 'what can you do?' shrug.

'Looks like it went the other way,' Georgia said.

'Yep.' Trickett drummed his fingers and looked around, his face darkening. 'It's a fucking morgue in here tonight. Damn. Sorry.'

'Oh, I don't know. Seems lively enough.' Georgia got up from her seat and sat down beside the big man. He radiated heat, and a faint sour smell that could have been stale beer.

He put his pint down and gazed at her with open astonishment. 'Hello. What's this then?'

'Whatever you like. Milfy, that's what you called me, wasn't it?'

'I don't believe I'm hearing this. And seeing it. Is this for real?'

'As real as you want it to be.'

'Are you... Is this you coming on to me?'

Georgia nudged him and giggled. He actually got a fright, his shoulders cinching in shock. 'Oh, I'm just sitting and having a conversation. That's all we're having. Unless you wanted a little bit more?'

'Well. Ah...' He took a drink, but he sported a look of almost child-like glee.

'As you say – not much happening in here. And it looks like you want something out of the evening. Unless you came to see the band?'

'I was meant to be watching 'em... Bit of solidarity. It's that Prat Spaniel nonsense again. Doing an acoustic set, the singer, Howie, and the guitar player. Wonder where they got that idea from?'

'Nothing stopping you leaving. Is there?' She sat closer again, and bent close to him. A little bit of cleavage; he took the bait, too, gazing at her with brutal fervour.

So fucking easy.

'I don't think I've done it with someone on the seniors tour before,' he said, quietly. 'Anything I should know?'

'Oh, it's nothing a seasoned groupie master like yourself can't handle, I'm sure. Unless you want mothering. Do you?'

'You kinky bitch! I love it. You're on.'

He leaned close to her, lips parted, the beard and the

battle-damaged T-shirt, and then God, that smell again, and of course she couldn't do it. She drew back, shook her head. 'Not here. But you can come with me.'

'What, now?'

'You got something better to do?'

'Fast work,' Trickett said. He gulped down the rest of his pint, lathered the suds into his beard, and grinned. 'Your place or yours, o Lady in Black?'

23

It's funny how you can change the parameters, the background, the ground you stand on, the very air you breathe... and they stay needy. Needy, jealous little boys. It never changes.

From the diary of Stephanie Healey

The big man had struggled to make it as far as the bed. Luckily, Georgia had plenty of practice when it came to moving people on top of blankets. She was more worried about getting the bedclothes in a mess – the soles of his boots were filthy. Unlacing them and letting them drop to the floor with dull sound, she imagined Boris Karloff as Frankenstein.

'Cosy here...' he murmured. His eyes were all but closed; only a glimmer of light hinted at animation, and his breathing was shallow, barely stirring the undergrowth at his nostrils. 'Nice 'n' warm.'

'That's right,' Georgia said. She turned the light out. The room was completely dark.

'Hey. Where... where you go?'

He had almost not got here. The taxi driver had shaken

his head as Georgia had sat him down and belted him in. 'He on something, love?'

'He's just had a couple of beers. I think he's been working hard.'

'Just as well he's got his mother to look after him. If he's sick, you pay, I'll tell you that now.'

'He's just a little sleepy.'

'Hell of a pint, that,' Trickett had muttered, resting his head on the window.

It had been a close-run thing. But she'd kept him awake.

Georgia waited for her eyes to adjust, then came closer. She could only make out the shape of the body on the bed.

'Sorry for the cloak and dagger,' she said. 'I thought it'd be difficult to get you to myself. Hope you don't mind.'

'You OK... you OK if we do it tomorrow? I'm kinda beered out,' he wheezed. 'Head's spinning. Might take forty winks. What's with all the lights? Like a fucking... fairground in here. Piccadilly or something.'

'Oh, stay with me a while longer,' she whispered. 'Stay with me.' She clicked a torch in his face. The eyebrows pinched, slightly, and she saw there was some movement behind the razor-cut of the eyelids, the way she might discern activity and animation at the bottom of her wheelie bin.

'That the one you shine in people's eyes?' He grinned. That wasn't so good; she wanted him stupefied, not sharp. 'When you check for things?'

'It's clinical equipment, you're right. This is the torch I use to check for souls.'

'What's the verdict, Doc? Long have I got?' he chuckled. 'Did you spike my drink?'

'What a crazy idea! Why would you think that?'

'This ain't no beer rush... Maybe it was the bitch with the kinky boots. Could have been, I guess.' He yawned, suddenly, jaw creaking.

'What happened to me the other night did give me a little idea, I do declare.'

'That the night when you went cray-zee?' He drew out the last syllable, and laughed at his own joke.

'Yeah. Funny how that can happen to a body. I thought we could have a chat, in fact.'

'You into dirty talk, that kind of thing? Guess I can... Go for it.' He turned to one side and yawned again, cuddling into a pillow.

Georgia slapped him. It was a hard thing to do, through his Mr Twit beard, but she got enough purchase in the blow to unshutter his eyes.

'No, no, no,' she said. 'Don't be fading out on me. It's not nighty-night time yet.'

'Did you just hit me?'

'No, you must have dreamed it. I want to talk about Stephanie.'

'Stephanie. Cold where she is.'

Instead of reacting, Georgia went along with it. 'And where is that?'

'Fuck knows.' He giggled. 'Speaking of which... where are we again?'

'How well did you know her?'

'Well enough. Didn't shag her, if that's what you're asking. Guess it's ironic, that, eh? Me being here and all that.'

'Very droll. Yes, I suppose there's something amusing in that. Did Riley shag her?'

'Just the once, I think. She weirded him out a bit. Too heavy into it, you know? Poets, what can I tell you? They're all the same. Wound up too tight. Riley's like that. He's not mellow, you know? Not too mellow. Not mellow like me. Can I sleep now?'

'You can't sleep. What happened the night of the fight?'

'What fight?'

'The night Stephanie vanished.' *Blockhead*, she muttered under her breath. 'The fight between Martin Duke and Riley. Was it over Stephanie?'

'Nah not really. Well, kinda. Duke was sweet on her; everyone knew that. He wrote a poem to the Hephaestians that was clearly about her. Embarrassing. I could hardly listen to it. Riley burst out laughing. Think that was the start of it, you know. The insult. The insult.' He yawned again. 'Anyway, think there was some sort of row about the other bitch.'

'What other bitch?'

'The little gothy piece. I think Riley went through her too. But she did it to spite Duke, cos he was sweet on Stephanie. I thought Colette was better-looking, but that's my opinion. It all got a bit… doof doof doof-doof doof doof-doof…' He mimed along to the *EastEnders* cliffhanger drumbeat, but it cost him a lot of effort to do so. His hands flopped back onto the bedspread.

'Martin Duke and Riley were fighting over Colette? Not Stephanie?'

'You disappointed?'

'I thought they were fighting over Stephanie.'

'Did someone actually tell you that? Or did you just think

it, and nobody corrected you? The mind's a funny thing… Funny thing.'

'Why wasn't Stephanie there?'

'Nobody knows. She was meant to be there. If someone knew, then we wouldn't be talking, would we? Shame. I was hoping her and Colette would have a showdown. Cat fight, you know?' Then he emitted a shockingly life-like feline screech; Georgia jumped, and almost dropped the torch. 'Was hoping they'd get into it. On the undercard. Titties flying everywhere. Bras and blouses ripped to buggery. I saw that once. In a movie. But no dice, mama. No one knows why she didn't turn up.' He yawned again. 'That's the big mystery, isn't it?'

'What about the lecturer?'

'Sillars? Yeah, he was there. Waded into the fight, broke it up actually. Quite handy, for a book-learnin' boy.'

'I thought you said it wasn't a fight? I thought Riley beat Martin up?'

'Nah… I say that just to protect his feelings. He sorta ran in and smacked Duke, then lots of people intervened. Bit like the other night. I wouldn't give Riley tuppence-worth of a chance against a cardboard cut-out of Martin Duke. He's a lover, not a fighter, I s'pose. I mean Duke's a ponce – he's just less of a ponce than Riley.'

'Did you see Stephanie before she went missing? Had she been seeing Riley, in the lead-up to it?'

'Nah, she was interested in other things.' He giggled.

'Like Cornfed?'

'Oh, the lady knows. How interesting.'

'Who is Cornfed? Tell me, Scott. I'll let you sleep if you tell me.'

'Ah, that's top secret.' He sniggered.

Georgia's temper came to the boil. She let it go – only a little. 'You know, you've probably got a nice bright future, Scott. Even though you're basically the fat friend of a better-looking boy, it's a good position to be in. Life will be good for you. I don't know how you manage it. I would only put you on a record cover with me to make me look better. Maybe that's what it boils down to.'

'Aww,' Scott said, in a mock-American dweeb accent, 'that's hurts my... feelings... nothing more than... feelings...'

'And I get it, the sick jokes, the weirdness. I understand you. You're basically a nonentity. You have to struggle hard for attention, even up there on a stage for your professional life. "Oh no, I didn't say that, did I? What am I like?" I've seen it all before. Riley will go solo before long – you know that? It's what happens.'

'Well aware of that. I know it's a short ride. But I'll ride it to the end.'

'You might make an interesting footnote to his career. Especially after you go missing.'

'What?' he said, dreamily.

Georgia clicked off the light. 'You know how I said I was going to take you back to my place? I kind of lied.'

She listened to him breathe for a moment or two. 'What?'

'We're not back at my place. You're in a caravan.'

'Caravan? Are you tripping as well?'

Georgia knocked the walls. 'Quite a tight squeeze in here. You hear that? Not much space to echo out. Very narrow walls.'

'Heh, I saw you knocking the wall... it turned into stars,

like bonfire night. What in God's name did you dose me with? It's good stuff, I'll say that. Nuclear grade.'

'Pharmaceutical grade, actually. It'll make you tired and confused. You'll see some visuals. You probably won't remember much of this. But you're present in the here and now. Which is good, because I want you to understand what happens, once I roll this caravan into Hunters Bar Reservoir.'

'You what?'

'You know Hunters Bar Reservoir, don't you? Steep drop-off. The thing about the drugs I gave you is, the effect is so much greater when you fight sleep. So, imagine how great the special effects will be when you try to swim in a great big coffin.'

'What? Where are you? I said, where are you?' He shuffled on the bed – but no more than that.

'Don't worry, I haven't gone. Not yet. I want you to think about it, Scott. You've got a vivid imagination. You tell me all those things about Stephanie. About her being in a grave. Or in the water somewhere. Well, you can be both. You can lie in here while the whole thing fills with water. You'll have a few seconds to think all about it. Before the real panic starts. Then you've got up to a minute, maybe two minutes, depending on how deep a breath you can take at the end. And how long you can hold it. Maybe like Stephanie did, too?'

'I didn't kill her. I don't know what happened…' Trickett's tone of voice had changed. Panic was there, now. 'No one knows what happened to Stephanie.'

'I know you didn't kill her. But I think someone did. Which is why I've brought you out here. Because you know something you're not telling me. And I'm getting fed up with being polite about things. I might be ready to do something desperate. So, unless you want to know what drowning feels like, you best tell me something.'

He struggled to a sitting position; Georgia guessed correctly where his chest was, and shoved him back onto the bed. The headboard reverberated.

'Who is Cornfed?'

Despite the impact, despite the panic, he managed a chuckle. 'You think it's a person? An actual guy?'

'I'll ask you once more – who is Cornfed?'

'Cornfed's not a who, it's a what.'

'What is it?'

'A code name. Shorthand. It's what Riley and me say when we want the Good Stuff.'

'Good stuff?'

'Yeah. It goes by a million names, that's one of them. Smack. Junk. Heroin. The big stuff.'

A bell rang out somewhere in Georgia's head – shrill, not sonorous. 'Heroin? Cornfed is *heroin*?'

'Yeah, that's it.'

'But Stephanie… When she talked about Cornfed, she mentioned…' Georgia's hand went to her mouth. 'She was taking it? Stephanie was *taking* heroin?'

'She took it, and she took *to* it, like the big beautiful goose she was, taking to water.'

'You're kidding. That can't be right, it can't be.'

'One hit is all it takes for some. Wouldn't touch it, myself. It was Riley's game for a while, but he was never a serious player. Tried it, loved it, didn't get over his head. Like those tits who tell you they only smoke on a night out. He got her into it. She liked the romance of it, he said. She thought she was like some beat poet in Paris or something. When in fact, all she was, from the get-go, was a fucking junkie. Don't you know this? Don't the police tell you anything?'

'No… My God, no.'

'It's true. Cornfed is the gear. And she was on it. Now… I think I'd like to go home.' He yawned. 'You're not really going to roll the caravan into the reservoir, are you?'

Georgia cracked one of the blackout curtains; streetlighting came in like a kick in the balls. They weren't up at the reservoir. They were in fact in Georgia's room. 'I'll call you a cab, Scott. Thanks for another lovely night. Make sure you get a good night's sleep, yes?'

24

When an angel sleeps
They stay afloat, somehow,
Wings folded, head resting on one shoulder,
But eyes wide open, rolled back
And then suddenly they're bent double,
Halfway between death and heaven
              Untitled poem, by Stephanie Healey

Georgia yawned, jaw cracking. Long day. Long couple of days. 'The big man would have found this ironic,' she muttered, starting the car.

There was an unseasonal bite in the air, a poison pen letter from winter where she reminded you in no uncertain terms what would happen once she was back. Uncertain about exactly where she was going, she turned on the satnav, cringing a little at the high volume as she made her way along quiet streets.

Bewley Street, like just about everywhere else, had attained a kind of respectability in recent years. It was a legal enclave, lots of double- and triple-barrelled names attached to signs, brass plates on the doors, high windows and closed curtains. Georgia remembered a lot of these old Victorian town houses had been run-down; one had even burnt out one night while she was a student here. The developers had come in, and the scuzz had gone out. The one notable exception was the girls standing under the streetlights at the wall.

This was the place she had come to the other night in the midst of her ravings, an event she saw more as a dream rather than something that had actually taken place. Somewhere that was the punchline to a million smutty jokes by knock-kneed young men, usually with a woman on the receiving end. *Bewley Street... She's off to Bewley Street to make up the rent this month... Sure I saw her getting kicked out a car on Bewley Street...* So on and so forth. The wall itself was behind a brick wall topped off with glass shards – Georgia always wanted to meet the people who designed such things – which hid a massive electricity substation from view.

Along a row of streetlights that lit up the ruddy-faced façade, the women stood in full view.

Not knowing where to start, Georgia picked the first one. It shouldn't have been a shock, but it was – she was pretty, and horribly young. High cheekbones and a clear brow; it might have been the face of a waitress, or someone serving you at an expensive bar. The girl frowned when Georgia came to a stop and opened the window.

'This a joke or something?' Local accent. A real edge on it.

Georgia cleared her throat. 'I'm looking for someone. It's...'

She pulled out the picture from her bag, but before she

could introduce her daughter, the girl said: 'Sorry, can't help you,' and began to step back.

'Please, just take a look at the picture. She was a writer, she... She had a project. It had something to do with Bewley Street. She's gone missing.'

'You deaf or something? I'd keep away from here, if I was you, love.'

Georgia moved the car on. They were all glaring at her. Suspicion, mistrust, and worse. This was a dangerous place. She marvelled that she'd gotten out of there without coming to harm. She'd been lucky.

One of the girls turned and walked away down the street, smartly. Another car further up the street suddenly revved up and tore off.

Two girls were stood beside each other under the second streetlight. They were still talking, but keeping an eye on Georgia's car. The first one, who looked as if she'd just been woken up out of a deep sleep, with a leopard-skin skirt and black tights, frowned at her. 'You looking for directions, dear? Wherever you're going, go straight on, fast as you can, and don't stop.'

Her friend shrieked laughter at this – a small, hard-looking blonde with a front tooth missing.

'I'm looking for my little girl.'

'You know how many times I hear that every night?'

Again, her friend laughed aloud at this.

'This is her. Stephanie. You might have heard.'

The woman in the leopard-print skirt came forward – her pumps were enormous, and possibly the wrong size for her – and stared at the pic. 'I know about this. Or I heard about it. I saw it on the telly.'

'Did you know her?'

The girl's face became serious. 'Bit before my time. I only arrived this year. Know about the case. She's gone, you know that, don't you? You're not going to get her back. You're wasting your time here. Someone's got to tell you. I'm sorry, love.'

'I only want to find out what happened. She spent time with people here – I know that for a fact now. I'll pass you a card, if you hear anything…'

The girl laughed again. 'Card? What do you think this is, a company meeting? Card, she says.'

Her companion sneered: 'Bank card? I'd accept that.'

'Your daughter's gone,' the girl in the leopard-print skirt said. 'I'm sorry, but it's true. She's in the river, or in someone's freezer. Someplace nice and quiet, anyway. I wish it wasn't true. But it is. Mind how you go, now. Mind how you go.' She waved, but it was an oddly robotic movement, her body and features stock-still barring the pendulous movement of her upper arm. Something in this gesture froze Georgia to the marrow, and she wanted to move off again up until the moment the girl two lights up approached, pointing at the car.

Georgia drove off, the laughter of the little blonde girl jagged in her ear, and caught up with the new girl. She was short and dark-skinned, possibly of Indian extraction, and she had long dark hair fashioned into intricate bunches down the side of her head. She was dressed all in black, and while she was not as pretty as the other girls, she looked more expensive. The thought was repulsive. 'Hey,' the girl said.

She was almost certainly in her twenties, though it would

have been difficult to pin down what end of the decade. She had a crumpled look around the eyes, and one look at the neck and the jutting bones visible just beneath told Georgia she was thin, dangerously so – even more of a giveaway than the stork's legs. This girl bent over and said: 'You're the lady who went crazy here the other night, weren't you?'

The way the girl framed the sentence, and the impudent jut of her chin, made Georgia fearful that a blow might follow these words. She said: 'That's right. I was here the other night.'

'Then I've got something for you, if you've got something for me.'

'What? Oh.' Georgia pulled out a twenty-pound note from her purse, and held it just out of reach. 'Get in, if you're getting in.'

The girl opened the door and got in, fast. Georgia resisted the urge to drive away at breakneck pace, and instead stayed put.

She held out her hand, a frank, quizzical expression on her face.

'Buckle up first,' Georgia said. When the girl did so, she asked: 'What's your name?'

'What do you want to know that for?'

'So I know what to call you. You know. What names are usually for.'

'Smart mouth,' the girl said. 'You can call me Judy.' She raised her eyebrows again, and gestured towards her outstretched hand.

Georgia fed her the twenty. 'Thanks for coming. There's more, if you tell me something I can use.'

'Use for what?'

'To find my daughter. The only thing I'm interested in. The only reason I exist.' Something caught in the back of her throat. She stared into the road, waiting for her eyes to demist.

A new element crept into Judy's voice after this – something not quite so hard. 'You could have come to grief out there. The other night, I mean. A few of the girls were wanting to wade in. And a few of their minders. They're around, you know.'

'I was out of my head. And I was desperate.' She glanced at the girl as she started the car. They turned onto one of Ferngate's main boulevards, a place of retail units and the bright lights of pizza parlours, multiplex cinemas and other large-chain delights, their lights oddly forbidding in the gloom of a quiet night. 'So. Stephanie. Did you know her?'

'I did. I got to know her through the scene.'

'Scene?'

'Yeah. The scene.'

'You'll have to explain that, sorry.'

The girl rolled up her sleeve. 'This scene.'

In the crook of her elbow were some sores that, even at a glance in the faint light, had a raised, angry appearance. The sores had an alarmingly fecund look to them, as if something living might crawl out. Georgia immediately indicated to go into a retail park next to a fast-food restaurant, and put on the handbrake.

'That's infected. Staph infection, maybe. You got any other symptoms?'

The girl shook her head. She became passive when Georgia examined her – the patient getting into her role as quickly as the doctor did. Georgia's hands sought her neck, the corner of her jaw. She saw a pulse jumping there. 'Your glands are swollen. Have you had any temperatures recently?'

'You know your stuff. You told everyone you were a doctor. I thought you were lying. Or one of those pretend doctors. Sociology or something. Yeah, I wasn't well the other night. Don't feel so bad now. Not great either, truth be told.'

'I'm going to write a note, and you're going to go to your GP tomorrow. If you aren't registered, go to A&E. Staph infections can be fatal.'

'It's not that simple,' the girl said.

'It's very simple – you don't look after yourself, you die. I'm not making any judgements here about using. I've seen it plenty of times. Abscesses, staph infections, HIV, the lot. Pick a problem, I've tried to sort it. Have you been injecting into the muscle?'

'Problems with my veins,' the girl said, softly.

Georgia nodded. Here was dread; God knew she'd seen just about every kind of infection and scenario involving drug users in her time, but this was away from the surgery and the panic button or any kind of help at all. 'Tell me how you met Steph. Did you know her?'

'Spoke to her a few times. She was… interested in us.'

'Where did you meet?'

'Would you believe, at church. She was in watching people light candles. I was in to say a prayer for my grandmother. She said hello to me. She seemed kind. Then I recognised her at a house party, thrown by Mr Riley Brightman. Local hero, take a bow. He dabbled in it. More into the gear at the time, than the women, but the two went together. That's why we end up on the streets – the stuff. That's why we do what we do.'

'Is that where Steph tried it? At one of his parties?'

'Yeah. I was there, the night she did it. Smoked it at first. She told me a funny story about fairies and dragons, while she was chasing one.' This statement struck Georgia like a blow. There was truth. 'But she wanted more. She got her own syringe. Said her mum was a doctor. I saw her go under, first time. She was on it from the start. It happens with some people.'

'Jesus,' was all Georgia could say. 'Jesus Christ.'

'She was into writing. She had a project. Said she wanted to do a portrait. I thought she meant painting, at first, or photography. I told her about all the books I loved when I was a kid. Ponies. Horse riding.' Judy's voice trailed off a little. 'She wanted to know all about me. Said I shouldn't be doing what I do. She was a fucking fine one to talk.'

'You're saying Riley Brightman got her into heroin?'

'Yeah. She had a weird name for it as well. You know what it was?'

Georgia shook her head.

'Cornfed. That's what she called it. Like an actual name, Cornfed. Meaning the good stuff, I think. "Get me Cornfed". "Best Cornfed you can get".'

'That sounds like her, all right,' Georgia whispered.

'Clever thing. Funny. Very droll. Pretty too, obviously. Had a way with words. Everybody raved about her. Well, boys mostly. She had the look, you know? Could have seen her on a catwalk. Think she'd done some photoshoots and stuff. Could see why. Weird, though – she doesn't look much like you.'

'How many times did you see her?'

'Two or three. She came to Riley to get the stuff. We all did. Whoever his supplier was, it was easy pickings. He had loads of it. He didn't take it himself. Thing is, I think he liked getting people onto it. The young girls especially.'

Georgia remembered the fresh young faces at the house party, the make-up, the best clothes, the glittery eyes.

'He even pretended he didn't want your girl to get into it. "Once some people go over the line, they're never coming back. After just one hit. And I think that's you." He told her that. And he was right. She went in anyway. She was all in.'

'She wanted to write about you, and your life? She told you that?'

'Yeah. Not me in particular. She was kind of fearless. Not a tough case or anything, but she spoke her mind. If people were rude, she told them they were rude. If she didn't like anything, she said so. But she wasn't, like, a fan of me, or anything. She was more into the big party, you know? The bigger scene.'

'Another scene? I don't follow you, sorry. You mean another drug?'

'No, the party. The one I'm not supposed to tell you about.'

'You've got to. What party is this?'

She knew, of course. Judy's face changed again, and she held out a hand. Georgia gave her a tenner.

'The party up at Chessington Hall. The one they have every year. I went last year, and the year before. But not this year. Too skinny, they told me. Try again next year.'

'What kind of party is it?'

'Use your imagination.'

'Tell me.'

'They round up a load of girls, and… You can imagine.'

'This is at Chessington Hall?'

'Yeah, it's some festival or other. Springtime. Funny costumes. I forget what it was in aid of.'

'You were there?'

'Yep. So was your daughter.'

'You're kidding!'

'Nah. Was a few days before she went missing.'

'You've told the police this?'

'There'd be no point to that.'

'Why not?'

'They turn a blind eye to it. And besides… there's nothing to tell. It's a private party, after all. There's a lot worse goes on in these kinds of places, I'll tell you that much. Quite pleasant, as it turns out. Really good money, considering.'

'There's the party this weekend. Is it run by Sir Oliver?'

'Private party, that's all I was told. Didn't see any lords or ladies, there.'

'Is it all… is it working girls?'

'Not all working girls, but there were a few of us there, yeah. That was the idea.'

'Tell me more – how did Stephanie get there? What happened?'

'That's all I know. She took part in… she was in at the party, for sure. I think she was thrown out, or something. Or asked to leave. I don't know. She said she was researching something, and there was a bit of a scene. Hey – what are you doing?'

Georgia's hands shook as she tapped something into her phone. 'Making a note.'

'You better not be phoning anybody.' Judy's hand clamped over her wrist. Georgia tore it away.

'I'm not phoning anyone. I'm making a note. God's sake, this is vital information. There was some kind of sex party up at Chessington Hall, and Stephanie was involved? Less than a week before she vanished down that road? Are you sure about this?'

'Not a sex party. Not exactly. I've told you enough. Now, you mentioned something about more cash?'

'Just a minute.'

'She was a good bit closer to the other lass. They both got into the gear on the same night.'

'What other girl?'

'Jasmine. Real name was Janina, which I think is a lot nicer. Shame.'

'Is she around tonight?'

'She's not around.'

'Do you know where she went?'

'No, I mean, she's not around. In terms of, you know, breathing.'

'She's dead? When?'

'Not sure when exactly, but they found her up at that old farm the other day. OD'd, they reckon. She went over the line. We'll all end up there some time.'

'My God. Stephanie knew this girl? They were friends?'

'Not exactly. I think Stephanie had her in mind for one of her portraits. Like, an article or something. Jasmine was pretty, you know? Popular around here, that's for sure. Curly hair. Really wild. The johns loved it.'

'Curly Sue,' Georgia whispered. From the diary. And Curly Sue was surely killed. With all the attention. Maybe she knew too much? She said: 'I need to know a bit more about this Jasmine…'

Someone rapped at the window, startling the pair of them. Georgia turned. There was a young, handsome man behind the glass. He had a clean-shaven, gym-honed look, impeccably groomed, and was wearing a suit that caught the light, as velvet or fine felt might. He might have been a contestant on a reality TV show she'd never heard of. The face was familiar in a way that filled Georgia with dread.

'What is it?' she said, keeping the window down.

The man grinned, and then pointed at Judy. 'You've got my property in there, love.'

'She's no one's property,' Georgia said. But the young man ignored her, and went around to the passenger side.

Judy looked terrified. Then to Georgia's astonishment, she wound down the window.

'We're just chatting,' Judy said, in a faux-bright voice on the verge of crumpling. 'I know this lady. She's taking me for a chicken feast.'

'Is she now?' said the young man, leaning his elbows on the inside of the open window. 'She looks like that mad old bird who was shouting and bawling over on Bewley Street the other night. You are, aren't you? The mother of that lass who went missing.'

'I'm trying to find my daughter,' Georgia said. She pulled out the photo. 'This is her. Her name was Stephanie. She…'

'I know who your daughter is. Seen it on the telly.' The young man spat out the corner of his mouth. 'Had that picture shoved in my face for two years. They not found her yet?'

'No. I was talking to Judy here; she knows about Stephanie.'

The young man nodded absently, then turned to Judy abruptly. He made a walking gesture with his forefingers on the door. 'Out you come, princess.'

Judy opened the door and got out. The young man in the sports coat smiled at Georgia. 'Good luck, love. I'm afraid Judy's too busy to have a chicken dinner. We'll have one for you later, though.' He laid a fraternal hand on Judy's shoulder; with the other he groped inside her jacket, brusque and crude, until he pulled out some notes. 'We'll have a chicken dinner, won't we, Judes?'

Judy said nothing. She allowed the young man in the sports coat to lead her away. Georgia triggered the button that brought the passenger-side window back up, took several deep breaths, and waited for the bells to stop ringing in her head.

She was exhausted. But something in the nerves was still going. She finished the note on her phone's memo pad.

'Party. Chessington. Working girls.' Then: *'Jasmine'*.

25

Everything's set. I could include a map at this point; I'll need to speak to someone who knows graphics.

From Stephanie Healey's untitled project notes, included in the diary

DI Hurlford gulped down at his coffee as if he needed it. He'd shaved, but the blue of his fine-cropped stubble matched the circles under his eyes. Georgia's first thought was that he had been out the night before. He scratched at his chin and said: 'I can only spare you a few minutes.'

'It's all I need.'

They were in the same coffee shop where Georgia had met Tony Sillars, the lecturer. It was quiet, apart from an elderly man, who had complained bitterly about the froth on top of his latte.

Georgia opened her phone and spun it around, highlighting a scan. 'I told you about Stephanie's project – the writing scheme. And how I think it's connected. I gave you copies of the diary she wrote, where she mentions it. Have you read it?'

'It's being looked at by several detectives.'

'That's not what I asked you. I said, "Have you read it?"'

Hurlford drummed his fingers; his nostrils fluttered as he took a deep breath. 'I've looked at bits and pieces of it.'

'Well. You'll be familiar with "Cornfed". We spoke about it before.'

'Yes.'

'I know what Cornfed is. Cornfed is heroin.'

Hurlford said nothing. He took the handle of his coffee cup between thumb and forefinger, but did not lift it towards his lips.

'Stephanie wasn't talking about a person at all. She was talking about drugs. Stephanie had gotten into drugs.'

'This was one area we were exploring.'

'So you knew. My daughter was on heroin, and no one thought to explain this to me, or make it clear?'

'We have to keep a number of things out of the public eye, Mrs Healey, when it comes to investigations like this. That sometimes means shutting out close family members, as well as the press and the general public. It isn't nice, but...'

'My daughter was on heroin!' She meant to keep her voice down to a whisper, but it came out as a hiss. '*My* daughter! And you didn't think this was worth telling me? What, did you think I'd go to the papers with it?'

'That was one angle we were keen to keep away from the press, yes.'

'What if I *had* gone to the papers? Surely it would have helped the inquiry? Jogged people's memories?'

Hurlford took a moment to consider his response. 'In inquiries of this type, if there has been some foul play – and

I would stress, this is not my belief – then it is important that you project the right image to the public.'

'Meaning what?'

'Sometimes, if there are lifestyle issues that your average newspaper reader might make a judgement about, rightly or wrongly, then it can hinder an inquiry.'

'Lifestyle issues,' Georgia echoed. She felt the tears coming again – but underpinned by something else. Brittle, icy fury.

'In a word, sexism, Mrs Healey. Had we made it public that your daughter had developed issues with drugs, then it makes it less likely that people might come forward. Public sympathy can lead to more people getting involved, as a result of more favourable press coverage. Painting someone as a drug addict can lead to editors losing interest, and from there, the public can lose interest. It wasn't relevant to Stephanie going missing.'

'How could it not be relevant?' Georgia spluttered.

'Because here is what I believe happened to Stephanie. I am not alone in this. We've gone over everything, and I mean everything. Stephanie was a depressive – you know this as well as anyone.'

'She had one or two issues but that is hardly the defining…'

'By definition, Mrs Healey, she was a depressive. She had sought treatment for it. She had sought treatment for it while she was a student in Ferngate. It was made worse by the fact that she had, for whatever reason, gotten herself into the drugs scene. During the week or so before she went missing, she had tried to come off it. She was not a heavy user, but I don't have to tell a medical professional about the dangers of withdrawal, especially after they had developed a dependency. She was suffering from severe depression. So here's what happened. She left her room in the halls of residence. She switched the phone off, left it behind. That point is very important: think about why someone would do that. Who leaves their phone behind, these days?

'She was seen leaving the building by several witnesses and her path was fully traced through CCTV. During a heavy storm, she walked up that road, whereabouts unknown. We don't know why she did this. There may have been extenuating circumstances – there was some trouble within her social circle that night. We know all about this – every bit of it. Regardless, she walked up that road, and it is my belief that she did this in order to kill herself. She did it at St Anthony's Ghyll, which would have been inundated with water at the time. She may have been swept out as far as Paveley Weir, which was also inundated that night, and it is more than possible she went into the River Dalton and from there could have been swept out to sea.

'There may have been foul play; it's a possibility. She may have met someone on that road who picked her up – perhaps this was even done with the best intentions. But we've traced every single vehicle that drove up that road, triangulated between several CCTV points, and we are satisfied that none of them had anything to do with what happened to Stephanie. The last points of contact all point to her walking up to St Anthony's Ghyll, And I truly believe that's where it ended. Her issues with drugs were a factor in what happened, but the simple cause and effect was – Stephanie intended to take her own life. And she did.'

He sat back, cleared his throat, and gazed at a spot over

Georgia's shoulder. She wanted to grip him by the face, to scream at him. Instead she said, in a calm voice borrowed from someone else: 'This is all circumstantial, isn't it?'

'It's circumstantial, but it's persuasive. I won't go over the amount of manpower or the number of hours people have put into this. But you better know this.' He stabbed a finger at his own chest. 'I've broken my back to find out what happened to Stephanie. Worked unimaginable hours. And my God, look... for what it's worth, I'm a professional, but I'm also a dad. I don't know what you're going through, but I have a good idea. I would have moved the mountains to find out what happened to Stephanie. I'd have dried up the river. But that's the best I've got. It isn't an idle fancy.'

'But it's still circumstantial. And following that line of thinking... You have Stephanie's writings, don't you? Her poems, the short stories, the little tales she'd write. I've seen them. You passed copies of them onto me, personally.'

'Sure.'

'She was writing up until the day she disappeared. Isn't that right?'

'Correct.'

'So if Stephanie meant to kill herself... Where's the note?'

He did not respond.

'My girl's life revolved around writing. No matter what issues she was having. Whether she was depressed or not. She wrote. It's what she loved. So where is the suicide note? Does it fit your theory that she wouldn't leave one? That she'd just get up and leave and not commit something to paper? For the world – or just for me?'

'I've told you all I can, Georgia. That's what I believe

happened to Stephanie. The conjecture fits all the facts. All that's missing is a body. I'm sorry – for what it's worth, I am so, so sorry you had to find out about your daughter's drug problem.'

'How bad was it?'

'Bad enough. In a short space of time.'

'And what are you doing about the source of the drugs?'

'I obviously can't comment on other departments or other detectives. Ferngate's drug scene is complex, and doesn't tend to advertise itself. Nor do I advertise the status of ongoing operations.'

'I'm not talking about dealers. I'm talking about the source of Stephanie's problem. I'm talking about Riley Brightman. Or Oliver Chessington Junior, to give him his Sunday name.'

'Riley Brightman had a brief flirtation with hard drugs, and soon saw the error of his ways – long before Stephanie did, it seems. He has been clean for a long time. He has voluntarily entered programmes of rehabilitation. He is active in recovery clinics and various other groups.'

'You know an awful lot about him.'

'It's my job to.' Hurlford looked as if he wanted to smile at this point, but thought better of it. 'Riley Brightman was questioned, in painstaking detail, about what happened to Stephanie. His every movement on the day she vanished, and on the days leading up to it, was checked and verified. His personal dealings with her were exposed, in every detail possible. The same was true of Martin Duke. And Tony Sillars. And Colette Browning. And Adrienne Connulty. And Scott Trickett. The same was true of everyone else you've contacted over the past couple of days. None of them abducted or killed Stephanie. None of them were directly involved.'

'You're missing something. I know it. You must know it, too.'

'All I'm missing, so far as I'm concerned, is a body. I am open-minded. I can be convinced. If the evidence changes, my mind changes, to paraphrase a clever man. But you'll have to do better than this. And so far as your suicide note theory goes... I'll share the details of a case I attended as a PC. Six weeks on the job. I had to break down the door of a shed where a man had decided to kill himself. Sunday afternoon. His wife and kids were inside the house. They'd just eaten a roast. I could tell you to this day how much of the roast he'd had, because they itemised every bit of it they found inside him in the post-mortem. He had been very quiet during the meal, his wife said. Hadn't said much. After he'd finished his food, he went into his shed, locked the door, blocked it with a heavy table that he used to maintain and repair his model rail collection, shut the curtains, took down a shotgun from a box on the top shelf, put the barrel in his mouth... I'm glad the wife and kids didn't see it. I can say that much.' He quickly drained the last of his coffee.

'Good story. But it doesn't apply here.'

'I must be going, Mrs Healey. I have other cases to attend to, today.'

'One more thing. About the girl they found the other day. Jasmine, her name was.'

'Long-term heroin user, Mrs Healey. Long-term. Worked on Bewley Street. A tragedy, but not the first time I've seen it.'

'Did you know Stephanie knew this girl?'

'Yes. They knew each other very briefly.'

'And did you know they had both gone to the party up at Chessington Hall? The weekend before Stephanie vanished?'

'Yes.'

'And this doesn't strike you as peculiar? That she kept it secret?'

'It wasn't secret. Stephanie had taken some work with an agency – bar work. They had given her a job up at the hall during Sir Oliver's annual party. She was looking after coats, in fact. This is all on record. She also worked a shift or two per week at The Griffony, with old Reg.'

'What? I didn't know that.'

'There's lots you don't know,' Hurlford said, quickly. 'And as for the girl – she called herself Jasmine, but Janina was her real name… And I'm going to do something unprofessional, now. I'll share this with you in strictest confidence.'

Hurlford pulled out a phone, and after a quick search – and a scan of the room to make sure no one else could see – he showed Georgia an image.

'This is her, after we found her at the deserted farmland. In an old barn, in fact. I'm sorry if this disturbs you.'

Georgia's expression hadn't changed. 'I'm a doctor. It's possible I've seen more bodies than you. If you want horror stories, I've got them.'

'She took a bad batch of heroin. Several other people became ill with it. Two others died. But Jasmine, as you can see there, was quite frail to begin with. The farmhouse has been derelict for years. It was a known place where users would squat.'

'And? What's the point of showing me this? To shock me?'

'She fell, Mrs Healey. She lost her way. That's what I'm trying to point out. It was horribly routine. I've seen it before. I'll see it again. There's no link between Jasmine's death and Stephanie's disappearance.'

'I never said there was.'

'But you were working up to it. I can tell, Mrs Healey.'

'Let's move on to the other unexplained thing, which I didn't know about until recently. What do you know of this party?'

He waited for her to continue.

'At Chessington Hall. All the big nobs go there, I'm told. Surely you know about it?'

'Of course I know about it. It's a big event on the social calendar up here.'

'Did you know prostitutes go there? That they were there, alongside Stephanie? What goes on up there, exactly? What sort of party is it?'

Hurlford snorted in astonishment. 'It's a charity event, Mrs Healey. Black tie. It's exclusive, sure, I'll give you that. But it's not secretive. It's just a party, an annual event. The spring ball. Been going on hundreds of years, in some form or other.'

'Oh, it's secretive all right. If it's a charity event, then why isn't it publicised? Why doesn't anyone know anything about it, bar some girls on Bewley Street?'

'It's a private party, Mrs Healey. And it has nothing to do with what happened to Stephanie. As I say – every movement has been checked. Every theory has been gamed out. Every piece of evidence has been weighed up and verified as far as possible. Stephanie worked on the cloakroom at Chessington Hall. She was one of dozens of temporary staff who got a job there that night. There'll be a few people working there this weekend, in fact. There's nothing sinister or unusual about it.'

Georgia sighed. 'I can see I'm not going to convince you. How could I convince someone who knows everything?'

'I wouldn't claim that. But I do know most things. Mrs Healey... Georgia... I'm sorry,' he said. His voice grew thick; he reached out on a sudden impulse and took her hand. 'I truly am. I want this case resolved. I want it over with. I want you to move on with your life. The toll is unimaginable. You're bereft, but you can't grieve. You know, but you aren't certain. It's corrosive, it's poison. I wish for better things for you. I really do. I'm sorry.'

He got up without another word, and left. Georgia sat back, stunned.

That's it, she thought. *That's it. That's all.*

Her own coffee lay still and dark in the cup, untouched since she'd laid it down on the table.

No. Not all, she thought.

She turned to her phone and looked up a number. On impulse, she dialled it.

It was picked up on the first ring, and a slightly harried-sounding young man said: 'Hi there. *Ferngate Ferret*, Ivan Bell here, music journalist, raconteur and warrior.'

'Just the man I want to speak to.'

26

*Neb and me… Neb and Magpie… Magpie and Ragdolly
Morticia… I'm really bored of this. I never much liked
soap operas. Time to burn it all down.*

From the diary of Stephanie Healey

'So – Adrienne's not back today?' Georgia asked.

Ivan Bell sat back in his seat, hands behind his head.
He was a pudgy lad wearing a shirt that was too tight
around the middle, with a couple of buttons taking on a lot
of strain. His hairstyle looked all wrong, too, long, straggly
curls that he was constantly blowing out of his eyes.

'Well,' he said, rolling his eyes, 'it's a safe bet that Adrienne
won't be back today. Or tomorrow. Or the day after that.
She's always got something on, has Adrienne.'

'Who runs the paper, then?'

Ivan beamed. 'What, on the ground, you mean? Day to
day? That kind of thing? The guy in the know? The man
with the plan? You're looking at him.'

'And her,' came another voice, at the far side of the
office. It came from a strikingly beautiful black girl with
close-cropped hair. Her skin tone, chin and cheekbones as

well as a slender neck was so striking that Georgia was sure she'd seen her somewhere before. Not more than twenty, she guessed. 'At the moment, you're looking at the senior editorial staff of the *Ferret*. While the, eh, senior editor does something else. Doing something else is what she does very well. It might be her talent, in fact. If she wasn't so good at other things.'

'Forgive my sexism,' Ivan said, 'this is Maria, the senior news reporter. Get a close look at her, because this face is going to be on the front cover of *Vogue*, mark my words. Come on, stand up...'

Maria waved him away, grinning.

'Aw, she's shy, but she shouldn't be, you know what I mean? Just look at her, for Christ's sake. Is that Britain's next top model, or what?'

Georgia couldn't help but smile. 'Going back to Adrienne...'

Ivan blew his fringe away from his forehead and folded his arms. 'Do we need to?'

'I'm afraid so. I need to know a little bit more about a project she was working on... Going back a couple of years, now. Do you have an archive or something – you know, files backed up on your editorial system?'

'Oh.' Ivan pursed his lips; looked over to Maria for guidance. 'You wouldn't be Stephanie Healey's mother, would you?'

'Yes, I would.'

'Well this is a bit...' He shared a glance with Maria. The tall girl got out of her seat and came over. She glared at Georgia as she crossed the office with a lethal, feline insouciance. *They must be friends*, she thought;

Adrienne Connulty would make friends with this girl, on the spot.

But then Maria pulled up a chair, sitting close to the only other people in the *Ferret*'s offices, and smiled. 'Yeah, there's an archive, Mrs Healey. Adrienne was looking through it the other day, in fact. She found pictures of your daughter. She was very beautiful.'

Georgia blushed, and stammered: 'Well, thank you. That's a kind, uh...'

'Thing is,' Ivan said, grinning, leaning close enough for Georgia to see a sesame seed lodged between his two front teeth, 'we've been in the archives, too. And not just the computer archives.'

'And we found one or two things,' Maria said.

Georgia became serious. She wanted to clutch the tall girl's arm. 'What about?'

'Well...' Maria checked over her shoulder. Someone walked past the frosted glass of the office door. After the silhouette had passed without pause, she said: 'We found out that our esteemed editor had ripped off your daughter.'

'How?'

'Stole from her,' Ivan said, his mouth twitching with the sheer excitement of it. 'Plagiarism. She stole an article. Stephanie had been working on something for the *Ferret* – an exposé of how badly sex workers are treated in Ferngate. How they get trafficked here; how they get put out on the streets and expected to earn back their fare. Straight up and down modern slavery.'

'Does that article sound familiar?' Maria asked, steepling her eyebrows.

'Well… I knew Adrienne had taken the idea, I mean that wasn't new…'

'Yeah, but she took it word for word. Verbatim. Adrienne took the report that Stephanie had filed, the interviews she'd conducted… Word for word, she copied it, after Stephanie disappeared. It had been meant to go in the last issue of the *Ferret* before end of term. Next thing we know, it's ended up on a national tabloid with Adrienne's face gurning alongside it.'

'How did you get this file? Was it on a computer?'

'No,' Maria said. 'It was hard copies, annotated, with Stephanie's handwriting. I can show you if you'd like.'

'How did you get a hold of it?'

'It was left in a filing cabinet. Adrienne's not that stupid… but she is quite stupid.' The tall girl grinned. 'She's great at giving the impression she's in control, but in actual fact she's all over the place, most of the time. She locked Stephanie's handwritten notes and a printout of what she'd written inside her filing cabinet. She didn't realise that there's a universal key for it – so we had a look one day. It's all in there. The printout makes it look like Stephanie had written her story on a machine in here, on the system.'

'No sign of it, before you ask,' Ivan said. 'We checked. Whatever it was has been deleted. Right off the system. No sign of it anywhere. It was completely wiped.'

'So Adrienne printed it off, and copied it over, and passed off the work as her own, then deleted it off the computer system?' Georgia asked.

'Yep. *Bitch*.' Ivan relished the syllable and its closing digraph, as if it was something he needed to spit. 'We couldn't believe it.'

Georgia pointed from one to the other of them. 'And how did you go about finding this out?'

Maria looked uncomfortable. 'Well...'

'We're journalists, is the answer,' Ivan said, unabashed. 'And by that I mean, we're nosy bastards.'

'And we hate her,' Maria said, nodding. 'Right to the tip of her tail. She's awful. You've got no idea...'

'I mean, the other day – that concert. I'm the music editor, right? The music editor. That's my title... I might even wear a badge. I could do, if I wanted to. Music editor. That's me. And she not only gets on the guest list for the biggest concert the Orchard has seen in decades, but she bars me from it, as well as the after-party, and makes me get a ticket with the plebs? Can you believe it?'

'That's not even the worst thing she did,' Maria said, head bent close to Ivan's. 'The other day the dean was coming to talk to her about something and she sent me out somewhere, to make sure I was...'

'Can I just cut in a second?' Georgia asked. 'How did you get the files you're talking about? How did you know about them?'

'We found loads of things,' Ivan said. 'It was just a fishing trip, I guess. We knew she just threw things in there then made sure she locked it up afterwards. She was always double-checking if we were looking, when she did it.'

'Which we were,' Maria admitted.

'This made us think that there was something locked up in there we should see. And to be fair... most of it was just a mess. Crap thrown in there, printouts, general rubbish. But there was some gold in there. We're left alone in here to crack on with doing her job for her while she makes a nice little career for herself. So obviously we're going to have a little nosy around.'

'And do you still have this?'

'I'll email you some scans,' Maria said. 'You should have them. I have to say, it probably has nothing to do with what happened to your daughter. But she was ripped off, we can say that for a fact.'

'Did you pass this onto the police?'

'Well… yeah. Straight away.' Ivan's manner grew serious, and he sat up straight. 'Could have been something worth knowing, for sure.'

'When was this?'

'February. She vanished for an entire week, left us to put the paper together…'

'And what did the police say?'

Maria scratched the back of her head. 'The copper, his name was Neal something…'

'Hurlford?'

'That might have been it. He said he already knew all about it, but thanked us for getting in touch.'

Georgia nodded. 'Operational issues. Gotcha.'

'We were going to pass it on to you,' Ivan said. 'I mean, morally, you know. The papers have gone missing recently, the bitch has moved them, but we've got scans and pictures of it. You have to know. You need to know… You should know that Adrienne's building a case on the back of what your daughter did. I never met Stephanie; I started after the summer, but… Well, everyone knows about that case. I saw you come in that day. She was very quiet about it… Course, I put two and two together.'

'Meaning I put two and two on the table for him, and

Ivan came up with four,' Maria said, not unkindly. 'I knew about you and knew about the case. Adrienne was very nervous about you coming here, in the lead-up to it. No matter how she appeared on the day.'

'Yeah. I think that's Adrienne Connulty, all right.'

'So,' Ivan said, 'now we've told you, we feel better. Don't we?'

There was a pause. Maria said: 'I guess,' but looked away from Georgia as she said it.

'I'll take a look at the scans. You've done the right thing.' Georgia smiled, kindly. 'Now there's something I can do for you.'

Maria and Ivan shared a look. 'What do you mean?' he said.

'I've got a story you might be interested in. An exclusive.'

Apart from the bar and coffee shop on the bottom floor, the building was lunch-hour quiet, that eerie calm a school building takes on once all the pupils have gone home. Georgia emerged into the sunlight. It wasn't everything, but it was something. Something new to think about; something to go on; a missing piece of the whole, no matter how trivial it might turn out to be.

Bitch, she thought, thinking of Adrienne Connulty's open, America's-sweetheart face. *Bitch is right.*

Georgia had only briefly clicked on the scans, but one in particular had pierced her defences. Just a single line in Stephanie's familiar hand, scrawled over the top of some photocopied transcripts of conversation with Jasmine. '*Hope this is OK for you xxx*' To Adrienne, almost certainly.

Georgia read the shy girl's hopeful tone, and saw in it the little girl from long ago, inviting other little girls around for tea. 'You do like the tea, don't you?' she'd asked. 'It's good tea, isn't it?'

Poor little mite, she thought, and choked back a sob.

And then there was someone behind her – a shadow detaching from the wall outside, something camouflaged, breaking cover.

Tony Sillars, his jaw tense, his eyes hard behind his pebble glasses.

'What do you want?' Georgia said, shocked out of her reverie, annoyed as much as alarmed.

'I need to speak to you, somewhere private,' he said.

'There's no one here, Tony, spit it out.'

'Come with me a minute, please.'

'I'm not going anywhere with you until you tell me what it's about.'

Sillars sighed. 'I want to confess,' he said.

27

In the olden days they used to catch butterflies by the dozen. It wasn't collecting so much as mass murder. These polite, precise Victorian men actually existed, outside of melodramas. They would catch them in nets, put them in jars, expose them to gases that might erupt from swamps on alien planets, and then, once the wings were stilled, pin them to a board. They saw nothing wrong with this. Even if the butterflies died by the hundred, in industrial quantities. Sometimes they'd even show them to their friends. You can still admire these transfixed flecks of colour at museums today. Their stilled life as a bequest, ownership passed on. And they would seem like the nicest, quietest men, these hunters. In other news, I wrote another poem on request.

From the diary of Stephanie Healey

Georgia didn't want to accompany Sillars back to his office. Nor did he wish to sit with her in the coffee shop. So, Sillars took her into an empty lecture theatre, after a conversation with a confused security guard.

Georgia remembered taking notes in here, with a spotlight

diagram of the four lobes of the brain pinned to the back wall. It was a grand arena, with vertiginously high tiers. The desks had survived Georgia's time till the present day, and were of course covered in graffiti. It was a place of browns and tallows, that would have perfectly suited gaslight.

He sat in the front row; she took her place in the row behind him, two seats away – far enough to avoid a lunge, and enough of a head start to make the exit, should it be necessary.

'If you're going to confess to something, I wouldn't shout too loudly,' she told him. 'The sound carries a long way in here.'

'I'm not confessing to a crime,' Sillars said. In the gloom he looked less than assured. Something had gnawed at him since the last time they'd been together in the same room – but it was a difficult quality to pin down. As with DI Hurlford, he was fastidiously groomed, dressed tidily and his shoes still shone – but there was something off about him, an angle on his countenance that didn't quite sit right. 'I told you – I have nothing to do with Stephanie's disappearance.'

'Then what are you confessing to?'

'We had a relationship that... crossed the line.' He swallowed. 'We didn't sleep together. But I kissed her once, after a cheese and wine event.'

'These cheese and wine parties. It's like the court of Caligula. The things that go on, eh?'

'It was unplanned. Not something I wanted to happen. Not something that I'm proud of.'

'Your next line is "It just happened," isn't it? "It just happened, it's just one of those things."'

'That's as far as it went. We shared a kiss. And it's not something I made a habit of. I'm…' He tinged a fingernail off the gold band on his finger.

'Not something you made a habit of. Just the once or twice, eh? Three times? A handful, let's say.'

'Aside from the petty morality, you have to appreciate we're all adults. I did not sleep with Stephanie. We had a situation that was… close. Too close. I appreciated that and I shut it down. You might have heard something else. You might have heard that she shut me out, or rejected me for someone else. Maybe even that I was the instigator, that I had come after her. I promise you it isn't true.'

'And the police know all this?'

'Of course.'

'And the faculty? You have regulations, don't you? You might not have broken the law, but you broke the rules.'

'As I've said before – there was no finding of impropriety.'

'Except there was impropriety. That's your confession, is it? Well, you've confessed to something I already know.'

'Partly. I also want to confess to something else. Intimacy. In a word.'

He reached into his jacket and brought out lined sheets of paper, torn from a refill pad. Georgia recognised the writing immediately; and also the drawings. Stallions in flight, manes flying away in the wind. Dragons, of course. A naughty pixie, floating above the lettering with a coquettish hand clamped to her mouth.

'Love letters?'

'No – poetry. We wrote poems to each other. Our relationship was… close, too close. I accept that, in person. I apologise for it. But it wasn't quite on a physical level.

It was closer than that. Cerebral. We enjoyed writing. We wrote poetry – she wrote poetry to me, and I responded. I don't know whether it was a game for her. I don't know whether she appreciated we couldn't be together in the way she wanted… The way we both wanted. But she wanted the closeness. She wanted to talk about it. This is… awkward. But it's true.'

'So, it was a platonic relationship? Apart from the kiss?'

'You can laugh about it, you can be suspicious of it, and you can hate me for it. But that's it. That's the truth. That's my confession. That's how close we were. And how close we *weren't*.'

Some of the lines on the pages ran faint; and the punch-holes were filled. 'These are photocopies?'

'The police have the originals,' he said. 'I think you should have them. But I wanted to speak to you, and explain. You mentioned something to me the other day, something about truth. It struck a chord. I've made mistakes, but I'm not dishonest.'

Georgia's breath caught when she saw something drawn in the margins of one of the verses: A kingfisher, beautifully detailed, standing proud, with a stickleback dangling from its beak. "We will dive," one of the verses alongside it began. "We will go deep in the river, and find our promised land."

Drivel, she thought, slamming the sheaf of paper shut.

'Thank you for passing these on to me,' she said, bitterly. 'Something else to make me cry. Something else to steal my sleep, and my appetite. It's one of these things that will kill me. Letters. Text messages. Emails. Fucking *footnotes*. Marginalia. It's a bullet with my name on it.' She wanted to dash the pages into his face.

'It's all I can do,' Sillars said. 'If I could take it all away from you, I would.'

'You can't do that. But there is something more you can do. More than you're telling me. You can tell me more about the fight and the love triangle... Or was it a square? I'm losing my bearings, in fact. There are a lot of points to plot in that one.'

'What do you mean?'

'Well, first of all, there's you. And there's Stephanie. So, you binned Stephanie off – against her wishes, you say. But she wrote special poems to you. Off the record, right?'

'That's fair enough,' he said, warily.

'Then there's Martin Duke. He adored Stephanie. She didn't adore him. Although they did have a fling of some kind. That isn't how he portrayed their relationship. It's a sore point for him.'

'That's also my understanding.'

'Then enter the rock star, Riley Brightman. Steamrollering them all. The caliph.'

This amused Sillars. 'Granted, he had his choice of the girls.'

'And his choice was Adrienne Connulty.'

His eyebrows knotted. 'Connulty? You sure about that?'

'Oh, she doesn't miss an opportunity, that girl. She sees what way the wind's blowing. She takes advantage and she takes control. That's who she is. Is this a surprise to you? For all I heard, they were quite open about their relationship. It wouldn't surprise me if it continued today. Casual or otherwise.'

He shrugged. 'I suppose that wouldn't totally surprise me, either.'

'Except it did surprise you – right then, when I mentioned it. So, were you sleeping with her too?'

'Absolutely not.' Angry, now. 'I might be a dreamer and I might be too open with people, but I'm not completely stupid. I can spot a wrong 'un. It wasn't for lack of effort on her part, I can say that for a fact.'

Georgia smiled. 'You know, this might be the first time you've told me something I completely believe.'

'That's entirely up to you. Yes, it was a mess. Yes, it was a soap opera. Between that lot and Colette Browning...'

'That's the girl who's with Martin Duke, now?'

'Yes... Dark hair, black clothes. Quite fragile-looking. Pretty, I guess. You've met her?'

'Once or twice. She was involved, in all that?'

'Well, yeah. She adored Martin Duke. It was clear from the very first. It gets embarrassing, sometimes. You see these things happen year after year. It's like a migration pattern. They're in an adult world and doing adult things, but a lot of these kids are, well... kids. They're still teenagers, in a teenage world. Colette was very young, very naïve. She told Martin Duke that Riley had been sleeping with Stephanie. I don't even know if it was true. She wanted to drive a wedge between Martin and Stephanie. Split them up.'

'And how did you come by this information?'

'Just gossip you pick up.'

'Gossip, from who?'

'Who do you think? Connulty.'

Georgia nodded. She indulged that feeling of things coming together. Of the pieces beginning to knit. 'Colette engineered the brawl between Martin Duke and Riley

Brightman? As a way of diverting Martin's attention from Stephanie?'

'That's the conclusion I arrived at.'

'And did you find this gossip titillating?'

'Stop being ridiculous.'

'Did you tell Adrienne that it didn't concern you, that you didn't want anything to do with it?'

'Yes – almost exactly in those terms.'

'And you didn't like being so intimate with your students when the consequences of all the friction and jealousy blew up in your face? Curious, that.'

'I've come here to tell you the truth – and I am telling you the truth.'

'Would you mind telling me a little bit more about the Hephaestians?'

'I'm sure we went through this the last time. It's a writer's circle – totally informal, open to anyone on any faculty. You just have to be a student at Ferngate to take part.'

'If I wanted to know who was part of the Hephaestians, then you could tell me?'

'I'm not sure that's legal, or within the rules... Data protection, and all that.'

'You just said it was entirely informal. And I refuse to believe you don't know who attended. You're pretty diligent when it comes to keeping hold of the material they produced. Like Stephanie's poems, for example. And the police must have made you go through the members' list, after all.'

'That's true. I can get a list to you. But I can tell you the hard core – Riley Brightman, Scott Trickett, Adrienne Connulty, Colette Browning, and Stephanie, of course.'

'No other people attended? Just those five?'

'There were others who put their name forward, but from that year group, they're the only people who submitted, and they're the people who attended the cheese and wine evenings and pub nights.'

Georgia sighed. 'I want to ask you one favour. Get me a list of people who put their names forward, too. Outside the hard core, as you phrased it.'

'I can do that for you. I don't know what it is you're aiming for, though. If you get caught doing something you shouldn't, like harassing people, then I'll deny ever having spoken to you.'

'We'll meet up again. You can give me a sheet with the names on them. Or you can whisper them in my ear, if you want to go the cloak and dagger route.'

Sillars thought for a moment, then nodded briefly. 'I can do that for you. I owe you that much.'

'It may be the very least you owe me, Dr Sillars. You have my number, I think.'

'Yes.' Then his expression hardened to the point of hostility. 'Now that I've agreed to what you've asked – I want you to do me a favour.'

'I'm listening.'

'Whatever it is you're trying to find out… I don't think it's going to provide any answers for you. There's no eureka moment here. There's no treasure map. I think you should give this up. And I'll level with you – you look terrible.'

Georgia wanted to spit at him. After a throbbing moment of utter rage, she managed to say: 'They did warn me you were a charmer.'

'You look as if you haven't slept in weeks. If someone

told me you hadn't eaten either, I'd believe them. You look like a dead woman walking.'

'That's a very interesting turn of phrase.'

'I mean it. I hesitate to tell you this, but I happen to give a shit what happens, so I'll come out with it. If you keep living your life in this way, you'll be in your grave before long. You're a doctor, aren't you? With your own practice? Get back to it, is my advice. Work hard. Work long hours. Think about other people. You've been given a terrible deal in life – I can't imagine what it even feels like. But I can see where it's going. Get out of this mindset. It's going to kill you.'

In a voice that seized her by the throat, having been perched somewhere else in the auditorium, Georgia said: 'The sooner the better.'

She left him in the gloom without looking back.

28

Silly kids, silly games. But the play can get a little rough, in our little group. Kisses are weapons, I've discovered. They cause casualties.

From the diary of Stephanie Healey

It took Georgia a while to spot her. She was in among a group of women about the same age. For once, she had blended into the crowd. Like them, she was still in her gym gear. She looked radically different with her hair tied back and her make-up removed.

Whereas she'd been anxious in her movements heading into the gym, her bag clutched close to her chest, now she was open, beaming and laughing as part of the group, her backpack slung over her shoulder. If Georgia had been this girl's mother, she'd have been pleased to see her at the centre of this scene, happy and relaxed and in lots of company.

The girl had changed out of the band T-shirt, ripped jeans and heavy boots she had arrived in, and now favoured those kind of camouflage-type Lycra bottoms that Georgia found a bit of an eyesore – purple, black and orange. Perhaps the design drew inspiration from the animal kingdom. Perhaps it was to baffle predators. On top of that was a fluffy hooded top with *Ferngate University* boldly embossed on the front – quite new.

She had her own car, tucked into one of the bays at the back of the sports and leisure department. It wouldn't quite have qualified for 'old banger' status, like the car Georgia had bought off an uncle who should have known better once she was out on placement in her senior years. It had seen plenty of mileage, though, and one or two bumps that were probably too expensive to repair, and not serious enough to warrant it – a parent's weekend runabout, donated for a noble cause.

Georgia caught up with her just after she slung her bag into the boot.

'Colette?'

Recognition was immediate. Colette slammed down the boot. 'What do you want?'

'I need to talk to you, if you have a spare five minutes.'

'I'm heading home for a run. I don't have any time.'

'It's about Stephanie.'

'Of course it's about Stephanie. It wouldn't be about anything else, would it?' There was a shrill note in Colette's voice. Georgia recognised it from years spent in the surgery, when she had to suggest an unpopular lifestyle change to a patient. As in that scenario, Georgia wanted to give the other person a good shake, but her training kicked in.

'I know it must have been difficult for you, Colette. It's not easy for anyone, when a friend just vanishes like that.'

'She wasn't really my friend. I couldn't say that.'

'But you knew her, didn't you? You guys all wrote. You

all loved writing for the Hephaestians. You had that in common, didn't you?'

'No, we didn't really have anything in common. I've said I'm busy. You'll have to excuse me.'

'I want to know why Stephanie didn't go to the cheese and wine night, Colette. The night she disappeared. The night of the fight.'

'I don't know what you're talking about.'

'You remember the cheese and wine night, Colette, don't you? The night you told Martin that Riley had been sleeping with Stephanie. The night it all kicked off. Everyone remembers that night, don't they?'

'I honestly think you need help. You're a sick person.'

'I *am* a sick person, Colette. Sick with worry, sick with fear, sick with dread. Imagine if every single time your phone went off, you got that jolt, and you thought: "This is it. This is when they tell me they've found a body. This is when I find out what happened to my daughter." Just think about that for a minute. This is every day of my life.'

'I'm sorry. For what it's worth, I would not have wanted anything to happen to Stephanie.'

'Except you did, didn't you? That night. You wanted something to happen to her, all right. You wanted her out of the way.'

'Shut your mouth. Crazy old witch. And brush your hair or something. Jesus. You look a fright. Have you been drinking?'

Georgia smiled thinly. 'Apart from one night just recently, I've had one… two glasses of wine. In the past two years. You see, I don't want to find out what'll happen if I have a lot to drink. I have a fear of that. Of doing something bad. I think I'll go off my head.'

'You're a long way past that, love.' Georgia had cut off the younger woman's path to the driver's side door of the car; seeing she was not going to give way, Colette turned and walked the long way round.

Georgia went after her, speaking to the retreating hooded top. 'I'm curious about the night Stephanie vanished. Because she was expected to go to the cheese and wine, but she didn't. And that suited you best of all, I think.'

'You're nuts. And if you try and stop me getting into this car, it's assault.'

'I haven't touched you, and I'm not going to. Just answer me this: how did you persuade Stephanie not to go to the cheese and wine night?'

'Keep taking the pills, Mrs Healey.' She reached the driver's side door. The car was so old it didn't have central locking; Colette slid a key into the lock.

'You arranged for Stephanie not to be there. And you made sure there was a confrontation of some kind at the party, while she was gone. You wanted to wreck the group, because you were after a man. I mean, making Martin jealous when you had it off with Riley, my God, that took some nerve. It makes you a determined little cookie, doesn't it? I think what happened was, you diverted Stephanie, somehow. You distracted her – or you set up some other meeting. Somewhere out of the way. Somewhere down that dark road. Didn't you?'

The girl's face quivered; blood suffused that pale skin, spreading across her throat. 'Shut your mouth. Just shut up!'

'All I need to know is what happened. I know you weren't there when she disappeared. But I think you were involved up to your neck in the drama that night. It fits. So, tell me – what happened? What am I not seeing?'

'You know what happened! So do the police! I had nothing to do with what happened to Stephanie – everyone knows it! Get fucking lost!'

Georgia licked her lips. Calm. She had to be calm, now. But it was difficult now she had the scent. Now that she knew her instincts were right. 'I'm on your side. Colette. Look at me. This is important. I need to hear you say it. How did it happen? Why didn't Stephanie go to the cheese and wine event? What made her stay away?'

'All right, I'll tell you,' Colette said. 'If it shuts you up, if it gets you off our fucking *case*, I'll tell you. It was a message system we had. In the Hephaestians. An actual message board. Not online. A cork board, like you'd have in your kitchen. At the department of English. Outside the refectory. We used it to keep in touch, to set things up. Daft messages. Cryptic things. We all had code names. I set one up for Stephanie.'

'What was hers?'

'Ginny Long Legs. I wrote to her, and I told her... I had something she wanted. I set up a meeting at Ferngate Bridge.'

'What was it she wanted?'

'What do you think?' the girl screamed. 'Her bloody Cornfed! The only thing she could think of! The only thing she could bloody talk about! She was hooked; she was an embarrassment. And Martin couldn't see past her. He thought she was God's gift. Thought it made her a poet. She thought it made her interesting. But she was a *disaster*. She went right off the rails. It took a matter of days. You should have seen the *state* of her. And she would have turned him onto it. She'd have ruined his life. She wasn't even into Martin, and she *was* fucking that horrible twat of a singer. Martin had no idea about that, none. And she didn't deserve him.

'So yeah. I set up the meeting that didn't exist. I pretended I was Riley. He had this weird script, I wrote, "No phones, no traces, just us. BAR." Burn After Reading. And she did. I also wrote some hint that the cops were about; that I was getting nervous. There couldn't be any phone record. That's why she didn't take the phone. As far as I was concerned, it meant she couldn't text Martin, and so Martin couldn't text her. It got her right out of the way. So yes – I wrote that. I told her I wanted to see her, and I had the Cornfed. But it wasn't me who met her, if anyone did. I was at the cheese and wine night. And I was with Martin from then on.

'I wanted her distracted. I did something a million other people do, every other day, to get that ungrateful witch out of my way. That's all. And the police know about it, before you ask. It wasn't my fault, whatever happened next. And you know something? If she hadn't been a filthy fucking junkie in the first place, none of this would have happened!'

Georgia's arm moved on reflex, a sudden surge from the elbow, as if a puppeteer had twitched her strings.

The slap was like a gunshot. Colette Browning sagged against her car, clutching her face. 'Oh!' was all she could say.

'What did you do? You silly, nasty little bitch. What did you do?' Georgia snarled.

'Get away! Get away from me!'

Before Georgia could say anything else, two hands gripped her shoulders and she was spun around, then hurled to the ground, the world twisting, then exploding. She sat up, and blinked, stunned.

Martin Duke's fists were clenched at the sleeves of his corduroy jacket. She didn't look at his face. She didn't want to.

'You,' he hissed. 'You again. Haven't you been told?'

Georgia stayed sat on the tarmac, legs splayed. She could only blink.

'I've a mind to sue,' he said. She felt droplets of spittle on her forehead. 'I'll definitely be calling the police. But I'll say it loud and clear. I'll shout it! For anyone else who's interested!' And he did, a terrible, deep sound like the lowing of a bull. '*Stay away from us*. Got it? Do not contact us again. Get out of town, and don't come back. You are over. So is your daughter. She's dead. What happened to her is no fault of ours.'

'Maybe not of *yours*,' Georgia said, getting to her feet. 'I'll give you that, Martin. But as for that trollop behind you – you remember, for the rest of your life… in the middle of the night, when these things really come back to haunt you… That it's *all* your fault.'

Georgia couldn't make out Colette; just an impression of a face in profile, comically marked with the palm of Georgia's hand, as the girl struggled to get into the car.

'Get out of here. Don't come back,' Martin Duke sneered. 'And don't say another word.'

'Dream on, son. I'm just getting started. Don't be getting in my way. Either of you.'

She did not get the chance to catch Colette's eye; the girl was already buckling herself into the front seat of the car. Martin Duke did not look back, easing his frame into the passenger seat. Then the little car started up and pulled away, fast.

29

I wonder what it would be like to just stop. That moment when everything fades out. I remember watching our old cat die, after it got an injection off the vet. I held it close, and looked right into its eyes while its inner light guttered and went out. I wonder if it would be like that. When you press the plunger and your whole life goes through the vortex. Everything contracting, everything black. It doesn't sound scary when I put it like that.

From the diary of Stephanie Healey

Georgia flew high overhead, watching the trees condensed into broccoli clusters, and the winding thread of the road pulled taut. Once she almost clipped the high branches, coming close enough to see them shot through with bright virgin green. More than once she saw her own shadow burning black spots in the heath as she banked this way and that in the sun. The irony was, she was a terrible flier in real life. She'd even medicated herself before one long-haul flight, that holiday they'd taken to Florida. She might as well have medicated herself for the holiday, too. But here and now, after she'd mastered a natural inclination towards vertigo, she got into it, and even knew delight as she soared, banked and turned. Took flight – that was the phrase. That was perfect.

She was sat in the car, parked in a lay-by off one of the high back roads, at the north side of Ferngate. Her laptop was plugged into the battery, and she was fully focused on the screen, her hands holding a peripheral joystick. Georgia was the type of person who never changed her ringtone, once she got a new phone. She only usually found out what she really needed on any handsets or computers and stuck to that. She couldn't have imagined herself piloting a drone, even a matter of weeks ago. She might have shown some rare weakness at this point, asking Rod to take control, or at least to show her the ropes. But a strange, natural fluidity had come in, a dexterity she would never quite have credited herself with before. She wasn't great with her hands, an attribute she had privately credited with the reason she hadn't become a surgeon, despite being encouraged in that direction by more than one senior house officer. But here and now, she developed a talent, or at least a working interest.

The dry-stone walls criss-crossed the countryside much as they had on the online maps. There was no disguising Chessington Hall on the overhead shots. Much as Georgia instinctively distrusted modern technology's insidious erosion of privacy, there was some democracy involved in that country estates could not altogether hide their location, their surroundings and their basic shape. But much like the OS2 map that Georgia had open by her side, these maps only provided so much information where publicly accessed thoroughfares turned into private roads. There, the 3D imagery and the precise kinks in the wires you could travel along gave way to mystery, flat images. She needed to know the topography, the magic OS2 maps could only hint at. She had to know the flaws, and the ways in.

She came across it quite by accident, distracted for a moment by a herd of sheep scattered beneath her like loose feathers in the wind. It was a part where a tributary flowed under a bow-backed stone wall. Georgia had a Scottish uncle who called such waterways 'burns', and this had stuck. Hovering high overhead with the dread persistence of a raptor, her drone focused on the point in the wall surrounding Chessington Hall. The adult sheep and their lambs nearby gave a good bit of perspective, and she was sure to keep them in view as the craft dropped slowly, and smoothly, towards the green grass below.

Strong afternoon sunlight was visible through the hole in the bridge. The aperture was big enough to admit one of the sheep, surely. Unless the breed was especially small, and the whole tableau was an elaborate perspective trick from a surrealist comedy show.

'That's the one,' she said to herself, taking the drone back into the skies, watching the sheep become tufted grass, become cotton wool, become snowflakes. 'It's worth a shot. Now: a new outfit.'

30

I just tried to put make-up on. I remember boys saying something horrible about me, something like, 'You can't get make-up on a donkey, can you?' Well, now I feel as if I've put make-up on a bad scarecrow. Or the scarecrow's wife, I should say. I actually slapped myself. How my hands shook; how bad I look. Cornfed. I wish I'd never met you, but we both know I can't leave. Still. I've got this job to do. I'm thinking this might turn into a book.

From the diary of Stephanie Healey

It was a bit of a squeeze, as it turned out. But she forced her way through it anyway.

Even before she reached the gap, she had considered not going ahead with this endeavour. This was the moment when she crouched at the other side of the wall, where she had been berthed for most of the afternoon. She'd come on foot, having parked the car at a tourist spot. She wore dark clothes – putting them on had felt ridiculous. Looking at herself in the mirror, she wanted to laugh. She was a facsimile of a cat burglar, perhaps copied from the pages of a child's picture book. A stripy top and a Dick Turpin number for her face wouldn't have seemed too outrageous an accoutrement. She had decided against the tight-fitting black beanie hat as she headed out the door into a lovely mild spring evening, realising that it should look obviously dodgy for anyone who happened to be watching.

She had heard voices in the woods as she approached Chessington Hall from the west side – ostensibly the wildest route through to the hall. She had gone through a 'PRIVATE – KEEP OUT' sign at a five-bar gate, and until she had reached the grounds proper, she had spent a good portion of her journey staring over her shoulder, expecting at any moment to be run down by a bull. But she encountered no one, until she heard the sounds of voices and laughter over the stone wall that bordered the property.

The marquee she'd seen during her interview with Sir Oliver was lit up from the inside, and shadows danced on the outside as people walked past the spotlights in the encroaching twilight. Music started from around 7pm, at around about the time Georgia had reached the hole in the wall.

There were so many ways this could go wrong, and she modelled all of them as she crouched and prepared to squeeze through. Her recent experience at the ghyll – that terrible squeezing sensation around her middle, as if she had been caught in the jaws of a monster – was fresh in her mind, and it struck her that being caught in this tunnel, and remaining stuck there forever more, was a possibility. Or perhaps remaining stuck, calling for help, until a sudden rain shower flooded the passageway. Or worse still, the ghastliest joke of all – perhaps she might meet a grinning skull in the dark – bones she'd never seen with her own eyes before, but bones that she knew.

As it was, she got to her knees, her waterproof backpack clutched before her, taking several deep breaths as she eyed the passageway. There was nothing much to it – two or three feet at the most – but it would be tight. And the fading light meant she was staring into a dark tunnel with no sign of anything at the other side. She got into the water, suppressing a cry as cold water clutched at her ankles over and above her boots. Then her hands were in the water, tricking down the faint decline. It touched her chin, and slapped her face. She gritted her teeth, pressed her mouth together, breathed deeply through her nose, and then went through.

There was a smell of mould, dank vegetation, and also of death. Undoubtedly, bacterial life forms that would have looked very interesting backlit under a microscope. Stones dug into the pads of her fingers, only slightly more unpleasant than the places where her fingers sank into unspeakable softness. And there was one part where the jaws of the trap closed in tight; she had to close her eyes and force her way through, the level of water reaching her mouth, then tickling her nostrils. She thought: *I will stay calm. I can edge backwards if I get stuck. If I can't go on, don't go on.*

Then her forehead touched metal.

That's when Georgia came closest to screaming. She reached out with her free hand and felt the edges of iron bars. Perhaps four or five of them, set into the gap, so as to ensure irrigation from the tributary but to block any dumb brutes and predators from trying to crawl through. Like her.

She felt a treacherous sense of relief. No option but to go back.

Then, as she released the bar, she felt it spring back just a little. She tried again, curling her hand around the bar. Thin. Textured – the smell of rust mingled with the other interesting scents of the channel. She pushed; it gave.

The bar snapped; it was almost rusted through. The others gave her more of a problem. She pulled these out towards her, thinking that this would make it easy for her crawling back out. Soon there was a gap, and she grunted as she forced her way through it, feeling the jagged edge of the broken bar slither the length of her back.

But it was soon over.

When she emerged out the other side, Georgia couldn't have said she felt reborn, exactly, unless it was with one eyebrow arched. But she felt a sense of elation once she'd crawled out of there, her front soaking wet and cold despite the warm air, her feet wet and uncomfortable. There, up ahead, was a thick line of trees with the marquee and the spotlit outline of Chessington Hall behind it. Every window was lit, and many of them had people passing through. Georgia hadn't realised that the treeline would be quite so sparse. On the online maps, and from a distance when viewed through the drone, it had appeared to be a thick line of trees, a natural border ended by the stone wall on the outside, which completely encircled the house. Judging by the stumps that angled out of the pine-needle-strewn forest floor, it would seem that some of these had been cleared recently.

Anyone looking out of that window could probably see me, she thought.

This made undressing even more of a fraught experience. She chose the biggest tree in the initial line next to the stone wall, and got changed into her second outfit of the night. This one was not quite so comical – and indeed, given its passage in her backpack, she had to be deadly serious about it. It might only have taken a minute or two to get completely changed, but she studied herself in a compact mirror, straightening her hair, straightening her clothes, making sure she didn't obviously look like she'd been dragged backwards through a hedge. Which might still happen, Georgia thought, wryly.

Taking care not to snap her heels, she stowed the backpack with her 'travel clothes' underneath some ferns. She had props, which had thankfully survived the trip in the backpack. Perfume and baby wipes had been another preparation she had made, but she doubted they'd make much of a difference when it came to the stench of the tunnel. So be it.

She darted from tree to tree, drawing ever closer to the hall. She was just about clear and preparing to collect herself when a man blocked out the light in front of her. He was tall, and dressed for the outdoors, with a heavy tweed jacket, boots and a flat cap. His face was lean, and hard-looking.

'You!' He bellowed, pointing. 'What are you doing out here?'

31

It can't be that bad, surely. It can't.
From the diary of Stephanie Healey

Georgia made sure to clink the glasses as she lifted them. 'Oliver sent me out to fetch some of the champagne flutes. We're running a little low. He said there had been a few left out here from earlier.'

'Out here?' If the man had a moustache, it might have bristled. 'Why would people be drinking out here?'

'Your guess is as good as mine, sir. Thankfully they weren't smashed.' She balanced the glasses on a tiny tray she held loose in her other hand.

'Quite. Well. Best you'd be getting back, now. You don't want to be out here when the fun starts, that's for sure.'

'Of course not, sir. Very good.'

She had no idea who this person was, or if she had cut the deference a little thickly. She had simply slipped into a role, one familiar from a lifetime of TV dramas and movies. It had been good enough, though, in that he hadn't seemed suspicious. There was only comeback at the end: 'Make sure you don't get yourself into a mess going through the trees. You look like you've crawled through a tunnel.'

She laughed, though her heart thundered. This, it turned out, was the wrong response, as he took a step closer to her and said, from a murky region lower down in his throat: 'You seem keen. Bit of experience to you, as well, if you don't mind me saying. And all the better for it. Ollie usually likes them a little young for my tastes.'

'Sir.' Georgia had a sudden inkling to run.

'Maybe at the end of the night, you might like to join me for cognac? Perhaps at the billiard rooms. That's where the reasonable adults like to go, after hours.'

'It's a long shift, sir. I'll keep an eye out for you once it's over.'

He showed no trace of excitement or furtiveness – he merely nodded, as if she had promised to have his shoes buffed before morning. 'Excellent. I'll look out for you. Your name is…?'

'Rachael, with an AE.'

'Well then, Rachael with an AE. I'll look forward to getting to know you later.'

She endured the brief intrusion of his hand on her back, gentle but still proprietorial. Then she made her way through the trees, out of cover, into the light.

The glasses and the tray had been props, a flimsy cover story, which had nonetheless gotten her so far. It was the only practice she'd put in. She had guessed the uniform for the serving staff, and she'd been just about on the money, to see some of the young women passing by the windows of the lower floor of the hall. Except they were all at least thirty years younger than Georgia, but they did at least have on white blouses, black shirts and black tights. Her heels had been a mistake – she cursed herself for an idiot for not thinking that sensible shoes were all the better for waitressing, and not heels – but she had gotten this far. One of the waitresses passed by with a tray of assorted drinks, and did not give Georgia a second glance.

Emerging fully from the forest, she took in the long, flat lawn, which had been studded with flaming lanterns, leading off towards the main thicket of woodland, at the other side of the estate. Huge gates at the bottom of the gravel drive and the twisting roadway were now closed, and manned by men in high-vis waistcoats.

Just off the main hall, the sound from the marquee made it seem like it was any other garden party or wedding. There were torches lit around the perimeter, giving the entire scene a cosy glow in the early night, a homeliness despite the vast scale.

There were security guards perched outside the tent, stolid and forbidding as Corinthian columns. Her natural instinct was to change direction, and was disturbed to note that this caught the eye of one of them. But they let her pass through, and she made her way down the gravel driveway towards the hall itself.

Georgia squeezed her way through a closing door behind one of the serving girls, who kindly held it open for her with her hip while holding onto two empty trays. 'Busier than last year, eh?' the girl said.

'Booming. Just as well, eh?'

'Surprised they won't hear the yelping back in Ferngate.'

'When's the main event, again?'

'Not too much longer. They tend to start after all the speeches are done, and they're just about over with.'

'Hope we get to see it,' Georgia said, following her through a tight passageway towards the sounds and smells of the kitchen.

'You must be joking! I'm locking myself in here when they sound the horn. Last place I'd want to be. Hey – let me take that for you. Whereabouts were these, then? I thought the tables were cleared.'

'Someone spotted them out in the forest. I was sent out to collect them. Ended up in a bit of a mess. Look at my tights.'

'Christ, you were taking a chance out there, love. Here, just balance the tray on the top of that plate – your tights are fine, but I'd go and sort your shoes out, if I was you,' she said, kindly. 'Oliver hates it when the staff don't scrub up right. Take a few minutes, if you can.'

'That's kind of you.' Georgia took a left turn back into what she suspected was the main hall, cursing the sound of her heels on the floor. She remembered a bathroom on the bottom floor, where she spoke to Sir Oliver the other day. The place was intimidatingly bright, like a hotel foyer. Several people in tuxedos and evening gowns were sprawled around the couches and alcoves set along the far side; one young man who had a whiplash fringe like a young Elvis was attempting a passable version of 'Wonderwall' on the piano. She saw the women's washroom, and made straight for it.

She found a stall and sat down on a seat, shaking, trying to control her breathing and rein in her pulse. She had only had a brief glimpse of herself in the huge, gilt-edged mirror borrowed from a Narnian princess, a flare of tied-back blonde hair and white blouse, but she dreaded to see the details.

From behind the door in the stalls, she heard two other women enter the toilet. Her tremulous breathing seemed louder than their whispers, but she soon tuned in.

'You been paid yet?'

'Yeah. Cash in hand.'

'How much? I hope you don't mind me asking.'

'Five hundred.'

'Me too.' A sigh of relief. 'I was worried I was getting ripped off. I heard some got a grand.'

'I didn't hear that. I think it's five hundred across the board.'

A low whistle. 'Some amount of cash on the go, here.'

'Look around you, darling.' At this, there was a jarring moment of recognition for Georgia; it was the girl in leopard-skin she's seen on Bewley Street.

'Well. It's nice to be in here for a change.'

'True.'

'Not a fan of the outfits, though.'

A harsh laugh. 'Fair play, you're spot on, there. I don't think I'll be asking to take this home.'

'We might not have any of it left to take home.'

'What do you mean?' There was a note of unease in that voice, now.

'Well, it gets a bit rough. That's why they're paying us.'

'They're paying us to bend over and then keep our mouths shut about it, darling. But what do you mean by "rough"?'

'After they let us go. They don't go easy. That's what I heard.'

'When you say don't go easy... what are you comparing it to, exactly?'

The door to the toilet banged open. 'What's going on in here?' said a harsh voice – a woman's voice. For a moment Georgia was back at school; she could almost picture one of her friends frantically stubbing out a cigarette.

'What does it look like?' came the truculent reply, from the girl with the leopard-skin outfit. 'I'm touching up my make-up, then I might go for a piss. All right with you?'

'You've got two minutes to do what you need to do – then you're heading out. Understood?'

'Heading out for what? A parade? Inspection?'

'Exactly right.' Two steps were taken – judging by the shift of the shadows beneath the stall door, Georgia guessed they were towards the girl she'd met at Bewley Street. 'Less than two minutes, now. If you're not out of here, you lose your fee and you get thrown out. And you don't get to come back next year. I hope that's all clear?'

'Yeah love. Don't worry. I'll be out in one minute and whatever.'

'Good. I am timing you.'

'Come on,' said the other girl.

Footsteps, out the door. Then the leopard-skin outfit girl sighed, and zipped up a handbag.

'You'll leave that in the foyer on your way out. And if any phones in your possession are still switched on...'

'Yeah, I heard the rules, love. Don't worry. I will comply. Are you a prefect?'

'I'm head girl.'

'Suits you.' The leopard-skin pattern skirt girl then left.

There was complete silence for a moment; Georgia

let a long, slow breath escape. She heard distant sounds, somewhere else in the building, and the almost subliminal buzz of the overheard lighting.

Georgia got to her feet. When her hand closed on the lock, the door rattled, right in her face.

'Who's in there?' It was the same woman, the "head girl".

'I'll just be a minute.'

'You've not got a minute, whoever you are. It's starting soon.'

'I'm coming.'

'What's going on in there? If you're in here, you're working, and that means you're coming out.'

'I'm busy at the moment!' Panic had crept into Georgia's voice.

Then she heard the lock to the door turn, and disengage. Georgia pictured it from the other side; a slot in the lock, wide enough for a penny, the doorman's friend. The person on the other side was opening the door.

She turned, fell to her knees and opened the toilet lid, just as a face appeared. She caught a glimpse of it.

And then she did feel genuinely nauseous.

She had recognised the voice of the girl in the leopard-skin print skirt from Bewley Street. But she had not recognised the voice of the woman blocking out the light in the open toilet doorway.

'What the bloody hell do you think you're doing?' asked Adrienne Connulty.

32

I wonder what the grounds would look like with row after row of statues in it. Women in veils, women with their faces covered. Wouldn't it look amazing in the mist? It'd take a brave person to walk through them, on their own. Who's the ghost – them or you?

From the diary of Stephanie Healey

Georgia expected a hand to clamp down on her neck. She jammed her face into the bowl, trying not to gag at the chemical and organic smells; and trying not to retch in genuine anxiety and fear.

It had been Adrienne, all right. In a camera-shutter moment, she'd seen that heart-shaped face, and a powder-blue trouser suit over the top of an open-necked blouse. She was dressed for work, not play.

And she had surely seen Georgia's face.

But then Adrienne said, gently: 'You need to get out on deck – that's the orders.'

'I'm sorry,' Georgia said, trying to make her voice thicker, more stricken. 'Nervous stomach… Maybe a bug.' And here she retched.

'God's sake,' Adrienne said, in genuine disgust. 'I don't want to catch it, do I? Please don't tell me you're working in the kitchen. You are, aren't you? Idiot. Get yourself cleaned up.'

'I'll be two minutes... I'm sorry.'

'I'm sorry too. Sorry you were born. What's your name?'

'Rachael.'

'Rachael what, smart-arse?'

'Rachael Quinn. Rachael with an AE.'

'OK. Rachael Quinn. I'll take note of that.'

The footsteps retreated. The bathroom door swished open and closed.

Georgia got to her feet, shaking worse than she had after she had emerged from the tunnel. A quick check of herself in the mirror yielded better than expected results. She used a spare clip to pin back her hair, the same way the red-haired girl had styled it, letting a lock fall across her forehead. It was the closest she came to wearing a mask; and how she wished for one at that moment.

She headed back across the foyer, cringing at the very notion of a powder blue trouser suit hovering into view. And then she saw it – moving out of the front door, and heading west, towards the mews.

Georgia headed right, towards the marquee. People were spilling out now, all men in tuxedos except for the serving staff in white. She stood near a large hedge fashioned into a geometrically precise gateway, almost completely denuded of its agricultural shape and function until she was close enough to touch it. She had a full view of the festivities from there, and there was no one else nearby.

The women were gathered in the long lawn and garden

space. There were perhaps twenty of them, with a variety of skin colours, although tending mostly towards white. Georgia saw that they all wore short white gowns, cut quite high on bare legs, and what appeared to be white pumps, even ballet slippers, on their feet. They were all young and beautiful; many were tall and statuesque, long legs and long hair let loose around their shoulders. They stood in a long, ragged row, chivvied by the same tall man in hunting tweed who had spoken to Georgia as she emerged into the woods.

Then she heard the horses. About twenty of them appeared, and a great cry went up, similar to the crowd effect on monochrome newsreel footage of a primeval football match, complete with caps waved in the air, as the steeds and riders appeared. The horses' flanks shone in the torchlight, and one or two bridled. As they trotted into the light, kicking up the stones of the gravel path like machine gun tracer fire, the riders became apparent in the light.

They wore red, traditional hunting gear and white jodhpurs. The only difference between this and a Boxing Day hunt was that they all seemed to be wearing sabres, and underneath the riding caps they had Dick Turpin-style masks fitted.

The riders hailed the roar of the crowd at the marquee with these swords. Georgia could make out worried expressions on the faces of the women on the lawn; one or two dropped jaws.

The horses all lined up, in better order than the women, at the foot of the lawn, only one or two shying among the former betraying signs of anxiety.

Someone broke away from the throng at the marquee,

a short, pugnacious figure who appealed for calm with his hands – and then demanded it, at the end of a loudspeaker.

'Right, gentlemen!' yelled Sir Oliver Chessington. 'Here we are, for the feast of St Walburga's Eve. If you're new to this event, I implore you – enjoy your night, get involved in the festivities, and have fun. If you're not new to this event... have your fun before the new guys figure it out.' He allowed the laughter to spread through the crowd, then appealed for calm again.

'Now it's incumbent upon me to make sure the up-and-coming youths of this country – men of prospects, one and all – to have their fun. I was told I should say, "Give youth its head," but I'm not that kinky, folks.

'There were also some suggestions that we should allow some women to ride this year, equality and employment rights legislation being what it is these days, but,' he said, hastily, cutting across some good-natured boos from the marquee, 'as I said, I'm not that kinky. As for our riders, who can say? They're here to have fun, and have fun they shall. So, without further ado, let's get this show on the road. Now I'm going to fire a live round in the air. If someone gets killed as a result, do feel free to register a complaint with the *maître d'* before you expire. Right! Let the Hunt of St Walburga begin!'

Sir Oliver raised his hand, and fired a pistol. It spat out a clear yellow flame straight up into the night sky; she saw the bullet arc into the air, white-hot, on its weird trajectory before fizzling out. She saw his hand buckle under the recoil, and the sound was incredibly loud, even carrying from a distance of maybe forty or fifty yards, and she cringed as if it had been fired at her.

The clenched fists of men bunched up as the marquee yelled encouragement. Whatever the man in the hunting tweed said to the women at this moment was lost amid the rest of the noise, but it had an effect; they all turned, and sprinted the length of the lawn, high skirts flapping, arms pistoning, towards the woods at the bottom of the lawn. The yells of the male spectators became feral; most of the heads in there were grey, Georgia saw. An actual scuffle seemed to break out among them. They were drunk, sagging against each other, jostling, almost exclusively white save for the red blotching.

One of the unfortunate women tripped on the lawn, sprawling face-first. This caused a chorus of mirth to spread through the spectators, a pratfall worthy of sustained applause. One of the other women, bless her, stopped to help the other girl up, and then they ran after the others as they began to disappear into the thick woodland.

The hunters on horseback stayed put. This tension seemed to whip the spectators into an even greater tumult. The front row of them were growling; one of them drooled openly, not even pausing to palm away the spit. The women were long gone, vanished into the dark forest.

Sir Oliver Chessington, a sly smile playing across his lips, checking a pocket watch for an unbearable minute or two. A born showman, he slowly raised the hand that still sported a pistol, sparking fresh enthusiasm from the guests. Then he looked straight at the line of hunters, and fired a second shot.

Then one of the masked figures put a bugle to his lips.

They released the dogs. A wave of hounds – mainly beagles, with the odd short-haired pointer and one or two

English setters – flowed down the same path the horses had taken, tails erect, yammering and barking as they picked up the scent. They poured across the lawn, yelping, heard above the shouts of the crowd.

Then the horses followed, one of them blowing a bugle, a mass of muscle and sinew tearing across the fields. The riders held sabres aloft, yelling in the wake of the hounds.

'Now then,' Sir Oliver said, as the riders began to follow the dogs into the woods, 'while the lads have their fun, let us men have ours.'

Sir Oliver pointed towards the landscaped archways and gates, where Georgia was positioned. He seemed to be pointing right at her, and she gasped. Turning, she saw that he was pointing towards a procession of people bypassing her, having come from the main door of the hall. She had not noticed or heard them, during the start of the hunt. It was another trail of women, this time dressed in more conventional, though perhaps not quite formal attire.

They walked towards the yelling, applauding, wolf-whistling phalanx of older men. A fair few of them broke ranks and actually ran forwards towards the women.

Georgia darted towards the far side of the arboreal gate; even in the low-level torchlight, her white blouse would have drawn attention like a spotlight. But it was too late. Someone spotted her; someone who was apart from the line of women now closing ranks with the men from the marquee. Someone else in a white blouse; the red-headed girl who'd kindly held the door open for her.

She pointed towards Georgia now. 'Yeah, that's her. The one I was talking about. There she is.'

Adrienne Connulty was with her, darting forward

daintily, despite wearing thick wedges. They added height, removed her petite quality, made her intimidating.

Adrienne spotted Georgia, and then stopped abruptly, recognising her at last. 'What the fuck?' she cried.

Georgia did not hesitate. She kicked off her heels, and ran barefoot along the back path, skirting the back edge of the marquee and the walled lawn, heading for the woods.

33

I passed the audition. Now all I have to do is stay sober and make notes.

From the diary of Stephanie Healey

Georgia ignored the pain in her feet – before she got to the rougher ground, anyway. The same way she tried to ignore the burning in her lungs, the torn tissue somewhere in her throat, its bitter blood taste. The woods stretched out before her, a thicket of impenetrable darkness. From within, she heard cries, the yelping of the dogs, and then a single scream.

Not that way. She turned, wincing as a stone dug into her foot at the softer skin somewhere above her heel, struggling to visualise the layout of the hall and its grounds – something she had tried to do earlier, in her room. There was a spiked gate at the west side, running along a single-track road; not an easy climb, but the only option she could think of. She began to move towards it.

Then she glimpsed a high-vis vest, tearing towards her. 'Hey!' the security guard yelled. 'Hold it right there!'

That decided it. The woods; the woods, with its shouts, bugling, horses, dogs and screams.

She travelled beyond the realm of pain in her feet. On flat, even ground, she was a lot faster than the large but unfit man labouring behind her. She reached the treeline, beyond the arboreal gates and around the edge of the wall, appearing in the flickering torchlight. She remembered how well the white gowns of the women had caught this light, how much attention she would surely draw out here.

The woods closed in like a grasping hand.

The boughs of sycamores and oaks bursting into life, as well as the thick hairline of the Douglas firs and other conifers, sturdy and verdant all the way through the year, had been planned out almost to the inch – so there was room for her to pass through, even the odd path to take. The ground was moist, although it hadn't rained since she had arrived in Ferngate, and it stung her where her feet were surely cut. She ducked this way and that, hoping to cover her tracks, or at least baffle whoever was following her.

A quick check over her shoulder showed that no one was following. She wondered if this might not have been the worst thing to happen; that they might not have wished to follow anyone into the woods, for all the money in the world. Then she ran off, trying to visualise the woods. They housed pheasants, she had read, getting fat ahead of the shooting season in the summer, but she heard no birds or animals in there. Except for one whinnying horse, and the constant yelping and barking. Again, there was a high spiked fence at the very back, but she might have had at least a mile and a half to cover before she got there.

That's it, she thought. *That's all I've got.* She would be lucky to double back towards the wall, now, especially if an alarm had been raised. Especially if the site foreman, chief groundsman or whatever the hell you called the man in tweed was around. She'd never get there in time.

She saw that there were silvery lights rigged on the trees at certain intervals, will o' the wisps that lit the way in stages, showing the ground's undulations and delineating the flat, steady pathways. Georgia did not trust these, and stole in among the trees. A million unpleasant things were underfoot – stones, moss, soft things, pliant things, then sharp things – but she had to ignore them now. There was no option.

A branch snatched at Georgia's shoulder and she cried out; in the darkness she hadn't even been aware it was jutting out. She might run at full speed into a branch, about eye level; she crouched low, scratching at a cut on her shoulder.

Then she heard someone approaching, off to her left.

Georgia's instinct was to hide, and she did, as best she could, behind stunted oak. She saw a weak, flickering white flame, seeming to reverberate off the tree trunks. A face came into view – a young blonde girl, surely no more than twenty, if that, her fine white hair as tangled as the vegetation she fought through. The girl did not see her. Her white dress – more of a smock, now that she saw it, crudely truncated at the legs – had a nasty tear at the shoulder. She'd possibly had the same experience Georgia had had a few minutes before.

Then came the barking. Two beagles tore after the girl and quickly ran her down. She cried out, a hand flung over her face, the other held out to ward off the dogs, as she went to ground, fast. Her dress tore, audibly.

Georgia got up to help, instinctively. Then she heard the horse coming down the pine-needle pathway. She ducked back into cover just in time, an overgrown fern tickling her forehead and stinging her eyes, before the black horse came into view.

The beast was pulled up short, flanks gleaming, an immense breed that might have been better ridden into battle, with its own breastplate. 'Heel!' its rider called. 'Donna! May! Heel!'

The two dogs backed off immediately, tails wagging, then circled the girl on the ground. Her shoulder was bare, the tear in the dress having been widened by the activity of the dogs. One of the creatures still had a flap of white material in its jaws.

The girl was sobbing, and still held her hands over her throat.

The rider dismounted and strode over. He removed his mask.

It was Detective Inspector Neal Hurlford.

His sword was sheathed; but he still took great care over it, one hand holding it steady as he approached. 'Heel,' he said, almost a growl in itself.

When Hurlford closed on the girl, she sat upright, sniffing. His voice was gentle, even fragile, at this point. 'Are you all right? It's all right, I'm not going to hurt you. I promise. You won't get hurt. Come back with me, it's over now. We'll have a nice night. OK?'

The girl did not respond, but got up, suddenly looking shame-faced at her terror. She took his hand meekly.

Georgia wanted to scream at her: *Run! Get away!* But she didn't. She hid, not daring to move, taking quick breaths from the diaphragm.

Hurlford whispered something to the girl, one hand on his back. Then he led her back to the horse. The dogs stood to, as he helped her climb up, just ahead of the saddle, before he joined her. Tears rolling down the girl's face caught the silvery light as the horse turned – a careful manoeuvre for such a huge beast.

Then one of the dogs' noses snapped up, and looked right at Georgia. Its tail stiffened; it bounded over, yelping, and its running mate joined it. Georgia's hands mimicked those of the girl who'd been pursued, covering her throat.

'Heel!' Hurlford called. 'Not that one! Heel! Home, Donna! Home, May!'

The dogs withdrew – reluctantly at first, then finally taking after their master as Hurlford turned back the way he had come on his horse, with his prize sitting in front of him in the saddle.

Georgia didn't even wait for the hoofbeats to disappear – she took to the path, heading in the opposite direction. She was aware she caught the light as she passed through the ghostly, insect-dappled silvery pools in her white blouse, but surmised that this was the quickest way to the edge of the estate, and a way out of the forest.

She grew more assured as the sounds of pursuit grew more distant; grew more confident that she wasn't being followed, and that she'd soon be on the road and back to her car in no time. The keys were still in a pocket at the back of her skirt; she had that advantage, at least. If she had to hit the road after that and get back home, so be it.

Georgia hadn't quite found what she was looking for, but she had found something that the people with the reins in Ferngate would not have wanted her to know. That was worth having. It might be worth using.

Then dogs barked, more than two, and all of a sudden, she knew the game was up. As quickly as that.

They closed in on her before she had a chance to determine which direction they were coming from. A sudden snapping of branches and a rustling of leaves wasn't enough information to make out in any detail, far less act upon effectively. Her blouse was seized at one arm, the material shredding; she wasn't sure what kind of dog the jaws belonged to, perhaps a springer spaniel, but she couldn't be sure. A smaller, more powerfully built dog had her by the backside, its teeth sinking in painfully, and she gave up. There were two other dogs around her, both beagles, both causing a fine row but not brave enough to challenge the other dogs for the spoils.

Two sets of horses' hooves beat out a complicated rhythm on the path.

'There's only one!' called out one of the masked riders, as he brought his horse to a stop. 'I was sure I saw two go in here.'

'One will do,' said the other rider, getting off his own steed. 'And I believe I've got first dibs, old chap.'

'That's a matter of debate!'

'You'll get yours, old son, don't worry.' He approached, and called the dogs off.

Georgia got to her feet. 'Fucking animals,' she hissed, rubbing at her backside.

The tall, slim rider laughed. 'Yeah, we've got them all.

Horses, bulls, and bitches.' Then he stopped short, seeing Georgia's face. He removed the mask.

'I'll be buggered,' said Riley Brightman. 'Scottie? Get yourself over, would you? We've got a live one, here.'

34

I'm imagining that place if it was a nature reserve; somewhere bird-watchers and botanists would go. A lazy boat pond, mayflies, herons splashing through the shallows. Somewhere you'd lie with your lover's head in your lap, and snap off the heads of buttercups, making living flesh glow, rather than making it livid. It could have been that kind of place.

From the diary of Stephanie Healey

Scott Trickett removed his mask, too, and walked through the phalanx of yelping dogs, oblivious to them. 'You have got to be joking. Seriously?'

Georgia said nothing. She backed away, hands held at her sides, as wary of the dogs as she was of the two approaching men.

'What are you doing here, Georgia?'

'Stay away from me, and let me go in peace.'

'She's not on the staff, is she?' Trickett asked. He reached out, and flicked a stray flap of her blouse.

'She's pretending to be on the staff,' Riley said. He had

grown very still. 'She's being a nosy parker in fact. Isn't that right?'

'Don't come near me, and don't touch me,' Georgia said, chin upthrust. 'I'm going to walk out of this estate, and if you try to stop me…'

'What will you do?' Brightman asked, incredulous. 'Call the police?'

'Yeah. For a start.'

'You're trespassing,' Scott Trickett said. 'You might have seen the signs around the estate, no? Either way, you're an intruder. On private land. This is the same as us creeping into your modest detached house on a red-brick estate. It's not allowed. We'd be within our rights to shoot you. Know what would happen to us, after we shot you? Fuck all.'

'Close your mouth,' Georgia said.

'Call the police if you like. There's loads of them here.' Trickett jerked a thumb in the direction of the horses.

'Shut up,' Brightman said.

'Don't tell me to shut up,' Trickett growled. 'Not in private. Not in company. Not even in your own imagination.'

Brightman said nothing to this. There was something in this acquiescence, in this restructuring of what Georgia had imagined the two bandmates' relationship amounted to, that struck her with sudden, solemn tones of doom.

'Is this what happened to Stephanie?' Georgia asked.

'I don't know about you, but I'm getting bored of this tune,' Trickett said, turning away in exasperation. 'For God's sake. Get it into your skull, once and for all – we've nothing to do with your junior squaw. We don't know anything about it. She's out having a swim, off the coast of Denmark or something. She's cuddled up with a pickled shark in Iceland. Give us peace!'

'I don't mean the night she vanished. I mean the week before it – when they held this party. Before she vanished. She was here. She knew about it, and she planned to write something about it. Didn't she?' Georgia ignored Trickett, directing the question at Riley.

'She worked here,' Riley said. 'Same as Adrienne Connulty's working here, now. She worked in the kitchens. She wasn't on the, eh...'

'The hunt. That's what this is. Some jumped-up hunt. You're hunting your women for the night.'

'This is a tradition that's been going on for hundreds of years,' Brightman said, indignantly.

'You could say the same about slavery, son. It doesn't make it right.'

Then Scott Trickett surged forward, right in her face. She smelled drink on his breath, something sweet like champagne, his beard close enough for her to reach out and pinch. 'Listen, Baby Jane: never mind the petty judgements. You think a nice Home Counties girl like you with your medical degree isn't a part of this world? This world shaped you, in ways you probably can't imagine.'

'Bullshit. What has this caveman crap got to do with me?'

'We own you, love,' Trickett sneered. 'We own your health boards, we own your industries, we own your money, we buy and sell the land you live on, we control your music and your TV shows and your movies, and Christ knows what else. This is the way the world works. There's nothing you or anyone else can do to change it. Get used to the idea. We're everywhere. We're in charge. And we're going nowhere.'

'I think Stephanie found out who was involved in this little party. I think she had some big names. I think she was going to expose you all.' Georgia felt something that wasn't quite courage rising in her breast, and wasn't quite rage. She expected Trickett to strike her at any moment, but she advanced on him anyway. One of the dogs began to growl. 'And I think she had you bang to rights. I think she used her contacts to find out about this, and she got in. I think what she saw shocked her. And I think she was going to tell people about it. She was going to expose you all. Now you tell me – is that a motive to make her disappear, Riley? What do you reckon, son?'

'Don't call me "son" again,' Brightman said, quietly.

'I've an idea,' Scott Trickett said. He drew his sword, and held it up to the light. The blade was thin, but not weak-looking. It was a sabre, not a rapier. It would cut cleanly, and deeply. 'I think we should do her in.'

Brightman shook his head. 'Fuck off, mate.'

'No, seriously,' Trickett said. 'We run her down, say she attacked us. Say she was a crazy woman. I mean, she *is* a crazy woman. Look at her, for God's sake.'

'Just let her go,' Brightman said.

'We can't let her do that. Think about it. She's got to go. Let's be honest here, Riles. We spoke about it before... This is the high we're looking for, isn't it? This is the buzz. Somewhere we've never been. It'll be a laugh. Let's do her in.'

'You two come fucking near me, I swear to God...'

Georgia backed away, and of course she tripped and fell flat on her back.

'You don't *swear* to God,' Trickett said, advancing, sabre held loosely at his side. 'You *pray* to God. That's what you'd better start doing.'

'This has gone far enough,' Brightman said. But he did not move any closer, or show any sign of helping her or obstructing his friend. 'Enough, now.'

'Executive decision,' Trickett said. 'For the good of the band. Now you, old sow, you'd better take to your trotters. Incidentally, just what was it you stuck in my drink that night? If you've got some more on you, I'd advise you to take them. All at once.' He giggled, obscenely, his dark eyes dancing in the light.

'That's enough,' Brightman said. He touched the handle of his own sword. 'Let her go.'

Georgia got to her feet, turned, and took off, ignoring the dogs encircling her.

She almost ran full length into a tall, forbidding figure. She screamed, and fell to her knees. This new arrival towered over her, swallowing up the light.

'Not sure I like this party,' said the dark man. 'Not my kind of thing at all, this.'

35

The nice boys are out there, of course. Just the other day,
this blond boy held the door open for me. Sure I've seen
him around. But I don't get the time to chat, much.

From the diary of Stephanie Healey

Jed Mulrine, the gamekeeper, stood in the shadow of the trees, taking a draw of his cigarette. He was standing close enough to Georgia to reach out and grab her, but he kept his free hand by his side. He was wearing the same clothes he'd been wearing when he helped Georgia out of the ghyll. His face was unreadable in the gloom.

'Oh for God's sake, it's Stig of the Dump,' Trickett said. 'Something we can help you with, old son?'

'Nothing in particular,' Mulrine said. He nipped his self-rolled cigarette and carefully placed it into an ancient tobacco tin, before tucking it into a pocket. Then his eyes met Georgia's. 'Only I was wondering if Mrs Healey here might fancy taking a walk with me?'

'That would be fine,' she croaked.

'Hold on a minute,' Trickett said, taking a step forward.

'This bitch is trespassing, Jed. She hasn't been invited. We ought to throw her over the fence and have done with her.'

'What for?' Mulrine asked simply.

'What for?' Here Trickett's tone changed completely. The indie kid with the slovenly T-shirts and trainers was gone; now there was an edge to his voice, something of the sadistic gamesmaster, something far more apposite to his personality. 'I'm not sure I like your tone, old boy. I think I'll be taking this up with Sir Oliver.'

'I don't think you'll be taking anything up with Sir Oliver,' Jed said, affably. 'Especially given what I've seen and heard here.'

'Don't say another word, or you'll be out of a job before the night's out,' Trickett said.

'You've got no authority over me, son. Or anybody else.'

'But *I* do,' said Riley Brightman, 'and I'm telling you to back off, Jed. Before something regrettable happens.'

'Regrettable like what, Oliver? You'll have to be very specific. The same way you were specific with Mrs Healey, here.'

'They threatened to kill me,' Georgia said, emboldened now that someone was in her corner. She stabbed a finger at Trickett. 'This idiot here, mainly. But they were both talking about doing it. Actually killing me. And how they'd get away with it.'

'Oh, don't worry, I heard what they said,' Mulrine went on. 'Every word of it.'

'I don't have time for this,' Trickett said. He puffed his chest out, and took another step forward. The dogs encircled Mulrine, yelping, but he held his ground. 'I won't tell you again.'

'You won't have to,' Mulrine said. He held out a hand to Georgia, and she took it. 'I'll escort Mrs Healey off the premises. And tomorrow morning – or whenever he's out of his bed – I'll speak to Sir Oliver about what happened here tonight.'

'And what do you think's going to happen then, Farmer Palmer?' Brightman said, roaring over the yapping dogs. 'You think he's going to accept that from you?'

'I'm sure of it,' Mulrine said. His hand was warm and dry, and roughly calloused. 'I've known Sir Oliver longer than either of you have been alive, and I'd bet pretty heavily that he'll listen to what I have to say about his son. And he will be *very* interested to hear what I say about his son's friend. Top ten records or not.'

'You got an invite for tonight?' Brightman asked. 'I don't remember hearing your name mentioned.'

'No, I've got a job to do, Oliver,' Mulrine said, stressing Brightman's real name with some insolence. 'Your dad tells me to keep an eye on the perimeter. So I do. He knows I don't care too much for this little ritual. Or the people who take part in it.'

'But still trying to get an invite or two for your own tribe,' Trickett sneered. 'Feather your own nest?'

'It's not necessary, son. Now I've had enough of the chat. You'd best be on your way. I'll be straight with you, here – if you want some kind of confrontation, it isn't going to end well for you.'

'I think this clown's threatening us,' Trickett said. He raised the sword, and for a single second Georgia was sure the heavy-set lad would charge. The horses and dogs seemed to sense something, too, the former beginning to whinny in the background. The dogs drew closer, with the English setter growling, inches away from Georgia's hand. She fought the urge to shy away, to cringe against Jed Mulrine's side. 'I think we should chase him off the estate. What do you reckon?'

'Not worth your while doing it,' Mulrine continued. 'And I'd put the shish kebab down. Or you'll lose it, and your hand.'

'You're actually looking for it,' Trickett said, his voice hoarse. He bounced on the spot, preparatory to charge. 'You've got big balls, I'll give you that.'

'Nah, not big balls. Just a bigger dog.'

Then Mulrine hissed in the back of his throat. Something shifted in the forest behind them. Something that growled, loudly.

The effect on the pack of dogs that slewed round them was near-supernatural. They drew back and then retreated as far as the horses, who both became agitated. Then Mulrine's Alsatian bounded forward at frightening speed, muscles quivering along its back. Trickett drew back along with the dogs, his eyes bulging beneath his hat.

'Lower the sword, I said,' Mulrine continued, in the same nonchalant tone. 'It's for your own safety, son. Put it in the sheath. And do it slowly. Saoirse's a good doggie most of the time, but when she gets some live game in her mouth, it can take her a while to drop it.'

Trickett did what he was told, joining Riley over at the horses. After controlling the animals, they turned around.

'We'll talk tomorrow,' Brightman said. 'If you have time tonight, I would think about writing a CV.'

'Or a suicide note,' Trickett said.

'Looking forward to it, lads,' Mulrine said, cheerfully. 'See you then.'

Georgia let out a long slow breath. Mulrine let go of her hand and soothed the dog, whose tongue lolled out and who allowed herself to be petted, once the horses and the other dogs had withdrawn into the trees. 'I thought, just for a minute, there...' she began.

'Don't you worry,' Mulrine said kindly. 'Pair of bullshitters, them two. Poor little rich boys. Think they've tasted the seamy side of life. Think they're romantics. Or existentialists. Or whatever they call being an arsehole these days.'

'I've got my doubts. The Trickett one, he was more of a ringleader.'

'Bad influence. Always said it. My boy, he always got on with Riley, but not Trickett. They both got thrown out of school, but I always thought it was the chunky lad's fault. His father was a bigger clown than he was, mind you. Something in the blood. Too much money for sense. Hope Oliver... or Riley... sees a bit of sense and splits from him. His dad's a good man, you know. Whatever you've seen tonight.'

'I think I have to get out of here. Can you get me over to the dry-stone wall on the west side? I've got some things I left there. My car's off the estate, in one of the lay-bys. It's a fair walk...' She looked down at her feet, her shredded tights, the dirt and dried blood encrusted there, and quickly looked away.

Mulrine shook his head. 'Whatever you've got there, and however you got in... I'd forget about it. You'd best get out of here, now.'

'Will they let us through the gates?'

'Nah, gates are shut. One route in and out, with a barrier and security guards.'

'Then how are we getting out?' She had visions of Mulrine's hut; she did not want to spend the night there. She did not want to spend another moment on the grounds of the estate.

'We'll go in my wagon.'

'But the gates are shut.'

'There's another way.'

With Saoirse by his side, he led Georgia through the woods. She did not trust the dark, and did not trust her saviour, either. Her nerves were stretched taut, and she was suddenly exhausted, totally at the end of her rope. Soon enough, they came to the end of the forest path, leaving the sounds of the hunt far away. Then Mulrine's Land Rover appeared, hidden behind a thicket of brambles near the edge of the estate.

'This goes on every year?' she asked him. 'The women? The dogs, the hunting?'

'I'm afraid so. Tradition.'

'So they basically round up some girls, then what? Take them back to the castle and have their way?'

'Mostly. I guess you can fill in the blanks.'

'It's appalling. How can it go on? In the twenty-first century?'

'Oh, Sir Oliver knows it doesn't fly these days, he's not silly. He fears it getting out. But it's important for the local community. Brings in a lot of money and investments. I wouldn't like to put a value on the heads at that marquee tonight – or on their sons, riding the horses. Lot of deals get cut here. Lot of investment for Ferngate. That's what they say, anyway. It'd cause Sir Oliver more trouble to *stop* holding it.'

We'll see about that, Georgia thought.

Soon they were in the Land Rover, and Mulrine turned expertly and headed down a rutted track along a brick wall. Georgia was thrown around in the passenger seat, clinging to the edge of the door. 'Is there an access road?'

'Not exactly,' Mulrine said, tersely. He switched to full beam as the end of the wall came into view. Part of it was overgrown with what looked like wisteria or ivy, trailing long dark fingers over part of the wall. Then he stopped the vehicle and put on the handbrake. Then he got out, leaving the headlights on, fully illuminating what he was doing.

Then Georgia saw it. And she gasped.

And things fell into place.

36

I'll tell you a bit about my mother. We aren't alike, and I know this annoys her. She might have preferred a little clone, a dolly to keep to herself. I don't say this in any pejorative way, of course. She loves me, and she's intense with it, but it can sometimes seem a bit like hate. I've seen her with people who've been her patients; their diseased bits have known the rough treatment of her hands, you could say. But her manner with them is delightful. She can turn the charm on, when she wants. She's top of the list for patients – old dears, growly working men, awkward teenagers, scared young mothers, they all want to see her before any of her colleagues, and she's proud of that; she tells me this all the time.

But it can hide a very keen, and sometimes cruel mind. She's so bloody upright, which I don't appreciate as much as I should. She is a very glamorous woman, when she puts her mind to it. My dad has travelled beyond jealousy at some of the attention she gets, and drifted into indifference. Think he's marooned there for good, now. God spare me that fate – a dead marriage, face-down in the water.

From the diary of Stephanie Healey

The next day, Georgia packed to leave; though she had no fixed departure date, she imagined that when she left Ferngate, it would be sudden. She had barely slept for the remainder of that night, imagining at any moment that the door to her cramped little room would be barged open, and an unspeakable horde would burst in. Perhaps they'd even arrive in their hunting regalia; perhaps they'd bring their dogs. But no one came.

Her phone – carefully hidden in the room, and so far as she could see, untouched – showed that she had missed several texts from Ivan Bell and Maria Case at the *Ferngate Ferret*. She had meant to check in with them over the course of the night, but had completely forgotten. She called Ivan.

'My God – we were so worried,' he said, voice running away with itself. 'We were even thinking of calling the police, all these things were going in our heads...'

'It's fine. We still on to meet today?'

'Did you get anything?'

'I certainly did. But there's something else – something I need from you guys. I'll have to meet you at the *Ferret*.'

'I don't know if that's a great idea,' he said, uncertainly. 'Adrienne was on the warpath yesterday. I don't know if she's got spies, or she's actually spying on us in the office, but she warned the whole office about you and told us not to speak to you.'

'I'll bet she did. No, I have to come into the office. Do you have access to the archives?'

'Some of them, sure.'

'Great. I'm going to bring in a pen drive, there's something I want to look at. And some other goodies that you and Maria might be interested in.'

*

At the *Ferret*, Ivan and Maria were hunched over at a huge desktop computer, one eye fixed on the frosted glass door and the corridor outside. Georgia sat up straight, utterly relaxed.

'We need to be quick, here – I'm looking for the master file that these photos came from. There's nothing from the metadata on the pictures that points out who took them – I know what issue they come from, and that's about it.'

She clicked open the folder from the pen drive Adrienne had given her. The stark, black and white images had a stroboscopic effect as she scrolled to the top and made the thumbnails larger. She felt a jealous, proprietorial pang at the nude image of Stephanie – her languid gaze, the liquid darkness of her eyes, her utterly unabashed stance – but she knew it would grab the attention of Maria and Ivan.

Georgia had no idea how instant this would be. 'I know this,' Maria said instantly. 'I remember the shoot. I know what issue this was from.'

'You weren't working here at the time?'

'No – I know the photographer, though. He asked to take pictures of me. Modelling.' She fidgeted uneasily and began to stammer, as if admitting she was beautiful was a terrible *faux pas. Bless her*, Georgia thought. *Imagine if she'd been Stephanie's friend, instead of those arseholes. Imagine that.* 'So I, eh, I checked out his past work, back issues. To be sure he was on the level.'

'You're sure you know him?'

'Absolutely – but let me check. The back issues will be saved in the cloud. We should access them here.' Maria scooted in to take over the mouse and keyboard, and Georgia moved aside.

Ivan cleared his throat, and blushed as he said: 'Your daughter was beautiful. I want you to know that.'

'She is,' Georgia said. 'And bless you for saying it.' She took the young man's hand, and was touched to see that he was the one who was welling up; he was the one who struggled to speak. She wanted to smooth down the curls on his head. There had been a strange shift in balance, here, a subversion of Georgia's everyday normality.

I am close, she thought. *I am close to the truth*.

'There it is,' Maria said. 'I knew it. The fashion issue. I think that's the one where Adrienne started to make her pitch for editor. It looked brilliant. I think it won awards. There's a couple of them up there.' She gestured towards Adrienne's desk, where various trophies adorned the shelves.

'You know, I thought they were butt plugs,' Ivan said. When both women stared at him, he shrugged. 'She *does* look the type. I would bet on it. But, um, I don't know for sure.'

'Hey...' Maria frowned, and sat up. 'There are no photo files. That's weird.'

Georgia nodded. 'Almost as if someone has removed them. Her?'

'Yeah. Good chance of it. I mean... our online filing system's pretty basic. It shows you the pages that were laid out, the images used... but all the images have been pulled.' She tapped the pen drive, attached to the USB port in the desktop. 'Where did you get these?'

'Adrienne found them in a cupboard. Wanted me to have them.'

'Weird that she should have them, and they're not on the system,' Ivan commented.

'It is. She was rooting through an old filing cabinet, and found old data pens. It dates from the time of the photoshoot, for the fashion issue. What I need is the photographer.'

'I can tell you who that is. I can't totally remember the name. He used to do a lot of work for the paper, for free. Build his portfolio. Quite talented. He's a bit of a Ferngate scenester. Sings in a band. Not the Megiddos. Howie something. I can't quite remember the second name...'

Georgia swallowed. 'Blond guy? White-blond, I mean? It's like a baby's hair. He looks about twelve? Howie Abbot. That's the name, I'm sure of it.'

'I think you've got it. But that's a stage name. His real name's something else.'

'Don't keep us in suspense like this,' Ivan said, drumming his fingers.

'It'll be up on the Wall of Shame.' Maria pointed towards a gallery of sorts along a back wall, framed front pages, some blown up to foyer poster size.

All three crossed over. On the picture they were looking for, two models stood in the same monochrome style, their faces blank. The male model was mixed race and striking, but horrendously stringy with barely any fat worth the name on his frame; he was tattooed and bare-chested, an undoubtedly beautiful man but not healthy-looking, to Georgia's eyes. She scanned the wrist for pockmarks, and saw none. The girl beside him was similarly attired, her hands covering her breasts, markedly shorter than the male model but even more striking, with deep dimples in her cheeks, thick dark eye make-up and strong bone structure.

The type of irritant who would have no need for filters or flattering angles at the chin in her life; someone who *takes a good photie*, as her Scottish granny would have said.

FASHION SPECIAL, blared the headline, black letterboxed in white.

Maria's fingers traced around the edges of the front page, corner to corner, before she found a tiny credit lodged at the far right-hand corner. 'There it is. Howie Abbot.'

The sound of a door being kicked open interrupted them.

It was Adrienne. She wore jeans, a hooded top and a baseball cap, and her skin was even paler than usual, if that was possible. She stood, frozen, a disposable coffee cup in her hand, biting the inside of her mouth for a second. Then she shrieked: 'Get that bitch out of here, right now!'

'I was just going, Adrienne.' Georgia strode towards her, and Adrienne backed away, towards the safety of her desk. 'Hey, you look a bit peaky. Have you had a long night?'

'I'm calling security.' Adrienne fumbled with her phone. 'First of all, I don't know what you two fuckers are doing here on a Sunday. On top of that, I don't know what the fuck she is doing here, when I specifically told you she shouldn't be within half a mile of this office!' As she dialled a number, she glared at Maria and Ivan, in utter fury. 'You're sacked, incidentally. Both of you. Right now.'

'Don't bother. We're resigning,' Maria said, coolly. 'We're not doing any more work for you.'

'We're mutually assenting,' Ivan corrected her – though he bore clear signs of distress and agitation, fidgeting with the collar of his T-shirt, eyes watering. But he went on, bravely: 'And we should have done it within five minutes of meeting you.'

'Whatever. Get the fuck out, all of you.'

Georgia moved over to the computer and closed down the files from the pen drive, and then removed it. Adrienne came over, squawking; her coffee cup rolled loose on the floor tiling, the grubby blue fibres gulping her drink down fast. 'Get your hands off my property! What were you doing here! This is a breach of security!' And the girl actually hit Georgia then, grabbing her upper arm and then turning the gesture into a punch, connecting painfully in Georgia's breast.

Georgia ignored this, pocketing the pen drive. Maria moved in between them, shoving Adrienne roughly. There wasn't much in this, but she staggered comically with the force of it, making a hilarious three-point turn, almost losing her balance entirely, twice, before she steadied herself on a desk.

The heart shaped-faced scrunched up, a parody of a spoilt little girl's, and she broke out into fierce sobs. 'You can't do that to me! You can't! I'll ruin all of you!'

Maria laughed. 'You going to get Daddy to fix us? How about your big brother?' She winked at Georgia and Ivan. 'Time we were going. Adrienne, can we count on you for a reference?'

Adrienne simply screamed; the sound wasn't like anything that would be made by a human throat. It couldn't be classed as syllables; it couldn't be written down. It reminded Georgia of a sound effect from a science fiction film, where aliens could take people over.

'Have a nice life, Adrienne,' Georgia said, heading towards the door. 'Keep hustling, won't you?'

★

'Mrs Healey, I thought I'd made it clear that we had nothing to gain from any more conversations? Every meeting I've had with you has ended abruptly and I've been made to feel I did something wrong. When I didn't.'

There was no warmth in Tony Sillars' voice, on the other end of the phone. Cold and civil would be as good as it got. *I am not making many friends on this journey*, Georgia thought. 'I understand that,' she said. 'I think you've been good with me, Tony, for what it's worth. You'll have to excuse my manners, given the circumstances. I just want one more thing from you. That's all.'

He sighed. 'I had half a mind to just hang up on you there. More than half. Go on. What is it you want to know?'

'You mentioned people who hung around on the periphery. There's one person in particular I am interested in. Someone who might have had access to your special message board? The one near the refectory?'

'I don't... how did you know about that?'

'Never mind. You haven't done anything wrong, as we've already established. I just want to trace this person. I want to be sure.'

'What person?'

'Name of Howie Abbot. One T, if that helps.'

'I don't quite recall... I don't recognise that name.'

'Funnily enough, the student roll doesn't seem to recognise him, either. He's never officially been a student, it seems. He sure has been busy around the campus, though. And other places, too. He sings with a band called Prat Spaniel. I don't think Howie Abbot is his real name. Maybe a description might help?'

'Sure.' She sketched him out, in as much detail as she

could. 'Key thing to remember is the hair. I think it's dyed – pure, stark white, like that horrible trend the footballers had years ago, when they all went for a bleach job.'

'That kind of rings a bell, but... Honestly, it could be a dozen people.'

'He takes photographs. He's good at it.'

'Now, that is kind of interesting. There is one guy that could be. He floated around the Hephaestians for a bit. He was interested in taking pictures of them; he sent some to us, so they could be shared. Communal message board, just between the Hephaestians. From the cheese and wine night. I spoke to him a few times. He said he was into poetry. He submitted a poem, after we had a chat one time, but of course, I can't be sure...'

'Are you in your office?'

'I am.'

'Can you check? Either the pictures, or the poems. If they're in your files. This is really important.'

'Of course I can. Hold on. I'll call you back.'

When he got back to her, he had it. 'Yeah, he sent me loads of pictures. He took them at a meeting – it was a feature for the student newspaper. He sent me one or two poems. I think he was a songwriter, or wanted to be. They were nonsense, truth be told. That's never stopped anyone making it in the music business, but he was no poet. Abbot wasn't his name, but... I think he submitted a poem or two in his real name. Or a different name, at least.'

'Tell me,' Georgia said. Her fist was clenched at her side. 'Give me the name.'

She could hear Sillars typing at his desktop. Then he said: 'Yeah this is it.'

He gave the name. Georgia could not suppress a gasp.

'That ring any bells?'

'It does, Tony. Bells and whistles. Thank you.'

'I don't appreciate this,' Lil Baikie said. Her hands were linked across the café table, fingers digging in tight among their opposite number.

'I appreciate you're busy,' Georgia said. 'It is important.'

'If it's important, and it's to do with your daughter, you should go to the police. I think this Nancy Drew bullshit is going to land you in trouble – maybe big trouble. Just my opinion.'

'Stuff your opinion up your arse,' Georgia said. Then, not bothering to wait for a response or even a reaction, she turned to the girl sat beside her.

Judy was even more of a fright during the daylight, and direct sunlight. The yellow skin, the dark eyes, the wasted frame, and somehow worst of all, the posture, was something that most people would be instantly repelled by. She wore a long-sleeved white top that was clean, but the kind of clean that came with extreme old age for a garment, edging towards bleached. It was of a style that might have been in at the same time as the Spice Girls, and might come back any day now. Judy was amused at seeing the hostel manager abused in such a way; perhaps that was something Georgia could work with.

'Judy,' she said, 'I want to know about any photographers who were involved with Stephanie. Anything you can remember.'

'That depends,' was all Judy said. She sat back and

folded her arms, smirking. There were three or four painful-looking sores at the corners of her mouth; one of them was open and red.

Georgia took out a twenty-pound note.

'No – I'm sorry, stop right there,' Lil said. 'That's not helping anyone'. She reached out to intercept the money, but Georgia snatched it out of her way, and then proffered it to Judy.

Judy took the money, still smiling. 'Yes, there was a photographer. He asked to take pictures of me. I said no. He kept telling me again and again that it wasn't the wrong kind of pictures, you know. Sleaze. Pervert stuff. I told him I didn't mind if he was that kind of photographer. I just didn't like him.'

'Did he give a name?'

'Yes. But I don't remember.'

'Did he look like this? This person?' Georgia opened her phone, and expanded an image she had saved in her files.

'Could be. I'm not sure.' She laughed aloud, sitting back in her seat, and folding her arms. Georgia saw that some of her front teeth were missing. Under the streetlights of Bewley Street, or in the gloom of her car, she had not spotted this. 'It was a while ago. I meet a lot of men.'

'Maybe this will help?' Georgia held out more notes – two tenners.

'Oh – that's it,' said Baikie. 'Get out, Georgia. Get out before I throw you out.'

'Shut up,' Georgia said simply, locking eyes with the taller woman. Then she turned back to Judy, and said: 'This is the last one you'll get, Judy. Tell me what I want to know.'

She took the money. 'Yes, Georgia. That was the

photographer. I am sure of it. He took pictures of lots of girls. He took pictures of Stephanie. He was with her – I thought they were a couple, but he was so interested in all the girls, and in me, that I thought maybe they weren't. Or maybe that didn't bother her. Stephanie was a strange girl.'

'Thank you,' Georgia said.

'OK, we're done here.' Lil slapped both hands on the Formica-topped tables, making the sugar bowl jump. 'I'd get out of here if I were you, Georgia. Fast.'

'Sure.' Georgia turned to Judy, and held out a hand.

Judy took it. Georgia took a firm grip, then sprang forward and yanked back the long-sleeved top.

Judy spat something in her mother tongue. She tried to twist her arm free, but Georgia applied more pressure, turning the arm over and presenting it to Lil.

'Look at that,' Georgia said. 'Look at the state of that. You work here, you know what that means.'

Judy screamed, a terrible sound; other people in the café gaped at the scene, alarmed; one man got to his feet, but stopped short of coming over as Judy jerked her arm free, got to her feet, gathered her bag and fled.

'I ought to bust you in the mouth,' Lil said to Georgia, radiating menace. 'She'll go to ground, now. You might have killed her, doing that. It'll be on you.'

'She'll be dead before long. You run that place. You know the score. What are you doing about it? What are you going to do to stop this from happening?'

Lil stood up, her face twitching with suppressed rage. 'Don't let me ever see you again, Georgia.'

'There is a huge problem in this town. What are you doing about it? Table tennis clubs? Knitting circles? What is it called, a fucking drop-in centre? Drop-in for what? A coffin? These people are going to die. They already are dying.'

Lil strode towards her, and Georgia had to fight the urge to shrink back. The taller woman stopped herself from striking out, but it was a close thing. Lil took a breath and said: 'What have I *done*? What have I *done*? What have I not done, you miserable bitch! Sitting there in your fucking Boden coat. What do you know about life for these girls? I've tried everything, everything to get them clean. I put everything on the line for them. I have done for years. And you know what I've learned? Do you? *I can't save them all*. I'll turn one or two of them around, every other year or two. That's it. That's all I can manage. Apart from that, they get a safe place, somewhere to sleep, a place they don't have to worry for a while. Somewhere to get washed, have a hot shower, brush their teeth. Somewhere they can find new clothes, underwear; somewhere they'll get their old clothes washed. And yes – somewhere they can use safely, sometimes. Somewhere they get clean needles. Would you rather the alternative? Would you rather I rounded them up in a big pen, maybe? Or a jail? Is that your solution? Don't you *dare* sit there and ask me, Mrs Country Doctor, what the fuck I'm doing about it! Don't you dare!'

Georgia weathered the retreating footsteps, the front door crashing shut; then the alarmed glances of the other people in the café, and the short, buxom woman at the till, whose good cheer and rosy colouring had utterly dissipated.

'Are you all right?' a man asked Georgia.

She dabbed away tears at the corner of her eyes. 'Yes,' she said. 'I'm fine. I have everything I need, now.'

37

And then Stephanie the Selkie travelled far from the sea she called home to the deep dark woods where the troll lived. Every step she took on dry land felt like you or I standing on a sharp stone.

From 'Stephane The Selkie's Magic Journey'

You wouldn't knock on the door of the dragon's lair, of course. She had to be canny. In reality, Georgia wasn't canny, but for a little while at least, she was lucky.

After walking along the same old road, watching out for cars in front and behind as before, she spotted the fake gate within moments. It was a case of knowing what you were looking for. The webbing and the fake fronds looked ridiculous close-up, though they probably wouldn't merit much of a glance when passing in a car. The real wisteria or ivy helped to complete the picture, snaking across from the dry-stone wall framing the gap. It took Georgia a while to work the mechanism, but soon she had slipped through and closed the gate behind her. Even though it was a mild day with plenty of blue visible in gaps above the clouds, the enclosed space seemed dank and soggy, and the path grew steep very quickly. She was out of breath by the time she had bypassed Chessington Hall and kept heading north, into the wilder woodland outside the grounds of the house.

'PRIVATE – KEEP OUT', read one sign. Georgia passed through, although it had the curious effect of making her feel more nervous than ever before from that moment. As if she had wandered into a minefield. *Here be tygers*, she thought.

The old OS2 maps had brought her here, rather than online ones. When patients' records had been fed into computer systems, Georgia had once wondered how much this placed the system at risk of utter catastrophe – either through data being lost to software corruption, or leaked out into the wider world through hacking. She had always thought that physical copies, no matter how unwieldy, were a failsafe that they should consider having. So it was for digital maps, which she knew didn't tell you the full story.

For instance – the secret gateway out into the main road from the Chessington estate. Not even close to where Stephanie disappeared, but within the 'mystery zone' she had been witnessed and recorded as entering, but not leaving. No one who had driven along that road, so far as CCTV and eyewitness accounts could account for what happened to Stephanie. No one was culpable. But Stephanie had still vanished. Georgia had long suspected that someone, somehow, had abducted her. That there was a piece of the puzzle missing.

And now she had a theory to match this fact. It was in fact perfectly possible to drive a vehicle onto the main road, abduct someone, and then drive away. It involved a terrible risk, of course. The A-road was quiet, but there was still the risk of the odd car coming past, even at that time of night, in those conditions.

The person who had taken Stephanie had been lucky in this respect.

There was no mention of the kissing gate, disguised by wisteria and overhung with netting, anywhere on any map, whether digital or paper. It had been a fine piece of work; abutting two other dry-stone walls that were also overhung with greenery, it wouldn't have merited any more than a double take.

'Just a shortcut,' Jed Mulrine had said, when he got back into the Land Rover after opening the gate. 'Rarely use it. Used to be a kissing gate. It's a handy road to have, if I'm working on the estate. Saved me a good twenty minutes; means I don't have to head north and skirt all the way around and come back on myself.'

It couldn't be Jed Mulrine, of course. He would have to be either jaw-droppingly slack, or perhaps have some secret death wish, a desire to get caught. Psychology was not Georgia's speciality, but she doubted Jed Mulrine had been making any kind of confession to her when he took her through the shortcut.

Georgia had triangulated where the hidden gate was located, based on where Jed had turned back onto the road (getting out and closing the gate behind him before getting back in – an activity that took less than a minute to complete, from getting back out the door and then driving off again), and how long it had taken him to skirt back around town and get her to the lay-by, where, mercifully, her car remained. Looking at the O2 map, she reckoned it was in a slight dog-leg bend. From the topography of the map, there was no indication of the narrow, rickety trail Mulrine had taken to get from the woods at the top of Chessington Hall to the gate, and freedom.

But there was on the online maps. You had to zoom in close on the overhead layout – of course, there was no 3D close-up map to guide you – but there was a faint trail running along the side of another dry-stone wall, demarcating where the sheep grazed and the woods stopped. There was a road there. It led directly to the road at the north of the estate, via an overgrown gap in the foliage. Looking at the photos on the 3D map, it didn't appear to be a natural gap, and the path wasn't taken much. It's possible only Jed Mulrine knew of its existence. Him, and the person who took Stephanie.

Close, Georgia thought, stepping through the high weeds. *You're close now.*

Even thinking of Stephanie in a grave somewhere in that place filled her with a treacherous kind of peace. She needed that link. She had to have the guilt proven beyond doubt; to see the bastard answer for himself. To look into his eyes.

Georgia followed the rickety road, marvelling at the hardiness that must have been required in a vehicle to take it up and down the stony, uneven path. She remembered being beaten about by it, thrown against Jed Mulrine more than once.

Perhaps Stephanie had been thrown around too, on that wild, terrible night. Maybe at that point she still thought she was safe. That someone she trusted had plucked her out of that spot. That he had something to give her to take away the pangs.

She stole in underneath the branches of some stout, tall

oaks. Then she saw something that she was sure she had imagined for a moment.

A house, among the trees.

'Kidding,' she whispered to herself. 'You're kidding.'

No; there it was, for absolute sure. It looked like the ruins of a cottage, leaning dangerously close to a tree that had grown around it, breaking its back to accommodate the grey slate roof and the stubby chimney. She saw that it had windows, and there were curtains.

It was tucked in among the trees, leaning against that old oak as she'd seen on the laptop screen earlier. There was something in its weathered, mossy façade that blended in beautifully with its arboreal framing – it was of a piece. It shared the same theme, the same stunted grandeur as the ancient, twisted oaks that hemmed it in protectively.

The cottage looked less obviously ruined the closer you got. From one angle – the one Georgia approached from – the place looked so run down that it might actually have drawn attention from ramblers – or that strange, new breed who called themselves urban explorers, people who sought out decay in buildings, office blocks just before they get taken down, crumbling terracing on ancient football stadia. A slated path left a jagged trail all the way up to a driveway which, Georgia saw with a start, was occupied.

Crouching low, Georgia referred to the OS map. She traced her finger along the route where she had travelled, but there was no cottage listed anywhere, and no sign of it among the tree canopy from the overhead shots she'd seen.

'And there you are,' she said simply.

There were bright yellow morning sun curtains in the window, but little sign of anything inside.

Closer, closer again.

And then something dark appeared in the bottom left. A figure; she saw it stop a moment, and then raise what must be a shotgun or a rifle to its shoulder, and then—

The tree exploded just above her ears, a second or two before she heard the shot. Something went into her eye, and she yelped; before she knew what was happening, she had hit the ground hard, then rolled through some of the waist-high weeds. She smelled rank mosses and damp, the detritus of the summer season, as if something was dead, nearby. Her cheek stung, but it was an irrelevance next to the irritant in her eye. Just a splinter, she hoped, as she ran back down the road, only some loose fragments, surely nothing worse...

Back in her car, she was suddenly fearful of the lay-by, and the rustling trees, and the absolute stillness and solitude of where she was sat.

Someone had taken a shot at her – high enough to scare her off without hitting her with the pellets, but not close enough to realistically pose a danger. A good shot, even if you were used to handling guns. She pictured someone at ease with bringing down a clay pigeon at pace, from a good distance. Or a real pigeon, for that matter. The splinters that had spiked her cheek were a fluke, she supposed.

He didn't recognise me, she thought. *If he had, he would have shot to kill. I'm sure of it.*

'Christ,' she breathed. 'Only one thing for it, now.'

She lifted her phone and dialled a number.

'Jed Mulrine,' said the voice on the other side. He sounded slightly out of breath; there were other voices in the background, male voices, and then a peal of laughter. Georgia envisioned a pub. 'That you, Mrs Healey?'

'It is. How are you, Jed? Listen, I wanted to say thank you for the other night.'

He chuckled. 'No need to say thank you. I was glad to help.'

'Was everything OK the next day? With Sir Oliver, I mean.'

'Oh yeah, nothing out of the ordinary there. Young master Trickett won't be joining the party next year, that's for sure. He won't be back at the hall, if Sir Oliver's wishes are granted, either. As for me – when Chessington the younger inherits the whole lot, then you could say my jacket's on a shaky peg, but for now, everyone's content. So please don't worry. Hey – you've done the state some service, Mrs Healey. Rest easy. Don't worry about me.'

'There is something I need to talk to you about, Jed. Something important. It's about Stephanie. My girl.'

'Oh?' He sounded faintly alarmed. 'Has something come up?'

'In a manner of speaking. It's something I need to ask your opinion on, more than anything else.'

'Well, of course. Is it something we can talk about now?'

'I'd rather not do it on the phone, Jed.'

'Fair enough. Want me to meet you somewhere? If you need somewhere private, then we could always head to my shack. Saoirse would love to meet you again.'

'I was thinking somewhere we could have a sit-down, and a bite of lunch.'

'The Griffony does a fine roast, if you've an appetite.' He sounded absurdly upbeat. *He thinks he's going on a date*, Georgia realised. *Oh, Jed.*

'I have a place I like to go in Runholme Bray. You know it?'

'Yeah… that's a bit far out though, isn't it?'

'It's on my way home. I'd like to thank you for what you did the other night, too – my treat. There's a place called The Merry Boar, do you know it?'

'I've been there once or twice – didn't know it was still open. Didn't it shut a while back?'

'Under new management,' Georgia said quickly, hoping that this was the case, and she hadn't simply pulled out an old webpage.

'Ah, I didn't know that. OK. The Merry Boar it is. What time? I'm free all day. Rare day off, while the rest of the estate clears up, for me.'

Georgia checked her watch. 'Two-thirty? I hope that isn't too late to eat.'

He chuckled. 'I'll forgo my lunch. The barman at The Griffony won't be pleased though.' Some cackling ensued, as Jed dealt with some banter over his shoulder. 'Heh. He's just asked me if I'm going out on a date, the cheeky sod.'

'I'll see you there, Jed. Look forward to it.'

After she hung up, Georgia set her teeth. Nothing else for it, now. The path was set.

She started the car, then pulled out of the lay-by. When she got to the edge of the road, she stopped. A black 4x4 car tore around the corner, stirring the low-hanging branches of the trees by the side of the road. The car jammed on the brakes upon sight of Georgia. She wondered if the driver had been baffled by the sight of a car coming out, and she actually reversed a little, to reassure the motorist.

Then the car stopped, blocking her from driving out. And

she understood, far too late, that this was entirely deliberate, as someone darted out of the driver's side door of the 4x4 and ran into view.

38

They actually had a row on the phone. While I called them. She was talking to me, made a couple of remarks, he made a few in response, and that was it. Seconds out, round one. I sat there with my chin in my hands, listening to them go at it. Secretly enthralled.

From the diary of Stephanie Healey

It was Rod. Rod, with a beanie hat and what looked like running gear. He looked a little more ridiculous than usual, with his stork's legs and his winkle in the middle far too well defined for his trousers to be comfortable.

For a split second, Georgia thought she might ram him. Simply let the clutch up too fast and jerk forward. It wouldn't take that much momentum to send him flying; possibly the 4x4 would go, too. Then she'd be off, and worry about the bodywork later. And the bodywork on Rod.

But of course, she didn't. She put the car in neutral and switched off the engine, letting down a window. 'What's going on? What are you doing here?'

'Hi,' he said, attempting a smile. 'I think we should talk.'

'OK. You could have called me on the phone, maybe.'

Something else occurred to her, then. 'You been following me?'

'Come on out, Georgia.'

'No, I will not. Rod… Rod!'

He had looped a hand through the window and disengaged the door, a fluid, reptilian move. The door gaped; he reached in.

Then it occurred to Georgia to be frightened. 'Rod! What's going on? What are you doing?'

He took a hold of her shoulder; she clamped a hand over his. His skin was warm and slick, as if he'd just come out of a shower. Sweat dripped off his temples. He jerked her out of her seat, and her phone spilled to the floor of the car.

A twist of his wiry shoulders, and she was sent sprawling, one hand braced against the tarmac, her hair trailing in her eyes. She saw his legs brace, and then she was pulled out of the car.

Georgia fought madly, kicking and bucking and screaming, over and over again: 'Rod! What are you doing? Rod!'

Her blows found no purchase on him; he caught both her wrists in one hand, incredibly strong, and then he heaved her off the ground as if she'd been a child. Her legs flailed; she thought to knee him in the face, but he mashed her body tight against his chest, removing the option. She tried to scratch his eyes, but he twisted his face away.

'This is it… This is over,' Rod said. 'It's over. You're going back. And what the hell happened to your face? Fighting again?'

'Leave me alone, you fucking psycho! Help! Help!' She shrieked at the top of her voice, until he clamped his hand over her mouth. She bit him then, and that got through: he grunted in pain and almost dropped her. Then he recovered, and stunned her by planting his own knee in the small of her back. She cried out, her limbs drawing in, and then he had the boot open and threw her in.

'Rod, my God. Was it you? Was it you?' She struggled onto her elbows.

'This has to stop,' was all he would say, his intonation something less than neutral, not too much above monotone. 'It's all over, all this. I spoke to them. I spoke to the police. They told me what you'd been doing. It has to stop. I'm taking you home, got it? I'm taking you home. I'll look after you for a bit. I'll do what I should have done six months ago. If I can't be your husband, I'll still be your protector. When I make a vow, I keep it. You'll be safe. We'll work through it. We'll sort you out, turn you around. I promise. It's a promise.'

Then another car screeched to a halt. Georgia saw Rod's head jerk away, startled. Then he closed the boot on her and left her in total darkness.

She heard only muffled conversation; a woman's voice.

'I'm in here!' Georgia said, hammering on the underside of the boot with her feet and hands. 'Help, he's got me in here! Help!'

There was some fumbling on the outside as someone felt for the release button. Then the boot flew open and Adrienne Connulty was there.

She grinned.

'Mrs Healey. You do pop up in some of the strangest places.'

39

*The most embarrassing night I've had over here was that
time I let the Magpie talk me into too many drinks, and
talked myself into too much talking.*

From the diary of Stephanie Healey

They'd taken Rod away quickly and without much
fuss, which was typical of the man in a way. He had
exercised his right to remain silent, although the crestfallen
expression on his face had been voluble enough. He looked
like a man who had gone past the stage of tears. He
looked empty. Georgia knew how he felt, although this
didn't quite amount to sympathy.

Rod had been taller than both police officers, and yet
had still appeared shrunken, his back hunched, as they put
him in the squad car that had arrived within minutes of
Adrienne Connulty appearing.

This was a vision of the old man he would become,
quicker than anyone knew.

Once the car had gone and Georgia had given a statement,
Adrienne had remained behind, stood beside her shiny new
Citroën. The younger woman had her arms folded but still

cut a relaxed figure as she leaned into the driver's side door of the car.

'To cut a long story short… I was following you. But I lost you. I drove past your car in the lay-by, saw you'd gone somewhere. So I went to the other lay-by, just up the road. I was keeping an eye on you. Aren't you lucky?'

'And you'll have gotten pictures of all of this,' Georgia said, numbly.

Adrienne shrugged. 'Sure I have. It's my job. And you know something? I've got this theory you absolutely bloody love it. Want to hear it?'

'I've a feeling you're going to tell me anyway.'

'I reckon you're just here to wind people up. I don't think you've got much of a plan. You just wanted to rattle a few cages and see what reaction you could get. Am I close?'

'Not too far away. I've got a theory about you, too. Want to hear it?'

Adrienne pursed her lips and shrugged. Georgia had to hand it to her; she didn't quite know what Adrienne had said to her husband when she pulled up and confronted him, just as he was stuffing his estranged wife into the boot of a 4x4, but it had an effect, all right. He had been ashen-faced, and stepped back. *Think about how Stephanie would react* – was that what she'd said? Or was Georgia filling in the blanks?

'I should thank you.'

Adrienne checked her nails. 'In your own time, then.'

'Thank you. I'm not sure what you saved me from, but… thank you.'

'You're welcome. Quite a story, all this.'

'Which newspaper's readers are going to hear all about it?'

'Not sure. Depends on their best offer. Look, Georgia, I know you don't like me. And no matter what I do, you still won't like me for it. I could cure cancer, and you'd say – oh, look. There's the bitch who cured cancer. But I'll say this to you, and you can take it to your grave: I want to find Stephanie. I want to know what happened.'

'I know you do, Adrienne. That's how your industry works, doesn't it? You've got the speed dialling record for police officers to turn up.'

'Catty. Such a low opinion of the police! Are you the type of person who writes in to national newspapers? For the letters page? I bet you are. I bet you've even been published. Feel free to tell me to fuck off, Georgia, but – what's his story? I mean, this afternoon. I don't want chapter and verse. Although I'm interested in that as well.'

'Brainstorm, I would say. Honestly. He's upright, solid, dependable, boring... all the major reasons for marrying him. A good man. I think he's lost his mind. He wanted me to go home, and get out of Ferngate... then again, that's true of just about everyone I've met in this miserable town.'

'It's good advice, Georgia.'

'Don't worry. I'll be out of here before long.'

'Mind if I ask what on earth you were doing out here?'

'Retracing my daughter's steps, I suppose. If I never have an answer about what happened, at least I'll have experienced the place. Got a feel for it. It's as close as I can get to her. Does that make sense?'

'I suppose. You will go home today, won't you, Georgia?'

'That an editorial leader speaking?'

'No. Just me.'

'I've got one or two loose ends to tie up first.'

'Try not to get yourself into any more scrapes while you're at it. Speaking of which – what's wrong with your face? Did he do that to you?'

'None of your business.'

'I'm just a private citizen voicing my concerns, Georgia. Nothing more.'

'Sure you are. Since you're speaking as a private citizen, would you kindly mind fucking off and leaving me alone? If you're not busy, that is. In case you're not getting the message – don't let me catch you following me again.'

'But you didn't catch me following you.' She grinned. 'In a way, I hope I never see your face again, Georgia. There's something about you that freaks me out.'

'Everyone says that. Funny.' Georgia returned to her car. She waited for Adrienne to start up; she flashed her lights, dazzling Georgia, as she turned out.

'Bitch,' Georgia muttered. But she waved, anyway.

Then she prepared herself for one more walk up the long dark road.

40

When they get to that stage, they're good for anything.
Everything becomes crystal clear to them. There's only
one thing they require. Give it to them now and again,
and you're golden. They love you for it. It's perfect.

His diary

Georgia took the steep, sheltered road, not deviating through a gap in the dry-stone wall the grounds as she had before. It meant she'd be absurdly easy to spot if anyone should be driving up it – but, counter-intuitively, she'd be well hidden from anyone who was looking for her anywhere else on the estate. It would be the last place someone with a gun would be looking.

Georgia was making good progress, congratulating herself on a good plan carried out well. Then a sudden noise startled her.

She gasped aloud. She clutched at the stone walls, uselessly. There was no escape hatch here, no hidden doors. A tiger pit might have sufficed, given the circumstances.

There was a car coming behind her – she knew which

one it was, too. And it was coming at pace, fast enough to obliterate her.

For a split second it crossed Georgia's mind to meet the vehicle in the centre of the path, arms raised – the only way she could possibly stop it.

But this was her last chance. She ran forward. There, maybe twenty yards up ahead and to the right, the stone wall was broken by another fence.

The crunched stone and the revving engine grew closer. Perhaps a tank might come over the brow of the hill, any moment – or something even more frightful, with foglamp eyes and a front grille studded with spikes.

Running full tilt, Georgia reached the gate and yanked on the latch.

It moved perhaps an inch or two, before a padlock rattled on the other side.

The Land Rover was almost there, judging by the sound. There was no chance she could even climb – so she made herself small, crouching into the bottom right-hand corner, just where the gate gave a little. She squeezed in tight to the wall, tucking herself in as much as she could. Where the slope levelled out, it would mean the vehicle could accelerate – there was a chance, just a small chance, that it might go past her.

It did; a blur of dark green. She didn't take in the driver's face, but she did take in that of the dog, behind chicken wire in the back of the vehicle.

Georgia expected screeching brakes; then she'd have to face the angry red tail-lights. *So sorry* – she heard herself say it, a dress rehearsal of sorts – *I thought I'd come up here for a break in the weather. It looked like such a nice path.*

And he wouldn't believe her.

But the Land Rover didn't stop. It carried on towards the cottage at the top of the road. It came to an abrupt stop.

Georgia stayed where she was, tight against the fence.

The door to the Land Rover opened, and she thought: *Oh no. The dog.* She heard it bark.

'Shut up,' Mulrine snarled, closing the door.

Georgia saw the dog's head bobbling up and down in the back window. Almost certainly, it had seen her. But Mulrine was distracted, and strode up to the door of the cottage in some anger. He hammered at the green-painted door, then stood back, fists clenched.

The door opened. Georgia couldn't see the figure who stood there.

'Yeah?' High-pitched and polite. The sound of a well-educated son.

'Want to talk to me about the Polish lass?'

'What Polish lass?'

'Don't get smart with me!' Mulrine bellowed. 'The one in the papers! The one I saw you knocking around with after Chessington's party last year! She turned up dead up the road. On the farmhouse I was planning on buying! Did you get her involved in that shit?'

The reply was so infuriatingly laconic, she expected Mulrine to take a swing at the person who uttered it. 'Calm yourself, old man,' the son said. 'That was a girl who got herself into a lot of trouble. Not all of it was my doing. You put that shit in your veins, it's only going to go one way. Unless you're made of the right stuff. She wasn't.'

'I don't believe you,' Mulrine snarled. 'Get out of the way.'

'Don't be cutting up rough, now... hey...' Mulrine barged past, but the son's voice remained an insolent purr. 'Don't make a spectacle of yourself.'

'I swear to God...' Mulrine began. Then the door slammed shut, cutting off his voice.

Georgia crept closer, bent almost double, trying to ignore the sight of Saoirse the dog barking and snarling at her, fit to chew at the window. She ducked under a side window and then stopped at a back gate, unlatching it. She could get in through there and hide at the back of the house – which was where she had wanted to be anyway. Sat on her haunches beneath the window, she could hear the conversation going on inside. The window was old-fashioned, single-paned.

Jed Mulrine's son said: 'Told you already, that's all going to get taken care of.'

'You'd better. Chessington had to talk nice to that bastard down the police station. You can expect the knock on your door any day.'

'You worry too much. It's sorted. No one's coming in here without a warrant. And if anyone gets a warrant, I'll know. It's all in hand.'

'It had better be,' Mulrine growled. 'This is your last warning. Take care of it. Right? I don't want to think about it ever again after this! I will not protect you any more. Sort it out.'

'I will. Be like taking out the rubbish, old man. Don't you worry. Clean as a whistle.'

There was a pause. Georgia was sure she had been spotted; or perhaps Mulrine had spotted that Saoirse was going nuts in the car, and become suspicious. She panicked, and prepared to run for the gate leading to the back of the cottage. But then Mulrine said: 'I've had enough of this. The lies. The panic. It's filthy, shameful. I'll never get it out of my mind.'

'She was asking for it. You know that. She found out too much. You'd have been caught in the flak.'

'You didn't have to speak to her.'

'Who?'

'The Tooth Fairy. Who do you think? The mother.'

'Her?' A snort. 'She's made a fool of herself from one end of this town to the other. Small wonder they haven't carted her off to a rubber room. No one will take her seriously again. A screaming banshee. She's turned into the village idiot. She's of no consequence. No one's listening to her. Not the cops... not Chessington... not the papers... nobody. Come on. Don't be moody, old man. Sit down, grab a cuppa. Maybe something stronger?'

'No.' Mulrine hesitated. 'Once you sort this out, I'm thinking about torching this place. Maybe getting some of the boys to put a bulldozer on it. These walls shouldn't stand any more. When I see the outline of it on the horizon, I want to be sick.'

'Chessington will be upset if you knock this place down. Good thing he doesn't know so much about it, mind. Happy to leave you to your own devices... and me to mine. Probably sting us for rent if he found out, the old bastard.'

'I've got to go. Remember what I said. Sort it out. Or I will.'

'You getting brave? Oh come on, old man. I can see you boxing the fruit-pickers' ears all right, but this isn't in your league. Let's not be a kidder.'

'Just sort it out. Or by Christ, I'll do something awful. Bank on it, boy.'

'Don't have a coronary.'

Quick footsteps near the door. This time Georgia sprang. She was through the gate quickly enough – but the new, silvery latch wouldn't fall over completely in time. She shrank back against the grey stone wall, looking out into a small, tidy back court, square patches of greenery hemmed in by old granite blocks.

Mulrine said nothing as he strode out the door. When he pulled open the driver's side door of the Land Rover, he yelled, 'Come on, daft girl, sit! Sit down in your seat!' Soon the Land Rover started up, turned in the driveway, then headed back down the way it had come.

Georgia hardly dared breathe. She hadn't heard the front door close.

Then she heard a long, slow, 'Hmmm...' Then footsteps approached the gate.

Georgia didn't move. She held her breath.

A matter of inches away, a hand reached out, flipped the latch closed properly, then tested the gate for good measure. The hand lingered for a second or two, fingernails tapping against the chrome-plated surface, and Georgia thought this is it, surely he knows what's happened, surely he'll come out, and then God knows what.

But the figure around the corner turned on his heels and strode off towards the door. Still, there was no sound of the front door closing. A lock was snicked, with the front door tugged once, twice, just to be sure. Footsteps returned – heavier-sounding, clad in boots – and then the alarm disengaged in the car. The front door opened.

It had been one of those big 4x4s that should have been on show, driven by men with mohawks and thick bacon necks. A glorified toy, the kind of thing that no one over the age of thirty should seriously admit to admiring, whether they did or not. Black paint, but silver suspension cages and gleaming alloys, the cab appearing far too high for someone Georgia's height to climb up to. She heard a driver's side door slam shut. And she might have had her suspicions confirmed, there and then, had she only been brave enough to stick her head out of the undergrowth far enough to get a look at the driver. But Georgia was not quite brave enough for that, not yet. The 4x4 started with a surly growl, and the broken slate on the pathway scattered as the wheels spun. The 4x4 moved down the track, heading away towards the main road and the circuit route back into town – or somewhere else.

It came so very close. The tip of Georgia's nose touched soil, was tickled by grass; brambles caught in her hair. Something moved across her cheek with multiple tickly legs, but Georgia did not flinch, did not give in to disgust.

The sound of the 4x4's engine was swallowed up by the trees at the far end of the pathway. All was silent.

She waited a painfully long time. She did not trust this development; saw subterfuge everywhere. She imagined the person behind the wheel of the 4x4 parked up at the false junction on the main road just up ahead, invisible behind the treeline, waiting for Georgia to make her move.

When she realised that the person in the 4x4 might in fact be heading to the petrol station for milk or to post a letter or some other short errand, Georgia quickly got to her feet and headed towards the ruined cottage.

Now here's what happened, she thought. *This is how it went. Princess Stephanie falls in love with a handsome prince, and he gives her the magical gift of Cornfed. The princess is a clever girl but she has a sweet tooth, and Cornfed can be so very, very sweet for people. So she falls under the handsome prince's spell. She meets some fallen pixies on the way who help her find Cornfed, and soon she needs more and more of it. Meanwhile, back in the magical kingdom, the handsome prince is drawing a lot of attention – and then there's poor Buttons, who only wants to marry Princess Stephanie, but of course he's too goddamned lame for her.*

So one night, a wicked witch decides to place a curse on princess Stephanie. She pretends to be the handsome prince, and tells Princess Stephanie there's a place he can meet her with the extra special Cornfed she's been wanting so badly. So Princess Stephanie does what the note tells her. She leaves her phone in her flat, and walks to rendezvous with the handsome prince in the middle of a terrible storm.

Except a goblin knew about Colette the wicked witch's plan. He'd been watching Princess Stephanie for a long time, and he'd wanted her for his own. And so he sees the message Colette the witch left for Princess Stephanie. And even though Colette the wicked witch planned to keep Princess Stephanie out of the way, she got more than she bargained for, when Princess Stephanie bumped into the goblin. The goblin knew a secret route back to his secret castle in the woods, and maybe something happened here to Princess Stephanie. Whatever happened, he surely took her away again before the knights could come and look for her.

But this was Georgia's version of the story. One she knew would be laughed out of the door by whatever policeman she told it to. Or perhaps she'd be told that the place had been searched; everyone had been spoken to and accounted for. Nothing to see here.

She peered in at the room with the yellow curtains, ultra cautious, standing on her tiptoes before the window. It looked into a cramped galley-style kitchen, clean, with a searing bright sunbeam cast across a marble effect worktop. The place might have been a holiday rental, with doily patterned filigree on the curtains and on a tablecloth at the back. Pale blue and white china stood in a crockery rack against the far wall. Beside that, a fully stocked wine rack.

Georgia crept around to the second window, with closed dark curtains. She looked in through a crack in the window. Gasped, and flinched. Bit her hand. She started forward, hands clasped to her face, drawing breath in great, frenzied gulps. She peered in through the crack in the window. Saw the same image. Had it confirmed.

There was a skeleton lying on a bed.

No, a cadaver, with sallow skin, appallingly bulbous eyes beneath tight-closed lids, hardly any lips at all. It wore some black pyjamas with limestone diamond patterning. The hair was longer, spilling over the wishbone shoulder blades, but still the same shade of black Georgia remembered. The corpse must have been preserved somehow, but clearly a corpse.

She was never sure if she screamed, then, or rattled the window. What she did know, was that the corpse on the bed's eyes flew open, and the mouth jerked open. Then the brown eyes blinked, stared, and saw.

Then it screamed, the voice carrying clearly through the window:

'*Mum!*'

41

One more adventure, I suppose.
Final diary entry

Georgia might have fainted; or might have been sent into some strange fugue; or perhaps been possessed. She saw Stephanie fall off the bed a shovelful of bones and tissue-paper skin, yellow as old wax, piled up on the floor. The hair completely covered her daughter's face, and soon a knife blade of her face reappeared. Pockmarked, blistered around the mouth, the tongue yellowed behind rotten brown teeth. Stephanie sat up, hands finding purchase on the carpet, and Georgia clawing at the window, trying to find purchase, looking for the clasp. But it was modern double-glazing. Georgia battered the window.

'Stephanie! You see me? I'm coming! Hold on... Get back...'

Georgia scrambled over the pathway, picking up shards of grey slate. She found one with the appropriate heft and edging to it, then bellowed at Stephanie: 'Cover your face! I'm coming in!' She was half-sobbing, half-hysterical with laughter. 'My darlin', I'm coming for you!'

She heaved the piece of slate over her head. It had a good edge on it, and she threw with all her strength. The window splintered, but did not break. It took several more to completely break through the window, and Georgia tore off her jacket, twisting it around her arm and punching out more shards. Then one razor-edged shard sliced down, with the lethal speed of a guillotine and the nasty angled cut to match. Luckily Georgia's hands were clear; and then there was a gap for her to get through. She used her jacket and then her training top as a barrier over the stray shards at the bottom of the frame, and then slid in, head-first. There was a nasty snag on her training top, once, but that was all. Georgia took the weight of the fall on her hands, then allowed her legs to fall in after her.

Stephanie was face down on the floor, palms flat on an ancient floral-patterned carpet. Georgia had seen people in this pose before, dumped at A&E when she was a trainee, and even once in a toilet at a shopping centre, where she had attended the discovery of a body. A drug addict at the end of their journey.

Georgia had seen it before, but her mind still strobed with unreadable patterns and tessellations, trying to work out that Stephanie was here, right now. And then she had the girl in her arms, feeling the slimy skin of her lips against her neck, the head lolling uselessly. Then she had pulled the girl up to her feet, as light as lifting a six-year-old, the rank hair against her cheek, filling her nostrils, and she did not care as she screamed, 'My baby, you're here! I'm here! I've got you! My precious girl!'

The hands only made it so far up Georgia's back. 'Mum,' she croaked.

'Just sit a minute, darling, sit on the bed.' Georgia eased her back down on the quilt cover – unwashed, like Stephanie's hair. And in a second, she took in the room, and saw, and smelt, and sensed, everything.

The dead flies garlanding the windowsill. The three-way combat of urine, excrement and strong bleach smells. The old vomit encrusting the carpet. The bucket under the bed, its contents unspeakable. And on a dressing table, a sick parade of syringes, some in plastic packets, some not. A fine mist of dried blood, surely shot from one of the syringes, pockmarked one wall. The mirror on the dressing table was webbed with stress fractures, but not enough to pop out a shard of glass.

'He kept you here. My God, he kept you here. I thought you were dead. I thought you were dead!' Georgia kissed the girl hard on the forehead and crushed her head into the crook of her neck. 'But now we have to go, my girl. We have to get out of here. If you can't walk, then I'll carry you. I'll carry you all the way home if I have to!'

Stephanie's head lolled on her neck, and her eyes struggled to point in the right direction. Georgia gasped at the hollows in her throat, at her cheeks. Even her strong jawline seemed obscene without flesh to cushion it. There seemed to be literally no fat whatsoever in her body. 'Mum...' she croaked again, then winced in pain.

'No – just wait. I'll get the front door open and we'll walk out of here. I'll call the police, and this will all be over. Don't you see? It's over! I've saved you!'

An expression of alarm and pure horror seemed to bring Stephanie back to life, and she jerked upright. 'No... no, please, don't, don't.'

Stockholm syndrome, Georgia thought. Or just the consequences of addiction, over a sustained period of time. The bastard kept her here! All this time! And nobody knew about it!

'It's all right,' Georgia said, holding up her hands, a placatory gesture. 'I understand. I'm going to help you. I'll make everything better. I swear on it. I swear my life.' Then she turned to the door, turning the handle carefully.

'No, I mean, don't... The door! No!'

Georgia hesitated. 'Is there someone still here?'

'No!' Stephanie said. Then she grew faint; her eyelids fluttered.

Georgia knelt beside Stephanie and hugged her close.

Stephanie sobbed, sagging. 'Take me away,' she rasped. 'Take me away now.'

'You've got it. Right now,' Georgia whispered. She took off her jacket, and covered her daughter with it. 'Can you stand?'

'Um. Please stay where you are,' said a man's voice. 'Both of you. Stay exactly where you are.'

Georgia looked up. There, stood in the doorway, was the man she'd been dreading.

42

If you're reading this, it means I've gone missing. I will almost certainly have disappeared in the same way Stephanie disappeared, as a result of the same person's actions. I'll explain where I went below, just so you can speak to the police, and finally get them to take me seriously. But first, I want to say how sorry I am that you've been left with the burden of us both having gone missing. Not to mention the suspicion, which will surely come your way. But Rod, I need you to know that however our lives ended up, we did love each other, very much indeed. I remember the first time we went to the Peak District – a tent, two battered cricket chairs and a gas stove that threatened to blow up on us, but my God, was there ever a holiday like it? I remember every sweet nothing that passed between us. And always remember, that this love, whatever it became, gave us our precious, beautiful daughter. There might never be an answer. There might always be torment. But think of the good things, whenever you can. Use them to fight the darkness. It's the only weapon you have, but it's a good one.

Georgia's final letter to Rod

Howie Abbot stood in the doorway – tall, blond, handsome, in that Jason Donovan sort of way, except that the shade of his hair was a touch too stark. Photographer. Singer of Prat Spaniel. Or to give him his real name, Dennis Mulrine. Jed's son.

He wasn't dressed for country living; he wore a pair of jeans with floral patterns stitched into the sides, a pretty kaleidoscope of yellow, pink and green. A bright red T-shirt with some black mandarin script stencilled on the front was stretched tight over his skinny frame. On his feet – besmirched by some mud he'd not long stepped in – were a pair of trainers. This hipsterish get-up was almost entirely undercut by the shotgun he cradled in his arms.

'Get up, slowly,' he said, his jaw working. His blue eyes were the same as his father's but devoid of the warmth. He pointed the shotgun right at Georgia.

Her entire body was braced for the appalling blast to follow, but Dennis's finger stayed on the trigger. Georgia spread her arms, slowly.

'Dennis… Let us walk away. This is over. People know I'm here.'

'People know you're here… so you broke in? Please. And did you think I didn't have precautions set up in here? You triggered an alarm on my phone.'

Georgia didn't think the young man had blinked once. The young man who hung around Ferngate, part of every scene, but not quite belonging to one. The gamekeeper's son, never quite part of the elite, not even a student at the university, but involved in university life. Playing in bands, piggybacking on the reputation of a genuine star, but never quite matching it. The one who took the pictures at the magazine. The one who took the pictures of Stephanie. The one who stalked her, and took his chance when he read something on the message board. The one who knew about the false wall, and the gate that led to the narrow, steep path, which led to his house – the ruined cottage either he or his father had renovated. Kept off-grid, off the books. The perfect place to hide the thing he desired most; the thing he wanted to possess above all other things.

'Killed her, didn't you?' Georgia asked. Her voice cracked, but she went on: 'The other girl. The one who knew about you and Steph. Jasmine, was her name. Or Janina – that was her real name. Stuffed her with a bad batch. Was it when I started getting too close?'

'Well, you were asking a lot of awkward questions. Maybe that one's on you?'

'And you knocked me into the ghyll. It was you.'

He smiled. It was an expression that might have been badly painted onto a doll. 'Strange thing is, I didn't know I was going to do it until the very last moment. I knew who you were. Total coincidence I came across you. I was trying to walk off a hangover. Then you actually bent over and looked into the ghyll. It was such a target. I couldn't resist. I know how a bull feels, when it sees red. It would have been beautiful if you'd gone down there, you must admit. Would have been poetic. Shame Dad had to come along when he did.'

'And you shot at me.'

'Yeah, I was hoping that was you. But you could have been anyone, of course.'

She licked her lips. 'Dennis, this is done. We're going to

walk out of here. I can get help for you. You're not well. You're clearly not well.'

'You're too right this is done. You and the pisspot, over there. The fucking latrine. Any last words, useless? That's right, stick insect. You, over there. Model material. Anything to say?'

Stephanie sank back onto the bed and moaned, the keening sound of an animal in a snare. Her eyes roiled again, and her shoulders sagged. Georgia saw her daughter drool, and a tremor activated the wasted body.

'Oh look – must be time for your jabs!' Dennis sneered. 'I'll sort you out with some lovely Cornfed after I've blown your mother in half. Keep an eye open, won't you? Half an eye, if you can't manage that.'

'If you kill me, will you promise to at least let her live? Keep her alive, Dennis. Please, at least do that much. Even if you keep her in this situation, make sure she lives. All right? Can you promise that? Let her live, Dennis. I'll beg if I have to.'

Something faltered in the young man's gaze. He looked as if he was about to say something. Then he put the gun to his shoulder and sighted along the barrel. Right at Georgia's face.

Georgia took a grip of her jacket sleeve, which still covered Stephanie. Then she twirled it into a compact spear, and swung it in a wide arc.

The movement caught him completely by surprise. The blow was not enough to knock the gun out of his hand, but it turned the barrel just enough, as he pulled the trigger.

The mirror on top of the dressing table disintegrated, and much of the wall behind it, plaster and splinters spat high into the air, in the colossal blast. Georgia flinched, nostrils filled with the reek of cordite; a laser line of pain had opened up across the same cheek she'd had punched through with splinters from the last time Dennis had taken a shot at her.

Stephanie shrieked, piercing the shrill ringing in Georgia's ears; then a feral expression erupted across her daughter's features and she sprang for him.

As it turned out, she was at the perfect height and distance for Dennis Mulrine to connect directly underneath her chin with a left jab. Her eyes rolled up in her head, and then Stephanie was spark out, a heap of tallow-coloured limbs on the bed.

Georgia used the distraction to close on Dennis Mulrine, gripping him on either side of his head, her nails parting his cornstalk fringe and splitting the skin. She plunged both thumbs deep into those flared, shocked blue eyes, and he screamed at the top of his lungs.

The meat of his forearm swung round and clubbed the side of Georgia's head, and her balance shifted somewhat. Then he had a hold of her hair, then his other hand found Georgia's neck, the shotgun dropping to the floor.

They grappled for a moment before he hurled her back against the dressing table. Its legs were already leaning at a crazy slant, before they gave way and the furniture collapsed, shards of glass from the disintegrated mirror pattering to the carpet.

From there, Mulrine overpowered her, easily, knees on her chest, his fingers clutching at Georgia's neck. On the bed, one of Stephanie's feet dangled off the edge. Georgia had a glimpse of the girl's toenails, painfully long and curved like talons; then Georgia bucked and tried to shake Dennis Mulrine off. She couldn't budge him.

He could not see; blood trickled down one side of his face as if he had wept it, but Georgia couldn't be sure if she'd punctured his eyeballs or not. She smashed her hands off his shoulder, but his head was thrown back, his neck muscles bulging, too high up to hit. She pounded at the arms, but they would not move.

Dennis Mulrine's hands tightened at her throat. Georgia's vision smudged. She tried to breathe and could not. He was strangling her; lightning bolts flared across her field of view, spectral fingers. Then purple lights undulated along the edge of her vision like interference on an old TV screen.

Her hands scoured the carpet around her for a piece of glass from the window or the dresser – anything to distract him. She heard her throat constrict with a ghastly click, just above the roaring and pounding in her ears.

'That's it. Just stop. Stop... Stop struggling. That's it.' His voice was almost soothing, although strain was etched across his face, in taut tendons and blue veins snaking across his neck. 'At least it's all over. All done for you. You don't need to worry. Just take it. Just take it. Accept it. This is the end. It'll be a relief. Won't it?'

Georgia's fingers closed around something. Something they recognised. Something they manipulated with reflex dexterity.

With a dreadful gurgling in her throat, she drove both hands up from between Dennis Mulrine's two arms; there was some give around her windpipe, just for a second, and she took a breath. Then she snatched at the collar of his T-shirt, pulling him towards her.

With her right hand she plunged a syringe full of air into his carotid artery, and jammed the button down.

Dennis Mulrine let her go. Then he undulated across the room, like a fire hose allowed to run free across the street while jetting water. He made the sound of the wind whipped up in a narrow street.

Georgia did not watch him die. She did not look at his face again. While he still writhed and hissed through clenched teeth, Georgia took her daughter in her arms and hugged her close.

'Mummy,' Steph said, eyelids fluttering. 'Mummy. You're back. Mummy.' Her fingers stroked Georgia's cheek.

The girl's mother covered the hand with her own, then stroked her hair until the room was silent.

She didn't hear any footsteps; didn't realise the Land Rover had pulled up; didn't hear Saoirse barking.

Jed Mulrine started speaking the moment he opened the door. 'Just me,' he said breezily. 'I meant to tell you...'

Then he must have seen something was awry. Or maybe it was the silence. Georgia stayed where she was, with her daughter near-insensible on her shoulder.

'What's going on here?' he screeched. Then he was at Dennis' side; the boy's head lolled horribly as his father tried to raise him from the floor.

'He's dead,' Georgia said. 'I had no choice. And I'm going to walk out of here, now. You're not going to stop me.'

Jed Mulrine began to sob, covering his face with his hands.

'You're a decent man, Jed. For what it's worth. I'm guessing you always thought you were doing your best. You were protecting your own.' Georgia lifted her daughter. It was so easy. There seemed to be almost no muscle tone to Stephanie's thighs. Despite the long, awkward limbs it felt no more difficult than lifting a doll. 'I am going to walk away.'

Jed didn't follow her. She left him sitting there, and walked out into the sunlight, cradling her daughter in her arms.

43

Today is January the first. Well, not really. Not by name. Not for a while, anyway. But from now on, every day is January the first.

I like January the first, to be clear. I like a fresh page, new images to discover on the calendar, new boxes to fill.

Jottings on a brand new notepad, by Stephanie Healey

The stitches had hurt. Georgia looked at the ugly black lines stitched across her face, stretching from the corner of her mouth up to her cheek, and tried to smile when she was shown to the nearest mirror. It especially hurt to do so.

'Got the scars to prove it,' she muttered. Then she allowed them to dress the wound in stinging antiseptic patches.

Despite this, she still took her time to help bathe and dress Stephanie in a hospital gown, taking care to comb her hair with her fingernails after washing it carefully. Stephanie was sedated – but in repose, with a slight breath shivering her nostrils to keep time with the heart monitor, and her long hair combed and clean, she looked peaceful.

'It'll take some time,' the doctor had told her, 'I don't really need to tell you that. She'll need some morphine in the short term – coming off it now could kill her. We'll figure something out.'

'It'll take as long as it needs to,' Georgia said. 'I'll be right here. Twenty-four seven.'

She refused to take a call from Neal Hurlford, although she did allow herself to be patronised by a twenty-one-year-old policewoman who kept repeating that she was a fully trained family liaison officer. By this point, Georgia had gotten into bed beside her daughter, holding her close, marvelling at the hands she had made, the face and neck and shoulders – even the arms, track-marked as they were, the veins a ruin. But Stephanie was warm, and fully hydrated from the drip, and by God, *alive*, and back with her.

'I think I should stay here,' the policewoman said, and Georgia didn't twig what she meant by that until the girl asked outright if she wanted him to be there.

'My God,' Georgia said, 'of course it's all right. Let him in, please. Dear God. Let him see her.'

Rod appeared, and collapsed on the instant. Georgia had seen people faint before, had seen people seized by utter anguish and grief, but she'd never seen someone collapse like that. She'd never quite understood what the phrase poleaxed meant, but she supposed it was appropriate here. He looked as if a mallet had been laid across his shoulders, and he fell to his knees, sobbing, taking Stephanie's limp hands in his own, then burying his face in her neck. Georgia joined them, her head on the other side of Stephanie's face. They stayed like that for quite some time, heads together.

Georgia noticed what he was still wearing. 'You berk…

who sold you that gear? You look like a strip club tout at a holiday resort.'

'Doing my fitness,' he said, muffled by his daughter's hair. 'Keeping busy running.'

She ran her fingers across his smooth scalp, just the once. 'It's over,' she said. 'This is the happiest day we'll ever have. God love us.'

When she finally felt composed enough to speak to Hurlford, in that very hospital room, Georgia only added one thing to her statement: 'When you see Jed Mulrine... Tell him I'm sorry. It wasn't what I wanted. I told him I'd meet him just to get him away from the grounds. I couldn't be sure if he was living at the cottage, himself, rather than his son. I just wanted to take a look. That's all. I didn't expect this to happen. He knew, but he wasn't to blame. He had a son. I don't think he's all bad. He did what he had to do to protect him, no matter what he'd done. I'd probably have done the same. In fact, I did do the same. I was on the very edge. Literally, when it comes to that bloody ghyll. I was going to go to any lengths to find out what happened to Stephanie. Who knows where I'd have ended up? Come to think of it, I had to kill someone to finish it. Maybe Jed Mulrine would have done the same. Maybe not. But it doesn't make him bad. Or... evil. Not like his son. Not a chance of it.'

'We'll be the judge of that, Mrs Healey.' Hurlford's eyes met hers for the only time that afternoon, and he said: 'For what it's worth, I'm sorry.'

'Not as sorry as you will be,' Georgia said, coldly. 'Not nearly as sorry. You're up to your fucking neck in it. I'd talk to a lawyer, if I was you. What I'll never know is – did you turn a blind eye because you're corrupt, or because you're stupid?'

He was taken aback. Blinking rapidly, he said: 'I'm glad you've got her back, truly I am.'

'Yeah. I sorted that out for you. Do you want to know how I did it? Where you and your hundreds of officers and thousands of hours didn't?' Without waiting for an answer, she said: 'I have something you don't. And you know what that is, don't you?'

'Yes,' he said. 'Instinct.'

'Got it in one.'

'Goodbye, Mrs Healey. I'm glad this was the right ending, for once.'

'Close the door, please.'

When he was gone, Georgia felt inside her jacket pocket for her purse. Inside the special compartment were some pills. She popped one, almost without thinking.

Epilogue

On a blustery morning back in her own house, Georgia read the paper with her eyes screwed tight, chewing the side of her mouth.

MY NIGHT INSIDE THE SHADOWY MANOR HOUSE CULT, by Adrienne Connulty

'There's a rude phrase itching to get out of that one,' Georgia muttered. She scanned the two-page spread until she couldn't bear it any more. She folded the broadsheet up, then placed it in a buff-coloured folder. Then she turned to the *Ferngate Ferret*, which lay on the seat beside her.

EXCLUSIVE: DETECTIVE IN SEEDY CHESSINGTON HALL RITUAL NAMED, by Ivan Bell

'Aw, good for you,' Georgia said. 'Listen to this: "DI Hurlford has been suspended pending an investigation." No shit, Sherlocks.'

There was a sidebar down the side of the page, without a byline. There was a picture of Tony Sillars, above a simple headline:

LECTURER SUSPENDED PENDING PROBE

Georgia said nothing about this.

RISING STARS SPLIT – MEGIDDOS NO MORE

Fans of one of Britain's hottest bands were left stunned after The Megiddos announced they had split, after just two years. The folk-rock duo's lead singer Riley Brightman said he was pursuing a solo career, and thanked guitarist Scott Trickett for "two amazing years at the top of the creative tree".

Trickett was arrested and interviewed over allegations of sexual harassment after comments emerged online about his alleged conduct, although he has not yet been charged with an offence.

'Now there's a career move, son,' Georgia said. She folded the *Ferret* up, and placed it alongside the broadsheet.

Sat on the opposite side of the room, Stephanie was painting her toenails, painfully slowly, on the armchair opposite, one long leg hooked over the armrest. Without looking up from her task – carried out so slowly she appeared not to be moving – she said: 'I see that bitch the Magpie has gone from strength to strength.'

'Never doubted it for a minute, did you? She might be doing well for now. But everyone will know what she did. And she's got a bigger problem than that.'

This time Stephanie did look up – a familiar, sardonic look in her black eyes. 'Her personality and general demeanour?'

'Spot on. You can't fake that for too long. She'll get found out.' Georgia sipped at her tea, and gazed out beyond the conservatory. The rain still dimpled the windows, although it had ceased falling outside. The trees were just starting to turn, and the sky was grey. There was something appealing in the wild country outside the family home – the one Rod had agreed she should keep, after all. So long as Stephanie stayed with her.

'You know, I don't mind a day like this now and again, so long as we're nice and cosy inside.'

Stephanie sniffed. 'I was more thinking about going horse riding again.'

Georgia brightened. 'Yeah?'

'Oh yeah. Seriously. A retro thing. Or a nostalgia thing.'

'Honey, don't take this the wrong way, but you were rubbish at horse riding.'

Stephanie snorted at the sheer affrontery; her purple nail varnish slithered across her neatly manicured toes. 'Back in the bosom of the family, and you're already tearing my self-esteem to pieces!'

'Well, I'll take you horse riding, then. But maybe we could go out for a nice lunch today?'

'Sure. I'll have the methadone.'

Georgia let this comment hang in the air, until her daughter coloured.

'Sorry, Mum.'

'Yeah. You know the score. Mummy's in charge, and that's official.'

'I, er, wasn't exactly joking. Pharmacy for me at 2.30.

Mr West is quite dashing, don't you think? Something of Christopher Plummer in *The Sound of Music* about him.'

'You and your bloody older men. That explains why you're finally doing your nails.'

'I meant for you, not me!'

'Well, we're both single, that's true. May the baddest bitch win.'

'You win.' Stephanie smiled – properly this time. 'Hands down.'

'Besides... I've got my own clinic to go to.'

'You sure about that? I mean... it isn't a competition thing, is it? I've been on smack for two years, and you try to one-up me with bloody painkillers!'

'We'll go through it together. You and me. We'll take the steps.'

Steph's face crumpled. Georgia hugged her again. She covered the top of that head with kisses. The hair had regained some of its shine, even though she had elected to get that bloody pixie cut once again. Georgia hugged her daughter closer, tighter. Every single hug was a blessing, a golden moment.

'I think I might be suffocating,' Stephanie said.

'Sorry. Mum's prerogative. If I could keep you safe, here, with me, all the time, I would. That's how it goes. So... any plans for tonight?'

'Writing, I guess,' Stephanie said, capping the vial of nail varnish perched on the end of the armrest. 'I'll start to write the whole thing. They advised me to do it. Not realising that I'd do it anyway. After I write it, I'll feel better. Then I'll see how we go. One day at a time, right?'

Georgia nodded. 'That's my girl.'

Acknowledgements

Many thanks to Dr Stephen Docherty for his advice on one or two medical matters. As usual I haven't applied his excellent advice as rigorously as I might have, so any errors relating to the body, illness and injury are entirely my own. This is why he's a doctor, and I'm writing this!

Thanks as ever to my wife Claire, my kids Helena and Rory and my mother-in-law Elaine for putting up with all the typing. If keystrokes were dollars... Many thanks to Angie and Ian as ever for all the encouragement. Angie, I hope to fulfil the prophecy in the thesaurus one day.

Holly, Hannah, Vicky, Rhea, Helena, Claire and all the squad at Head of Zeus are absolute diamonds – thank you so much for all your support and help, and thank god you haven't seen how bad my mullet has got.

About the Author

P.R. BLACK lives in Yorkshire, although he was born and brought up in Glasgow. When he's not driving his wife and two children to distraction with all the typing, he enjoys hillwalking, fresh air and the natural world, and can often be found asking the way to the nearest pub in the Lake District.

His short stories have been published in several books including the Daily Telegraph's Ghost Stories and the Northern Crime One anthology. He took the runner-up spot in the 2014 Bloody Scotland crime-writing competition with "Ghostie Men". His work has been performed on stage in London by Liars' League.

@PatBlack9